"Tell me what g

"Don't, Benjamin. Do_____ secrets I might have, _____ I am. Trust me when I tell you that you wouldn't like what you uncovered."

"I find that hard to believe."

"Good night, Benjamin," she said, then left the kitchen.

Benjamin deserved better. He deserved more than she'd ever be able to give him. She had no intention of ever loving again. She didn't want to risk the chance of loss once more. Even with a man like Benjamin. Especially with a man like Benjamin.

She had to keep him out of her heart. She needed him at the moment, but hopefully soon they'd figure out what was going on and she'd be free to leave Black Rock and Benjamin behind.

Dear Reader,

We hope you enjoy the Western stories *Cowboy Deputy* and *The Cowboy's Secret Twins,* written by *New York Times* bestselling Harlequin Romantic Suspense author Carla Cassidy.

Harlequin Romantic Suspense books feature strong and adventurous women, brave and powerful men and life-and-death situations that bring them together.

And don't miss an excerpt of Carla Cassidy's *The Colton Bride* at the back of this volume. Look for *The Colton Bride,* available October 2013.

Happy reading,

The Harlequin Romantic Suspense Editors

COWBOY DEPUTY
&
THE COWBOY'S
SECRET TWINS

Carla Cassidy

HARLEQUIN® ROMANTIC SUSPENSE

ISBN-13: 978-0-373-68918-7

COWBOY DEPUTY
& THE COWBOY'S SECRET TWINS

Recycling programs
for this product may
not exist in your area.

Printed in U.S.A.

HARLEQUIN®
www.Harlequin.com

CONTENTS

ABOUT THE AUTHOR

Carla Cassidy is an award-winning author who has written more than one hundred books for Harlequin. In 1995 she won Best Silhouette Romance from *RT Book Reviews* for *Anything for Danny*. In 1998 she also won a Career Achievement Award for Best Innovative Series from *RT Book Reviews*.

Carla believes the only thing better than curling up with a good book to read is sitting down at the computer with a good story to write. She's looking forward to writing many more books and bringing hours of pleasure to readers.

COWBOY DEPUTY

Chapter 1

It was only when she saw the dancing swirl of cherry-colored lights in her rearview mirror that Edie Burnett glanced down at her speedometer. She was going forty miles an hour. As she eased off the gas pedal and pulled to the side of the street in front of a little dress boutique, she caught sight of a sign that indicated the speed limit was twenty-five.

Muttering a curse beneath her breath, she came to a stop at the curb. This was just the icing on the cake of crud that had become her life.

The official car pulled up behind her and she watched in her rearview mirror as the driver got out. Tall and lean, his khaki shirt tugged across broad shoulders as he walked toward her driver window with purposeful strides.

An errant curl of dark hair flopped onto his broad forehead and it only took that single glance in her mirror to know that the man was a hot piece of hunk.

Still, at the moment she didn't much care what he looked like. She needed to figure out the best way to talk him out of giving her a ticket. She wasn't sure she could afford lunch, much less a fine for speeding.

Cute or pathetic? She quickly decided to reach for cute and clueless and then resort to crying if necessary. It had worked for her more than once in the past.

"In a hurry?" His deep, pleasant voice resonated inside her and she looked up to see long-lashed eyes the color of rich dark chocolate gazing at her.

"Oh, wow, I'm so sorry. I had the radio on and it was a really good song and I guess my speed just kind of got away from me." She gave him a bright bewildered smile. "I didn't notice the speed limit sign until I saw your lights flashing in my rearview mirror."

"But surely you noticed you'd entered the heart of town," he countered.

"I'm such a dunce," she agreed, once again giving him her friendliest grin.

"Driver's license please," he said, no returning smile curving his sexy lips.

Her own smile faltered as she dug into her oversize purse for her wallet. Damn. He was obviously going to give her a ticket. She handed him her license and watched in her mirror as he returned to his car, unable to help but notice that he looked just as good going as he had coming.

Now was the time she'd usually summon up fake tears and hope she could find a soft spot in his heart. But as she stared blindly out the front window the tears that blurred her vision were achingly real.

The past seven months of her life had been an utter nightmare, culminating in the call from somebody here in town that her grandfather needed help.

It had been two years since she'd last seen her grandfather, Walt Tolliver. At that time she'd come back to the small town for her mother's funeral. That particular trip back had been brief and so filled with grief she now scarcely remembered it. Since that time she'd tried to call the old man every weekend, yet in the past six months with her own life falling to pieces, Edie hadn't talked to her grandfather.

A sob escaped her and was quickly followed by another. By the time the deputy returned to her car window, she was blubbering like a baby.

"Hey, there's no need for that," he exclaimed as he held her license out to her. "I'm just going to issue you a warning."

"It's not that," she replied, the words choking out of her between sobs. She grabbed the license and tossed it into the dark recesses of her purse. "It's my life. It sucks. A year ago I was too stupid to live. I thought my creep of a boyfriend loved me and I wanted to do something special for him for his birthday so I gave him my credit card and told him to buy himself the stereo system he'd been drooling over. He bought the stereo all right, and half the store. He maxed out my card and disappeared.

I used most of my savings to pay off the card and then I lost my job."

The words tumbled from her lips as if of their own free will as tears continued to cascade down her cheeks. "Then this morning as I was packing up to drive here, my landlord appeared with a thirty-day notice for me to get out. He's selling the house where I rent an apartment and I have to go."

She suddenly looked up at him, appalled by the gush of her personal problems to the handsome stranger. God, how embarrassing was this? She swiped her cheeks with the back of her hands. "I'm sorry, this isn't your problem. I'm sorry I was speeding and I appreciate you just giving me a warning."

"Are you okay to drive the rest of the way to Walt's house?" he asked.

She nodded. "I'm fine."

He stepped back and motioned for her to pull away from the curb. It was only when she was back on the road that she wondered how he knew she was headed toward her grandfather's place.

How embarrassing, to totally break down in front of a stranger and spill the sordid details of her life. She hadn't cried a tear with each bad thing that had occurred over the past year. It seemed unfathomable that she'd had a mini-breakdown in front of a stranger.

At least she hadn't told him everything. She hadn't told him that the credit card debt Greg had left her with had been the least of the heartache he'd left behind.

She dismissed both Greg and the hot deputy from

her mind as she turned off Main and onto a tree-lined residential street. Black Rock was typical of many small Kansas towns, with the business section taking up two blocks of the main drag surrounded by picturesque side streets lined with mature trees and pleasant, well-kept homes.

When she'd been young she and her mother had often visited her grandparents for a week or so each summer. Her mother and her grandmother would spend much of that time in the kitchen and Walt would entertain Edie by teaching her to play chess, bird-watching in the backyard and gardening.

Those had been some of the happiest days of Edie's life. But when she'd been a teenager, she'd opted for spending time with her friends instead of visiting grandparents. Then the years had slipped away and everything had changed.

Her grandmother had passed away, her mother was gone and now the only family she had left was Poppy, and according to the brief phone message she'd gotten from somebody here in town, he needed her. The problem was she wasn't in a place where she could be much help to anyone.

As she pulled up in front of the familiar two-story house, her heart fell. Even the forgiving glow of the late-afternoon sun couldn't take away the air of neglect that clung to the place.

The lawn needed a good mowing and the house itself screamed for a fresh coat of paint. Weeds had choked the last of the fall flowers in the beds that lined the walkway to the front porch.

She got out of her car and tried to ignore the

sense of being overwhelmed. Was he ill? Poppy was seventy-one years old. Was he too old to be living on his own? How was she going to help him when she could barely help herself?

She knocked on the door, hoping he was at least well enough to open it. "Who is there?" The deep voice resounded with energy from the other side of the door.

"Poppy, it's me, Edie."

The door flung open and Edie breathed a sigh of relief at the sight of her grandfather, looking older, but robust and healthy. "What a surprise! If it isn't my favorite girl in the whole wide world." He pulled her into the foyer and into the loving embrace of his arms.

He smelled of cheap cologne and menthol rub, of early autumn air and sweet childhood memories, and as she hugged him back she wondered why she had stayed away for so long.

He finally released her and motioned her to follow him inside. "Come on, then. I need to check on my dinner."

As she followed behind him toward the kitchen she noticed that the inside of the house was neat and tidy and the scent of a roast cooking emanated from the kitchen.

Maybe it had been a cranky neighbor who had called her because of the condition of the exterior of the house and the yard. She couldn't remember the caller giving his name but it was obvious that he had overreacted. Thank God her grandfather seemed fine.

She'd take the next couple of days and mow the

lawn, weed the flower beds and maybe get a couple gallons of paint to spruce up the place. She made a commitment to come visit every two months and resume her weekly phone calls.

"Got roast and potatoes for supper," he said as he went to oven and opened the door. "And green beans from the garden. Go on, sit down while I stir these beans and add a little bacon grease."

"Are you expecting company?" she asked, noticing that the table held two place settings. Unless Poppy had suddenly become a psychic, the extra plate hadn't been set for her.

"Benjamin is coming over. He stops by two or three times a week for dinner and some chess." Walt smiled at her. "It will feel like a regular party with you here." He finished stirring the beans and then grabbed a plate from the cabinet and added it to the table.

"I was beginning to think you'd forgotten all about your Poppy," he said with a touch of censure in his voice.

"You know the phone lines go both ways," she replied.

"I know, but I figured if a young girl like you wanted to talk to an old coot like me, you'd call." He eased down in the chair next to her at the table. "What are you now, twenty-three or twenty-four?"

"Twenty-nine, Poppy." Although the past year of her life, she'd made the mistakes of a teenager and suffered a woman's grief.

One of his grizzly gray eyebrows lifted in surprise. "Twenty-nine!" He swiped a hand down his weather-worn face and shook his head. "Seems the past couple of years have plum gotten away from me. That means it's been almost ten years since I lost my Delores and over two years since we lost your mama." For a moment he looked ancient, with sadness darkening his blue eyes and his paper-thin lips turned downward.

The sadness lasted only a moment and then his eyes regained their usual twinkle. "I hope you're going to be here long enough for me to teach you a lesson or two in chess."

She laughed. "I'm not leaving here until I win at least one game."

"Good," he said, obviously delighted. "That means it's going to be a nice long visit."

Although Edie was glad she was here, again she was struck by the thought that he seemed just fine and whoever had called her saying he needed help had definitely overreacted.

He jumped out of his chair and walked over to the oven and opened the door. "Benjamin should be here soon and we'll eat. Are you hungry?"

"Starving," she replied. Her lunch had been a bag of chips she'd eaten in the car. "Is there anything I can do to help?"

"There are a couple of nice tomatoes in the refrigerator. If you want to, you can slice them up and put them on the table."

As she sliced the tomatoes, they chatted mostly about the past, playing a game of *remember when* that created warm fuzzies in Edie's heart.

She shouldn't have stayed away for so long. Poppy

was the only family she had left in the world. Her home in Topeka was just a three-hour drive to Black Rock but somehow her personal drama and heart-break had taken over and the last thing on her mind had been her Poppy.

"You'll like Benjamin," Poppy said as he took the roaster out of the oven and set it on hot pads in the center of the table. "He's a good guy and a mean chess player."

And probably eighty years old, Edie mentally thought, although she was grateful her grandfather had a friend for company. Maybe this big house was just too much for Poppy. Maybe it was time for him to think about an apartment or someplace where he didn't have to worry about maintenance and upkeep. Time to talk about that later, she thought as the door-bell rang.

"That should be Benjamin," Walt said and left the kitchen to get the door.

Edie wiped off the countertop and then pasted a smile on her face as Walt came back into the kitchen. The smile fell as she saw who followed at his heels, not an old, gray-haired man with stooped shoulders and rheumy eyes, but rather the very hot deputy who had pulled her over and witnessed her mini-breakdown.

"Edie, this here is my friend Benjamin Grayson. Benjamin, this is my granddaughter who surprised me this evening with a visit," Walt said.

"Hello, Edie, it's nice to meet you." He stepped forward and held out a hand, obviously deciding to play it as if he'd never seen her before.

He'd looked great earlier in his khaki uniform but now with worn tight jeans hugging his long lean legs and a blue cotton shirt clinging to his broad shoulders, he was pure sin walking.

"Nice to meet you, too," she replied as she gave his hand a short, curt shake.

"Go on, sit down," Walt said. "Let's eat before the roast gets cold."

Edie slid into a chair at the table and tried not to notice the clean, male scent mingling with a woodsy cologne that wafted from Benjamin.

He might have smelled good and he might have looked great and in another place and time she might have been interested in him. But Edie had sworn off relationships and men and sex for the rest of her life. Besides, her intention was to be in Black Rock for only two or three days.

As the men joined her at the table and filled their plates, Walt and Benjamin made small talk about the weather and the forecast for a harsh winter to come.

Although Edie was glad she'd gotten the phone call that had prompted her to come for a visit, she still didn't see any real issue where her Poppy was concerned.

"Any word on that missing girl?" Walt asked.

Benjamin shook his head. "Nothing. It's like she vanished into midair."

"Missing girl?" Edie looked at Benjamin curiously.

"Her name is Jennifer Hightower, a twenty-two-year-old who went missing three weeks ago," Benjamin replied.

"And she's not the only missing girl in town," Walt said. "Benjamin's own sister went missing over two months ago."

Edie saw the darkness that crawled into Benjamin's eyes as he nodded. "That's right, but surely we can think of something more pleasant to talk about while we eat." There was a note of finality in his tone that indicated this particular subject was closed.

Walt immediately began to talk about the fall festival the town was planning in the next month. As Edie ate, she found that her focus tugged again and again to Benjamin.

His face was tanned as if he spent a lot of time outdoors rather than inside at a desk or seated in a patrol car. He had nice features, a no-nonsense slight jut to his chin, a straight nose and lips that looked soft and very kissable.

There was no question that she was curious about his sister, felt a tinge of empathy as she imagined what it must be like to have a family member missing.

Edie didn't know about missing family members, but she was intimate with grief, knew the sharp stab of loss, the ache that never quite went away.

She could only assume that Benjamin wasn't married and she questioned why a handsome man like him would choose to spend a couple nights a week playing chess with an old man.

"How long are you planning to visit?" he asked.

With those gorgeous, long-lashed eyes focused intently on her, a small burst of unwanted heat ignited in the very pit of her stomach.

"Just a couple days or so," she replied, grateful her voice sounded remarkably normal. "I need to get back home and take care of some things." And he knew exactly what those things were because she'd spewed them out in a mist of tears when he'd pulled her over.

"You still managing that restaurant?" Poppy asked.

She hesitated and then shook her head. "Unfortunately a couple weeks ago I showed up at the restaurant and found a padlock on the door and a note that said the place was out of business." She tamped down the residual anger that rose up inside her each time she thought of that day. There had been no warning to any of the employees, no hint that the place was in trouble.

"So, have you found a new job?" Poppy eyed her worriedly.

"Not yet, but when I get back home I'm sure I won't have any problems finding something," she assured him with a quick smile. The last thing she wanted was for him to worry about her.

Thankfully dinner went quickly and as Poppy stood to clear the table, Edie shooed him away. "You two go on and play your chess. I'll take care of the cleanup."

"I won't argue with you. I like the cooking but hate the cleanup," Poppy said.

"I could help. It would only take a minute," Benjamin said.

Edie shook her head. "I've got it under control." The last thing she wanted was to be butting elbows with him over the sink. He was too big and too sexy for her and she didn't want him close enough that she could smell him, feel his body heat.

She breathed a sigh of relief as the two men left the kitchen and disappeared into the living room. It took her only minutes to store the leftovers in the refrigerator and then stack the plates for washing.

There was no dishwasher and as she got the dish drainer rack from the cabinet, she remembered all the times she'd stood at this sink and helped her grandmother wash dishes.

It hadn't been a chore; it had been a chance to talk about the day, about the weather, about life with a woman Edie had considered wise and loving.

The last time Edie had been here she'd been thirteen years old and madly in love with a boy named Darrin. It had been a case of unrequited love. Darrin had preferred video games to girls.

"It's not a mistake to love," her grandmother had told her. "But you need to love smart. Choose a man who has the capacity to love you back, a man who can make you feel as if you're the most important person in the world."

As Edie washed and rinsed the dishes, she wondered what her grandmother would say about the mess Edie had made of her life. She had definitely loved stupid, choosing to give her heart to a man who not only didn't have the capacity to love her back, but also had all the character of a rock. The price she'd paid for loving stupidly had been enormous and she'd been left with the determination to never put her heart in jeopardy again.

A burst of deep male laughter came from the living room as she placed the last dish in the drainer. It sounded as if the two of them were enjoying their game.

Darkness had fallen outside and Edie realized she hadn't brought in her suitcase from the car. As she entered the living room both men looked up from the chessboard. "What are you doing, girl?" Poppy asked. "Come sit and watch a master at work." He gave her a grin that twinkled in his eyes.

She returned his smile. "I gather from the smug look on your face that you're winning."

"I've been playing him a couple nights a week for the past six months and I have yet to win a game," Benjamin said.

His gaze slid down the length of her, the quick once-over that a man might give a woman he found attractive.

She felt the heat of his gaze and quickly moved toward the front door. "I'm just going to get my suitcase from the car."

"Need any help?" Benjamin asked.

She quickly shook her head. "Thanks, but I can get it." She scooted out the front door and into the cool September evening air.

For a moment she stood on the porch and stared up at the night sky. Here in Black Rock the stars seemed brighter, closer than they did in Topeka.

"Make a wish, sugar," her grandmother would tell her whenever the two of them had sat on the porch and gazed upward.

Edie reached up and grabbed the small charm

that hung on the gold chain around her neck. The gold was cool in her fingers but warmed quickly as she held it tight.

There was only one wish she'd like to make and she knew it was one that could never come true. She released her hold on the charm and headed to her car in the driveway.

Behind her car was parked a large black pickup she knew must belong to Benjamin. Funny, she would assume he was more the sweet little sports car type than the big bruising truck.

She'd packed light and grabbed the small suitcase and overnight bag from her backseat, then headed inside the house. She heard no sound from the living room. Apparently the current chess game was intense enough that both men were concentrating.

She carried the suitcase up the stairs, the third and seventh steps creaking beneath her weight as they had when she'd been a child. She entered the last bedroom at the end of the hall, the room where she'd always stayed when she and her mother had come for a visit. The dusty pink paint on the wall and the pink floral spread covering the double bed brought another wave of memories.

Every night that she'd slept here she'd been tucked into bed lovingly not only by her mother, but also by her grandmother. And often Poppy would come upstairs to sneak her a cookie or a little bowl of popcorn. In this house she'd always felt loved like nowhere else on earth.

It took her only minutes to stow her items in the

dresser and closet, then she headed back downstairs where it sounded as if the chess game had ended.

As she entered the living room, Benjamin and Poppy got up from the small game table. "He beat me both games," Benjamin said. He smiled at Edie, a warm, sexy smile that once again fluttered a faint heat through her veins.

"Maybe you and Edie could play a few games together, you know, practice so eventually you can beat the master." Poppy grinned.

Benjamin laughed. "I'd love to hang around and play a game of chess with Edie, but unfortunately I've got some reports that need to be written before morning."

The twinkle in Poppy's eyes faded as he looked at Benjamin seriously. "You know how to find those girls. Find the aliens and you'll find out what happened to that Hightower young woman and your sister."

"Aliens?" Edie looked from her grandfather to Benjamin with curiosity.

Poppy nodded. "Space aliens. I keep telling Benjamin and his brothers that they've landed here in Black Rock and until we get them rounded up, nobody is safe."

A sick feeling swept through Edie as she stared at her grandfather, hoping to see the familiar twinkle of a joke in his eyes. But there was no twinkle—only a faint tinge of fear coupled with the determination of an intergalactic warrior. And then she knew why somebody had called her to check on her Poppy. It was because he was losing his mind.

Chapter 2

Benjamin saw the dismay that swept over Edie's features at Walt's words. She was a pretty woman and he knew her statistics from looking at her license. She was five foot four and weighed 117 pounds. Her hair was auburn and her eyes were green.

But those statistics didn't begin to really describe the woman who stood before him. Yes, her short curly hair was auburn, but it shone with a luster that made his fingers itch with the need to touch. *Green* was too ordinary a word to describe her eyes, which sparkled with tiny shards of glittering gold.

The orange sweater she wore complemented the burnished highlights in her hair and intensified the color of her eyes. Something about her stirred him in a way he hadn't been stirred in a very long time.

"I'll walk you out," she said, casting a meaning-ful look at him.

"Walt, as always, thanks for the meal and the chess game," Benjamin said.

"Thanks for the company," Walt replied, obvi-ously unaware that his previous words had upset his granddaughter. "Edie, you can pull your car into the garage. I sold my car a year ago. I got tired of pay-ing for insurance."

Edie nodded. "Thanks, Poppy, I'll do that."

As Benjamin walked out with Edie, he caught a whiff of her perfume, something subtle and spicy that reminded him of tangy fall air and cinnamon.

"I'm the one who called you," he said when they were far enough away from the front door that Walt wouldn't hear. "I've been worried about him."

In the illumination from a nearby streetlight, he could see the confusion on her pretty face. "I didn't catch the name of the person who'd called me and once I got here I thought maybe it was just a cranky neighbor upset because the yard needs some work. He seemed so normal."

"He appears to be normal in every way except for the little issue that he thinks space aliens are trying to take over Black Rock. It wouldn't be a big problem but he's often out in the middle of the night alien hunting and I'm afraid he'll get hit by a car or fall down someplace where nobody will be able to help him."

"How long has this been going on?" she asked. She still looked overwhelmed by this news and as he remembered the things she'd told him when he'd pulled her over for speeding, he had a crazy desire to take her into his arms and assure her that everything was going to be all right.

Instead he rocked back on his heels and frowned thoughtfully. "About six months. My brothers and I have tried to assure him that there are no space aliens in town, but he's adamant in his belief and gets downright cranky when you try to tell him different. Look, I'd recommend you take him into his doctor and get a full checkup done. Maybe this is some sort of a medical issue."

"I guess that's as good a place to start as anywhere," she replied. "Well, thanks for all your help with him. I guess I'll see you around over the next couple of days, but hopefully not in my rearview mirror with your lights spinning."

He grinned at her. "As long as you're not a fast woman, we won't have any problems in that area. But I can't promise I won't follow you just because I think you're pretty." Someplace deep inside he recognized he was flirting a little bit.

She must have realized it, too. But her eyes cooled and she took a step back from him. "I am a fast woman, probably way too fast for a small-town deputy."

He wasn't sure who was more surprised by her response, him or her. Her lush lips compressed as she frowned once again. "Thanks again for you help. See you around."

She turned and headed back to the house in short quick steps that swayed her shapely hips. Benjamin watched until she disappeared behind the front door and then released a sigh as he got into his truck.

He had no idea what had possessed him to attempt a little flirt with her. It was obvious by her response he wasn't very good at it. Still, her cool response had surprised him.

Since his brothers Tom and Caleb had hooked up with their soul mates, Benjamin had become the toast of the town when it came to the single women. But all the women who were interested in him left him cold.

He'd been cold since his sister, Brittany, had disappeared over two months ago. Tom, his oldest brother and the sheriff of Black Rock, still held out hope that she would be found alive and well, but even though Benjamin never said anything out loud, as each day had passed with no word from her, he'd lost hope of ever seeing his little sister again.

As he backed out of Walt's driveway, he tried to ignore the stab of grief that always pierced his heart when he thought of his missing sister.

And now they had another one missing. Tom was reluctant to tie the two disappearances together, but Benjamin had a bad feeling about the whole thing. He was afraid Black Rock was in for dark days, and the darkness had nothing to do with Walt's imaginary space aliens.

As he headed for the ranch his thoughts returned to Edie Burnett. For a minute as he'd seen her tears after he'd pulled her over, he'd thought she was faking them to get out of a ticket.

Old Mabel Tredway did it on a regular basis. The eighty-two-year-old woman shouldn't be behind the wheel of a car and whenever Benjamin pulled her over for crossing the center line or going a little too fast, she wept like a baby. But the one time he'd given her a ticket, the fake tears had stopped on a dime and she'd cussed him, his dead mama and all the cattle on his ranch.

However, Edie's tears had been real and as she'd burped up the details of her life with each sob, he had decided not to write the ticket.

She had enough to deal with in deciding what to do with Walt. Benjamin and his lawmen brothers had come to the end of their rope with the old man. Nobody wanted to see anything bad happen to him, but they all felt it was just a matter of time before he got hurt.

As he pulled into the gates that led to the family homestead, he felt the familiar sense of peace the place always brought to him. The house itself was an architectural anomaly. What had started as a simple two-bedroom ranch had become a sprawling complex as rooms were added with each birth of a child.

There was also a small cottage just behind the house where Margaret Kintell, a sixty-eight-year-old widow, lived. Margaret had worked as a housekeeper for the Grayson family for as long as Benjamin could remember. Her husband, John, had worked as a ranch hand until he'd passed away several years ago, and even though Benjamin had encouraged Margaret to retire she insisted that her job was still taking care of the Grayson children.

Unfortunately Benjamin was the only Grayson child still living in the family home and he wasn't

exactly a child at thirty years old. His brothers Tom
and Caleb lived in town. Brittany had been living
in town at the time of her disappearance and Jacob
was holed up in a small cabin nestled in a grove of
trees on the ranch property.

The porch light was on so he knew Margaret was
probably still in the house rather than in her little
cottage. As he walked through the front door, the
scent of apples and cinnamon filled his nose and Tiny
came running toward him, barking a happy greeting.

"Hi, Tiny." He bent down on his haunches to pet
the mixed-breed mutt who had stolen his heart six
months ago. "Margaret?" he called as he stood. As he
walked through the living room toward the kitchen,
Tiny followed close at his feet.

She greeted him in the doorway and gestured him
into a chair at the table. "Go on, now, sit down. I
made fresh apple cobbler and I know that nutcase
Walt probably didn't feed you good and proper."

Benjamin smiled and eased down at the table.
"Actually, he had a very nice roast and potatoes for
dinner." Margaret had been mad at Walt since last
year's fall festival when his apple pie had beaten out
hers for a blue ribbon.

She harrumphed as she scooped up a healthy serving of the cobbler into a bowl. "Probably got the
recipe from one of those space aliens of his. I don't
know why you have taken that man under your wing.
You're too soft, Benjamin. That's always been your
problem. All Walt Tolliver needs is a stern talking-
to." She placed the bowl in front of him and then went
to the refrigerator and pulled out the jug of milk.

"Maybe his granddaughter can talk some sense into him. She arrived in town today."

"Really?" Margaret placed a glass of milk in front of him and then sat across from him. "That would be Julie's girl."

"Edie," Benjamin replied. "Her name is Edie Burnett."

"That's right. Julie married that no-account Kevin Burnett. He was a drinker, that one, and a womanizer. The marriage lasted just long enough for Julie to get pregnant. It was a shame, her dying like that in a car accident. So, what's Edie like?"

Hot. With tantalizing eyes and a body that could make a man weak in the knees. He spooned some of the apple cobbler in his mouth in an effort to think of a more reasonable response.

"She didn't seem to know what's been going on with Walt and when she realized he thought Black Rock was being invaded by space aliens, she seemed a little overwhelmed by it all," he finally replied.

"She in town to stay?"

"No. I imagine she'll just be here long enough to figure out what needs to be done with Walt and then she'll go back home."

"What's she like? Julie was a pretty woman and sweet as that cobbler."

"She's nice-looking," Benjamin conceded, "but I think she might have a little bite to her." He thought about how her gaze had frosted over when he'd attempted a little light flirtation.

If he were a man who liked a challenge, he might have pursued a little more flirting just to see if he could melt that frost. But Benjamin was a man who'd never felt enough passion to work too hard for anything. Except this ranch.

"She's got her work cut out for her in straightening out that old man," Margaret said as she rose from the table. "I'm going to head to my place. It's time for this old broad to call it a night."

Benjamin smiled. "Good night, Margaret." The old woman had the heart of an angel and the saltiness of a sailor, but she helped to keep the ranch and Benjamin's life running smoothly.

Once she was gone the silence of the house pressed in on him. Growing up with all his siblings in the house, he'd longed for silence.

But lately the silence in his life had felt oppressive, ushering in a loneliness he'd never felt before. His brother Jacob had closed himself off in the cabin in some form of self-imposed isolation. Brittany was missing and Tom and Caleb now had beautiful bright women to fill the silences in their lives.

He got up from the table and carried his bowl and glass to the sink. As he rinsed the dishes and placed them in the dishwasher, he thought of all the things he needed to get done in the next couple days while he was off-duty.

Of course, the law enforcement team in Black Rock was so small that all of the men were often called in on their time off. He left the kitchen and doused the light, then headed toward the master bedroom.

As always, when the silence pressed in the heaviest, his thoughts turned to Brittany. A little over two months without a word, without a clue as to what had happened to her. They'd found her car hidden in an abandoned barn a month ago and it was at that moment that any hope he might have entertained in seeing his sister alive again had died.

With intentions of rising before dawn to start the catch-up on chores around the ranch, he shucked his jeans and shirt and got ready for bed. Tiny sat next to the bed and looked up at him expectantly.

"You know you have your own bed to sleep in," he said to the dog, who cocked his head as if he didn't understand. Benjamin pointed to the dog bed in the corner. "Go on, get to bed."

Tiny remained in place for a long moment and then finally slunk slowly to his bed. He got in and then looked at Benjamin with mournful brown eyes.

"I don't know why you look so sad," Benjamin said. "We both know you'll be curled up in my bed at my feet before morning."

Minutes later, as he eased down onto his king-size bed, his thoughts returned to Edie Burnett. She'd been quiet during the meal but he had a feeling quiet wasn't really in her character.

He burrowed down and closed his eyes. It was just his luck that the first woman in a long time who had stirred something inside him was only in town for a couple days.

From what she'd told him, she'd have a mess on her hands when she got back home. She had to find a new job and another place to live. He didn't want to think about what she was going to do if Walt's problem wasn't a quick fix.

He drifted off to sleep with visions of lush lips and green eyes playing in his dreams and was awakened some time later by the ringing of his phone on the nightstand.

He was awake instantly, his heart drumming a rapid beat. He glanced at the clock as he fumbled in the dark for the receiver. Just after midnight. Nothing ever good came from middle-of-the-night phone calls.

"Yeah," he answered as he sat up.

"It's me," his brother Tom said. "I'm at the hospital. Somebody beat the hell out of Walt Tolliver and he won't talk to anyone but you."

"I'm on my way." Benjamin hung up as he climbed out of bed. As he pulled on his clothes he wondered what the hell had happened to Walt and where the hell Edie had been.

Edie rolled over and looked at the clock next to her bed. Just before midnight and she still hadn't managed to fall asleep. When she'd come back into the house after Benjamin had left, she'd grabbed her keys and then moved her car into the garage. When she'd returned she'd wanted to ask Poppy more questions about the space aliens he thought were trying to take over Black Rock, but she was afraid to indulge the delusion. She was hoping to talk to his doctor and ask how she should handle the situation.

Even if she'd wanted to talk to him about it, the opportunity didn't arise. Immediately after, Poppy had gone to sleep in the bedroom just off the living room.

She'd climbed the stairs to her room, but knew that sleep would be elusive. She'd taken a long hot shower and tried not to think about Benjamin Grayson. But thoughts of the man kept intruding.

She'd been rude to him with her little remark about being too fast for a small-time deputy, but even though she'd just met him, she'd felt an inexplicable need to distance him from her. His smile had been far too warm, his eyes had been too brown and for just a moment, she'd been afraid that he might make her forget that she'd sworn off men for the rest of her life.

She'd been an accident waiting to happen when she'd met Greg. Reeling with grief over her mother's unexpected death, she'd met him in a bar two weeks after the funeral. It had been love at third drink.

They'd dated for two months before he'd moved in with her and she realized now she'd been far too naive, hadn't asked enough questions and instead had believed everything he'd told her about himself.

They'd talked of marriage and children and he'd filled the loneliness that the absence of her mother had left behind. He'd told her that he was an entrepreneur between projects and that his money was tied up in his latest endeavor. God, she'd been such a fool.

One thing was clear, she didn't need anyone in her life. When she got back home she'd focus on finding a new job, a new place to live and cleaning up her messes. She would be just fine all alone for the rest of her life.

She must have fallen asleep because she knew she was dreaming. Pain ripped her body, but it was a pain tempered with a sense of joy. A bright lamp

nearly blinded her as the pain intensified. A mur-
mur of voices took on an urgency that was suddenly
terrifying and at the same time a bald-headed man
wearing a doctor's mask glared at her with accusa-
tion and a phone began to ring.

She awoke with a gasp, the taste of overwhelming
grief and crushing guilt thick in her mouth. Disori-
ented for a moment, she looked around the moonlit
room. Then she remembered where she was and that
the phone she'd heard in her dream was actually the
phone ringing in the house.

As it rang again…and again, she realized Poppy
either didn't hear it or didn't intend to answer it. She
looked at the clock. Twelve forty-five. Whoever was
calling was persistent, for the ringing didn't stop.

She jumped out of bed and left her room. Flip-
ping on the hall light, she ran down the stairs and
grabbed the receiver of the phone in the living room.

"Hello," she said half-breathlessly.

"It's me, Benjamin." His deep voice sounded irritated. "I'm here at the hospital with Walt."

"What?" Confusion sifted through her as she
looked at the closed door of Poppy's bedroom. "But
he went to bed earlier."

"Apparently he went out. Somebody beat him up
and he managed to flag down a car that brought him
to the hospital. He's going to be all right, but I think
you should be here."

"I'm on my way. Where is the hospital?"

"Go straight down Main to Chestnut and turn left.
It's about halfway down the second block. You can't
miss it."

She murmured a goodbye and then raced back up the stairs to get dressed. Her heart beat an uneven tattoo as she thought of somebody beating up Poppy.

Why, oh, why, had he left the house in the middle of the night? This delusion of his about space aliens obviously had a dark undertone.

Within minutes she was dressed and in her car creeping down the darkened Main Street, seeking Chestnut. Benjamin had sounded angry, as if it were somehow her fault that Poppy had been out wandering the streets. What did he expect her to do? Strap the man into bed at night?

She found the hospital, a two-story brick building with a large parking area near the emergency room entrance. She easily found a parking space, and as she hurried into the door she prayed that Benjamin was right and Poppy was going to be okay.

Once again she kicked herself for staying away for so long. She didn't need Poppy, but it was obvious he needed her. The first person she saw when she walked into the waiting room was Benjamin.

His dark thick hair was tousled as if he'd just climbed out of bed, making him look even sexier than she remembered. He jumped up from the plastic chair he'd been in as he saw her.

"Where is he?" she asked.

"Where were you?" he countered, his shoulders rigid with tension. "Didn't you know he had gone out?"

"He went to bed just after you left. I went upstairs to go to sleep, as well. What was I supposed to do, tie a little silver bell around his neck so I'd know if he was on the move?" she asked belligerently.

The tension slid off his shoulders and he smiled. "You'd need a ball and chain because I'm afraid he'd be able to get a little silver bell off." He rocked back on his heels and slid a hand through his unruly hair. "Sorry, I didn't mean to come at you like that."

"And I'm sorry I didn't have a ball and chain on Poppy," she replied, reluctantly charmed by his apologetic smile. "How is he? Can I see him?"

Benjamin nodded. "He's been waiting for you. He refused to talk to me until you got here. Come on, I'll take you to him." He placed his fingers just beneath her elbow, and she felt the warmth of the touch burning her through the sweater she'd pulled on. She tore her arm away from him.

What was it about this man that made her feel defensive and prickly? Maybe she was overly sensitive to him because he was the least of her problems. She had a life in Topeka that was in complete and total chaos and a crazy grandfather in Black Rock that she somehow had to fix before she could go home.

She heard Poppy before they reached the exam room. "I'm fine. I just need to go home and rest a bit." His voice held the raspy edge of frustration.

As she and Benjamin stepped into the exam room Edie's breath whooshed out of her at the sight of Poppy, who sat upright on the examining table. One of his eyes was blackened and swollen shut and his jaw held a massive bruise that appeared to grow darker as she stared at him.

"Oh, Poppy," she exclaimed, her heart squeezing tight in her chest. "What happened?"

He shifted positions and winced. "One of the bastards caught me."

"Where were you, Walt?" Benjamin asked.

The doctor, an older man with a receding hairline and a kind smile, held up a hand to halt any questioning. "Before we get into that, I'm Dr. Drake. I've been Walt's doctor for the past twenty years." He held out a hand to Edie, who introduced herself.

"Other than what's obvious, what are his injuries?" she asked.

"A couple of cracked ribs and a lot of bruising along his left side. I'd like to keep him here under observation for a night or two."

Edie breathed a sigh of relief at the doctor's words, but Walt took exception. "I don't need to stay overnight. I want my own bed in my own house."

"Walt, as your doctor I'm afraid I'm going to have to insist," Dr. Drake said firmly. "You took quite a beating and I wouldn't be doing my job if I just let you out of here without running a few more tests."

The mutiny on Poppy's face eased into something resembling resignation. "I'm not going to wear one of those damn gowns and this place better have cable television. And I want a pretty nurse."

Dr. Drake smiled. "I think we can handle all that. Now I'll just get out of here and let Benjamin conduct his investigation."

"Dr. Drake, before I leave, I'd like to have a word with you in private," Edie said.

He nodded. "I'll be in my office at the end of the

hall, and if I'm not there just grab a nurse and have her hunt me down." He left the room and Edie turned back to Poppy as Benjamin stepped closer to the bed.

"Where were you, Walt?" he asked again.

"Out by the cemetery. I thought that might be a hot spot for those creatures and damned if I wasn't right. I was only there about an hour when one of them showed up. Either I made a sound or those suckers have some kind of extrasensory stuff 'cause even though I was hiding behind a bush, he came tearing after me." He looked from Benjamin to Edie. "I think it's best if you leave town, Edie. Those creatures are violent and this town isn't a safe place anymore."

"I'm not going anywhere, Poppy," she replied. "At least not until I know you're safe and well."

"This space alien, what did he look like?" Benjamin asked.

"Like an alien," Walt exclaimed, seeming to get more agitated with each question.

"Poppy, you need to be more specific," Edie replied. "Was he little and green?"

Poppy shot her a look as if she'd lost her mind. "He wasn't some damn cartoon Martian. I couldn't tell much what he looked like. He was wearing all black. His face didn't have a nose or mouth, just big eyes."

"Where exactly in the cemetery were you?" Benjamin had pulled out a small notepad to jot down the pertinent information.

"I was hiding behind that big burning bush at the entrance and the alien was just inside the gate."

"What was he doing?" Benjamin asked.

"Just walking," Walt replied.

On and on the questions went. To Benjamin's credit he didn't lose patience even when Walt got cranky and insisted they needed to call in more law enforcement for the small town.

When the nurse came in to move him from emergency into one of the regular rooms, Edie and Benjamin were shooed out. Edie gave Poppy a gentle kiss on the top of the head and after promising to visit him the next morning, she and Benjamin left the room.

"You didn't get much to go on," she said to Benjamin as they walked down the hall toward the doctor's office. Nervous energy jangled inside her. She'd managed to hold it together in front of Poppy, but she felt perilously close to losing it now.

"I'm sure it wasn't a space invader on a nefarious mission, but *somebody* hurt Walt and I intend to find the person responsible," he said with an intensity that somehow calmed her.

"Why would somebody want to hurt him like that? He's an old man. He's not a threat to anyone." She was horrified to feel the ominous burn of tears in her eyes. God, she'd only been with Benjamin three times and she refused to be in tears yet again.

"Are you all right?" he asked. There was a softness in his eyes, a gentle but steady light that made her want to fall into it. He raised a hand, as if to touch her hair or cheek, but dropped it as she stiffened her back and took a step away from him. Someplace buried in her mind she recognized that this man was definitely dangerous to her.

"I need to speak to Dr. Drake. Please keep me updated on the investigation." Without waiting for his reply, she turned and hurried down the hall, away from him…away from temptation.

Chapter 3

The Black Rock Memorial Cemetery was located about two miles from Walt's home. It was a peaceful plot of land, shady with large trees and with several stone benches amid the headstones.

The grass was neatly mown and the flower beds without a weed. The place was maintained by Josh Willoughby who lived in a small house next to the cemetery. He was an affable man who worked at the feed store and took care of the cemetery on the weekends and on his days off.

Benjamin's parents were here. They'd been killed in a helicopter accident six years ago and as Benjamin approached the front gate, he made a mental note to stop by their graves before he left.

The bush that Walt had told him he'd hidden be-

hind was next to the front gate, a burning bush that
had fully flamed into red leaves with the fall air.

The grass was too short and dry to show any signs
of the struggle that had taken place between Walt
and his space alien. He bent down on one knee next
to the bush and began to comb the grass with his
gloved hand, looking for some sort of evidence that
might help identify Walt's attacker.

As he worked he couldn't help but think about
Edie. She'd been foremost in his thoughts since he'd
left her at the hospital near dawn.

He'd been impressed by how she'd handled the
situation at the hospital. She'd remained calm and
patient with Walt even when he'd gotten downright
cantankerous.

It was only as they'd stepped out of the room that
he saw a crack in her composure. She'd looked small
and lost and overwhelmed by everything that was
going on. Benjamin had fought the impulse to pull
her into his arms and hold her until somehow her
world was magically set right.

His family teased him about his penchant for picking up strays. Dogs and cats and people needing help
always seemed to find their way to Benjamin.

But his crazy attraction to Edie Burnett had nothing to do with his desire to help her through a tough
situation. The very scent of her excited him, her
nearness half stole his breath away and her mouth
seemed to beckon for a taste. He was like a teenager in heat and wasn't quite sure what to do with
his desire for her.

He'd wanted to kiss her, right there in the hospital

hallway. He'd wanted to pull her up against his body and wrap his arms around her and hold her until that frightened, lost look in her eyes changed to desire.

It was a new feeling for him, the instant chemistry he felt toward her, and one he was reluctant to deny.

All thoughts of Edie flew out of his head as his hand touched something metal. He pulled the item from the grass and gazed at it thoughtfully. It appeared to be part of a key chain, a flat black circle with the initial *A* in silver in the center.

He placed it in a small evidence bag. There was no way of knowing if it might have come off Walt's attacker or had been dropped by somebody else at another time.

"Problems?"

The deep voice coming from just behind Benjamin spun him up and around, his hand automatically reaching for his gun. "Jeez, Josh, you scared the hell out of me," he said as he relaxed. "I figured you were at work."

"It's my day off. I saw you skulking around and wondered if there was a problem."

"Walt Tolliver got the tar beat out of him here last night."

Josh frowned and hitched up his jeans around his bulging belly. He was a big man, an inch taller than Benjamin's six feet and at least fifty pounds heavier. "I've been trying to keep an extra eye out here lately but last night me and the wife went to bed early."

"So you didn't see or hear anything?"

"Only thing I heard was Marylou's snores. The woman sounded like a freight train with brake problems last night, not that I'd like you to mention it to her." He gave Benjamin a pained smile.

"Why have you been keeping an extra eye out here?" Benjamin asked.

"A few times over the past couple weeks I thought I saw lights. I figured it was probably kids fooling around. There was never any damage or any sign that they were there in the mornings so I wasn't sure if it was just my imagination."

"The next time you think you see something, you call the sheriff's office," Benjamin said.

"Is Walt okay?" Josh asked.

Benjamin nodded. "Banged up, but he'll survive."

"He wasn't able to tell you who attacked him?"

"Don't ask," Benjamin said darkly.

A slow grin swept over Josh's broad face. "Let me guess, it was a space invader."

Benjamin nodded. "I'm headed over to the hospital from here to see if he can give me more details this morning than he was able to last night."

"Good luck with that," Josh said. "I'm going back home. Just call if you need anything else from me."

Benjamin watched as the big man lumbered back in the direction of his house, then Benjamin walked toward his parents' graves.

He didn't visit here often. In truth Benjamin had been closer to his siblings than he had been to his mother and father. His parents had loved to travel and once their kids all got old enough to fend for themselves, they were often away on one adventure or another.

He stood at the foot of their graves and wondered

if they were both whirling around in spiritual unrest with Brittany's disappearance and Jacob's isolation from life.

Brittany's case had come to a painful standstill due to a lack of leads. As far as Jacob, Benjamin held out hope that eventually Jacob would tell him why he'd quit his job with the FBI and closed himself off from the world.

It was just after noon when he left the cemetery and decided to stop for lunch before going to the hospital. As he walked into the café he spied his brothers Tom and Caleb in one of the booths.

As he walked toward where they were seated, he nodded to Larry Norwood, the town's newest vet, and raised a hand to Billy Jefferson, a neighboring rancher.

"We were just sitting here wondering if our resident alien buster had been successful in his hunt," Caleb teased as Benjamin slid in next to him. "Any sight of the little green men?"

"I'll have you know that Walt specifically said that the alien wasn't a cartoon Martian. He wasn't sure what planet the aliens are from."

"It was somebody from this planet who beat him up," Tom said, his features stern. "And I want that person found and charged. I don't like things like that happening in my town."

Benjamin knew how personally Tom took the safety of the residents of Black Rock. It was what made him a respected and beloved sheriff. "I spoke to Josh," Benjamin said. "He mentioned that he thinks maybe kids have been hanging out at the cemetery after hours."

"I'm not surprised," Caleb said. "Halloween is only weeks away. There's nothing better than taking a girl to the cemetery and scaring her with ghost stories that make her squeal in fear and jump right into your arms."

"Does Portia know you hang out in the cemetery and scare girls?" Benjamin asked with a wry grin.

Caleb smiled. "She was the girl I was scaring in the cemetery."

Portia Perez and Caleb had been high-school sweethearts who had broken up when Portia had gone to college. Recently the two had gotten back together again and seemed more in love with each other than ever.

"What about Walt's granddaughter? What's her name?" Tom asked.

To Benjamin's surprise he felt his cheeks warm. "Edie. Edie Burnett."

"What's she like?" Caleb asked curiously.

Benjamin shrugged. "Attractive. Overwhelmed. She's pretty much alone in the world other than having Walt."

"Uh-oh," Caleb said. "Sounds like a perfect candidate for the Benjamin-to-the-rescue club."

Tom grinned as Benjamin shot his younger brother a look of irritation. "It's not like that at all," he protested. "She's only in town for a few days and she doesn't seem like the type who would want a man to run to her rescue. Is there anything new on the Jennifer Hightower disappearance?" he asked in an effort to change the subject.

"Not a damn thing," Tom replied.

As the three brothers ate their lunch, they discussed the latest disappearance of a young woman. Jennifer Hightower had gone to work at the convenience store on the edge of town as usual and had been scheduled to work until closing time at midnight. Her car had been left in the parking lot at the store, but she was nowhere to be found.

"The interviews with her friends have yielded nothing. We got nothing from her car. The surveillance tape from the store showed that she was alive and well at midnight when she closed up the place." Tom listed the facts one after another, his voice deep with frustration.

"She doesn't have a current boyfriend and her ex has a solid alibi," Caleb added. "It's like she vanished into thin air."

"Or somebody was waiting just outside for her," Tom said. "Too bad the convenience store doesn't have cameras outside."

"Have we decided that this case is connected to Brittany's?" Benjamin asked. It was the question that they'd all danced around for the past couple weeks.

Tom frowned, as if in pain. "There's no real evidence that they're connected. Jennifer doesn't look anything like Brittany. But the fact is we have two missing women. I don't want to believe they're connected, but I guess we have to consider the possibility."

His words caused a knot of anxiety to form in

Benjamin's chest. If the disappearances were connected, then that meant there was a possibility that
somebody in town was kidnapping pretty young
women. What he was doing to them was anybody's
guess. Until a body was found it was impossible to
speculate about what had become of the victims.

All he knew was that there was a new pretty
young woman in town and the fear of an unknown
darkness walking the streets of Black Rock.

Edie cursed beneath her breath as the lawn mower
died for the fifth time in the past hour. She was exhausted, but wanted to get the lawn finished before
calling it a day.

She'd been working at it for the past two hours.
The problem was twofold: the lawn mower was an
antique and the grass was so tall it kept gumming
up the motor and conking it out.

Deciding to take a break, she eased down on the
top stoop of the porch, thirsty but too tired to walk
inside and get anything to drink.

She'd spoken with Poppy several times during
the day. He wasn't a happy camper. "The nurse isn't
pretty and I think she might be a vampire," he had
groused. "Every time I turn around she's taking
blood from me."

Edie had soothed him, grateful that the doctor
had agreed to run a battery of tests to see if Poppy's
delusion was somehow a medical issue.

And if it wasn't? A little voice nagged in the back
of her head. What did you do with somebody who
thought they were seeing space aliens? Send them

to therapy? Somehow she doubted that Black Rock had a resident therapist who might specialize in alien delusions.

All she could hope for was that Dr. Drake would find something with his tests that would account for the delusions and that whatever it was could be fixed with a pill.

All thoughts of her grandfather fled from her head as a familiar black pickup pulled into the driveway. Instantly her heart did an unexpected tap dance as Benjamin got out of the driver's seat.

Surely it was just because she'd been alone all day, she told herself. It had nothing to do with the fact that he was clad in a pair of killer jeans that hugged the length of his long legs and emphasized his lean abdomen. It had nothing to do with the glint in his eyes that perfectly matched the sexy, lazy grin that stretched his lips at the sight of her.

"Who's winning? You or the grass?" he asked as he drew closer.

"Definitely the grass," she replied as she got to her feet.

"It's too tall and the lawn mower is too old and I'm exhausted," she admitted. "What's going on? Did you find the person responsible for beating up Poppy?"

"I wish, unfortunately I don't have much to report." He stepped closer to her, close enough that she could smell his cologne. "I went out by the cemetery and looked around. The only thing I found was what looks like a part of a key ring bob. It's engraved with the letter *A*, but I can't know if it had anything to do with the attack on Walt or not."

"Don't tell him what you found. He'll swear that the *A* stands for *alien*," she said dryly.

Benjamin laughed.

He had a nice laugh, deep and robust, like a man who enjoyed laughing.

"Actually, I just came from a visit with Walt."

"I spoke to him a couple hours ago and he wasn't too happy." She was overly conscious that the knees of her jeans were grass stained from weeding and she was wearing one of Poppy's oversize flannel shirts over her T-shirt. She didn't have on a stitch of makeup and the fact that it bothered her, bothered her.

"He's still not happy. He wanted me to stop by and pick up a pair of sleep pants that he says are more civilized than the ones at the hospital. He said they're in his top dresser drawer."

"Come on in and I'll get them for you." He walked too close behind her, not stopping in the living room but rather following her into Poppy's bedroom.

She hadn't been in this room for years and it was nothing like she remembered. When her grandmother had been alive the room had been a typical bedroom with the bed covered in a floral print spread and matching curtains at the window. The nightstands had held dainty little lamps and a trunk at the foot of the bed had contained a variety of sofa blankets that her grandmother had crocheted.

Now the bed was shoved against one wall and the nightstands and trunk were gone. A large desk took up much of the room. The top of the desk was cluttered with maps of the galaxy and of the town, notes jotted in Poppy's nearly illegible hand and an instant camera.

"It looks like headquarters for an alien hunter," Benjamin said as he picked up one of the maps of the stars.

"I'm really hoping the doctor will be able to find a medical reason for this craziness." Edie pulled open the top dresser drawer and found the pair of plaid sleep pants Walt had requested. She leaned her back against the dresser, every muscle in her body sore from her fight with the lawn mower.

"Too bad Walt didn't have this camera with him when the attack happened. He could have taken a picture of his assailant." Benjamin looked up from the desk. "You look tired. Why don't you let me finish up the lawn in the morning and you go take a shower and come with me for dinner at the café?"

"The grass isn't your responsibility. I couldn't ask you to finish," she replied.

"You didn't. I offered and you'd be a fool to turn me down," he said lightly.

"Okay, I'll let you finish the lawn in the morning, but I can just grab a sandwich here for dinner." She didn't want to think about going out to dinner with him. It would feel too much like a date and she had no intention of dating ever again.

"Edie." He took a step closer to her. "A nice hot meal will do you good. Besides, the special tonight is lasagna and it's terrific."

Lasagna definitely sounded yummy, and she was starving. She hesitated a beat and then nodded.

"Okay, I'll meet you at the café," she finally said. At least that way she could eat and run.

He looked at his watch. "It's four-thirty now. Shall we meet in an hour?"

"Sounds perfect," she said as she followed him out of the bedroom. When they reached the front door, he turned back to look at her.

"You aren't going to stand me up, are you? I really hate when that happens."

She doubted that this man had ever been stood up in his life. "I'll be there," she replied.

The moment he left she raced up the stairs for a long hot shower, already regretting the agreement to meet him. She should have just stayed home and eaten a sandwich. There was something about Deputy Sheriff Benjamin Grayson that definitely put her on edge.

At five-twenty she drove slowly down Main Street looking for the café. She found it nestled between a taxidermy business and a veterinarian's office. As she pulled into a parking space down the street, a knot of nerves twisted in her stomach. *It's ridiculous to be nervous about a quick meal,* she told herself. She'd just eat fast and then get back to Poppy's house.

The evening had cooled a bit as the sun began to sink and she was grateful for the gold sweater she'd pulled on over a clean pair of jeans.

As she walked by the taxidermy store she shivered slightly at the animals in the window. A stuffed wolf looked ready to pounce on prey and a squirrel stood on its haunches with a nut between its paws. She'd never understood the desire to hang a deer head on a wall or stuff Fluffy to keep forever.

Dead was dead and no amount of stuffing and saving could change that. Her hand slid up to grip the charm around her neck. As always an edge of grief threatened to swell inside her, but she shoved it away, refusing to give it power.

Before she opened the café door she smelled the savory scents of frying onions and sweet tomato sauce and her stomach rumbled in response.

The minute she walked in the door, she saw Benjamin leaning against the long counter and talking to an attractive blonde waitress.

At the sound of the bell tinkling above the door with her entrance he turned and smiled at her, that sexy grin instantly heating places in Edie that hadn't been warm in a very long time.

He murmured something to the waitress and then approached Edie. "You came."

"I told you I would. I always do what I say I'm going to do. I'm hungry and too tired to fix something at home. This seemed like the most convenient thing to do." She was aware she sounded not only defensive, but more than a little bit cranky, as well.

It didn't seem to bother him. His eyes twinkling with good humor, he took her by the elbow and led her to an empty booth toward the back of the busy place.

As they made their way through the tables, he was greeted by everyone they passed. It was obvious Benjamin was well liked in the town he served. Not that she cared. He was just a hot, sexy blip on her radar who would be nothing but a distant memory weeks from now.

Once they were seated in the booth she picked up the menu, needing something to look at besides him. But the food listings were far less appealing than Benjamin.

She closed the menu and shoved it to one side. "Don't you have a wife or a girlfriend you should be having dinner with?"

"Don't have either," he replied and then grinned. "But thanks for being interested enough to ask."

"I'm not really interested. I was just making casual conversation." Awkward, she thought. This whole scene felt awkward. She should have made herself a sandwich at the house and called it a night. But the truth was the house had felt far too quiet without Poppy there.

"So, tell me something about Edie Burnett," he said.

"You know more about me than I'd intended for anyone to know," she replied darkly.

"All I really know is that you've had a run of bad luck lately, but I'm sure there are far more interesting aspects to you."

She leaned back in the booth. "Why are you doing that?" she asked flatly.

He frowned in confusion. "Doing what?"

"Flirting with me." Although she wanted to look away she boldly held his gaze. "I don't know what you're looking for but you won't find it with me. I'm only in town for a short period and, besides, not only am I never going to date again, but I also intend to stay celibate for the rest of my life."

His eyebrows rose and then fell back into place. "A lot of men would consider that a real challenge," he said with that wicked glint in his eyes. The glint dimmed and he shook his head. "He must have hurt you very badly."

"It doesn't matter now, that's so in my past." She was grateful that the waitress appeared at that moment to take their orders.

They both ordered the lasagna special and when the waitress left, Edie took the reins of the conversation. "I pretty well spilled my life story to you when you pulled me over for speeding. Why don't you tell me something interesting about you?"

"Probably the most interesting thing about me is that I have three brothers and one sister and all of us went into law enforcement."

"Was your father a cop?" she asked.

"No, Dad was a genius when it came to buying and selling stocks. He worked the ranch and invested and did very well. When all of us kids got older, he and my mother traveled a lot."

"I know that one of your brothers is the sheriff. What about the others?" She began to relax a bit with the conversation steered away from her.

"Tom is the oldest and he's the sheriff. Then there's Jacob, who became an FBI agent. Caleb is a deputy like me and so was…is Brittany." He winced as he caught himself, but it was obvious to Edie that he wasn't expecting a happy ending where his sister was concerned.

"I'm sorry about your sister," Edie said softly.

"Yeah, so am I. And I was sorry to hear about your mother's death. My housekeeper told me that your mom was not only pretty but also a nice woman."

"She was the best," Edie said, then picked up her glass of water to take a sip and swallow her grief. "You've told me an interesting thing about your family. But tell me something about you personally." She was determined to keep the conversation on him, to focus on anything but herself and all the challenges she faced.

"Let's see." He leaned back against the booth and gave her that lazy smile that never failed to light a tiny fire inside her. "I like a horseback ride at sunset and big juicy steaks cooked outside. Green is my favorite color and I've got a dog named Tiny who thinks he's master of the world. I've never had a broken heart and I don't think I've ever broken one. How's that?" he said.

"Unbelievable," she replied. There was no way a man who looked like Benjamin Grayson could have gone through his life so far and not broken a heart or two.

At that moment the waitress arrived with their orders and their conversation moved to more general things. He was pleasant to talk to and for a little while, she forgot all that was facing her. But she remained on edge, far too conscious of the allure of his flirtatious eyes and the warmth of his smile.

When her plate was empty she was ready to run. He offered to pay for the meal and after some argument, she accepted.

As they walked out of the café and into the deepening twilight of evening, he insisted he walk her to her car. "It's really not necessary," she protested. "I'm only parked down the street a little bit."

"I know, but it's a gentleman's duty to see a woman to her car," he replied lightly.

When they reached her vehicle, she pulled her keys from her purse, ready to bail and get away from Benjamin. "Thanks for dinner," she said as she unlocked her car door and then turned back to face him. "I appreciate everything you've done, but I can handle things now and you can get back to your own life."

"You aren't getting rid of me that easily," he replied. "I'll be over first thing in the morning to finish mowing the lawn. That was our deal."

She hesitated, not wanting to take anything more from him. He took a step closer to her. "Edie, you don't have to be in this all alone." He reached up and gently pushed one of her errant curls away from her forehead. "Walt is my friend and I'll do whatever I can to support you."

He dropped his hand back to his side but didn't move away from her. She felt as if she'd stopped breathing the moment he'd touched her and she forced herself to breathe now. "I appreciate that. Okay, then I guess I'll see you in the morning."

She'd let him finish the lawn and then she'd have nothing more to do with him. The last thing she needed in her life at the moment was another complication and Benjamin definitely felt as if he could be a big complication if she'd allow it.

For a moment he stared at her lips, as if he wanted to kiss her, and for that same amount of time she almost wished he would. Instead she jerked open her car door and wondered when she'd lost her mind.

"Edie, before you go take this." He pulled out a card from his pocket. "This has my personal cell phone number on it. Don't hesitate to use it if you need anything."

She took the card and dropped it into her purse and then slid in behind the steering wheel, eager to make her escape from this man who made her think about hot kisses and the sweet sensation of skin against skin.

She drove away without looking back, knowing that it was going to take her all night long to forget the feel of his warm fingers against her forehead, to get the very scent of him out of her head.

When she got back to Poppy's place, she called to check in on her grandfather, who was as cranky as she'd ever heard him, then she decided to vacuum and dust the living room.

She needed some sort of activity to occupy her and hopefully keep thoughts of Benjamin from her mind. But he was difficult to cast out of her head.

He was nice. He was definitely sexually drawn to her. She knew it by the look in his eyes, by the fact that he seemed to have trouble keeping his hands off her. Was he only being nice to her because he wanted to get her into bed?

Somehow he didn't strike her as that type and that was what worried her. She reluctantly had to admit that she liked him and that was on top of the wild physical attraction she felt toward him.

By the time she'd finished with the housework she was exhausted and she'd finally managed to banish thoughts of Benjamin from her mind.

She locked the front door and then headed upstairs for bed. Tomorrow she intended to call Poppy's doctor and get an update on the tests they had run on the old man. She prayed that Dr. Drake would be able to find an easy fix for Poppy's obsession and that Benjamin and his brothers would find and arrest whoever had assaulted her grandfather.

Even though she was exhausted, once she was in bed her mind whirled with all the things waiting for her when she got back to Topeka. First and foremost on her list of things to do was find another job.

She'd loved managing the restaurant, but wasn't sure she wanted to go back into the same field. In truth she didn't know what she wanted to do with the rest of her life. A year ago she'd thought her future was all planned out. She'd marry Greg, be a wife and mother and decide on a career when their children went off to school.

Greg was on board right up until the time he disappeared from her life. Just like her father. She punched the pillow and closed her eyes, determined to get a good night's sleep without any more thoughts of betrayals from men.

I deserve it, a little voice whispered in her head. *I'm not good enough to be with anyone.* Emotion swelled up inside her but she steadfastly shoved it back down and squeezed her eyes more tightly closed.

She awoke suddenly, her heart pounding with unexpected adrenaline and her body tensed in a fight-or-flight response. Immediately she knew something had awakened her and as she remained frozen in place, she heard a faint noise coming from downstairs.

Somebody was in the house. The thought thundered in her brain. She knew she'd locked the front door before she'd come upstairs. But as she heard more noise she knew with certainty that somebody was there.

She swung her legs over the side of the bed and stood, then quietly crept to the top of the stairs. The noise was definitely coming from the direction of Poppy's bedroom.

Was it possible Poppy had somehow managed to talk the doctor into releasing him? She glanced at the clock on the nightstand, the luminous dial letting her know it was after one. Surely nobody would have released him in the middle of the night. It was more likely that Poppy had left on his own, slinking out like a thief in the dark. He could be so bullheaded at times.

She ran lightly down the stairs, aided by the bright moonlight that flooded in the living room windows. As she gazed toward Poppy's bedroom, she frowned in confusion. There were no lights on, but she saw the faint glow of a flashlight.

"Poppy?" The single word fell from her lips.

The flashlight whirled toward her, blinding her

as it hit her eyes. She raised a hand in defense, but gasped as a big body collided with hers.

The force of the collision lifted her off her feet and as she fell, the back of her head slammed into the floor and she knew no more.

Chapter 4

Benjamin sat in his easy chair in the living room and channel-surfed. It was late and he should be in bed, but he was too restless to sleep and it was all thanks to Edie Burnett. Something about the woman had him twisted in knots.

He'd hated to tell her goodbye after dinner and was already eagerly anticipating going to Walt's in the morning to see her again.

It was a new feeling for him, this sweet anticipation, and one he'd never felt for a woman. It had heartbreak written all over it, but knowing that didn't seem to make him cautious.

He'd dated plenty over the past couple years but none of the women he'd seen had shot him full of the simmering excitement like Edie.

But she claimed she wanted nothing to do with men. Or sex. He'd never met a candidate less likely for celibacy. Those lips of hers were made for kissing and her curves were meant to be stroked and loved.

She definitely had some sharp edges that he guessed disillusionment had formed in her. It was that sharpness she used as a defense whenever he got too close.

As they'd eaten dinner, more than once when she got uncomfortable with the conversation, she'd reached up and touched the charm hanging on a gold chain around her neck. The charm was a pair of angel wings that he guessed was a symbol of the mother she'd lost.

He stroked Tiny's soft fur as he changed the channel for the hundredth time and realized that television in the middle of the night sucked. Tiny released a long-suffering sigh, probably wondering why they were in the chair and not in bed.

The ring of his cell phone jerked him upright. He fumbled in his pocket, pulled it out and answered.

"Benjamin, can you come over here?"

It took him a moment to recognize Edie's voice. She sounded strange, stressed to the max and needy. "What's wrong?"

A small burst of laughter escaped her. "I think the aliens have landed."

His stomach clenched with nervous energy. "I'll be right there." He didn't bother to ask her any more questions but instead hung up and was in his truck and headed to Walt's within minutes.

There was no question that something had happened, something that had her spooked enough to call him. He tightened his hands on the steering wheel as he sped down the dark deserted streets.

At least he knew that whatever had happened, she was physically all right, at least enough to make the phone call to him. But emotionally she'd sounded fragile and he couldn't get to her fast enough.

When he pulled up the driveway, he saw her standing in the doorway. As he got out of his truck, she stepped on the porch. She was clad in a navy nightshirt that barely skimmed the tops of her thighs and her face was as pale as the moon overhead.

"What happened?" he asked as he reached the porch.

"Somebody was in the house, in Poppy's bedroom. I was in bed asleep and I woke up when I heard the noise. I thought it was Poppy, that maybe he'd left the hospital." She frowned and raised a hand to the back of her head.

He took her by the arm and led her into the house and to the sofa. "Are you hurt?" he asked, a new knot in his chest growing bigger. Her skin was cool and her arm trembled beneath his hand.

He wanted nothing more than to pull her against him and hold her tight until she was warm. But his first role was as a responding officer to a crime scene.

"I hit my head," she said. "He shoved past me and knocked me down and I hit my head on the floor."

He reached up and felt the back of her head and muttered a curse as he fingered the goose egg there.

"We need to get you to the hospital and have that checked out," he said as she waved him away from her.

"It's fine. I'm fine. I was just out for a minute or two."

"Out? You mean like unconscious?"

She winced. "Stop shouting. I said I was okay."

Benjamin took a step backward, shocked as he realized he had been shouting and he'd never been a shouting kind of man in his life. He sat on the sofa next to her. "Tell me exactly what happened."

He listened and took notes as she told him about waking up and thinking Walt had come home. As she told him about seeing the intruder in Walt's bedroom and that person slamming into her, his blood went cold.

Thank God the intruder hadn't used a gun. When he thought of all the horrible scenarios that might have occurred, he went weak in the knees with relief.

"Did he take anything?" he asked.

"I don't know. I didn't go into the bedroom. When I came to, I just grabbed my purse from the kitchen counter and found your card."

He was grateful to see that some of the color was returning to her cheeks. "I'm going to call my brother and get him out here," he said. "And I'll see if I can rouse Dr. Drake to come over and examine you."

"That's really not necessary," she protested.

"I think it is. It's either see Dr. Drake here or head to the emergency room at the hospital. You were knocked unconscious. You need to be checked out."

She managed to glare at him. "You sound pretty bossy."

"At the moment I'm feeling pretty bossy." As she leaned her head back and closed her eyes, he made his phone calls. When he was finished she raised her head once again to look at him.

"Maybe it was somebody who heard through the grapevine that Poppy was in the hospital and decided to take advantage of the situation by robbing the place," she said. "My car is in the garage. I don't think the person knew I was here."

"That's possible," he agreed. "I'm going to check out Walt's bedroom. I'll be right back."

"I'll go with you." She jumped up off the sofa and a flash of pain momentarily twisted her features.

"Why don't you sit and relax? It's obvious you have a headache." Once again he fought the impulse to take her into his arms.

"I'd feel better staying with you."

Her words let him know just how spooked she still was. She followed close behind him and together they went into Walt's room. "Don't touch anything," he cautioned as he used his elbow to turn on the light in the room.

"Don't worry," she said dryly.

Two things struck Benjamin as he looked around the room. The first was that all the windows were still intact and locked, indicating the point of entry had been someplace else in the house. The second was that it was obvious somebody had been in the room. The papers that had been on top of the desk were now strewn across the floor. Drawers hung open with clothes spilling out and boxes had been pulled off the shelves in the closet.

"If they were looking for something of value, they came to the wrong house," Edie said.

"Can you tell if anything is missing?" he asked.

He watched as she gazed around the room and frowned. "Nothing that I can see. Wait...remember the camera that was on the desk? I don't see it any-where now."

He walked around the desk, checking the floor to see if perhaps the camera had fallen off, but it was nowhere to be seen.

"What on earth has Poppy gotten himself involved in?" Edie asked softly.

"I don't know, but somehow we're going to figure it out," he replied.

At that moment Tom arrived at the scene, followed closely by Dr. Drake. As the doctor examined Edie, Tom and Benjamin got to work processing the scene.

The entry point was the front door, which held an old lock that had been jimmied open. Whoever had come in had apparently gone directly to Walt's bedroom, for there was no indication that anything else had been disturbed.

Dr. Drake pronounced that Edie probably had a mild concussion and would be fine and then he left. By that time Tom had dusted the front door for prints and Benjamin had dusted the bedroom. Benjamin had little hope of lifting anything. Whoever had bro-ken in was probably smart enough to wear gloves.

Edie had nothing to offer as far as what the per-son had looked like. It had been dark and everything had happened too fast. All she could be sure of was that he'd been big and dark and had hit her like an NFL tackle.

It was after three when they had done all they could for the night and Tom left. Edie was curled up in one corner of the sofa, looking small and exhausted.

Benjamin sat next to her. "How's your head?"

"Better than it was. At least now it's down to a three-piece band instead of a full percussion orchestra." She released a weary sigh.

"You need to get a new lock on the front door. It probably wouldn't hurt to put a new one on the back door, as well. I'll get somebody to take care of it first thing in the morning."

"Thank you," she replied. "I have to confess, I'm a little bit nervous about staying here all alone for the rest of the night without the locks fixed."

He knew better than to think she was issuing an invitation for him to spend the night with her, but he couldn't stop the slight flush of heat that filled him at the very thought.

"I guess you have two options," he said, pleased that his voice sounded normal. "I can either take you to a motel for the rest of the night or I could stay here until morning."

She shot him a narrowed glance and he did everything possible to keep his features without any expression. The last thing he wanted her to think was that he was somehow taking advantage of the situation.

Releasing another deep sigh, she sat up straighter. "I guess it would be stupid to go to a motel at this time of the night. I'll get you some blankets and a pillow so you can bunk here on the sofa."

"Or, just for your information, I've been told I make a terrific snuggle buddy."

"Deputy Grayson, surely *snuggle buddy* isn't in your job description," she said as she rose to her feet.

"It could be," he replied as he also stood.

"That's so not happening," she said. "But I might share a little conversation with you over a cup of tea before I turn in."

"Sounds like a plan," he agreed easily. As he followed her into the kitchen, he admitted that he'd much prefer a place in her bed, but as she'd reminded him moments before—that was so not happening tonight.

The hot tea didn't quite banish the chill that had taken hold of Edie since the moment she'd come to on the living-room floor.

"Talk to me, Benjamin, tell me more about the ranch where you live," she said, needing something, anything, to take her mind off the fact that somebody had been in the house while she'd been asleep and vulnerable.

What might have happened if she hadn't awakened when she did? Would the intruder have eventually crept up the stairs and found her? Would a simply robbery have escalated to something worse—her rape? Her murder?

As Benjamin began to talk about his life at the ranch, his eyes took on the sparkle of a man who

loved that life and his deep voice filled with a vi-
brancy that was vastly appealing.

As he talked of cattle and horses and his daily routine when at home, she felt herself begin to finally
relax. There was something solid about Benjamin
and the life he led, something that reminded her of
all the hopes she'd once possessed, all the dreams
she'd once had for herself.

She'd once wanted the kind of life he was describ-
ing, one of normal routine and peace, filled with the
love of family and the kind of happiness that came
from knowing where you belonged.

It had been a long time since she'd felt as if she
belonged anywhere. Looking back now, she recognized that there had always been a little part of her
that had suspected Greg wasn't the man for her. But
she'd been desperate to be loved, tired of being alone
and had clung to him despite her reservations.

Greg hadn't been her first mistake. Before him
had been Charles, a man she'd dated for almost a
year, a man who hadn't known the meaning of fidel-
ity. Loving stupid, that was what she was good at,
and it was better to never love again than continue
making the same mistakes.

Her head began to pound again as if in protest of
her thoughts and exhaustion slammed into her with a
force that made her long for the comfort of bed. "I've
got to go to bed," she said as she pushed back from
the kitchen table. "The extra blankets are upstairs in
the closet. I'll just get what you need for the sofa."

He got up, as well. "I'll follow you so you don't
have to make an extra trip down the stairs."

"Thanks," she replied and wondered if he was always so nice. She was far too conscious of him behind her as she climbed the stairs.

"Blankets in there?" He pointed ahead of them to the hall closet. "I'll take care of myself," he continued as she nodded. "Let's get you tucked into bed."

She walked to her bedroom doorway and then turned to face him. "Thank you, Benjamin, for agreeing to stay here for whatever is left of the night. I'll be fine once the new locks are installed."

"It's not a problem." He took a step closer to her, so close she could smell the scent of him, feel the heat that radiated from his body. "You had a scare and I'm glad to do whatever I can to make you feel safe."

She felt wonderfully safe and intensely in danger with him standing so close to her. "I guess I'll say good-night."

"Wait, there's just one thing I've been wanting to do all night." He reached out and pulled her against him, close enough that she could feel his heartbeat beneath the solid wall of his chest.

She held herself stiffly but as his hand slid up and down her back as if to comfort, she allowed herself to relax against him. She hadn't realized just how badly she'd needed a hug until now.

The feel of him against her, so warm, so strong, finally banished the last of the chill that had resided in her since the moment she'd awakened and realized somebody was in the house.

Moments passed and the slide of his hand over her

back slowed and instead of being comforted, Edie felt a new tension building between them.

She raised her head to look at him and saw the flames that filled his eyes. Instantly she knew that she should step out of his arms, gain some distance from him.

She did neither.

As his mouth descended toward hers, she opened her lips to welcome the kiss, telling herself she could always justify the madness by claiming brain numbness from her fall.

His mouth plied hers with a welcome heat, his tongue touching hers as he tightened his arms around her. *Falling,* she felt herself falling into him, consumed by him as all other thoughts fled her mind.

She tasted his desire for her, a desire tempered with a tenderness that threatened to be her undoing, and that was ultimately what made her halt the kiss.

A small groan escaped him as he dropped his arms from around her and took a step back. "Are you sure about this celibacy thing?" he asked with a teasing grin.

"One little kiss isn't about to change my mind," she replied. "Good night, Benjamin." She escaped into the bedroom and closed the door behind her, needing to gain some distance from him.

She fell into bed, exhausted by the events of the night, but sleep refused to come easily. The kiss. It was that kiss that haunted her. And the man.

Benjamin Grayson was like no man she'd ever known before and he scared her. She needed to keep her distance from him until she left Black Rock to return home.

But how soon could she get back home? With Poppy getting beaten up and the break-in tonight, how could she possibly consider leaving? She wasn't sure what worried her more, the mess of Poppy or the insane attraction she felt for Benjamin.

She fell asleep with the taste of him on her lips and awakened with the sun streaming through her window and the sound of the lawn mower growling from the front yard.

By the time she'd showered and dressed for the day, the noise outside had stopped. She found Benjamin in the kitchen, seated at the table and sipping a cup of coffee. The very sight of him brought back the memory of the devastating kiss and an irritation surged up inside her.

"Shouldn't you be at work chasing bad guys?" she asked sharply. "This town is obviously infested with them."

One of his dark eyebrows rose. "Sounds like somebody got up on the wrong side of the bed." A blush warmed her cheeks as she headed for the coffee. "I contacted Ed Burell, the local locksmith. He'll be here in the next half hour or so to take care of changing the locks."

"Thanks, I appreciate your help," she said as she joined him at the table. It was impossible to be cranky with him when he was going out of his way to make her life easier.

"My brother Caleb is already out interviewing the neighbors to see if they saw anyone or anything suspicious last night. Tom has been talking to some of the high-school kids to see if they know anything about Walt's attack and I've already alerted everyone in town who processes film to give me a call if somebody brings in an instant camera. There's not much else that can be done at the moment."

"I didn't mean to sound like I thought you weren't doing your job," she replied. "I just wish we could figure out what's going on."

"We will." There was a fierce determination in his voice. "Sooner or later the person who attacked Walt will be caught and charged with the crime. This is a small town and eventually somebody will say something and we'll have our man."

"And hopefully the doctor will tell me all Poppy needs is a pill to fix him right up and I can get back home."

"Now, I've got to admit I'm not in any hurry to see you go." He stood and carried his cup to the sink. "But speaking of going, I need to get out of here." He turned back to face her. "Do you want me to wait with you until the locksmith arrives?"

"No, I'll be fine," she assured him. "I do appreciate everything you've done. Just keep me informed about the investigations and that's all I really need from you." It was an obvious dismissal. "An occasional check-in phone call would be great."

Once again that well-shaped dark brow rose and a twinkle filled his eyes. "That kiss was either very, very bad or very, very good."

The familiar warmth of a blush heated her cheeks.

"That kiss was stupid, the result of a head injury that didn't have me thinking clearly."

He laughed. "If that's what you need to tell yourself to get through the day, then so be it. I'm sure I'll talk to you later."

She remained seated at the table as he left the house, trying to ignore the slow burn that he created inside her. Okay, she could admit that she was intensely physically attracted to him, but the kiss they had shared was the beginning and the end of acting on that attraction.

She'd only been seated at the table for about ten minutes when Ed Burell arrived to change the locks on the doors. He left after handing her the new keys.

Edie left soon after that, deciding a visit to Poppy was in order. As she drove down Main Street, she found herself looking at the various businesses.

There was a cute little dress boutique, the Canyon Pizzeria, the café and dozens of other businesses. Unlike many small Kansas towns that had fallen on hard times, Black Rock seemed to be thriving despite the current economic climate.

Edie parked on the street next to the small hospital. She walked inside and headed to the second floor where Poppy's room was located. When she entered his room, she was surprised to see him dressed and seated on the edge of his bed. A plump nurse with a pretty smile greeted her.

"I just tried to call you," Poppy said. "I can go home. Fit as a fiddle, that's what I am, other than my black eye and cracked ribs. Dr. Drake gave me all kinds of tests and says he wishes he was as healthy as I am."

Edie looked at the nurse, who nodded in affirmation. "He's good to go," she replied. "Dr. Drake should be in any moment if you have any questions."

Moments later a talk with the doctor in the hallway let Edie know he'd found no medical reason for her grandfather's delusion. There was nothing more he could do but release him.

A half hour later they were back home. As Walt prepared lunch, Edie sat at the table and listened to him regaling his hospital adventure to her.

She tried not to be depressed as she realized she was no closer to solving the problem of Poppy than she'd been before his attack. Granted, somebody had beaten up the old man, but it definitely hadn't been a space alien.

As they ate she brought him up-to-date on the break-in and the new locks on the doors. When she told him that the only thing that had been missing was his camera, he blew a gasket.

"The bastards knew I had pictures of them. The night before you arrived here." He got up from the table with jerky movements that spoke of his irritation. "I was going to take that camera down to Burt Smith's discount store to get the pictures developed."

"Poppy, you have to get this idea of aliens out of your head," Edie exclaimed.

"Out of my head? I'm not about to get those bastards out of my head. Tonight I'm going hunting again and this time I'm going to take my gun."

Edie stared at him appalled. Just what Black Rock needed, a crazy man with a gun out in the middle of the night.

Chapter 5

It was just before midnight when Edie and her grandfather left his house. Edie knew it was madness but at least she'd managed to talk Poppy into leaving his gun at home. The good people of Black Rock should give her an award.

"Where are we headed?" she asked once they were in the car and pulling out of the driveway.

"Go south on Main Street, I'll tell you where to turn off when we get there," he replied. He was clad all in black, like a ninja warrior ready for battle.

"Are we going back to the cemetery?"

"Nah, lately on Friday nights they've been in Devon Moreland's clearing," he replied.

Not for the first time since agreeing to this madness, Edie's thoughts turned to Benjamin.

Edie had considered calling Benjamin to ask him to come over and help her change Poppy's mind about going out tonight, but after some thought she'd decided against it.

What worried her was the idea that perhaps she wanted to call Benjamin not because she needed his help with Poppy, but just because she wanted to see him again.

Earlier she'd listened to Poppy talk about his time in the hospital and while he'd napped she'd watched television, but no matter how she tried to keep her mind occupied, thoughts of Benjamin and the kiss they'd shared kept intruding.

He'd kissed her as if he'd meant it, as if it were a prelude to something hot and wild, yet something tender and enduring. She didn't want to believe in the promise of his kiss and if what he'd told her about himself was right, she didn't want to be the first woman in his life to break his heart.

And she would break his heart if he tried to pursue anything with her. Even if he thought he might be the right man for her, she definitely knew she was the wrong woman for him.

At this time of the night the streets were dark and deserted. Edie drove slowly, wishing they were back at the house and not on some crazy hunt for aliens.

"This is the kind of night they like," Poppy said, breaking the silence. He leaned forward to look up at the sky through the windshield. "See them clouds chasing across the moon? They like cloudy nights. Turn left up ahead."

She made the turn and tried not to feel as if she

were indulging Poppy's fantasy. They both should be home in bed, but she was hoping that she would see whatever it was that made the old man insist there were aliens in town. Then maybe she'd be able to make him understand that he'd been mistaken.

"How are you doing with that boyfriend of yours?" Poppy asked.

Edie tightened her hands on the steering wheel. "We broke up," she said, pleased that her voice remained neutral.

"Turn left here," he said. "So, does that mean you have a new beau?"

"At the moment I'm footloose and fancy-free, and that's just the way I want it," she replied as she focused on the narrow road they traveled.

"Turn right up ahead," Poppy said.

She felt as if they'd entered a forest. Trees crowded together so closely that the moonlight was obscured overhead. "You can park right up there under that oak tree and we'll walk the rest of the way."

"How did you find this place?" Edie asked as she parked her car and shut off the engine.

"I didn't find it, the aliens did and I found them. It took me a couple months to figure out their routine. Some nights they're in the cemetery and then some nights they're out here." He grabbed the flashlight he'd brought with him and opened his car door. "Come on, I've got a perfect hiding place where you'll be able to see them."

Edie left the car and followed close behind Poppy as he took off walking through the thick woods, his flashlight beam bouncing in the darkness with each step he took.

No wonder Poppy was in such good physical shape, she thought. On the nights he went alien hunting he must walk miles. They didn't go far before he gestured her down behind a large bush.

"See that clearing?" He pointed the flashlight beam forward to reveal a small break in the woods. "That's where I've seen one of them several times before." He shut off the flashlight and sat in the grass, indicating that she should do the same. "Now we wait and see if one of the bastards show up tonight."

Edie settled in next to Poppy and for the next few minutes the only sounds were those of a soft breeze stirring the leaves overhead and insects buzzing and clicking their night songs.

"You know you won't find a better man than Benjamin," Poppy whispered, breaking the silence.

Startled by his words, she tried to see his face in the darkness. "I'm really not looking for a man, Poppy."

"I'm just saying. Most of the women in town seem to find him attractive, but he's not a trifling man. Out of all the Grayson men he's always been my favorite. Tom is a take-charge kind of guy and Caleb is impulsive and easy to rile. Jacob was always a loner but Benjamin is solid as the earth and has a good heart."

As Poppy continued to extol Benjamin's virtues, all Edie could think about was the dark chocolate color of his eyes as they filled with desire and that crazy hot kiss they had shared.

"I keep telling him he should forget his deputy job

and work full-time at the ranch. That's what he loves, working with the animals and the land."

Edie remembered the passion that had filled his voice when he'd talked about the ranch. "If that's what he loves to do then why isn't he doing it full-time?"

"Don't know. I can't ever get a solid answer from him."

They both fell silent once again. The minutes ticked by in agonizing slowness. After half an hour of sitting, the ground seemed to grow harder beneath Edie and sleepiness began to creep in.

They both should be home asleep, not sitting outside in the brisk autumn night air waiting for aliens to appear. She should especially not be out here thinking about Benjamin Grayson, warmed by the memory of the kiss they had shared.

"Poppy, let's go home," she finally said when another fifteen minutes or so had passed. "It's really late and I'm tired."

He sighed, obviously disappointed. "I wanted you to see one of the aliens. I want you to know that I'm not crazy. I know everyone in town thinks I've done gone around the bend, but I'm not nuts."

"Poppy, I don't think you're nuts," she protested softly.

"You're just like your mama, Edie girl. You have her good heart," he replied, a smile obvious in his voice. "I've missed you, Edie. I've missed your phone calls. You're the only family I've got left."

Edie's "good" heart squeezed tight in her chest.

Was it possible this whole alien thing was nothing more than a manifestation of Walt's loneliness?

"I've missed you, too, Poppy. And I promise I'm going to be better about keeping in touch with you," she replied.

Before he could answer, the sound of a low motor filled the air. "Here they come," Poppy exclaimed.

Edie peeked through the brush and in the distance saw a small lit vehicle approaching the clearing. It took her only an instant to realize it was an off-road ATV, but with the lights radiating out from it, she could easily see how a confused old man might think it was some kind of a space terrain vehicle.

"Poppy, keep down and keep quiet," she said as the vehicle came to a stop. Her heart slammed against her chest in a frantic tattoo. What would somebody be doing on an ATV in the middle of the woods at this time of night? Certainly nothing good, she thought.

The ATV shut off and Edie gripped Poppy's arm tightly, hoping and praying the old man didn't suddenly jump up to confront the driver.

Her curiosity turned to fear when the lone man stepped off the ATV and she realized he wore some sort of full hazmat suit. No wonder Poppy had thought the aliens had landed.

With the moonlight playing on the silver suit and reflecting off the mirrorlike face of the helmet, the man looked not only otherworldly but also ominous. What on earth was going on?

He carried with him a small spade and some sort of bag that held an eerie yellow-green glow. As Edie and Poppy watched, the man quickly dug a hole and dropped the bag inside.

"I'll bet that's the one who beat me." Poppy's voice was far too loud for the silence in the clearing. The man's head lifted as Edie held her breath and squeezed Poppy's arm even harder.

The man raised a high-beam flashlight and began to shine it in their direction as he pulled a gun with his other hand. Edie gasped as the light found them.

"Poppy, run," she said urgently. She got to her feet and yanked up the old man by his arm.

At the same time she heard the crash of brush ahead and knew the man was coming after them. A scream released from her as the crack of a gun splintered the air.

Thankfully Poppy was spry and seemed to know the woods. They held hands and ran as fast as their legs would take them. In the distance she heard the whine of the ATV and knew their pursuer had stopped his foot chase but intended to continue on the ATV.

The lights from the all-terrain vehicle bounced off the trees as the engine whined and crashed through the brush. With each step she took, Edie feared a bullet in her back.

Poppy's beating had obviously been some sort of warning, but the fact that the man had shot a gun at them let her know he wasn't warning anymore.

She nearly sobbed in relief as they made it back to her car. Poppy fell into the passenger's seat while she threw herself in behind the steering wheel and punched the key into the ignition. As the engine roared to life she slammed the gear shift into Reverse.

The tires spun as she wheeled the car around for a quick escape. At the same time the ATV burst through the trees just behind them. Edie screamed and Poppy cursed as their back windshield shattered.

"Drive, girl!" Poppy yelled. "Put the pedal to the metal!"

Edie did just that, flooring the gas pedal and praying that the old clunker didn't pick this particular time to conk out. She flew down the road, barely making the turn that would eventually lead them back into the heart of the town.

"Yee-haw," Poppy yelled. "We lost him."

Edie looked in her rearview mirror and released a shuddering sigh of relief, but there was no relief from the fear that still torched through her. There was only one man she wanted to see, one man who could make her feel safe in what had become a crazy world.

"Tell me how to get to Benjamin's," she said. She wasn't sure what bothered her more, the fact that some crazy man in a hazmat suit had tried to kill them or her desperate need to be with a man she knew she shouldn't want.

He was dreaming about her. Somewhere in the back of his sleep-addled mind Benjamin knew it was a dream and that he didn't want to ever wake up.

Edie was in his arms, her green eyes glowing with smoky desire. His head filled with the scent of her, that slightly wild spicy fragrance that drove him half-wild.

Her skin was warm and silky against his and he wanted to take her, possess her in a way he'd never possessed another woman.

He was just about to do that when a loud banging broke the dream. Tiny began to bark and jumped off the foot of his bed and raced out of the room.

As the last vestige of the dream fell away, Benjamin leaped out of bed and grabbed the jeans he'd shucked off before going to sleep. As he yanked them on, the knocking at the front door continued. He grabbed his gun from the nightstand and then hurried out of the bedroom and down the hallway, turning on lights as he went.

What the hell? As he pulled open the door Edie and Walt tumbled inside. "He tried to kill us!" Walt exclaimed as Tiny's barks grew sharper. "The bastard shot out the back window of Edie's car."

Benjamin had no idea what was going on or what had happened, but Walt's words ripped a surge of unexpected protectiveness through him as he looked at Edie.

Her eyes were wide, her face pale and he quickly placed his hands on her shoulders and then ran them down her arms, ending with her trembling hands in his. "Are you all right?"

She gave a curt nod of her head. "I'm okay, and it wasn't a space alien, but it was a man in a hazmat suit on an ATV."

"A hazmat suit?" Walt looked as bewildered as Benjamin felt at the moment.

"Come on, let's all go into the kitchen and you can tell me what's going on." Reluctantly Benjamin released Edie's hands and they headed toward the kitchen.

Once there Benjamin gestured them into chairs at the table and as he sat, Tiny curled up at his feet, obviously exhausted by his earlier frantic barking. "Now, start at the beginning and tell me exactly what happened."

As Edie told him the events of the night, a hard knot of tension formed in his chest, first that she and Walt would be foolish enough to venture out in the middle of the night and second because something terrible was obviously going on under the cover of night in the small town he loved.

"Where exactly did this happen?" he asked.

"That little clearing on Devon Moreland's land," Walt said with a frown. "So, they aren't space men?" He looked at Edie and for a moment appeared older than his years.

She reached out and covered the old man's hand with one of hers. "No, Poppy. The man in the woods was definitely human."

Walt frowned and shook his head. "I feel like such a damned old fool."

"He looked like a spaceman. Anyone might have made the same mistake," Edie said gently and then looked at Benjamin. "He was burying something in the clearing. When he saw us, he pulled a gun and shot at us, then chased us on his ATV. He stopped chasing us when we hit Main Street."

"But not before he blew out the back window of her car," Walt added.

"I don't suppose there's any way you could make

an identification?" Benjamin asked, although he knew the answer even before she shook her head.

"Impossible. With that suit on I couldn't even swear that it was definitely a man and not a woman," she replied.

Benjamin scooted back his chair from the table. "I don't want you two going home tonight. Why don't I get you settled in here and we'll talk more in the morning."

"I am tired," Walt agreed as he also got up from the table. "I don't like putting you out, but I have to confess I'd feel more comfortable at your place tonight."

"I'll just wait here while you get him settled in," Edie said.

It took only a few minutes for Benjamin to make Walt comfortable in one of the guest bedrooms. As he headed back into the kitchen, his head reeled with all the information he'd heard. The idea of how close Edie and Walt had come to disaster horrified him.

He found her still in the chair at the table with Tiny in her lap. "What a sweet baby," she said as she stroked Tiny's dark fur.

"Don't let him fool you. Beneath that goofy grin of his is a mutt determined to rule the world." He was glad to see that she looked better than when she and Walt had initially flown through his front door.

"I hate to even ask this, but do you think you could take me back to where you and Walt were tonight? It's been years since I've been anywhere near Devon Moreland's property."

"I think so," she replied.

"I need to make some calls, get things lined up and then we'll head out." Although the last thing he wanted was to drag her out of the house once again, he needed her to show him exactly where all this had gone down.

He wasn't worried about Walt somehow sneaking out again. As he prepared to leave he checked on the old man, who was snoring up a storm. Besides, if he awakened, the ranch was too far out of town for him to try to walk anywhere.

The first thing he did was call Tom and fill him in on what had occurred then made arrangements to meet both Tom and Caleb at the sheriff's office in thirty minutes.

He pulled on a shirt and a jacket, checked on Walt one last time and then he and Edie got into his truck to make the drive back into town.

"I'm sorry you got involved in all this," he said.

"Me, too. Although I'm more than a little curious to see what *all this* is," she admitted. "That scene in the woods tonight felt like something out of a science fiction movie."

"You and Walt could have been killed," he said with a touch of censure.

"I know, we shouldn't have been out there, but Poppy's original plan was to take his gun and go alien hunting. I got him to agree to leave his gun at home by going with him."

Benjamin fought a shudder as he thought of the old man armed and running amok in the darkness. "I guess I should thank God for small favors."

She released a sigh. "I was hoping that I would see

something that had a logical explanation, something that would make me able to convince him there were no aliens in town."

He glanced at her and then back at the road. "I don't want you out again that late at night."

"Don't worry. I can say for sure that tonight was the first and the last of my alien hunting," she replied dryly.

"I'd also like for you and Walt to stay at the ranch until we figure out what's going on," he added.

"Surely that isn't necessary," she protested.

"I think it is," he replied smoothly but firmly. "Those were real bullets that were fired at you tonight. We have to assume that the break-in at Walt's is related, and that means he knows who you are and where you live. You saw him doing something he obviously didn't want anyone to see and now he'll see you as a real threat."

As a deputy sheriff he wanted her at his place because he thought it was the best place for her to be. But his desire to have her stay at the ranch transcended his role as a deputy.

As a man he needed to protect what was his and even though he'd only known her for a couple days, somehow in that span, he recognized that he'd claimed her as his own.

He glanced at her again and saw the frown that whipped across her features. She sighed with weary resignation. "I guess I'd be a fool not to stay here."

At that moment they pulled up in front of the sheriff's office where Tom's car was already parked. "I sent Caleb over to the fire department to pick us up a couple suits," Tom said after he'd greeted them. "I figure if the perp felt the need to wear a hazmat suit when he was disposing of whatever he had, it's best if we have them on when we dig it up."

"Good idea," Benjamin replied with a reassuring glance at Edie. She offered him a weak smile and at that moment Caleb arrived and they all headed to the area where Edie and Walt had encountered the man.

Tom and Caleb rode together in Tom's car and followed Benjamin and Edie. "It sounds like Walt stumbled on some sort of illegal dumping," he said as they left Main Street.

"At least we've solved the mystery of the space aliens and I know Poppy isn't crazy." She reached out and directed the heater vent to blow on her face.

"Cold?"

"Just chilled by everything that's happened. Turn left ahead."

He made the turn and checked his rearview mirror to see his brother's car right behind his. "I suppose with everything that's happened lately now wouldn't be a good time to ask you if you've considered moving to Black Rock."

"Why would I consider doing that?" she countered.

So I'd have the opportunity to see you every day of my life. The words played in his head but thankfully didn't make it to his lips. "I know you're going to be looking for a new job and a new place to live. I'm sure Walt would love having you here in town."

"Maybe, but that's not in my plans. We parked up there next to that tree." She pointed ahead.

Benjamin pulled to a halt and cursed himself for being a fool. He seemed to be suffering his first major crush on a woman and other than her response to his kiss, she appeared fairly oblivious to his charms.

He only hoped that this crazy, giddy feeling he got whenever he was around her would fade as he got to know her better.

They all departed their vehicles and it was quickly decided that Benjamin and Tom would don the hazmat suits and go into the clearing while Caleb stayed with Edie.

The minute Benjamin was suited up all thoughts of romance and Edie fled from his mind. This was business and the fact that he and his brother wore hazmat suits meant it was serious business.

Together he and Tom made their way slowly into the clearing, their high-powered flashlight beams leading the way. The woods were still, as if any creatures had long left the area and were afraid to return.

Benjamin had his gun in hand, although he didn't anticipate any trouble. Whoever had taken a couple shots at Walt and Edie from this clearing would be long gone.

Tom carried a metal container specifically designed to transport anything toxic they might find and in his other hand he carried a shovel. Edie had indicated that the person had buried something in a bag, so they weren't looking for some kind of dump of liquid chemicals.

Once they reached the clearing, Tom set down the container and shovel and shone his flashlight on the ground. Benjamin did the same, seeking evidence of a burial site.

It didn't take them long to find not one, but three different areas where it looked as if the ground had recently been disturbed.

Tom picked up his shovel and approached one of the areas. As Benjamin kept his light focused on the ground, Tom began to dig.

He'd removed only three shovels of dirt when Benjamin saw the glow Edie had told him about, a faint yellowish-green glow that definitely looked otherworldly.

He exchanged a worried glance with Tom. What in the hell was going on out here? What on earth could be the source of the weird glow?

His chest tightened with tension as dozens of crazy speculations raced through his head. There were no factories in town, no businesses that might generate any form of glowing toxic waste.

Another swipe with the shovel exposed a white plastic shopping bag with the name of the local grocer printed on the side. It was loosely tied at the top and together the two brothers crouched down to get a closer look.

It was obvious that the glow was coming from whatever was inside the bag. With a dry throat, Benjamin leaned over and untied the bag. As he looked inside a gasp of horror spilled out of him.

An arm.

An arm complete with a hand.

A tattoo of a snake decorated the skin just above the wrist, a tattoo Benjamin immediately recognized.

The arm belonged to Jim Taylor, a seventy-eight-year-old man who had finally lost his battle with cancer two weeks ago, a man who had been buried in the cemetery about ten days earlier.

Chapter 6

"Walt Tolliver, what in blazes are you doing in my kitchen?"

The strident female voice pulled Edie abruptly from sleep. She remained buried beneath the blankets, reluctant to rise since she'd only gone to bed a couple hours before. A glance at the window let her know the sun was just beginning to break over the horizon.

"What do you think I'm doing? I'm looking to make myself some breakfast," Walt replied.

As their voices grew softer, Edie closed her eyes once again, but sleep refused to immediately return. It had been after three when Caleb had finally driven her back to the ranch. Benjamin and Tom had remained in the woods and all Caleb would tell her was that the clearing was officially an active crime scene.

She had no idea what kind of crime had occurred there, but the thought that she'd seen part of it in progress chilled her to the bone.

She must have fallen asleep again, for when she next opened her eyes, the sun was shining fully into the room and she felt rested.

Sitting up, she looked around the room where she had slept. Caleb had told her that Benjamin wanted her in the guest room with the yellow bedspread. It was on the opposite side of the house from the bedroom where Walt had slept and across the hall from the master bedroom.

She knew it was the master bedroom because when she'd been looking for her room she'd gone into it first. The king-size bed looked as if somebody had jumped up in a hurry, the blankets and sheets tossed carelessly aside. The entire room had smelled of him and for just a minute as she'd gazed at the bed, she'd wanted to crawl into it and be enveloped by his scent.

The room where she'd slept was pleasant enough, with buttercup walls and yellow gingham curtains at the window. She had no idea what to expect from the day, but was eager to hear from Benjamin about exactly what they had discovered in the clearing.

She got up and went into the bathroom across the hall for a quick shower. As she put on the same clothes, she made a mental note that if they were going to stay here another night she needed to go to Poppy's place and pick up some clothes for both of them.

She left the bathroom and headed down the hallway and into the living room, where she looked around, interested in the place Benjamin called home.

The requisite flat-screen television hung above the stone fireplace and the sofa was a brown and black pattern. She knew instinctively that the black recliner would be Benjamin's seating of choice. She could easily imagine him there, his long legs stretched out before him and Tiny on his lap.

Thinking about the dog, she wondered where he was this morning. When she entered the kitchen she got her answer. Poppy sat at the table eating what smelled like a freshly baked blueberry muffin and Tiny sat at his feet, obviously waiting for any crumb that might fall to the floor.

The dog wagged his tail at the sight of her and at the same time a gray-haired older woman who stood at the stove turned and smiled. "There she is," she exclaimed.

She bustled to Edie's side and led her to a chair at the table. "I'm Margaret, honey, not that your grandfather would think of making an introduction."

"Hell's bells, Margaret, you didn't give me a chance to introduce you," Walt grumbled. "She can talk a body to death, that one can," he said to Edie, but he had a distinct sparkle in his eyes.

"Don't listen to him," Margaret said. "How about I whip you up some breakfast? Maybe some pancakes or eggs and toast?"

"If Edie wants breakfast I'll be more than happy to fix her something," Walt said as he began to rise.

"This is my kitchen," Margaret said in a huff. "I'll do the cooking around here."

"Poppy, finish your muffin, and thank you, Margaret, but I'm really not hungry. However, a cup of coffee would be great," Edie said.

Margaret got her the coffee and then sat at the table across from her. "You look just like your mama, God rest her soul," she said. "A sweet girl she was and I was sorry to hear about her death."

"Thanks," Edie replied. "Is Benjamin home?"

"No. That poor boy isn't home yet. Walt told me some of what happened last night." She cast the old man a begrudging glance. "Guess he's not as crazy as we all thought he was."

"Just stupid, that's what I was," Poppy exclaimed. "Thinking a hazmat suit was some sort of a space suit."

"It's a mistake anyone could make," Margaret said gruffly as a faint pink stained her cheeks. Poppy looked at her with surprise and then down at his muffin as a slight blush colored his cheeks, as well.

Edie sensed a little attraction in the air between the two. Good, she thought. If Poppy had a woman friend to keep him company, then Edie wouldn't feel so bad about eventually going home.

And shouldn't she be thinking about going home? Poppy's mental health was no longer an issue. Whatever crime had been committed had absolutely nothing to do with her and there was really nothing else holding her here.

Still, maybe she'd stick around another couple days just until Benjamin thought it was safe for Poppy to return to his own house. Her decision to stay had nothing to do with the fact that Benjamin's chocolate-colored eyes made her yearn for things she knew better than to wish for, nothing to do with the fact that his kiss had stirred her on levels she'd never felt before.

It was just after the three of them had eaten lunch when Edie stepped out the front door and sat in one of the two wicker chairs on the porch. The afternoon sun was unusually warm and the air held the scents of fresh hay, rich earth and fall leaves.

In the distance she could see a herd of cattle grazing and several horses frolicking in circles. Peaceful. The scene, the entire place, felt peaceful and enduring.

It would be a wonderful place to raise a family and it wasn't a stretch to think that Benjamin would make a terrific father.

He'd shown incredible patience with Poppy and his affection of his dog spoke of a man who could love easily. Love and patience, the most important things that children needed to grow up healthy.

She reached to hold the charm that dangled in the hollow of her throat. It was cold, like the shell that surrounded her heart.

He was a man who deserved children and that was just another reason for her to steer clear of him. There would be no children in her future.

As she gazed out she saw a plume of dust rising in the air, indicating a vehicle was approaching. She steadfastly ignored the quickened beat of her heart as Benjamin's truck came into view.

She remained seated as he parked and got out of the pickup, his weariness evident in the stress lines down his face and the slight slump of his shoulders. Still, he offered her a warm smile as he stepped onto the porch.

"Long night," she said as he eased down in the chair next to hers.

"You have no idea." He pulled a hand through his hair, messing it up and yet only managing to look carelessly sexy.

"Can you tell me what you found?" She found it difficult to look at him as the sleepy cast to his eyes only made him look sexier and brought to her mind the memory of the kiss they'd shared.

"You won't believe it. I still don't believe it myself." He drew in a deep breath and released it with a sigh. "We found an arm, a foot and a hand each buried in the clearing and all of them glowing like they could power a car for ten years."

Edie sucked in her breath in shock. "Do they belong to somebody who was murdered?"

"We think the arm belongs to Jim Taylor. He died of cancer and had a proper burial a little over a week ago. We don't know who the other hand belongs to, although it's definitely female. And we don't know about the foot."

She stared at him in stunned surprise. "And you don't know why they were glowing like that?"

He shook his head. "My brother Jacob arranged for a contact at the FBI lab in Topeka and Sam Mc-

Cain, one of the other deputies, is transporting them there as we speak."

"What do you think it all means?" She fought the impulse to reach out and stroke her hand across his furrowed brow. He looked as if the weight of the world suddenly rested on his shoulders.

"It's too early to be able to tell what any of it means," he replied. "But we're wondering if maybe somebody is conducting some sort of experiments on Black Rock's dead."

Edie fought the chill that attempted to waltz up her back. "Any suspects?"

He barked a humorless laugh. "At the moment, only everyone in town." He sighed again, a weary sound that blew through her.

"Why do you do this?" she asked curiously.

He turned and looked at her. "Do what?"

"Why are you a deputy? It's obvious that your heart is here at the ranch. Even Poppy said he doesn't understand why you aren't ranching full-time."

He gazed out in the distance and shrugged. "Working law enforcement is what we Grayson men do. Sure, I love the ranch, but in this town, people know me as a man with a badge. That's who I am." He said the words almost belligerently, as if he were trying to convince himself of something rather than her. "So, how has your day been?"

"Okay, although there seems to be a territorial war going on over the kitchen. I thought Poppy and Margaret might come to blows over who was going to fix lunch."

"Who won?" He leaned back in the chair and some of the tension in his shoulders appeared to ease.

"Definitely Margaret. In fact, she threatened to blacken his other eye if he touched one of her pots or pans."

He smiled then, a tired smile that erased the worried lines that had tracked across his forehead. "I'm not surprised. She's a feisty one."

"There seems to be some strange energy between her and Poppy. It's like they're kids and he pulls her hair and she kicks him in the shin but beneath all the aggression is some kind of crazy attraction."

"They've both been alone for a long time. I think it would be great if they hooked up."

"I can't believe we're talking about my grandfather *hooking up,*" she said dryly.

He laughed but quickly his laughter died and he gazed at her with smoldering eyes. "It would be nice if somebody around here was hooking up."

For a moment gazing into his eyes she felt as if she couldn't breathe. It took conscious willpower to force herself to look away from him but it was impossible for her to reply.

"I need to get some sleep," he said. "I have a feeling as this case unfolds it's going to take all the energy we have to give." He stood and once again looked weary beyond words.

"Aren't you afraid of nightmares?" she asked as she also got up from her chair.

He took a step closer to her, so close their bodies almost touched. Once again her breath caught in her chest as he reached up and touched a strand of her hair. "There's only one thing that would definitely keep nightmares at bay, and that's if you were in bed with me as my snuggle buddy."

He dropped his hand and stepped back from her. "But since you've indicated that's not happening, then the best I can do is hope that my dreams are pleasant." He didn't wait for a reply but instead turned and went into the house.

She stared after him and finally released a shuddering sigh. For just a moment as she'd gazed into those magnetic eyes of his, as she'd felt the heat of his body radiating out to warm hers, she'd wanted to be his snuggle buddy. And that scared her almost as much as eerie, glowing body parts buried in the woods.

"Can you tell me where you were Wednesday night around one in the morning?" Benjamin asked Abe Appleton, the local retired chemist. Abe's current claim to fame in the town came from the programs he presented to elementary-school classes about chemistry and physics.

"On any given night at one in the morning I assure you I can be found in my bed," Abe said. "Is this about that mess on Moreland's property? Why on earth would you think I had anything to do with that?"

"We're talking to anyone in town who has a background in chemistry," Benjamin replied. The two men stood on Abe's porch. It was just after eight in the morning.

When Benjamin had arrived in the office that

morning, Tom had handed him a list of people he wanted Benjamin to interview. Abe had been the first name on the list.

Deputies were still working the clearing, digging to see if there were any other surprises buried there. It would be days before they heard back from the FBI lab on what exactly had caused the glow to the body parts, but the investigation was ongoing.

The small-town rumor mill was working overtime with the gossip ranging from a serial killer in their midst to a mad scientist conducting unholy experiments on murder victims.

"You want to come in, check my alibi with Violet? She sleeps light and would know if I wasn't in bed on the night in question," Abe said. "Benjamin, I make volcanoes out of baking soda for the kids. I suck a hard-boiled egg into a bottle. I have no idea what happened in the woods."

"You know anyone else who might have a background in chemistry?" Benjamin asked.

Abe frowned thoughtfully. "Not off the top of my head. 'Course I don't know exactly what you found. When Violet and I were at the café early this morning, we heard everything from a leg that got up and danced on its own to a hand that grabbed Tom around the throat."

Benjamin grinned. "Sounds fascinating, but it's hardly close to the truth." His grin faded as he considered the truth. "Still, it looks like somebody was doing some sort of experimenting, somebody who might have a background in either medicine or chemistry."

"Can't think of anyone, but if I do I know where to contact you," Abe replied.

"Thanks, Abe. I may be back with more questions."

Abe smiled. "In that case you know where to contact me."

Minutes later as Benjamin backed out of Abe's driveway, he thought of all the arms this investigation entailed. While he was interviewing potential suspects, Caleb was following up with Josh Willoughby at the cemetery. There was no question that the arm they'd unearthed belonged to old Jim Taylor and that meant, at the very least, that there was some grave-robbing going on.

Tom had another deputy assigned to checking the sales of hazmat suits. The suits were not cheap and hopefully they'd get a lead through that avenue.

A different deputy was assigned to interview doctors and nurses at the hospital. Since they didn't know what they were dealing with there was no way of knowing if they were spinning their wheels or not.

As he headed toward the taxidermy store in town, his thoughts turned to Edie, who was never really out of his mind. He was thirty years old and more than ready to be in love, ready to start a family. He wanted to fill the house with children who he could teach to love the ranch as much as he did.

Edie had asked him why he wasn't ranching fulltime and Benjamin hadn't been completely honest with her. The truth was he was afraid of what was beneath his badge, afraid that there might be nothing.

Being a deputy gave him a sense of purpose and

more than a little respect in the town. Without that what would he be? What would he have?

He dismissed the crazy thoughts from his head as he parked in front of the taxidermy shop. When they had been making the list of people to interview, Abe's name had come to mind first because of his background in chemistry, and after some careful thought Big Jeff Hudson and his son, Little Jeff, were added to the list. None of the deputies had any idea what kind of chemicals were used in the taxidermy business, but Benjamin intended to find out now.

A tinkling bell above the door announced his arrival as he stepped into the shop. This was his least favorite place in town. Dead animals stared at him from all directions. He found the whole thing rather creepy.

"Benjamin!" Big Jeff greeted him from behind the counter in the back of the store. "What a surprise. I rarely see you in here."

Benjamin made his way around a standing deer to approach the thin, older man. "How's business?"

"Not great, but we'll be swamped soon with deer season opening. What brings you into my little shop of horrors?"

"I need to ask you some questions. I suppose you've heard about the crime scene on Moreland's property."

"Is anyone talking about anything else?"

"It does seem to be the topic of the day," Benjamin agreed. "Is Little Jeff around?"

"He's in the back unloading some supplies, but

he doesn't like to be called Little Jeff anymore. He goes by Jeffrey Allen now. You want me to get him?"

Benjamin nodded and immediately thought about the key fob he'd found by the bush at the cemetery the morning after Walt's beating. *A* for Abe? For Allen? The idea of either man beating the hell out of Walt seemed a stretch, but Benjamin wasn't about to close off his mind to any possibility.

Big Jeff disappeared into the back room and returned a moment later followed by his son. It had been years since the nickname of Little Jeff had been appropriate for the hulking thirty-four-year-old who had been primed to take over the family business when Big Jeff retired.

"Hey, Benjamin," Jeffrey Allen greeted him with a friendly smile. "Dad said you wanted to talk to me. What's up?"

"I wanted to ask the two of you about the chemicals you use in processing animals. Any of them considered toxic?"

"By no stretch of the imagination," Big Jeff replied easily.

"Any of them contain some sort of fluorescent properties?"

Jeffrey Allen laughed. "Not hardly. I don't know one of the local hunters or fishermen who want their prize catch to glow in the dark."

By the time Benjamin left the shop he knew more about taxidermy than he'd ever wanted to know. The rest of the day was more of the same, asking questions of people and getting nothing substantial to help with the case.

It was going to be difficult to pin down alibis of anyone they might suspect for the night that Walt and Edie had been confronted in the woods. At that time of night most people would say they were in bed asleep and that was difficult to disprove.

After talking to the people on his list, he returned to the office, where he was updated by his brother Tom. There had been nothing else found in the clearing and Devon Moreland had claimed complete ignorance on what had been happening there.

The bullet that had shattered Edie's rear window had come from a .38 caliber handgun, definitely common to this area. Tom had assigned one of the other deputies to check gun and ATV owners in the area but it would be several days before he'd have a definitive list.

He'd made arrangements for Edie's back car window to be replaced that morning.

It was just after seven when he finally made his way to the ranch. Weariness pulled at his muscles and hunger pangs filled his belly. Breakfast had been a muffin and a cup of coffee and he'd skipped lunch. He was sure that Margaret would have a plate waiting for him when he got home.

As he approached the house he saw Edie sitting on the porch, the last of the day's sunshine sparking in her hair. Pleasure swelled up inside him, banishing any thought of food or rest.

He could get used to coming home to her. There was no question that she touched him on all kinds of levels. As he parked his truck and got out, she rose from the chair and smiled.

That smile of hers eased some of his weariness and replaced it with a simmering desire to learn more about her, to taste her mouth once again, to somehow get beneath the defenses she'd wrapped around herself.

"Long day," she said. It was a comment, not a question.

"I have a feeling they're all going to be long for a while."

"Anything new?"

He shook his head. "Nothing specific. Let's get inside. It's too cool to sit out here once the sun goes down."

The second he opened the door Tiny greeted him with a happy dance that had both him and Edie laughing. "He's become my buddy when you're gone," she said as Benjamin bent down and picked up Tiny.

"Do you like dogs?"

"I love Tiny," she replied. "Where did you get him?"

"Found him in a box on the side of the road. Somebody had dumped him. He was half-dead and I wasn't sure he was going to make it but all he needed was a little tender loving care."

Edie stepped closer to him and scratched Tiny behind one of his ears. "Poor little thing. I wonder if he has nightmares about the bad things that happened to him before you found him."

"I like to think that with enough time and love, bad memories no longer hold the power to give you nightmares," he replied. It didn't escape his notice that this was the second time she'd mentioned night-mares, making him wonder what haunted her sleep at night.

They walked from the living room into the kitchen, where Margaret and Walt were seated at the table with cups of coffee. Margaret jumped up at the sight of him. "The rest of us already ate, but I've got a bowl of beef stew all ready for you, along with some corn bread that will stick to your ribs."

"Thanks, Margaret." Benjamin set Tiny down on the floor and then went to the sink to wash up to eat. "Walt, that eye is looking better," he said once he was seated at the table. "How are the ribs?"

"Still sore, but not as bad as they were. Have you caught the creep who beat me up yet?"

Benjamin was aware of Edie sliding into the chair next to him, the spicy scent of her filling him with a hunger for something other than beef stew. "Not yet, but we're working on it," he said to Walt.

For the next few minutes, as he ate, he told them what he could about the investigation. He finished eating and Margaret took his plates away and then announced that she and Walt were going to her cottage to play some rummy.

"I think we'll know more about everything when we get some results back from the FBI lab," he said to Edie once the older people had left the house.

"But that could take a while, right?"

"Unfortunately," he agreed with a nod of his head. "In the meantime we'll keep interviewing people and hope that somebody knows something about what's been going on."

Edie leaned back in her chair. She looked as pretty as he'd ever seen her in a deep pink sweater that enhanced her coloring. "I think it's time I go home."

"Do you really think that's a good idea?"

"Whoever chased us the other night must realize by now that we couldn't identify them. Plus I know that Poppy isn't crazy and he's insisting I go home."

He wanted to protest. He wanted to ask her if she'd stay for him. But they'd shared only a single kiss and he really had no right to ask her to stay.

"So what are your plans?"

"I'll stop over at Poppy's place in the morning and get my things and then head on back to Topeka." She frowned. "I hate to leave him like this and I was wondering if it would be okay with you if Poppy remains here a couple of days. He is healing nicely, but I think the attack shook him up more than he's saying. I tried to tell him I wanted to stay at least until he gets back on his feet, but he went ballistic."

"He's welcome to stay until he feels like he's ready to go home," Benjamin said.

She nodded. "I appreciate it."

"And if I need to talk to you? About the investigation?"

"I'll give you my cell phone number and when I get settled in a new place, I'll let you know my address."

"I'll be sorry to see you go." The words escaped him before he realized he intended to speak them.

Her gaze didn't quite meet his. "You're a nice man, Benjamin, and you deserve a nice woman in your life." She got up from the table. "Believe me,

I'm the last person on earth you need in your life in any way. I'm not a nice woman and it's time for me to get back to my life."

Before he could respond she turned and left the kitchen.

Chapter 7

It was after eleven when Edie finally left Benjamin's ranch the next morning. Margaret had insisted she have a big breakfast and it had been difficult to say goodbye to both her and Poppy.

She might have stuck around if she thought that Poppy really needed her, but she sensed a bit of romance taking place between him and Margaret, a romance that could fill any loneliness Poppy might have entertained.

Benjamin had already been gone when she'd gotten out of bed and she'd remained in her room the night before after she'd left him in the kitchen.

She'd been afraid to spend any more time around him, afraid that somehow he'd talk her into staying, afraid that he might kiss her again and make her want him even more deeply than she already did. It was definitely time to get out of Dodge, but her heart was heavy as the ranch disappeared in her rearview mirror.

She could have been happy there, she could be happy with Benjamin, if she deserved happiness. But deep in her soul she knew the truth.

Still, she was grateful she hadn't had to face him one last time that morning. It was easier this way, with no long, drawn-out goodbyes.

By the time she entered the outskirts of town she was thinking of the problems that awaited her in Topeka. Thank God she had a little bit of savings put away, just enough to get her into another small apartment.

She wasn't too worried about a job. She'd flip hamburgers if necessary to get by until she found something more permanent. It would have been nice if she'd gone to college, but there had never been enough money at home, and the minute she'd graduated from high school she'd started working to help out her mother.

When she reached Poppy's place she parked in the driveway and got out of the car, surprised when a neighbor hurried out of his house and toward her.

"Hi," he said with a smile of friendliness. "I'm Bart Crosswell, Walt's neighbor. I was just wondering how he's doing. Me and my wife heard about him getting beaten up but we haven't seen him since then."

Bart was about sixty with a broad face that looked as if it had never held a frown. "He's staying with some friends for the next couple days," she replied, "but he's doing just fine."

"Glad to hear that. And I noticed you cleaned up the yard real nice. We didn't want to complain or say anything, but it was obvious that it had kind of gotten away from him over the past few months."

"I'll try to make sure that somebody is keeping on top of it from now on," Edie said, grateful that the neighbor appeared to be a nice guy.

"I don't mind mowing it whenever I mow my own. I just didn't want to step on Walt's toes," Bart said.

"That's very kind of you. When he gets back home maybe the two of you can work out an agreeable arrangement," she replied.

"Will do." He lifted a hand in a friendly goodbye and then began to walk back to his house.

Poppy would be fine, Edie thought as she let herself into the house. He had friends and neighbors that obviously cared about him. He didn't need her. Nobody needed her and she didn't need anyone, she reminded herself as she climbed the stairs.

She pulled her overnight bag from the closet and set it on the bed. It wouldn't take long for her to gather her things and leave town.

Leave Benjamin. She couldn't help the little pang in her heart as she thought about him. In another place, in another time, she might have allowed herself to care about him. But, she couldn't think about that now.

She went into the bathroom across the hall and gathered the toiletries she hadn't taken to Benjamin's and then returned to the bedroom and placed them in her overnight bag.

Once she had all her clothes folded and packed away, she sat on the edge of the bed and allowed herself to think about Benjamin once again.

He'd asked her if she'd considered relocating to Black Rock now that there was really nothing holding her to Topeka. In the brief time she'd been here as an adult, she recognized that Black Rock was a pleasant town filled with friendly people.

It was easy to imagine living in Black Rock. She could get an apartment close enough to the downtown area that she could walk to the stores on nice days. She could enjoy regular visits with Poppy and build a pleasant life here.

There was only one fly in the ointment: a hot sexy deputy with soft brown eyes and hot kisses that made her want to forget her vow of celibacy, forget that she'd given up on finding any real happiness.

No, she wouldn't even consider relocating here. Benjamin Grayson was too much temptation and believing she could ever have a loving relationship with anyone was nothing but utter foolishness.

She rose from the bed and froze as she heard it— the soft, but unmistakable creak of the third step. Her blood chilled as she realized somebody else was in the house, somebody who hadn't announced their presence but was quietly creeping up the staircase.

Her breathing went shallow as she grabbed her purse and shot a wild gaze around the room, seeking something that might be used as a weapon.

There was nothing. And as she heard the distinct

creak of the seventh step panic clawed at her. There was no question in her mind that whoever it was had no good intentions, otherwise they would have said something to announce their presence.

Clutching her purse, she silently moved across the room and into the closet. She closed the closet door and sat on the floor with her back against it and her legs braced on the other side.

For a long moment she heard nothing but the frantic bang of her own heartbeat. God, she'd been careless. She hadn't locked the front door behind her when she'd come inside. She hadn't thought there was any danger.

If it were Bart surely he would say something. Agonizing moments ticked by and she heard nothing. Her heart rate began to slow a bit. Had she only imagined those creaks? Had it just been the house settling?

At that moment a fist crashed into the closet door. "Come out of there, you bitch," a deep voice snarled.

Edie swallowed a scream and pressed her back more firmly against the door. Help. She needed help. Oh, God, her cell phone.

She wildly fumbled in the bottom of her purse for her cell phone. A deep sob escaped her as she scrabbled to find the instrument that would bring help.

He grabbed the door handle and turned it, then threw himself against the door with a force that shook the door frame. "You and that old man ruined everything! I'm going to make you pay if it's the last thing I do."

Deep and guttural. She didn't recognize the voice.

As he slammed into the door once again she managed to get hold of her cell phone.

"I'm calling the sheriff," she cried out as she punched 9-1-1.

When the operator answered she gave them Poppy's address and then screamed as the door shuddered once again.

"You won't get away from me no matter where you go." The voice shimmered with rage. "I'll find you wherever you are and make you pay for screwing up my life." There was a snap of wood as the frame broke and then silence.

The only noise was her gasping breaths and uncontrollable sobs. Was he gone? Or was it a trick? Was he waiting for her to venture out of the closet so he could hurt her? She shoved the back of her fist against her mouth as tears blurred her vision.

Who had it been? And what had she done to warrant such intense hatred? Would she be safe going back to Topeka or would he find her there to merit out some form of twisted revenge?

Benjamin was grabbing a quick cup of coffee in the café when he heard the call for a responder to Walt's address. He tore out of the building and jumped into his car, his heart hammering so fast he could scarcely catch his breath.

There could only be one person who would have made that call. Edie. He knew she'd be stopping by Walt's on her way out of town, although he hadn't known specifically what time she might be leaving.

If anything happened to her, he'd never forgive

himself. He should have talked her out of leaving town, insisted that she stick around until they had a handle on the whole situation.

It took only minutes for him to arrive at Walt's. He went through the open front door with his gun drawn, anticipating trouble.

He heard nothing. The silence of the house thundered in his head as he slowly made his way from room to room. He didn't want to call out. If somebody was inside, he didn't want to announce his presence or exacerbate whatever the situation might be. He damn sure didn't want to force somebody to hurt Edie.

When he'd cleared the lower level of the house he crept up the stairs, wincing as two of them creaked beneath his weight. When he reached the first bedroom, his heatbeat crashed so hard in his ears he feared he wouldn't hear anything else.

He cleared the bedrooms and bathroom until there was only one left at the end of the hallway. His heart jumped into his throat as he saw Edie's overnight bag on the bed. He finally called out, "It's Deputy Grayson. Is anyone here?"

She exploded out of the closet and into his embrace. Trembling arms wrapped around his neck and she buried her face in his chest and began to weep.

He held her tight with one arm and his gun with the other. "What happened?"

"He was here. He said I ruined everything and he was going to make me pay." The words escaped her on a trail of tears as she squeezed her arms around his neck.

"Who, honey? Who was it?"

"I don't know. I didn't see him."

He felt her physically pull herself together. A single deep breath and she moved out of his embrace. But her face was achingly pale and her eyes were wide and red-rimmed from her tears.

"I had just finished packing when I heard somebody on the stairs." Her voice trembled. "I got scared. Thank God I grabbed my purse and hid in the closet." Tears welled up in her eyes once again. "I sat on the floor and braced myself as he started to slam into the door. I thought he was going to get in before anyone got here to help."

"Let's get you out of here," he said. As she grabbed her purse from the closet, he picked up her overnight bag and wondered who in the hell had come after her.

"We're going to the sheriff's office to file a report and then I'm taking you back to the ranch," he said once they were in his car. "You aren't heading out of town by yourself until I'm certain that you're no longer in danger."

"If you're expecting an argument, you aren't going to get one," she replied.

"You didn't recognize his voice?"

She shook her head. "It was just a deep growl." She wrapped her arms around herself as if to fight off a shiver. "He sounded so angry, like he would easily enjoy strangling me to death with his bare hands."

Benjamin tightened his hands on the steering wheel as a rage began inside him. The idea of anyone putting their hands on Edie made a rich anger burn in his gut.

When they arrived at the sheriff's office, Tom sat down with them and Edie told him what had occurred. Tom immediately dispatched two deputies to Walt's house to fingerprint the closet and talk to Bart. They hoped Bart might have seen whoever entered the house.

Confident that the investigation side of things was under control, within an hour Benjamin and Edie were back in his car and headed to the ranch.

"I know you were eager to return to Topeka and get things settled there," he said.

"Funny how somebody trying to kill you can change your mind." She offered him a weak smile.

A healthy dose of respect for her filled him.

"I have this terrible fear that if I go back to Topeka now this creep will somehow find me there and I won't have my own personal deputy to ride to my rescue," she added.

Benjamin tried to find a responding smile, but there was absolutely nothing humorous about the situation. "I shouldn't have let you go," he said. "I shouldn't have let you go to Walt's to get your things alone. I should have been with you or I should have talked you out of leaving altogether."

She reached out and placed her hand on his arm. "How could you have known that I might be in danger? Who could know that he'd be after revenge for me somehow screwing things up for him. I just wish I knew what it is he thinks I messed up." She removed her hand from his arm.

"If we knew that, we'd probably have all the answers." Benjamin wheeled through the entrance that led to the ranch. He didn't want to tell her that the thing that worried him now was that whoever had come after her would eventually know she and Walt were staying here.

If it came down to him doing his job or keeping her safe, the job could go to hell. He'd already lost one woman in his life. Brittany. He had no hope of ever seeing his sister again.

Edie had made it clear to him that she didn't want him in her life on any kind of a romantic basis, but his heart was already taken by her and the idea of anything happening to her nearly shattered him.

"You'll be safe at the ranch, both you and Walt. I'll make sure of it," he said firmly.

"I don't doubt that at all," she replied.

As Benjamin parked in front of the ranch his mind whirled with all the ways he could ensure their safety. Tom certainly didn't have men to spare given the magnitude of the current investigation.

Maybe it was time to have a talk with Jacob, see if he could enlist his brother's help in keeping an eye on the ranch.

When they got into the house Benjamin sat down with Walt, Margaret and Edie and told them how important it was that the house remained locked at all times, that they keep an eye out for trouble and that obviously the threat to Edie and Walt wasn't over.

He didn't anticipate any trouble immediately, so after making sure all the doors were locked up tight, Benjamin left to go talk to his brother.

Jacob had holed himself up in a small cabin on the property almost three months earlier. He'd quit his job in Kansas City with the FBI and had come home with deep haunting shadows in his eyes and had refused to discuss with anyone what had happened to him.

The only thing he'd told his brothers when he'd arrived in Black Rock was that he didn't want anyone to know he was back. He lived like a hermit and Benjamin and Margaret provided the supplies he needed.

It took only minutes for Benjamin to pull up in front of the cabin that was nearly hidden in a thick grove of trees. At one time this had been a caretaker's cabin, but during Benjamin's childhood it had been used as a guest cottage and an occasional romantic getaway for his parents.

He found his brother where he always found him, in the small living room in a recliner with a beer in his hand and the television playing.

Jacob's cheeks and chin were covered with whisker stubble and his dark hair was longer than Benjamin had ever seen it. He looked like a man without pride, a man who had lost the ability to care about anything.

"You look like hell," Benjamin said as he came through the front door.

"And a good afternoon to you, too, little brother." Jacob gestured him into the chair opposite him and turned down the volume on the television. "What's going on?"

"I need your help." Benjamin eased down into the chair.

Jacob raised one of his dark eyebrows. "I hope it doesn't require me leaving this chair or my beer."

A flash of irritation swept through Benjamin. He'd always looked up to Jacob but the shell of a man who had returned to the ranch was nothing like the man who had left.

"Actually, it does require you getting away from the beer and out of your chair," Benjamin said.

"Then the odds of me being able to help you out are pretty slim."

"For God's sake, Jacob. Pull yourself together," Benjamin exclaimed with a burst of uncharacteristic anger. "I need you to help me keep a woman safe."

Jacob took a sip of his beer and eyed Benjamin with interest. "Something in your voice tells me this is a special woman."

Benjamin felt a faint heat crawl into his cheeks. "She's in trouble through no fault of her own. Somebody attacked her today and I don't think the perp is finished yet. I've got her at the house but I'd like an extra pair of eyes watching things there."

"Does this have to do with the Moreland mess?"

Benjamin nodded. "I've got both Walt Tolliver and his granddaughter at the house." He leaned back in the chair and released a sigh. "I'd assumed since they couldn't identify the culprits that they were safe from harm. But I was wrong." He told his brother what had taken place at Walt's house.

"So he didn't go after her to somehow protect himself. He went after her for revenge." Jacob shook his head. "That's a nasty motive for an attack. I'd say whoever you're looking for has a history of a short fuse, maybe some sort of persecution complex. You know the type, the whole world is against him and whatever troubles he has is always somebody else's fault."

"Not much of a profile to go on," Benjamin said.

Jacob shrugged. "Not much information yet to go on. Tom called me last night to give me the latest on what's been happening with the case."

"Right now my main concern is keeping Walt and Edie safe. I'm hoping Tom can spare me so I can hang out at the house, but I'd feel better knowing you had my back."

Jacob set his beer down and his eyes were as black as night. "I got your back," he said simply. "Just let me know when you need me around and I'll be there."

"Are you ever going to tell me what brought you home?" Benjamin asked softly. Jacob broke eye contact and for a long moment said nothing. Benjamin leaned forward in his chair. "Whatever it is, Jacob, we can help you."

His brother looked at him with a wry smile. "Nobody can help me."

"Just tell me this. Are you hiding from somebody or are you hiding from yourself?"

Jacob's eyes widened and then narrowed into slits. "Maybe a little bit of both." He picked up his bottle of beer once again. "Just give me a call if you need me to keep an eye on the house." He picked up the remote control and turned up the volume on the television in an obvious dismissal.

As Benjamin headed back to the ranch house he

couldn't help but worry about his brother. He felt as if they'd already lost Brittany and if something wasn't done, somehow they were going to lose Jacob.

It wasn't right for a man to wall himself off from everyone. It wasn't right for a man to be alone with just his beer and his thoughts. Jacob needed something, but until he asked for it nobody could give it to him.

As he once again parked in front of the house and got out of the truck, his thoughts turned to the woman inside. For some reason he felt as if she and Jacob shared that common trait. He thought that Edie needed something from somebody but was afraid or refused to ask.

He only wished it was him that she needed, that she wanted. But he had resigned himself to the fact that the only thing he could do for her was to keep her safe. And when the danger passed, he would send her off to live her life without him.

Chapter 8

Edgy.

That was the only word to describe what Edie felt as she sat in the kitchen. It had been two days since the attack on her, two days of confinement with Benjamin. He hadn't left the house or her side for the past forty-eight hours.

She'd been in bed, but had gotten up a few minutes ago and decided to make herself a cup of hot tea.

She sat at the table with the hot brew in front of her with only the oven light on. This was the first time she felt as if she could breathe, without his overwhelming presence by her side.

Familiarity was supposed to breed contempt, but in this case that old adage was wrong. The sexual tension between them had grown to mammoth proportions. She felt his hot, simmering gaze on her like a hand on her thigh, a palm on her breast, and with each moment that passed she wanted it, wanted him.

And in the past two days Margaret and Poppy had become best buddies, sharing the kitchen like two top chefs, playing card games and giggling like teenagers.

She felt a desperate need to get out of town, but each time she thought about leaving all she could think about was that man hunting her down and making her pay.

There was no question that being here in this house with Benjamin made her feel safe. He'd even insisted Margaret move into the bedroom across the hall from Walt's for the time being rather than stay in her little cottage behind the house. He didn't want anyone to somehow use her to get to Poppy and Edie.

She leaned forward in the chair and took a sip of her tea that warmed her all the way down to her toes. No matter how she tried to keep thoughts of Benjamin at bay, he continued to intrude into her brain.

As if summoned by her thoughts alone, he appeared in the doorway of the kitchen, Tiny at his feet. "I thought you were asleep," she said.

He moved from the doorway to the table and sat next to her. Tiny curled up on the rug between them. "I was on the phone with Tom getting updates."

"So what's new?"

"Not enough to solve the case," he said with frustration. "We know now that the arm definitely belonged to Jim Taylor, the old man I told you about who died of cancer. The other two body parts still haven't been identified. We haven't heard anything from the FBI lab on what chemicals might have been involved."

"Then there's really no news," she said and lifted her cup for another sip of tea.

He forced a smile. "Nothing concrete but they're all gathering information that hopefully will eventually crack the case."

"You should be back in the office instead of hanging around here with me," she said.

"Right now you and Walt are our best clues to what might be happening. If somebody comes after you here, I'll be ready for them. I'm doing my job by making sure you and Walt are safe."

"How come you don't have any workers around here?" she asked curiously. She'd noticed that she never saw anyone in the yard or in the pastures or corral.

"I'm a small operation. I've been able to handle things myself for the past couple of years."

"Tell me about your sister." She'd been curious about the woman who had gone missing, a woman he barely mentioned. "What's she like?"

For just a brief moment a smile curved his lips and his eyes warmed. "Beautiful, impulsive and headstrong. We all spoiled her terribly. But she's also bright and tough and has a great sense of humor."

His smile fell and his eyes darkened. He placed a hand on the table, his long fingers splayed on the top and stared down. "She was working as a deputy like the rest of us. Initially when she missed work none of us panicked. She'd occasionally oversleep or get screwed up with her schedule and forget to come in until we called her. It wasn't until a full day went by with no word from her that we all started to get a little concerned."

He leaned forward and his fingers curled into a tight fist. "By the time two days had gone by with no word from her, we knew she was in trouble. There had been no activity in her bank account, her cell phone wasn't picking up and that's when true panic set in."

She was sorry she'd asked, saw the pain that radiated from his features and his lips compressed tightly together. Her heart ached with his pain but before she could find words to comfort him, he continued speaking.

"I can't explain to you what it felt like when the realization struck that she had met with foul play. Suddenly every minute that passed was sheer torture. It was impossible to eat, impossible to sleep. I tried making deals with fate. You know, if she'd just show up safe and sound then I could be struck dead. If she would just be returned to us then fate could take this ranch from me and I'd happily live in a hovel for the rest of my life." He released a short, strained laugh. "God, I've never told anyone this stuff."

She reached across the table and covered his fisted hand with her own. "I'm sorry, Benjamin. I can't imagine what it must be like to not know what happened to somebody you love."

He uncurled his hand and instead entwined his fingers with hers. "Eventually the gut-ripping desperation passes and you find that you have to eat, you have to sleep, that life goes on no matter what." He gazed at her with sad eyes. "My brothers all hold on to the hope that she'll eventually be found alive, but not me. The day we found her car hidden in an old abandoned barn, my gut told me she's dead."

For a moment Edie didn't know what to say to comfort him, but her need to take the pain from his eyes was visceral. She understood his grief, awakened with her own each morning and went to bed with it each night. "I'm sorry, Benjamin. I'm so sorry that you're going through this."

He tightened his grip on her hand. "Thanks. It actually helped to talk about it. Now, why don't you tell me what puts the sadness in your eyes?"

She forced a laugh and gently pulled her hand from his. "Life," she said. "My life really started to crumble when my mother died." Edie once again wrapped her hands around her teacup. "We were very best friends. My father walked out on us when I was just a baby and it was always just her and me."

"She never thought about remarrying?" he asked.

"Not that I know of. I don't think she ever dated. She had a circle of girlfriends and when she wasn't with them, she seemed content alone. I met Greg in a bar two weeks after Mom's death."

She paused to take a sip of the tea that was now lukewarm. There was something intensely intimate about sitting at the table with everyone else in bed. In the semidarkness of the kitchen it seemed easier to let her guard down, to open herself up to him.

"I was grieving and vulnerable and ripe for the picking. He moved in and I became one of those too-

stupid-to-live women I abhor. I made every mistake
a woman can make. I believed whatever he told me
about his money being tied up in some high-dollar
business. He fed me what I needed to hear but it was
nothing but lies." She shrugged and offered him a
crooked smile. "It felt tragic at the time he left me,
but now I realize he did me a big favor by getting
out of my life. I'm like my mother. I'm good alone."

Benjamin's gaze lingered for a long moment on
her face. "I wish I'd met you first," he finally said
softly. "I wish I'd been the man in your life before
Greg ever entered it."

There it was, that deep yearning to fall into his
gaze, to feel his strong arms wrapped around her, his
heartbeat against her own. It was a palpable want,
melting something inside her she didn't want melted.

"It wouldn't have made a difference," she said,
surprised that her voice didn't sound strong and sure,
but rather breathy and faint.

He leaned back in his chair and released a sigh.
"Tell me what gives you nightmares."

She looked at him in surprise and gave an uneasy
laugh. "What makes you think I have nightmares?"

"I don't know, I've just had the impression that
you do."

"Staying up too late and drinking tea gives me
nightmares about tea bags," she said as she got up
from the table. She carried her cup to the sink, aware
of his gaze remaining on her.

She rinsed the cup and placed it in the dishwasher
and then turned to face him once again. "Don't, Benjamin. Don't pry to find out any secrets I might have,

the kind of woman I am. Trust me when I tell you that you wouldn't like what you uncovered."

"I find that hard to believe," he replied as she walked toward the kitchen door.

"Good night, Benjamin," she said and then left the kitchen. As she went through the living room toward the hallway she fought against the sudden sear of hot tears at her eyes.

The charm around her neck seemed to burn her skin, a painful reminder of loss and grief. It had been her fault. She should have never gotten pregnant. She obviously wasn't meant to be a mother.

Even though the doctor had told her that sometimes these things happened for no discernible reason, when the baby died Edie had known the truth, that somehow she was responsible, that it had been her fault that her baby had been born dead.

Benjamin deserved better. He deserved more than she'd ever be able to give him. She had no intention of having children. She had no intention of ever loving again.

She would admit it, she was a coward. She didn't want to risk the chance of loss once again. Even with a man like Benjamin. Especially with a man like Benjamin.

As much as it pained her, she had to keep him out of her heart.

It had been another long day. After the discussion with Edie the night before, Benjamin had gone to bed with a heavy heart.

He felt that over the past several days he'd gotten

to know her as well as he'd ever known any woman. She was kind and warm and giving. She had a wonderful sense of humor and was bright and so achingly beautiful. And yet, he sensed a darkness in her that he couldn't pierce.

She'd been distant with him all day, as if punishing him for getting too close the night before. Tension had sparked in the air between them until he'd felt he might explode.

The tension had eased when after dinner the four of them had sat at the table and played poker. The laughter the games created was a welcome relief.

There was no doubt that there were sparks between Walt and Margaret. They had begun to act like a couple who had been married for fifty years, finishing each other's sentences and exchanging warm gazes. He had a feeling when this was all over and done he might just lose his housekeeper, but he couldn't feel bad about it. He was only glad that Walt and Margaret had found each other to share companionship in the golden years of their lives.

He now sat in his recliner, Tiny on his lap. Edie had gone into Walt's bedroom to check the wrap around his ribs and Margaret had gone to bed.

A man needed companionship. Men weren't wired to be alone and he believed Edie wasn't wired to be alone, either. There was no question in his mind that she was attracted to him, that she had feelings for him. He knew it in her gaze, felt it in her touch, sensed it radiating from her as they warily circled one another.

But he didn't know how to get beneath her defenses. He didn't have the tools to know how to get to her heart. Tiny whined, as if sensing Benjamin's growing despondency.

"Shh." He scrubbed the dog beneath his ear, which instantly halted the whine. Too bad a scratch behind Benjamin's ear wouldn't solve the depression he felt settling around his shoulders like an old, heavy shawl.

Maybe the problem was a lack of sleep, he told himself. He felt as if he needed to be on duty twenty-four hours a day and he'd only been catching catnaps throughout the long nights.

Most of the hours of the night he wandered from window to window, looking outside, wondering if danger lurked anywhere near.

For the moment the investigation was proceeding without him, although he'd kept in close contact with both Tom and Caleb. It was impossible to trace ATVs through motor vehicle records because they were for off-road use. But Sam McCain had come up with a list of people they all knew had the vehicles in town.

Jim Ramsey, another deputy, was checking gun records and collecting the names of everyone who owned a .38 caliber gun. They were still waiting on results from the FBI lab that would hopefully tell them more about what they were dealing with.

The explosion of gunshots and the shatter of glass lifted him from his chair. Edie's scream ripped into his very heart as he raced down the hallway, Tiny barking wildly at his heels.

He ran into the bedroom where Walt had been staying to see the old man on the floor, his upper arm covered with blood and Edie on the floor at his side. The window was shattered into a hundred sparkling shards on the floor.

"Stay down," he yelled. "Margaret, call 9-1-1." He didn't wait for her response but instead raced out the front door, determined to find the shooter.

Edie would do what she could for Walt until the ambulance came, but this might be Benjamin's only chance to catch the person who seemed intent on destroying Edie and Walt.

Thank God he'd still had on his holster. He drew his gun as he left the house. The night was cold and dark and he ran around the side of the house where the shooter would have had a view of Walt's bedroom window.

He tried not to think about Walt and the blood and prayed that the old man wouldn't die before the ambulance could get here.

On this side of the house there were two structures in the distance, a shed and the barn, both perfect cover for a shooter aiming at the bedroom window.

Benjamin stayed low to the ground, grateful for the cloudy conditions as he raced toward the shed. But before he was halfway there, he heard the sound of an engine, the tinny whine of an ATV.

He flew around the side of the shed and nearly collided with another figure. "Halt!" he yelled, his finger itching to fire his gun.

"Benjamin, it's me," Jacob said. "I heard the gunshots. He had the ATV waiting. He's gone."

Benjamin cursed soundly. "Did you see who it was?"

"No, he was too far away when I spotted him, but he was a heavyset guy."

"I've got to get back inside. He hit Walt." Benjamin was grateful to hear the sound of a siren in the distance.

"I'm going to check around out here," Jacob said as Benjamin nodded and hurried toward the house.

Dammit. Benjamin's heart raced as he went back inside. He found Edie and Walt and Margaret in the hallway. Apparently the two women had managed to drag Walt out of the bedroom.

"He got me right in the shoulder," Walt said as he saw Benjamin. The old man's face was pale as Edie pressed a towel to the wound.

"He's losing a lot of blood." She looked up at Benjamin with wild eyes.

"The ambulance is on its way." Benjamin felt helpless, filled with a rage barely contained as he crouched down next to Walt. "Hang in there, Walt. I still need to beat your ass at chess."

Walt offered him a weak grin. "Don't worry, I'm not planning on going anywhere."

At that moment the ambulance arrived along with Tom and Caleb. Caleb followed the ambulance with Edie and Margaret in tow while Benjamin remained at the house to explain the events to Tom.

He'd just finished when Jacob came in the door. Tom raised an eyebrow at the sight of his reclusive brother. "First time I've seen you out of the cabin," he said.

Jacob shrugged. "Heard the shots and knew Benjamin might be in trouble. The perp parked the ATV behind the barn. He must have walked closer to the house to fire the shots. When I was running up, I saw him heading for the ATV. But before I could get close enough to get a shot or see who it was, he was gone."

"You get a general impression...height...weight?" Tom asked.

"I'm heading to the hospital," Benjamin said before Jacob could reply. "I didn't see anything, I can't help you here," he said with frustration.

Tom nodded. "Go. Jacob and I can take care of things until you get back."

Minutes later in his truck, Benjamin's thoughts weren't on the perp, but rather on Walt and Edie. He'd let them down. He'd promised he'd keep them safe and he'd screwed up. He shouldn't have been sitting in his chair, he should have been walking the floors, checking the windows and keeping vigil.

He shouldn't be a deputy. It wasn't where he belonged. He'd known it for a long time now, but he'd been so afraid of being nothing, he'd held on to the legacy that his older brother had begun. And people had nearly died. At least he prayed they'd gotten Walt help in time.

By the time he reached the hospital he was sick with worry. He went in through the emergency room doors and immediately saw Edie and Margaret sitting side by side.

"What's going on?" he asked.

"They won't let us back there and nobody has told us anything," Edie said. Anguish was thick in her voice.

"The doctor said he'd speak to us as soon as he

could," Margaret added. She reached over and patted Edie's knee. "Walt is strong and he's too onery for the devil to want him. He'll be fine." Although she said the words with a lightness in her tone, her dark eyes were filled with worry.

Benjamin shoved his hands in his pockets and leaned against the wall, anger battling with guilt inside him. "I should have done things differently," he said in frustration. "I thought the ranch would be safe. I thought if you were inside the house nothing bad would happen."

"Don't," Edie said. "Don't blame yourself for this."

"I can't help it," he replied. "It would have been different if we'd had enough manpower to station men around the ranch. I should have realized that I wasn't enough to keep you and Walt safe."

At that moment Dr. Drake came out to speak to them. Edie jumped up from her chair and stood next to Benjamin. "He's fine," Dr. Drake began. Edie sagged against Benjamin in obvious relief. "Thankfully the bullet entered and exited the fleshy part of his upper arm. We're going to give him a blood transfusion and keep him here so we can watch the wound for infection."

"I'll see that a guard is put on him during his hospitalization," Benjamin said. One way or another Tom would have to arrange for protection for the old man.

Margaret stood from the chair. "And I'll be staying with him as long as he's here," she said and raised her chin as if to argue with anyone who might protest. "Nobody's going to hurt him while I'm on duty."

"Can I see him?" Edie asked.

Dr. Drake nodded. "Go on back."

Edie started through the door and then turned to Margaret. "He'll want to see you, too."

Margaret offered her a grateful smile and together the two women disappeared behind the door.

Benjamin raked a hand down his face as Dr. Drake offered him a commiserating smile. "Bad night."

"Could have been worse," Benjamin replied. "If that bullet had hit Walt an inch lower, an inch to the left, then I'd be having a conversation with the coroner right now."

The two men turned as the door whooshed open and Tom walked in. "How's Walt?" he asked.

"A lucky man," Benjamin replied. As Dr. Drake said his goodbye and left, Benjamin looked at his older brother. "I've promised a guard here on Walt for as long as he remains in the hospital."

"Done," Tom agreed. "I'll make the arrangements."

Benjamin frowned. "There is something I don't understand. Whoever is behind this has to know that Walt and Edie are no threat to them. Why the attacks on them?"

"Jacob seems to think we're dealing with somebody who's so angry that the body parts have come to light that it's more about revenge than anything else."

"Whoever it is, he's a nasty piece of work," Benjamin replied.

"I've got several of the men checking out the ATVs in the area to see if any are still warm from riding. Walt should be safe here with a guard at the door, but what are we going to do about Edie?" Tom asked. "Maybe it's time she head back to Topeka."

"She doesn't want to go home yet. She's afraid, Tom, afraid that the person will follow her back there. With what's happened tonight, I don't feel comfortable telling her that's an unwarranted fear." Once again Benjamin raked a hand across his jaw. "I think the best thing to do is to check her into the motel for a couple days. I'll stay there with her and make sure she'd safe."

"She'll agree to that?"

Benjamin hesitated a moment and then nodded. "Yeah, she'll agree to it. What I need is for you and the others to solve this thing as soon as possible."

"Jacob is leaning on his contact in the FBI lab so hopefully we'll get some ID results from those body parts sooner rather than later. And by the way, he said to tell you that you should do whatever you need to do and he'll make sure Tiny is taken care of."

Benjamin frowned, thinking of all the logistics. "Maybe we should leave my truck here, make sure we aren't followed, and you can drop Edie and me off at the motel. That way hopefully nobody will know we're there except Brett, and he won't tell anyone if we ask him not to."

"On another note, I think we might have another missing young woman," Tom said.

Benjamin wouldn't have thought his tension level

could climb any higher, but this news sent it through the roof. "Who?"

"Suzy Bakersfield. Her boyfriend called a little while ago and said she should have been home from work an hour ago. I've got Dan Walker checking it out."

Suzy Bakersfield was a twenty-four-year-old who worked as a waitress at Harley's, a rough-and-tumble bar at the edge of town. "Let's hope she just decided to go home with somebody else and didn't want her boyfriend to know." Benjamin shoved his hands in his pockets and stared at his brother. "You think these missing women are tied to whatever else is going on?"

Tom's frown deepened and for a moment he looked older than his thirty-six years. "I don't know what in the hell is going on in this town. It's impossible to know if the two are related until we have more information. All I really know is that I have a terrible feeling that things are going to get much worse before they get better."

Benjamin clapped a hand on his brother's shoulder. "We'll get through this, Tom. Just like we got through Mom's and Dad's deaths, just like we got through Brittany's disappearance. We'll get through it because that's what we Grayson men do."

Tom flashed him a grateful smile as Benjamin dropped his hand back to his side. "Let me know when you're ready to take Edie to the motel. In the meantime I'm going to step outside, get on my phone and make some arrangements."

Benjamin watched him go and then sat in one of

the chairs to wait for Edie. It could have been her. That bullet could have easily hit her, killed her.

How could he protect her from an unknown assailant? One who was so filled with the need for some twisted revenge that he'd stop at nothing?

Within thirty minutes Sam McCain walked through the door. His coffee-colored face offered Benjamin a smile. "You okay?"

"As okay as I'm going to get."

"Tom tagged me for the first guard duty on Walt."

"Hopefully it will be a quiet, uneventful shift for you."

"There hasn't been a quiet, uneventful moment in the past couple of days," Sam returned.

"You got that right," Benjamin replied.

As Sam left the room to find Walt, Benjamin returned to his chair. His head spun with thoughts. Who the hell was behind all this? More importantly, would he be able to keep Edie safe until the guilty were behind bars?

Chapter 9

Two things struck Edie as she left Walt's room and returned to the waiting room. The first was that she was filled with a sick adrenaline that she didn't know what to do with and the second was that she could feel a queasy guilt wafting from Benjamin.

He rose from his chair as she entered. "Is he all right?" he asked.

She nodded. "He's going to be just fine, and I have a feeling that if he needs anything at all then Margaret will make sure he has it. What happens now?"

"I've made arrangements for Tom to take us to the motel. We can stay there for a couple days without anyone knowing we're there. I'm confident by then we'll have all this figured out." His gaze held hers, as if anticipating an argument. "Or maybe the best thing for you to do is to find another hotel in a different town."

She considered her options. The idea of running away from danger was definitely appealing, but she didn't want to leave Poppy. Besides, she had a terrible fear that no matter where she tried to hide, she'd eventually be found by the madman who was after her.

"I can't go," she finally said. "I don't want to leave Poppy. At least here I know you have my back."

He frowned. "Yeah, a lot of good that did you tonight."

She grabbed his hand in hers. "Don't do that, Benjamin. Don't blame yourself for what happened. There was no way you could have anticipated this happening." She released his hand. "Let's just get to the motel and get some sleep."

The adrenaline that had filled her from the moment the window had exploded and Poppy had fallen to the floor began to ebb a bit.

She knew she should be terrified that there was obviously somebody who was determined to kill her or Poppy or both of them. She also knew that Poppy would be safe here in the hospital. Deputy Sam McCain had assured her that nobody would get into his room unless they were hospital personnel and even then they would all be scrutinized carefully.

It took nearly an hour for them to finally leave the hospital and get checked into the motel. The room was ordinary with two double beds, a small table shoved against the wall and a wardrobe holding a television.

"Brett Hatcher, the man who owns this place, will make sure that nobody knows we're here," Benjamin said once they got inside.

Edie nodded and sat on the bed nearest the door. She was exhausted and yet keyed up at the same time. Even though it was late she knew she wouldn't be able to sleep for some time.

Benjamin moved to the window and pulled the curtains tightly closed and then turned back to look at her. "Normally I'd have you sleep in the bed nearest the window so that I'd be between you and anyone who might come in that door, but with the events of tonight still fresh in my mind I don't want you anywhere near the window."

"I trust your judgment," she said.

"You shouldn't," he replied with a touch of bitterness as he sat on the bed opposite her. "I should have never put you two at the ranch without a dozen guards on the property."

"Benjamin, I know how small this town is, how many men are working for the sheriff's department. There wasn't the manpower to post guards. You can't beat yourself up about this. It certainly hasn't shaken my confidence in you."

She watched as some of the tension in his shoulders eased. "I swear to God, Edie, I'd take a bullet in the chest before I'd let anything happen to you."

The depth of his feelings for her was there on his face, shining from his eyes and tangible in the air. She felt it wrapping around her and for several agonizing seconds she forgot how to breathe, she couldn't catch her breath.

"I know," she finally managed to say and then jumped up off the bed. "I'm going to take a shower before going to sleep." She escaped into the bathroom where she leaned weakly against the wall.

She'd sworn she didn't want or need anyone in her life, but at the moment her need for Benjamin filled her up inside. She wanted him to hold her, to stroke fire into her veins, to kiss her until she was mindless with pleasure.

She wanted to believe that her need arose from the night's events, from the fact that death had come so close, but she knew the truth. This need, this want of him, had been a slow, steady burn that had been building with each and every moment she spent with him.

Turning on the water in the shower, she tried to tamp down her desire for him. Hopefully in a week or so this would all be over and she would be back in Topeka figuring out her life.

Benjamin deserved more than a temporary woman; he deserved more than her. She stepped into the hot, steamy water and welcomed the relaxing spray that slowly unkinked taut muscles.

She just needed to get into bed and go to sleep. She needed to not think about the fact that Benjamin would be in bed only three feet from her.

At least he'd gotten a room with two beds. Sharing the room for a couple days was going to be difficult enough, but if they'd had to share a bed it would have been nearly impossible.

After several minutes she turned off the water, stepped out of the tub and grabbed one of the fluffy white towels that awaited her. She dried off and then ran her fingers through her wet hair to rid it of tangles.

She hated to put on her same clothes, but had no other choice. When she finally got beneath the sheets she'd take off her jeans and sweatshirt and sleep in her bra and panties.

When she left the bathroom she found Benjamin seated where he'd been when she'd left the room, on the edge of his bed. "At the hospital Tom told me that we might have another missing woman," he said.

"Oh, no! Who is it?" She sat on her bed facing him, so close she could smell his scent, that slightly woodsy cologne that had become as familiar as the beat of her own heart.

"Her name is Suzy Bakersfield. She works as a waitress at Harley's, a bar on the edge of town. She was due home from work a couple hours ago and her boyfriend called when she didn't come home."

"Do you think these missing women are related to the other stuff?" she asked.

He blew a deep sigh. "I don't know. I asked Tom the same question, but we just don't know enough at this point. What worries me is that if they aren't related, then we have two separate criminal issues going on here in Black Rock. I figure now isn't the time to talk to my brother about quitting."

Edie looked at him in surprise. "You're really thinking about it? I hope your decision doesn't have anything to do with what happened tonight."

His eyes were dark as he held her gaze. "It's something I've been thinking about for a long time, but I've been afraid."

"Afraid?" She couldn't imagine a man like Benjamin being afraid of anything.

Once again he released a sigh and averted his gaze from hers. Instead he stared at the wall just to the left of her, a frown racing across his forehead. "I've wanted to ranch full-time for a while now, but I've been scared of what people might think, about what might lie beneath my badge."

"I don't understand," she replied.

"The badge gives me respect in this town. People know they can depend on me and they like me. I've been afraid that if I take off the badge, then I'd be nothing. I'd lose the respect of my friends and neighbors."

"Oh, Benjamin, people like and respect you because you're a good man with a good heart. You're warm and friendly and solid and any respect you've earned has nothing to do with your badge," she exclaimed.

He offered her a smile. "You're the reason why I've decided when these cases are finished, then I'm handing in my badge."

"Me?" She looked at him in surprise. "What did I do?"

His eyes took on a new warmth, a sweet depth that was intoxicating. "I know you're afraid and yet you've handled all this with such courage and grace. Fear isn't stopping you from doing whatever it is you feel you need to do. I figure if you can do that, then so can I."

This time it was she who broke eye contact. "You should do whatever it is that makes you happy, Benjamin. Happiness is so fleeting and when it stands in front of you, you should embrace it with all of your being."

She got up from the bed and pulled down the spread. She needed to stop the conversation, needed to distance herself from him. She didn't want him to admire her. She didn't want him to look at her with his soulful eyes that made her want to fall into his arms and somehow believe that happiness might be hers to embrace.

He seemed to sense her need for distance. "I think I'll take a fast shower," he said as he got up from the bed.

"I'm sure I'll be asleep when you get out so I'll just say good-night now," she replied. She turned off the lamp next to the bed, plunging the room into darkness other than the light spilling in from the bathroom.

He hesitated at the doorway of the bathroom, as if he wanted to say something more to her. She refused to look at him again, afraid that somehow, someway, he'd break down her defenses. He finally murmured a good-night and retreated into the bathroom.

She quickly took off her jeans and T-shirt and got into her bed. With the covers pulled up around her neck, she squeezed her eyes tightly closed and tried not to think about the look she'd seen in Benjamin's eyes.

As she lay in the darkness of the room, she recognized what she felt from him, what she saw whenever he looked at her.

Love. And it made her realize that no other man had ever looked at her in that way, that she'd never truly been loved by a man before.

She'd thought Greg loved her and she'd believed she'd loved him. But looking back on that relationship, she recognized it had been emotional need that had driven her into his arms and financial need that had driven him into hers.

In all her relationships before, the missing element had been the kind of love she saw shining from Benjamin's eyes whenever he looked at her.

He'd said he wished he'd met her before Greg and she wished the same. Perhaps then her heart would have been opened to taking what he seemed to be offering her, open to giving back to him tenfold.

But it was too late.

He was too late.

Still, a little part of her wondered what it would be like to make love with somebody who truly loved her.

Benjamin stood beneath the spray of the shower until it began to cool. Somewhere in the span of the events of the past couple days he'd made his decision to turn in his badge. He wouldn't do it now, with Tom so overloaded by what was happening, but within the next few months he would follow his heart and become a full-time rancher.

When he thought about spending all his days and

nights at the ranch in all his imaginings, Edie was there at his side.

He could easily see himself walking up the lane from the pasture and her seated on the front porch waiting for him to return. It was easy to imagine the two of them on horseback, her laughter riding the fresh-scented air and her eyes sparkling with that light that made him weak in the knees.

He'd never felt this way about a woman before, suspected he would never feel this depth of love again. She was a burn in his soul, a song in his heart and he knew that no matter what happened between them, she'd transformed him as a man forever.

He stepped out of the shower and quickly dried off, his head still filled with thoughts of Edie. She'd shown him that he was capable of love, of great passion for a woman. He'd begun to believe that it wasn't in his character to feel those emotions. She made him feel more alive than he had in all his years of life.

He didn't bother putting his shirt back on but pulled on his briefs and his jeans and left the bathroom. The room was dark and silent and he thought she must already be asleep.

He shucked his jeans to the floor and placed his gun on the nightstand, then slid in beneath the sheets that smelled faintly of bleach and fabric softener.

He was exhausted but he instinctively knew that sleep was a long time coming. His mind whirled not only with the shooting of Walt, but also the possibility that another woman had gone missing.

Hopefully Suzy Bakersfield had just gone off with a girlfriend and hadn't checked her plans with her boyfriend. That she was alive and well and would have some explaining to do when she eventually returned home.

But he couldn't dismiss the sick feeling that she was just like Brittany, just like Jennifer Hightower, and she'd somehow disappeared into thin air.

As always thoughts of his missing sister caused a deep grief to rip through his heart. The idea of never seeing her smile again, never hearing her babble about men and work and life, left a hole inside him that he knew would never completely be filled.

"Benjamin, are you asleep?" Edie's voice whispered across the darkness of the room.

"No."

"Me, either," she said and released a deep sigh.

"Things on your mind? Do you need to talk?" He rolled over on his side to face her direction.

She was silent for a long moment. "I'm reconsidering this celibacy thing."

Every muscle in his body froze. He was afraid to speak, afraid to hope what her words might mean. He realized she was waiting for some sort of a response from him. "Oh, really?" he finally managed to utter. "What's changed your mind?"

"You."

He heard her change positions and knew that she'd turned to face his direction. "How did I change your mind?" he asked. His breath was painful in his chest as he tried not to anticipate what might happen next.

"I don't know, you just did," she said with a hint of frustration in her voice. "I want you, Benjamin. I want you to make love to me."

Joy leaped into his heart, but it was a joy tempered with caution. "Edie, I don't want a bullet through the window to force you to make a decision you'll regret later." As much as he wanted her, he didn't want to be just another mistake in her life.

"As long as you'd understand that it's a one-shot deal, that there are no promises or strings attached, then I wouldn't regret it."

Funny, most men would have jumped at the chance for sex with no strings, no commitments, but Benjamin had hoped for more, had desperately wanted more from her.

"Benjamin?" Her whisper held both a wealth of longing and more than a hint of self-consciousness.

He'd take what he could get of her, he thought as he threw back the sheet and got up and then grabbed his wallet from the nightstand. He had a condom tucked inside it, compliments of his brother Caleb who insisted the Grayson men were always prepared.

He was surprised to discover his fingers trembling slightly as he pulled the condom out and placed it on the nightstand next to her bed.

He hesitated, wishing there was some illumination in the room so he could see her face. "Edie, are you sure?"

Her hand reached out and touched his, then her fingers twined with his and she tugged him into her bed. As he got beneath the sheets he felt nervous, excited and as if he were about to make love for the very first time.

He pulled her into his embrace and she came willingly, eagerly. She was all heat and soft curves against him as she hid her face in the crook of his neck.

He stroked his hands up the length of her back, unsurprised that her skin was as silky as he'd imagined. He wanted to say words of love, wanted her to know just how much he cared about her, but he knew that would only drive her away.

She needed this not to matter and so he told himself it didn't, that it was just a hookup for mutual sexual pleasure and nothing more.

Still, when he found her lips with his he drank of her, his heart filling with her taste, the clean soapy scent of her and the warmth that raced through his veins.

"I knew you'd feel so good," she said as he left her mouth and rained kisses down the side of her jaw. She released a small moan as he found a sensitive place just below her ear.

"And I knew the same about you," he murmured.

Her arms tightened around him and she stroked her fingers down his back, increasing the flame that threatened to consume him.

His hunger for her wanted to move fast, to rip the panties and bra from her body and take her with hard, fast strokes. He wanted to possess her in a way she'd never been possessed before, in a way that would make her cling to him now and forever.

But his need was tempered with the desire to go slow, to savor each and every moment that he held her in his arms, for he knew this moment probably wouldn't happen again.

He captured her mouth again, their tongues swirling together in a deeply intimate kiss. At the same time his hands moved to her bra fastener. He hesitated, waiting to make sure she wouldn't suddenly protest. When she didn't he unfastened the whisper of fabric.

She shrugged it off and tossed it to the end of the bed, then went back into his arms. His heart banged against his chest at the feel of her warm breasts against him.

She fit neatly against him, as if they were made to fit together. She leaned back slightly and stroked a hand down his chest. "So strong," she murmured and pressed her lips against his collarbone.

He wasn't strong, not where she was concerned. He felt weak and vulnerable and needy as he captured her breasts with his hands. "So beautiful," he whispered. "You make me weak, Edie."

"I don't want you weak right now. I want you strong and powerful."

Her words merely increased his raging need of her. He bent his head and took the tip of one of her nipples in his mouth, enjoying the gasp of pleasure that escaped her.

Her nipple hardened and extended in his mouth as she tangled her fingers in his hair and moaned. She pressed her body into his and he knew she had to realize that he was fully aroused.

Rather than warding her off, his erection seemed to intensify her desire. She grabbed his buttocks, her fingers burning through the thin cotton of his briefs.

He ran a hand down the flat of her belly and slid

it under the slick silk of her panties. Hot and damp, she arched up to meet his touch.

A sudden impatience snapped through him. He wanted to be naked and he wanted her naked. He tugged at her panties to remove them and she aided him by lifting her hips.

He then took off his own and pulled her back into his arms, reveling in the feel of bare skin against skin.

Again he touched her damp heat and she caught her breath and then moaned his name. His heart expanded with love for her. Wanting to be the best lover she'd ever had, he increased the pressure of his touch, felt the rising tide of sensation inside her.

He ran his lips across her cheek, down the length of her neck and moaned in pleasure as she reached her climax. She shuddered and cried out his name once more as she went limp.

She didn't stay that way for long. As she reached out and encircled his hard length with her hand, it was his turn to gasp in pleasure.

Control it. He was definitely going to lose control if she continued to touch him that way. He slid away from her and reached for the condom on the nightstand, mentally thanking his little brother for insisting that he be prepared for the unexpected.

When he was ready he crouched over her and framed her face with his hands. He could easily imagine how her eyes looked at the moment, emerald and glowing with fire. He kissed her lips, her cheek and then her forehead as he slowly eased into her.

Engulfed in exquisite pleasure, he whispered her

name again and again and began to stroke in and out
of her sweet heat. She gripped his buttocks, drawing
him in deep with each thrust.

Lost. He was lost in her and he never wanted to
be found. But all too quickly he felt the rise of a tidal
wave building up inside him, sweeping him toward
completion.

When it came, he took her mouth with his in a kiss
that held all the emotions he had inside. And when it
was over he slumped to the side of her in awe.

Benjamin had enjoyed sex plenty of times in his
life, but never with the kind of love he felt for this
woman. His Edie.

No, not his. The deal was that this meant nothing to her. Just physical release without any strings.
She'd made it clear in a hundred different ways that
she had no intention of loving him back.

But that didn't mean he couldn't try to break
through her defenses and win her heart. He rolled
over and kissed her, then slid out of bed. "I'll be right
back," he said and went into the bathroom.

He washed up and then stared at his reflection in
the mirror. He'd never seen her coming. He'd had no
way to prepare himself for the tremendous emotion
Edie evoked inside him. He'd been utterly helpless
to stop himself from loving her.

And he was equally helpless to stop her from leaving him. The sad truth was the people you loved
didn't always love you back. But he wouldn't stop
trying to win her love until she left town. He'd hold
her through the nights, keep her safe and as happy

as possible during the days and maybe, just maybe, his love would win.

He turned out the light and left the bathroom. "Good night, Benjamin," she said as he stepped back into the room. Any thought he had of holding her through the night vanished as he realized she didn't want him in her bed again.

"Good night," he replied and crawled beneath the covers on his own bed. He smelled of her and he wanted to keep that scent in his head forever. But he knew that eventually this case would be solved and just like Brittany, she'd be gone from him forever.

"You have to stop crying," Brittany said to Jennifer Hightower. "You're going to make yourself sick."

"What difference does it make," Jennifer cried. "He's going to kill us anyway."

Brittany snaked her fingers through the bars that separated the two women and attempted to stroke her hair. Jennifer had been crying since their captor had brought in Suzy Bakersfield about an hour ago. Suzy was now unconscious on a cot in the third cell of five in what appeared to be an old, converted barn or shedlike structure.

Brittany had lost count of the days she'd been held captive, although she thought Jennifer had been with her for a couple weeks. She knew from experience that Suzy would remain unconscious for the rest of the night and would awaken sometime tomorrow to horror.

Horror had become an intimate companion to Brittany. When she'd initially awakened in the small cell, she'd screamed herself hoarse and had desperately tried to find a way out, but there was none. The structure was sound, with no apparent weaknesses that could be exploited. Each cell had a cot and a toilet and nothing else that could be used as a weapon or for escape.

They were usually fed a small meal once a day by their captor, but several times there had been nothing for two or three days. Each time he came in, Brittany tried her best to identify him, but he always wore a hat and a ski mask that made it impossible. His voice sounded vaguely familiar but no matter how she racked her brain she couldn't place it.

"Jenny, you didn't eat the food he brought. You need to stop crying and eat. We have to keep up our strength so that if an opportunity arises we can escape." Brittany pulled her hand back from Jenny's head and instead gripped the metal bars that separated the two.

"You can't give up hope," Brittany said, even though she struggled with that, as well.

"There is no hope," Jenny sobbed. She raised her head and looked at Brittany, her eyes swollen nearly shut and her skin splotchy from her tears.

"There's always hope," Brittany said fervently. "As long as we're alive, there's hope."

Brittany had to believe that, she had to believe that somehow her brothers would find them before the last two cells were filled with women, for it was then that she knew their captor intended to begin his game—and the game meant death to them all.

Chapter 10

It was impossible to tell what time it was when Edie awakened the next morning. She knew that Benjamin was already awake. She could hear him in the bathroom and apparently he was talking to somebody on his cell phone.

She'd known making love with him was a mistake, albeit a glorious mistake. Her body still tingled with the memory of his every touch, his every kiss, and there was no way to deny that he was in her heart as deeply as anyone ever had been.

She'd made glorious love with him and she now could no longer deny her love for him and yet, really, nothing had changed. She couldn't magically undo her past and she refused to let down her guard.

Benjamin was a good man who deserved a good

woman. The charm around her neck suddenly felt as if it burned her skin. She reached up and grabbed it in her hand and for a moment allowed the pain to race through her.

The charm wasn't a symbol of her mother's death, but rather the death of her baby, the daughter who had died without drawing a breath.

A medical mystery, the doctor had said with sympathy in his eyes. A tragedy, the nurse had replied as she'd gently wrapped the perfectly formed infant in a pink blanket.

But Edie had known better. It had been her fault. Somehow she'd done something wrong. She'd been so stressed over the bills and Greg's abandonment. She knew in her heart of hearts it was all her fault.

"They'll be other babies," the doctor had said when he'd signed her release papers. "You're young and healthy and I'm sure there are healthy babies in your future."

But he'd been wrong. The day Edie had buried the daughter she'd named Mary, she'd buried any hope she had, any expectation she might entertain for happiness.

Before the grief could completely overwhelm her, she released the charm and drew a deep breath. This was her secret. Oh, the few friends she had in Topeka knew that she'd lost her baby, but after the birth she'd distanced herself from them all, unable to stand the sympathy in their eyes, the platitudes that rolled so easily off their tongues.

She'd just wanted to be alone with her grief, and there was a part of her that still felt that way. She reached over and turned on the lamp on the nightstand, then got out of bed and quickly pulled on the clothes she'd taken off the night before. She felt better prepared to face the day, to face Benjamin, dressed.

When the door to the bathroom opened, she tensed. The last thing she wanted was a morning after, a rehash of the mistake she'd made the night before.

"Oh, good. You're awake," he said as he came into the room. He walked over to the window and opened the heavy outer curtains, leaving the gauzy inner curtains in place. Sunshine poured in but it was impossible to see out or into the room.

"I was just talking to Tom. He called to tell me the lab report came in." He sat on the edge of the bed and smiled at her and in his eyes, in the warmth of that smile, she saw the memories of their lovemaking.

"Did the results tell you anything about the person responsible?"

"First of all, the good news is that nothing was radioactive. In mixing some of the chemicals a reaction occurred that created the fluorescent glow, but nothing was radioactive. The bulk of the chemicals were ones used almost exclusively by taxidermists, so Tom was on his way to the taxidermy shop to speak to Jeff Hudson and his son, Jeffrey Allen."

"You think they're responsible for this?" she asked. She didn't want to look at him, didn't want to remember the feel of his warm lips against hers, the stroke of his hands across her naked body.

"I think it's a good lead," he replied. "Maybe it won't be long before this is all over." He stood. "In the meantime I called Brett and he's going to bring us some coffee and breakfast in a few minutes."

"Room service? I didn't know motels offered that."

He smiled again, the warm, wonderful grin that made her want to run into his arms, or run as far away from him as possible.

"We've used the motel off and on over the years when we've needed to stash somebody away. Brett is very accommodating when that happens."

As if to punctuate his sentence, there was a knock on the door. Instantly tension replaced Benjamin's warm smile as he drew his gun from his shoulder holster and motioned her into the bathroom.

He peered out the window and instantly relaxed. "It's okay. It's Brett."

He unchained and unlocked the door to admit the older man who carried with him a large shopping bag. He nodded at Edie and walked over to the small table. "Got you some coffee and egg muffins and a couple of sweet rolls," he said.

"Thanks, Brett, we appreciate it," Benjamin replied.

"No problem. Just call the office when you need something else and I'll be happy to do food runs for you." With another nod to Edie he left the room.

Benjamin locked the door behind him as Edie began to unload the food. Maybe she'd feel better after a cup of coffee. A caffeine rush would surely banish her desire to be back in Benjamin's arms.

They sat at the small table and ate, talking little

until the food was gone and they were left with the last of their coffee.

"The good news for the town is that the wooded area where the body parts were found wasn't contaminated and won't require an expensive cleanup," he said. "Something like that could bankrupt a small town like Black Rock."

"That is good news for you," she replied.

"And we'll have good news for you soon," he said softly. "This is going to be over and the person who attacked you will be behind bars."

"From your lips to God's ears." She took a sip of coffee and broke off eye contact with him. It was there again in his eyes, a soft vulnerability, a sweet longing that scared her.

"Edie." The longing she'd seen in his eyes was now in his voice.

She closed her eyes, refusing to look at him. "Benjamin, don't." She was afraid of what he was about to say, didn't want to hear whatever he thought might be in his heart.

"I have to," he said, obviously knowing exactly what she meant. "My lack of real passion used to worry me. I've watched two of my brothers fall in love. I saw the passion in their eyes, heard it in their voices whenever they saw or talked about their women. I thought something was missing inside me. I'd never felt that for any woman I'd dated, until now. Until you."

There it was, out on the table, the one thing she didn't want to hear from him, the last thing she'd wanted to hear. She forced herself to look at him

and the emotion in his eyes was raw and open for
her to see.

"I love you, Edie. I love you passionately, desperately and I want you to stay here in Black Rock with
me. I want you in my life today and forever."

It was exactly what she'd feared. She was going
to be his first heartbreak and she hated it; she hated
herself for not being the woman he needed in his life.

"Benjamin, you're just feeling that way because
of last night," she said. "I'll admit, the sex was great.
We obviously have a physical chemistry, but I've told
you all along, I'm not looking for a relationship."

"Sometimes when you aren't looking for love it
finds you anyway," he countered. He reached across
the table for her hand, but she pulled away, not wanting his touch, which would simply make things more
difficult. "Edie, I'm a simple man, but I believe you
love me. I see it when you look at me, I tasted it
in your kisses last night. I've had sex with women
before, but last night we made love, both of us together."

She desperately sought the words to deny her own
feelings for him, but they refused to rise to her lips.
Once again she looked down at the top of the table,
finding it impossible to look into his eyes without
drowning in his feelings for her.

"It doesn't matter. Don't you see?" She got up
from the table and stepped away from him. "It
doesn't matter what you feel, and it doesn't matter
what I feel. I'm still going back to Topeka and living my life alone."

A sudden grief clawed up her throat, burned in

her eyes, the grief of knowing she was turning her back on love and the darker, deeper grief of overwhelming loss.

She gripped the back of the chair, her knuckles white as she fought for control. But the fight was in vain. Tears began to run down her cheeks as an agonizing pain ripped through her. "Please, Benjamin, leave it alone," she managed to gasp. "I'm not the kind of woman you want. You deserve better than me."

She looked around wildly, needing to escape not only from him, but also from her own dark thoughts, from the incredible pain that threatened to shatter her into pieces.

He got up from his chair and took her by the shoulders, forcing her to look up at him. "What are you talking about, Edie? You are the woman I want and we both deserve to be happy together. I'll ranch full-time and you can do whatever makes you happy as long as each morning I wake up to see your face and each night I fall asleep with the sound of your breathing next to me."

He moved his hand to her cheek and softly stroked there. "We'll build a life together. We'll laugh and we'll love. Each night when the weather is nice, we'll sit on the front porch and watch the horses play as the sun sets. It will be a wonderful life, Edie, if only you'll share it with me."

It was magical picture he painted with his words, one she wanted to step into and embrace and she felt her resolve fading, her defenses crumbling.

"Come on, Edie. You know you love me. Let's raise cattle and children together."

Of all the things he might have said, this was the one thing that exploded apart the picture of happily-ever-after, and her weeping began in earnest.

She didn't want to tell him. She'd never wanted to tell anyone. But she was certain it was the one thing that would turn him away in revulsion, the one thing that would change his mind about loving her.

And ultimately that would make it so much easier on her. If he'd just stop loving her. Then perhaps she wouldn't want him as desperately, as frantically as she did.

"Talk to me, Edie. Why are you crying?" He used his thumbs to wipe at the tears on her cheeks.

She wasn't sure what she was crying for, if it was because she had every intention of walking away from this wonderful man or if she cried for the child who had never been, the sweet baby daughter she'd lost.

He attempted to pull her into his arms, but she whirled away from him, wild with her grief. She headed for the bathroom, needing the privacy, but before she went inside she turned back to face him.

"You don't know me, Benjamin. You don't know what I've done."

"Then tell me. I know nothing you can say will change the way I feel about you. Nothing that you have done will make me not love you."

He was like a shimmering mirage in the veil of her tears, a mirage that looked like love but she knew if she let him close enough it would disappear.

"I killed my baby, Benjamin. That's what I did."
She watched his eyes widen and saw the shock that
swept over his features just before she escaped into
the bathroom and locked the door.

Benjamin felt as if he'd been sucker punched in
the gut. Of all the things he'd anticipated she might
have said, there was no way he could have anticipated this.

The one thing he knew was that there was no way
Edie could intentionally harm anyone, especially her
own baby. He stared at the closed bathroom door,
the sound of her weeping drifting through the door.

She'd hit him like a speeding, out-of-control
driver and then had left before checking for damage or explaining why she'd been reckless in the
first place.

After everything they'd been through he deserved
more from her. He knocked on the bathroom door.
"Edie," he said, steeling his heart against the sound
of her crying. He tried the doorknob, unsurprised
to find it locked. "Edie, come out here and talk to
me. I haven't asked you for much, but you owe me
an explanation."

Her sobs were gut-wrenching. He heard her gasping for air, hiccupping as they began to subside. He
remained standing outside the door until there was
finally silence on the other side.

"Edie, please talk to me," he finally said. He
stepped back as the doorknob turned and the door
opened. The ravages of pain were on her splotchy

face, in her red-rimmed eyes, and he wanted nothing more than to take her into his arms.

She didn't meet his gaze as she moved past him and sat on the edge of his bed. She stared down at the carpet beneath her feet, her shoulders slumped forward in utter defeat.

"I was almost seven months pregnant when Greg abandoned me." Her voice was flat, as if she'd forgotten all her emotions in the bathroom. "I was reeling with the financial mess he'd left me, still grieving for my mother and wondering how I was going to deal with being a single parent."

He wanted to sit next to her, wanted to pull her into his arms and tell her everything was going to be okay, but he sensed her need to do this alone, to tell her story without the comfort he might offer her.

"For the first couple weeks after he left and the creditors were calling me, I did nothing but cry." She laced her fingers together in her lap, the white knuckles letting him know how difficult it was for her to talk.

"I finally quit crying and decided I was going to be just fine. I'd be a terrific mother and I was strong enough to do it all alone." She raised her head to look at him and in her eyes he saw a woman's grief, a mother's despair.

"Everything seemed normal. I went into labor a week before my due day and got to the hospital. Halfway through the delivery I knew something was wrong. The atmosphere in the room changed and nobody was smiling or joking anymore. Eventually she arrived, a beautiful baby girl who was stillborn."

He could no longer stay away from her. He sat next to her but when he attempted to pull her into his embrace, she jerked away.

"Edie, I'm so sorry for you. I'm so sorry for your loss." His heart ached for her and he wished there was some way he could take away her pain, banish the haunting that darkened her eyes. "What did the doctor say?"

She released a bitter laugh. "That these things happen, that it was a tragic medical mystery that sometimes occurs."

"Edie, you didn't do anything wrong. Sometimes bad things happen for no reason, but that doesn't mean you should blame yourself, that you should punish yourself for the rest of your life."

She jumped up from the bed, her entire body trembling. "But I did do something wrong. In those two weeks that I was so broken, there was a night I thought for just a minute that everything would be so much easier if I wasn't pregnant. I was big and fat and uncomfortable. Don't you see, Benjamin, I wished the baby away and she was gone."

He got up off the bed and pulled her against his chest. She fought him, trying to get away, but he held tight until she collapsed against him as she cried uncontrollably.

He now understood the shadows he'd sometimes seen in her eyes and the significance of the charm she wore around her neck. What he didn't know was how to take away the misplaced guilt she felt, how to make her understand that to deny herself happiness for the rest of her life wasn't the answer. He simply held her tight, waiting for her storm of tears to pass.

Eventually she stopped crying and simply remained exhausted in his arms. He led her back to the bed and together they sat, his arm still around her shoulder.

For several long minutes neither of them spoke. Her heartbreak hung thick and palpable in the air. He stroked her shoulder although he knew she was beyond the place where physical connection might comfort her.

He drew a deep breath. "The day before Brittany disappeared I had a fight with her. As usual she was late to work and I'd had to cover some of her shift. I was ticked and I told her that there were times my life sure would be less complicated if she'd just get out of it for a while."

He paused to draw another breath, emotion thick in the back of his throat.

Edie was as still as a statue against his side. "What did she say?" she finally asked.

"She laughed and patted my cheek and told me not to be such a grumpy bear. It was the last time I talked to her. Am I to believe that in that moment of anger I somehow made her disappear for good?"

"Of course not."

"Then why would you believe that a moment's thought had the power to make sure your baby didn't live?"

She didn't answer. Her head remained bowed and her body felt boneless against him and he knew that he hadn't broken through to her.

"Edie, don't throw your life away because of a tragedy. You deserve to be happy, and if it's not with me, then open up your heart to somebody else."

She finally raised her head to look at him and in her eyes he saw the strength of her defenses back in place. She moved away from him and stood, her back rigid and her mouth pressed together in a grim line.

"I'm not strong like you, Benjamin. I can't forget what happened, what I lost." She reached up and touched the charm that hung around her neck.

"I don't expect you to forget," he countered. "Your daughter was a part of you, a part of your heart for nine months. You don't forget those you love and lose. You remember them and sometimes you ache for them, but life goes on and the only way to truly honor their memory is to be happy."

A panic welled up inside him as her walls climbed higher. He was going to lose her before he'd ever really had her. "Edie, for God's sake, let me in. Let me show you happiness and love."

For just a brief moment her eyes shimmered with the love he knew was deep in her heart for him. Hope filled him, but was quickly dashed as she shook her head and the emotion in her eyes vanished.

"I'm sorry, Benjamin, but when this is all over I'm going back to Topeka. I don't need love in my life. I don't want it. I just want to live the rest of my life alone, without risk."

Once again she headed for the bathroom and disappeared inside. And this time Benjamin didn't go after her.

There was nothing more he could say, nothing more he could do, and for the first time in his life, Benjamin knew the pain of heartbreak.

Chapter 11

Edie would have liked to hide out in the bathroom forever. At least in there she didn't have to look at Benjamin, didn't have to see the love light in his eyes.

It hurt. Her love for him ached in her chest. She'd never wanted anything more in her life than a future with him, a chance to grow old with him at her side.

But she was afraid to love again, afraid to seek happiness. She couldn't forgive herself and she didn't trust that his love wasn't just some illusion to torment her.

She took a shower and lingered after dressing. She didn't want to go back inside the room and see the pain she'd inflicted on him.

She'd never wanted to break his heart. He was

such a good man, as solid as the day was long and with a tenderness that was a gift to anyone who knew him.

For a moment if she closed her eyes and let herself go, she could see a future with him, she could hear the days of laughter, feel the love that would fill her world.

The moment was shattered by his knock on the door. "Edie, Tom just called. It's over. Jeffrey Allen confessed to everything."

She sagged against the door. Over. It was all over. Now there was nothing to keep her from going back to her lonely life. She straightened and opened the door. "Good, let's get the hell out of here so I can go home."

"Tom and Caleb are on their way to bring me my truck," he replied. "They should be out front in a few minutes."

"If you don't mind, I'd like to stop by the hospital on the way to the ranch. I need to tell Poppy and Margaret goodbye before I leave."

"You're leaving today?" He looked at her in surprise.

She nodded. "As soon as I get my things at your place I'll be on the road."

"That breakfast we had earlier left me hungry. Come to the café with me and eat a good lunch before you take off. I'll tell you everything Tom told me when he called."

"Only on one condition," she said. "That you don't try to talk me into staying."

The smile he gave her was a weary one with a

touch of disillusionment. "I gave it my best shot, Edie. The ball is in your court. I won't try to talk you into anything."

An hour later they were seated at a table in the café. She'd said her painful goodbyes to Poppy and Margaret and in her mind she was halfway out of town already. She'd only agreed to this meal because she had a long drive ahead of her and had to eat something before taking off. Besides, she was curious about the crime that had kept her in town, the man who had beaten Poppy and terrorized her.

"According to what Tom told me, Jeffrey decided to dabble in a little chemistry and see if he could come up with a way to better preserve flesh," Benjamin said after they'd placed their orders with the waitress.

"Apparently he was hoping to come up with some kind of cream that would work on human flesh, a beauty product that would take the world by storm."

"And so he stole body parts from the cemetery?" she asked.

Benjamin nodded. "That's what he confessed to. From what Tom said, Jeffrey believed that somehow he'd created a radioactive reaction in his experiments, hence the hazmat suit to dispose of the botched batch."

"So why did he go after me and Poppy? He had to know that we couldn't identify him."

"Interestingly enough, Tom said those two things were what he was most reluctant to admit to. When he did, it was just like we suspected, sheer anger that drove him to attack the two of you. If he'd been successful in his experiments he would have eventually become a very wealthy man. Beauty is a big business these days and he thought he was going to discover a fountain of youth, something that would keep skin from aging."

Edie fought back a shiver as she remembered hiding in the closet while Jeffrey had banged on the door and threatened her.

"You okay?" he asked as if he sensed the fear that suddenly crawled up her back.

"I'm fine, just glad this is all over and I can go back home without looking over my shoulder."

At that moment their orders arrived. Their meal was interrupted several times by people stopping by their table to ask about Walt or talk about Jeffrey's arrest.

Benjamin introduced her to Larry Norwood, the town vet, and to Hugh Randolf, who owned the feed store. She met Karen Patterson, who worked at the bank, and Lisa Rogers, who was a beautician.

Each and every person greeted her with open friendliness and sent home the fact that if she'd chosen differently, Black Rock would have been a wonderful place to call home.

They were just leaving the café when at the door they met a big guy in overalls and a red flannel shirt. Benjamin introduced him as Josh Willoughby, the groundskeeper at the cemetery.

"Hope you're planning on staying in town," he said to Edie. "I know Walt would love having you around."

"Actually, I'm on my way out of town in just a

little while," Edie replied. "This was just a visit gone crazy."

Josh smiled. "Seems to me the only one who went crazy is Jeffrey." He looked at Benjamin. "I guess we've solved the mystery of the lights I thought I saw once in a while at the cemetery. Must have been Jeffrey skulking around the newest graves."

"Must have been," Benjamin agreed. "At least this particular issue has been solved."

"Yeah, now all you have to do is figure out what happened to those missing girls," Josh replied.

Edie felt the weight of concern in Benjamin as he released a deep sigh. "Yeah, we definitely need a break where the disappearances are concerned."

Goodbyes were said and then Edie and Benjamin got back into his truck and headed for the ranch. They were both silent for part of the ride. It wasn't a comfortable silence but rather one filled with tension.

Telling him goodbye was going to rip out her heart, but she was determined not to change her course, not to alter her future.

"So, what are your plans when you get back to Topeka?" he finally asked, breaking the miserable silence.

"Find a job, find a new place to live," she replied. "Those are my two immediate concerns."

"You'll let somebody here know where you move? We might need you to come back when this goes to trial."

"You have my cell phone number. That won't change, so you can get hold of me if you need to."

As the entrance to the ranch came into view she steeled her heart against a sense of homecoming.

It felt like home. It looked like home, but she reminded herself it was just an illusion. Her grandmother had always cautioned her to love smart, but she'd already made the choice not to love at all. And that was the smartest choice of all.

When they got inside she went to the bedroom where she'd stayed and began to pack her bags while Benjamin headed for the kitchen. She was grateful he didn't hover near her as she placed the few articles of clothing she'd brought back into her suitcase.

She took a clean pair of jeans and a long-sleeve emerald blouse into the bathroom and quickly changed, grateful for the clean clothes after being stuck in the others for two days.

When she left the bathroom she nearly bumped into Benjamin. "I just wanted to let you know that I called Jacob and asked him to bring Tiny back. I thought you might want to say goodbye to the mutt."

A new ball of emotion swelled up in her chest at thoughts of the little dog. She nodded and walked back into the bedroom. She grabbed her suitcase but Benjamin took it from her and together they went to the living room.

At that moment Jacob came in the door, Tiny in his arms. The dog vibrated with excitement at the sight of Edie and Benjamin. As Jacob placed Tiny on the floor he ran first to Benjamin and then to Edie.

She scooped him up in her arms and hugged him as he licked the side of her neck. She smiled at Jacob, noting that the man looked rough with a whisker-darkened jaw and the darkest eyes she'd ever seen. "Thanks for bringing him here for a goodbye."

He nodded and then turned and left the house as Edie placed the dog back on the floor.

"You'll have to excuse my brother. He's not the most social creature on earth," Benjamin said.

"That's okay. Well, I guess it's time for me to get on the road." She didn't quite meet his gaze.

"Edie, if you ever need anything, if you change your mind about me…about us, I'll be here." The yearning in his voice nearly broke her.

She picked up her suitcase and overnight bag and clung tight to the handles so that she wouldn't be tempted to throw her arms around his neck and cling tightly to him. "*Thank you* seems so inadequate for what you've done for me and Poppy, but I'm so grateful, if this had to happen to us, that it happened here with you."

She looked at him then, memorizing his beautiful brown eyes, the strong, handsome features that were permanently etched in her mind. Years from now on cold lonely nights she would remember him and the expression on his face and would be comforted by the knowledge that she'd once been loved.

Together they left the house and he stood next to her car as she stowed her suitcase in the trunk. She dug her keys out of her purse, opened the driver's door and then turned back to look at him.

"Well, I guess this is goodbye." She refused to cry in front of him even though tears began to well up inside her. "I hope you do take up ranching full-time, Benjamin. You come alive when you talk about it."

He nodded, his eyes filled with a sadness it would take her a long time to forget. "And I hope you find peace, Edie. I hope you find forgiveness for yourself, even though you did nothing to be forgiven for. Be safe, Edie, and try to find some happiness for yourself."

He stepped away from the car and she slid in behind the steering wheel and closed the door. As she started the engine, she swallowed hard against the tears that seemed determined to fall.

Refusing to look in her rearview mirror as she pulled away, she kept her focus on the road ahead. Still, by the time she reached the entrance, her vision was blurred with the tears she could no longer contain.

She believed she was doing the right thing and yet there was a tiny voice deep inside her screaming that she was making the biggest mistake of her life.

"Shut up," she muttered to the voice. Still the tears continued and she angrily swiped at them with one hand. There was nothing to cry about. This was her decision, the right decision.

If you never looked for happiness, then you were never disappointed. If you never sought love, then your heart would always remain intact. It was the safest way to live, wrapped in a cocoon of isolation.

By the time she reached the narrow stretch of highway that would lead out of town, her tears had stopped and she kept her mind focused on all the things she needed to take care of once she got back to Topeka.

She was the only car on the road so it was easy to

let her mind wander. She might try the apartments down the street from her current address. She was going to miss that smile of his. She tightened her hands on the steering wheel and consciously forced thoughts of Benjamin out of her head.

She hadn't driven very far when she saw a truck approaching fast behind her. As he got on her tail he honked and then shot into the left lane to pass her.

When he got up next to her she recognized him as the man she'd met earlier at the café. Josh something, the cemetery man. He pointed at the back of her car and gestured wildly as if something was wrong.

Terrific, just what she needed…car trouble that might keep her here for another day or two. She pulled over to the side of the road and Josh pulled in behind her.

He got out of his truck as she got out of the car. "Your back tire is going flat," he said.

"Terrific, and I don't have a spare," she exclaimed. She walked toward the rear of the car and bent down to look at the tire he'd indicated. She frowned. The tire looked fine to her.

Before she could straighten up, something slammed into the top of her head. She sprawled forward to the ground, as pinpoints of light exploded in a growing darkness. Her last conscious thought was that they'd all been wrong.

It wasn't over.

Benjamin wandered the house like a lost man, Tiny at his heels. He'd been alone for most of his adult life but he'd never felt such loneliness.

He'd told Tom he was going to take off the next couple days. With Jeffrey Allen behind bars and that particular crime solved, there were plenty of deputies who could work on the disappearance of the women. He wasn't really needed.

She didn't need you. She didn't love you enough. The words whispered through his brain, bringing with them an ache he'd never felt before.

He'd held out hope until the moment her car had disappeared from his view and it was only then that the last of his hope had died.

He thought about heading to the cabin and talking to Jacob, but realized he wasn't in the mood to talk to anyone, especially Jacob, who seemed to hate life as much as he hated himself at the moment.

There was plenty of work around the ranch that he could do and maybe that was exactly what he needed—physical labor to keep his mind away from thoughts of Edie.

He wanted to make himself so exhausted that when he closed his eyes to sleep that night he wouldn't think of her warm laughter, wouldn't smell her enticing scent and wouldn't remember how she'd felt in his arms.

As he left the house and headed for the barn, his thoughts turned to his sister. He would always have a little bit of guilt inside him about the last conversation he'd had with Brittany, but he knew it wasn't his fault that she'd gone missing.

Just like it wasn't Edie's fault that her baby had been stillborn. He couldn't imagine the anguish of a woman who had carried and loved her baby for nine months, gone through the agony of childbirth and then ended up with nothing.

An experience like that could definitely scar a heart, but it wasn't supposed to destroy a heart. He shook his head as he opened the barn door. Edie had allowed the tragedy and her misplaced sense of guilt to define her, and there was nothing he could do to change that.

Always before he'd found peace and comfort in the barn where the air smelled like leather and hay and horse, but this time there was no peace, no solace to be found. The only scent he wanted to smell was the sweet fragrance of Edie and she was gone from him.

He pulled out his saddle, deciding to oil the leather. He didn't know how long he'd been working when his cell phone rang. He fumbled it out of his shirt pocket and answered.

"Benjamin, we've got a problem." Caleb's voice nearly vibrated with tension. "Is Edie with you?"

Tension filled him. "No, she left here about an hour ago. She was headed back to Topeka. Why?"

"Her car is out on the highway, but she's not around."

Benjamin's heart crashed to his feet. "I'll be right there." He clicked off and then hurried for the house and his keys.

He was on the road in minutes, telling himself to calm down, that there had to be a logical explanation. She had car trouble or she ran out of gas and took off walking back to town, he thought.

But she had your phone number. Why wouldn't

she have called for help? Surely she would have put all personal issues aside if she'd needed help.

By the time he pulled to the curb behind her car, he was half-wild with suppositions. Both Tom and Caleb were there, their cars parked in front of Edie's vehicle.

"There's no damage to the car," Caleb said. "And the keys are in it. I started it up and the engine purred like a kitten, and the gas tank is full."

His words shattered Benjamin's hopeful speculations. His panic must have shown on his features. "There's no blood inside, no signs of a struggle," Tom said.

"There weren't any signs of a struggle in Brittany's or Jennifer's car," he said. Was it possible she'd become the latest victim to a madman who was collecting the young women of the town? "We have to find her," he said with an urgency that made him feel half-sick. He'd lost her because she didn't love him, but he couldn't imagine losing her to this kind of fate.

For the next two hours the three officials walked the area, seeking some clue that might lead to her whereabouts. Tom had people checking in town to see if anyone had seen her. During that time Benjamin's mind raced as his heart grew heavier and heavier.

What were the odds that they'd keep her safe from one madman only to have her fall prey to another? It looked as if she'd pulled the car over on her own. What or who would make her stop?

Was it possible this wasn't another disappearance, but rather tied to the case they'd thought was closed? But Jeffrey had confessed to everything, he reminded himself.

Dammit, he'd thought she was safe, that the danger was over. He looked at Tom, who hung up his phone and shook his head. "Nobody has seen her in town."

"I want to talk to Jeffrey," Benjamin said.

Tom looked at him in surprise. "Why? He's locked up and couldn't have anything to do with this."

Benjamin frowned thoughtfully. "I know that, but I've known Jeffrey all my life and I've never seen him lose his temper, never seen him hurt a fly." His head was a jumble of thoughts, ones he should have entertained the minute Tom had told him Jeffrey had confessed.

"The beating Walt took was vicious and Edie said the man who tried to get at her in the house was filled with rage. That just doesn't sound like Jeffrey. Besides, you said he readily confessed to the experiments and illegal dumping of the body parts yet was reluctant to confess to hurting Walt and attacking Edie."

Tom raised a dark eyebrow. "Are you thinking about a partner?"

Benjamin nodded. "Maybe somebody he's trying to protect or somebody who scares him more than time in jail."

"Let's go have a talk with him," Tom replied.

As Benjamin got into his truck to drive back to town, he prayed they'd find some answers that would lead back to Edie. He prayed that it already wasn't too late for her. He prayed that she wouldn't become another missing woman, that she wouldn't just seemingly disappear off the face of the earth and he would never know what happened to her.

Chapter 12

Edie regained consciousness in pieces of confusion. She moaned as a sharp pain raged in the back of her head and then realized moaning was all she could do because her mouth was taped closed.

Panic pumped her heart in a frantic rhythm as her eyes snapped open. Her ankles were tied, as were her hands behind her back. She sat on the dirt floor of a small shed and for several agonizing seconds she couldn't remember how she'd gotten there.

Then she remembered being in the car and heading out of town when Josh the cemetery man had caused her to stop. But why had he done this? What did he want with her?

She struggled in an attempt to free her hands, but

they were bound tight and her efforts only made the ties tighter and cut off her circulation.

How long had she been unconscious? Minutes? Hours? Did anyone know she was in trouble? Was anyone even looking for her?

Benjamin. Her heart cried his name. Had Josh taken the other women, as well? Would she become just another woman in the town of Black Rock who had disappeared without a trace?

Tears welled up in her eyes, but she shoved them back, afraid that if she began to cry she'd choke. If her nose stuffed up she would suffocate. She would have laughed out loud at this thought if it were possible. Which would she prefer, suffocation by tears or death at the hands of a crazy creep?

She couldn't wait for help to come. It might never come. She needed to do something to help herself. Wildly she looked around the dim, dusty shed. There were picks and shovels leaning in the corner, but nothing that appeared sharp enough to cut the ropes that held her.

There was a machine standing nearby, bigger than a lawnmower and with a small bucket on the front. Her blood went icy cold as she realized it was probably used to dig graves.

Was that what had happened to those other women? Were their bodies under the ground, hiding in a secret grave that Josh had dug on the cemetery property?

A new panic seared through her. Maybe she could use the blade of one of the shovels to free herself, she thought. At least she could try. She attempted to scoot across the floor but instantly discovered that her hands were not only tied together behind her back but were also anchored to something that held her in place.

Frustration added to her fear as she realized there was no way she could do anything to get out of this mess. She was at the mercy of Josh and fate.

She froze, her heart nearly stopping in her chest as she heard somebody approaching. *Please, please let it be somebody here to rescue me,* she thought. *Please, let it be Benjamin or one of his lawmen brothers who walks through that door.*

The door creaked open and her heart fell as Josh walked in. She raised her chin and gave him her best stare of defiance. He laughed, an ugly sound that twisted in her guts.

"You can glare at me all you want," he said as he leaned against the door and eyed her in amusement. "But the way I see it, I've got the upper hand here and you should be begging me for your life. Not that it would do any good."

His pleasant expression morphed into one of rage as he took a step closer to her. "You stupid bitch, you and that old man of yours ruined everything!"

He began to pace just in front of her. "Jeffrey Allen was on the verge of producing a product that would have set the cosmetic industry on its ears. I was supplying Jeffrey with body parts and he'd agreed to pay me half of whatever he made."

He stopped in front of her, his eyes wild with hatred. "You know how much they pay me for my work here in the cemetery? Next to nothing. I got to

work another job just to put food on the table. I was
going to be rich but you and Walt had to stick your
nose into things."

He leaned down so close to her that if her mouth
hadn't been bound she would have bitten his nose
off. In his eyes she saw not only a deep-seated rage
but also a hint of insanity.

"You screwed up my plans." His breath was sick,
fetid in her face. "And the price for that is death." He
straightened and walked back to the door. "After dark
tonight I'm going to do a little work in the cemetery.
That gives you several hours to think about what it's
going to be like to be buried alive."

Horror washed over her, making her slump back
against the wall as he left the shed. She wondered
what time it was, how many hours she had left before darkness fell.

Her head pounded with intensity and the taste
of terror filled her mouth. She should have never
stopped the car. But she'd had a false sense of safety
and hadn't sensed danger.

Closing her eyes, she realized what she'd heard
was true. When facing death your life flashed before your eyes. She thought of those starlit nights
with her grandmother and sweet loving moments
with her mother.

She regretted all the time lost with her Poppy and
hoped that he and Margaret would form a lasting
connection that would keep them both company until
their deaths.

And she thought about Mary, the daughter she'd
lost, the daughter she'd loved. She'd loved her baby

and had wanted her no matter how difficult it would be as a single parent.

She'd planned for Mary, had stroked her own fat belly and sung to the baby. She'd never wished Mary away. She'd been beating herself up for something that hadn't been her fault.

In this moment of facing her own death, she realized Benjamin was right. Mary's death was a tragedy, just like Benjamin's sister's disappearance. Both had been tragedies without answers, without blame.

Tears formed in her eyes once again as she realized she'd had happiness right there in her hand. All she'd had to do was reach out and grasp it, grasp him.

Benjamin. Her heart cried out his name. She'd been a fool to let fear keep her from immersing herself in his love, for not wallowing in her own love for him. And now it was too late.

Fate had given her a chance to be with a man who loved her to distraction, a man who made her happier than anyone else on the face of the earth. It had given her the possibility of other babies and beautiful sunsets and a man who would love and support her. And she'd walked away. She'd loved smart and acted stupid and now it was too late to change things.

She looked at the cracks around the door where faint daylight appeared. How many hours until nightfall? How many hours left before she found herself in the horror of a grave?

Jeffrey Allen Hudson looked like a broken man when Tom led him into the small interrogation room. His shoulders slumped and his broad face was pale, as if some terminal disease was eating him from the inside out.

Tom placed him into a chair at the table and gestured Benjamin toward the chair opposite Jeffrey. Benjamin didn't sit.

"I don't know what you want from me," Jeffrey said. "I've already confessed to everything." He stared down at the tabletop, refusing to look at either man.

"Jeffrey, tell me about the attack on Walt Tolliver's granddaughter." Benjamin placed his hands on the table and leaned forward.

"I already told Tom I did it, so what else is there to say?" He still didn't look up. "Why don't you just leave me alone? I'll face whatever punishment I have to, but I don't have anything else to say."

"If you cooperate with us, maybe I'll put in a good word with the prosecutor," Tom said.

Jeffrey drew a deep breath and finally looked up. His eyes were filled with torment. "What do you want from me?" he asked wearily.

Benjamin ran everything over in his mind as he tamped down the urgency that screamed inside him. "I just need to know one thing. When you stabbed Edie in the leg, did you use a paring knife from Walt's kitchen or was it a pocketknife?" He ignored Tom's look of surprise.

There was no denying the look of confusion that crossed Jeffrey's features. It was there only a moment and then gone as he focused again on the top of the table. "A pocketknife," he mumbled.

Benjamin slammed his hands down on the table.

Jeffrey jumped and scooted his chair back an inch. "You're lying, Jeffrey. Who are you protecting? A friend? Your father?"

"No! My dad has nothing to do with this." Jeffrey grabbed the sides of his head with his hands.

"Jeffrey, Edie is missing. Her car was found on the side of the highway and we think she's in trouble. If you know anything, you need to tell us. Jeffrey, you don't want to be a part of her getting hurt or worse." Benjamin wanted to rip Jeffrey from his seat and shake him until the truth rattled out of his teeth.

Tears formed in Jeffrey's eyes. "He told me that he'd kill my dad if I said anything." The words were a mere whisper. "He's crazy, you know. I didn't realize it until we were both in too deep. I promised him half of what I made. He thought he was going to be rich and he was so angry when it all fell apart."

"Who, Jeffrey. Tell me who," Benjamin exclaimed, his anxiety through the ceiling. But before Jeffrey could reply the answer came to Benjamin.

"It's Josh Willoughby, isn't it?" he asked.

Panic swept across Jeffrey's face and Benjamin knew he had his answer. He looked at his brother. "You'd better send somebody with me to Josh's place, because if I find out he's harmed Edie I'm going to kill him."

He didn't wait for an answer but instead strode out of the room and out of the station. He was on the road to Josh's house when he saw Caleb's patrol car following him.

He'd meant what he'd said. If Josh had hurt Edie…

or worse, Benjamin wouldn't blink twice as he beat the life out of the man.

Josh Willoughby. They all should have realized he had something to do with this. He was in charge of the burials at the cemetery. It would have been easy for him to provide Jeffrey with the body parts before the caskets were covered with dirt.

From the moment Benjamin had heard that Jeffrey had confessed, he'd found it hard to believe that he was responsible for beating Walt and attacking Edie. It was completely out of character.

It wasn't out of character for Josh. Josh was known to have a temper and he also owned an old ATV. It made sense that Jeffrey was involved on the science end of the experiments and Josh was the one who did the dirty work.

The day was slipping away, the sun sinking low in the western sky. It would be dark soon and the thought of Edie someplace out there in the dark and in danger was almost too much for him to bear.

You're probably too late, a little voice whispered in the back of his head. He tightened his grip on the steering wheel and tried to ignore the voice. He couldn't be too late for her. He couldn't be.

He'd already lost Brittany. He couldn't lose Edie. It didn't matter that she didn't want to spend her life with him. It was just important that she have a life to live.

The cemetery came into view and just after it was Josh's small house. Josh's truck was parked out front, letting Benjamin know the man was home.

Benjamin parked in front and raced to the door

where he pounded with his fist. Caleb parked just behind him and hurried to join his brother.

Josh's wife, Marylou, answered the door. She was a small, mousy woman who didn't socialize and was rarely seen in town. She eyed Benjamin and Caleb with more than a bit of trepidation. "Yes?"

"We need to talk to Josh," Benjamin said.

She didn't look surprised, just weary. "He's out back."

Benjamin leaped off the porch and headed around the side of the house, his heart beating so fast he was nearly breathless. Caleb followed just behind him. "Don't do anything stupid," he said.

"Don't worry, I plan on being smart when I beat the hell out of him," Benjamin replied tersely.

They found Josh in the backyard, a hammer in hand as he worked on a rotting windowsill. "Damn house is falling apart," he said as they approached. "What are you two doing here?"

"Put down the hammer," Caleb said as he drew his gun.

"Hey, what's going on?" Josh asked.

"Where is she?" Benjamin asked as Josh slowly lowered the hammer to the ground.

He straightened back up and looked at Benjamin with confusion. "Where is who?"

Benjamin hit him in the chest hard with both his hands. "You know who I'm talking about. Where is Edie?"

Josh stumbled back a step, his face flushing with color. "Hey, man, what's the matter with you? I don't know what you're talking about."

A white-hot rage flew through Benjamin. He slammed Josh on the chin with his fist. "We can do this the easy way or we can do it the hard way," Benjamin said.

Josh grabbed his jaw. "What's wrong with you? You're crazy, man." He looked at Caleb. "Aren't you going to do something?"

Caleb smiled. "Yeah, I'm going to watch."

Josh dropped his hand from his face and fisted his hands at his sides. "Listen, I don't know what's going on. I don't know what you're talking about." A flicker of rage darkened his eyes. "But if you hit me again, I'm going to sue you and the whole town for abuse."

Benjamin jabbed him in the chin once again. "So, sue me."

"Turn around and put your hands behind your back," Caleb said. "Your partner in crime, Jeffrey Allen, is singing like a canary right now and you're under arrest for assault on Walt Tolliver and a bunch of other crimes that will be detailed later."

"Jeffrey Allen is a lying piece of crap," Josh exclaimed. "He's just trying to get away with everything he did."

"Turn around, Josh," Caleb repeated, his easygoing smile gone.

Josh looked at Benjamin, a small smile curving his lips. "Gee, hope you find what you're looking for." His gaze slid from Benjamin and to the cemetery in the distance.

It was a quick glance, almost imperceptible, but it shot a bolt of electricity through Benjamin, along with a horrifying sense of dread. "Get him down-town," Benjamin said just before he took off running.

"You're too late," Josh's voice rang out. "The bitch ruined everything. She's dead, Benjamin. You hear me? She's dead and buried."

Benjamin nearly stumbled as grief ripped through him. "No. No. No." The single word escaped him over and over again with each step he took.

Too late.

Too late.

The words thundered in his head and his grief was so intense he thought he might puke. The sun had sunk beneath the horizon and twilight had slammed in without warning.

The distance between him and the cemetery seemed agonizingly big. He ran so hard, so fast that a stitch in his side appeared.

Too late.

They'd all been too late for Brittany. They hadn't known she was in trouble until she'd been gone for too long. They were probably too late for Jennifer Hightower and Suzy Bakersfield.

But this isn't the same case, he reminded himself. Edie wasn't one of the women who had disappeared without a trace. She'd been taken by Josh to punish her for destroying his dreams of wealth.

He released a sob as he flew through the cem-etery entrance, his gaze seeking a fresh grave. It was not only grief that ripped through him but also a killing guilt.

They'd all told her it was over, that she was safe. They had taken Jeffrey's confession without ask-

ing the hard questions, without doubting the verac-
ity. He'd put her in her car and sent her on her way.
This was his fault.

He careened up and down the row of graves, seeking something that looked suspicious as darkness
continued to fall. He'd always had a secret fear that
he didn't have the capacity to feel deep emotion, to
love with every fiber of his being. But as he hurried up and down the feet-worn paths between the
graves, tears blurred his vision and he wished he
couldn't feel.

He finally reached the end of the graves and didn't
know whether to be relieved or disturbed that he'd
found nothing. Where was she? Dear God, where
could she be? He knew she was here somewhere,
knew it with a sickening certainty.

Tom's patrol car pulled up, the lights of the vehicle cutting through the encroaching darkness. "Find
her?" Tom asked as he hurried out of his car.

"No." The word worked around the lump in Benjamin's throat.

"Did you check the shed?"

Benjamin stared at him in confusion. "What
shed?"

"Beyond that rise there's a little caretaker's shed."
He pointed in the direction.

Benjamin took off running. He'd forgotten about
the shed, which was tucked out of sight from the
cemetery proper. He heard the sound of Tom's footsteps behind him and was grateful when his brother
turned on a flashlight to light the way.

The old shed came into view and once again he

felt like throwing up. *Please,* he begged. *Please let her be inside there. Please let her be okay.*

He tried not to think about all the places Josh could have buried her body. The cemetery was surrounded by land and he tried not to think about how long it might take before a burial site would be found.

Too late.

The words once again screamed in his head. *Please, please don't let me be too late.* He sent the prayer into the air and hoped that somebody was listening.

Darkness.

It surrounded her and invaded her soul. He'd said he'd come for her when it was dark, when nobody would see him bury her alive.

Her wrists were raw and bloody from working the ropes and the last piece of hope she'd entertained was gone. The darkness had arrived and the monster would arrive anytime.

Edie leaned her head back against the wall. Her head still hurt and she was more tired than she'd ever felt in her life. It seemed ridiculous that all this had happened because Poppy had thought he was seeing space aliens.

It also seemed ridiculous that she was going to be killed not because Josh wanted to protect himself, but because he was angry with her. Killing her was simply about revenge.

People were crazy, but she had been one of the craziest to walk away from Benjamin and love.

"Love smart, Edie girl." Her grandmother's voice whispered through her head.

I did, Grandma. I loved smart when I fell in love with Benjamin and now it's too late for me, too late for us.

She stiffened and snapped her head upright as she heard the sound of running footsteps. He was coming. She closed her eyes and tried to become invisible in the darkness. A moan erupted from her as the door crashed open. She opened her eyes and saw only a dark shadow in the doorway.

Death. He had come for her.

"Edie."

She shivered at the voice that spoke her name, a cruel trick for he sounded like the man she loved.

Another body appeared in the doorway and a flashlight beam half blinded her. "Edie!" He rushed toward her and she realized it was Benjamin, not Josh.

She began to cry as he took the tape off her mouth. "It's okay, baby. It's all right. You're safe now. I promise you're safe." He pulled her forward into his arms as Tom got behind her and worked at the ropes that bound her.

"He said he was going to bury me alive," she cried as Benjamin held her tight. "He said I ruined his life so he was going to take mine."

When Tom freed her hands she wrapped her arms around Benjamin's neck, clinging to him as the fear slowly shuddered away.

Tom cut the rope that held her ankles and Benjamin scooped her up in his arms. "Let's get you out of here," he said as she buried her face into his broad chest.

The night was dark and cold, but she felt warm and safe in his arms as he carried her toward the house in the distance where the cars were parked.

"He drove up next to me," she said. "He motioned that something was wrong with my car. I was stupid to stop, but I thought it was safe." She clung tighter. "He told me my tire was going flat and when I bent over to look at it, he knocked me unconscious. I thought I was going to die."

When they reached the car, he placed her in the passenger's seat and then hurried around to the driver's door. "Josh?" she asked as he slid in behind the steering wheel.

"Is in jail and I'm taking you to the hospital to get checked out."

She didn't argue with him. Her head pounded and her wrists were encircled with dried blood from her attempts to get loose. "Why did Jeffrey confess to something he didn't do?"

"Josh threatened to kill Jeffrey's father if he talked," he said.

She leaned her head back against the seat and closed her eyes, trying to process everything that had happened, trying to forget how close she'd come to death. "How did you find me?" she asked, not opening her eyes.

"We leaned on Jeffrey and he came clean about Josh. Then I went to talk to Josh and leaned on him a bit."

She cracked an eye open and looked at him. "Leaned hard, I hope."

He smiled grimly. "I would have killed the bastard if Caleb hadn't been there."

She nodded and closed her eyes, satisfied with his reply. She was exhausted, her emotions a jumbled mess. The taste of horror still clung to the roof of her mouth and all she wanted to do was fall into a deep, dreamless sleep.

Two hours later her wrists had been treated and she'd been checked into a hospital room for a night of observation. "You and Walt are becoming familiar faces around here," Dr. Drake said when she was settled in a hospital bed. "You took quite a hit on the back of your head and I want to check those wrists again in the morning to make sure there's no infection setting in."

At that moment Benjamin appeared in the doorway. "I just brought Walt up to speed on everything. He said it's a good thing we arrested Josh, otherwise he would have had to release himself from here and kick his butt."

Edie gave him a weary smile. "That's my Poppy, ready to take on the bad guys and any space aliens that might invade his town."

"Get a good night's sleep, Edie," Dr. Drake said. "You've been through trauma and rest is the best medicine." He turned and gave Benjamin a stern look. "Don't you stress her with your questions. There's time enough to finish your investigation tomorrow."

"Don't worry, Doc. I'm just going to sit here for

a little while until she falls asleep." As Dr. Drake left the room, Benjamin eased into a chair next to the hospital bed.

"You don't have to stay here," Edie protested as she fought to keep her eyes open.

"Yes, I do," he replied. "I need to sit here and watch you sleep. I need to assure myself that you're really okay. I just need to sit here and listen to you breathe." Emotion thickened his voice. "I've never been so afraid as when I saw your car parked on the side of the road. I don't ever want to be that afraid again."

She reached out a hand toward him and he grasped it in his. "I do love you, Benjamin," she said and then fell asleep.

She awakened to a sliver of early morning sun drifting through the window. Benjamin sat slumped in the chair, looking incredibly handsome and equally uncomfortable as he slept.

Her headache was gone and she felt ready to get out of here, ready to face life with all its joy and with all its heartache.

As she looked at Benjamin her heart swelled as for the first time she truly allowed herself to embrace all that was in her heart for him. Love. It fluttered through her with sweet warmth, filling up all the cold, empty places in her soul.

She gripped the charm around her neck and held tight. She would never forget the baby girl she'd lost, would always have an edge of grief where Mary was concerned. But she couldn't allow that tragedy to define who she was, to determine her future.

Benjamin's eyes fluttered open and for a moment she wanted to drown in the brown depths as he gazed at her. He straightened in the chair and quickly raked a hand through his tousled hair. "Good morning. How are you feeling?"

"Ready to get out of here and get on with my life," she replied.

"I had Tom take your car back to the ranch," he said as he stood. "I'll just get Dr. Drake in here and see if you're ready to be released."

Before she could stop him, he disappeared out the door. A niggle of doubt shot through her as she got up from the bed and headed for the bathroom.

Maybe he'd decided she was just too much trouble. He'd been emotional last night, but now he'd seemed a bit detached, as if he'd already moved on in his mind.

She changed into her clothes and checked her wrists, grateful that they looked less raw this morning. She finger-combed her hair and rinsed her mouth, then returned to the room to wait for Dr. Drake to come in and release her.

Benjamin came back through the door. "Looks like you're all ready to take off," he said as he leaned against the far wall.

"I told you, I'm ready for a fresh stab at life." She got up from the bed and took a step toward him.

He jammed his hands in his pockets, his expression unreadable. "You should be back on the road within an hour or so."

"Actually, I've been thinking about that. Being locked in that shed for hours, I did a lot of thinking."

She took another step toward him, her heart suddenly beating almost painfully fast. "I thought about the fact that we've both suffered from loss, me with my daughter and you with your sister. I grieved for both of us and then realized how silly I'd been to try to protect myself from life…from love. I do love you, Benjamin, with all my heart."

His eyes lightened just a touch and he shoved himself off the wall. "Yeah, you told me that last night but I figured it was the result of whatever drug Dr. Drake might have given you."

She smiled. "He didn't give me any drugs. I meant what I said. I love you, and if it's not too late I want to be a part of your life. I didn't think I needed anyone, but I need you. I need my snuggle buddy."

He seemed to freeze in place. "Are you sure you don't feel that way because I pulled you out of that shed? Because of some misplaced sense of gratitude?"

"Benjamin, I loved you when I got into my car to leave Black Rock. I loved you the night we made love. I feel like I was born loving you and that when I die, I'll feel the same way." She took another two steps forward, standing close enough to him that she could feel the heat radiating from him, smell the scent that made her think of warm male and home.

"I was afraid, that's why I was running away. I was afraid to believe that I deserved to be happy, but while I was sitting in that shed I knew I deserved happiness, that I deserve you."

He had her in his arms before her heart beat a second time. "I'll make you happy, Edie," he said and his eyes shone with a passion that nearly stole her breath away. "I love you, Edie, and I can't think of anyone I want more by my side for the rest of my life."

His lips descended on hers in a kiss that tasted of shared sunsets and fiery passion and love, sweet love. This was where she belonged, in Benjamin's life, in his strong arms.

When the kiss ended he reached out and touched the charm around her neck. "It's okay if you don't want to have children," he said. "I'll understand if that's what you choose."

He took her breath away. She knew that having a family was important to him and the fact that he was willing to make this sacrifice for her only spoke of the depth of his love.

She placed a hand on his cheek and smiled. "No way. We're going to fill that ranch house full of kids. Mary would have wanted lots of brothers and sisters."

He kissed her again and the kiss was interrupted by a deep clearing of a throat. They sprang apart to see Dr. Drake standing in the doorway. "Well, I guess I don't have to worry about her being in good hands," he said dryly.

"Trust me, Doc, she's in the best of hands," Benjamin said as he pulled her against his side.

"Edie, you're good to go," Dr. Drake said.

"Great, then let's leave," she said to Benjamin. She was ready to start a new life with him.

They left the hospital and stepped out into the cool autumn morning sunshine. Once again Benjamin pulled her into his arms, his eyes filled with love and more than a touch of amusement. "I can't believe we owe all this to Walt and his space aliens."

"Maybe that means this was written in the stars," she said.

"So, you're willing to hitch your star to a full-time rancher?" he asked. "I'm not sure what I am without my badge."

She smiled up at him. "Oh, Benjamin, I'd hitch my star to you no matter what you did. I know what lies beneath your badge—a man with honor and compassion, the man I love with all my heart." She backed out of his arms. "Now, are you going to make me stand around in this hospital parking lot all day or are we going to the ranch and start practicing for those babies we're going to make?"

She laughed in delight as his eyes sparked with a fiery need and he tugged her toward his truck and into the future that she knew would be filled with laughter and passion and love.

Epilogue

"I still think we should have done corn bread stuffing," Poppy said as he and Margaret worked to stuff the giant Thanksgiving turkey.

"Sage dressing is traditional," Margaret said, her voice brooking no argument.

Edie smiled as she stood at the window and watched Benjamin as he approached the house from the pasture. It had been two months since the day she'd left the hospital, and in that two months much had occurred.

Benjamin had driven with her to Topeka to pack her belongings and bring them back to his place. Margaret had moved out of the cottage and into Poppy's house and the two seemed satisfied with their slightly contentious, but very caring companionship.

Benjamin still wore his badge, although he'd told his brother that he was resigning in the spring. For Edie, the past two months had been magic. Her love for Benjamin had simply grown deeper, more profound, with each day that had passed.

All the facts of Josh's crimes had come to light. Jeffrey Allen was cooperating with authorities, hoping to get a lighter sentence when he came to trial.

Josh had provided the body parts for Jeffrey's experiments with the understanding that he would share in whatever proceeds Jeffrey eventually made. It had been Josh who had beaten Walt in the cemetery, an attempt to scare the old man into leaving things alone. It had also been Josh who had shot at them in the woods when he'd been burying the botched experiments.

Pure and simple it had been rage and greed that had driven Josh, and Edie was comforted by the fact that he would be in prison for a very long time to come.

Later this evening Tom and his fiancée, Peyton, were coming for dinner, as were Caleb and his fiancée, Portia. They had invited Jacob, but Benjamin had warned her that he probably wouldn't show up, that he'd prefer his isolation in the small cabin.

The front door opened and Benjamin came in, as always his face lighting up at the sight of her. He pulled her into his arms for a welcome kiss and then smiled as he heard Poppy and Margaret arguing about sweet potatoes. "I hear that our master chefs are at it again."

"At least we can be thankful to know that the dinner is probably going to be amazing," she replied.

"It will be nice to have everyone here," he said, but his eyes darkened just a bit and she knew he was thinking about the two who would be missing—Jacob, who for some terrible reason that he refused to discuss had isolated himself from life, and of course, Brittany.

The darkness in his eyes lasted only a moment and then was gone, replaced by the light of love as he gazed at her. "I have a lot of things to be thankful for this year, and the main one is you."

As his lips met hers, her heart swelled with her own thanksgiving, happy that she'd been smart enough to open her heart to happiness, to love.

He was escalating his timeline.

When their captor brought in the fourth woman, Brittany realized the last two had been taken within a short span of time. She recognized the latest victim as Casey Teasdale, a young woman who worked as a receptionist in the dental office.

The masked man whistled as he carried the unconscious woman into the cell across from Brittany. Both Jennifer and Suzy went crazy at the sight of the new woman, one begging and the other cursing the man who held them.

Brittany sat silently, watching his every move, looking for something that might help her identify the man behind the mask. But as always, nothing he did led to an identification.

He locked the door of the cell where he'd placed

Casey and then headed back toward the door of the barn where they were being kept. He stopped in front of Brittany's enclosure and she felt his sick energy, his excitement as he looked at her.

"Almost time," he said. "I only need to add one more to my collection and then the games will begin." He began to whistle again as he left the building.

Brittany stared after him, knowing that time was running out for her, that time was running out for them all.

* * * * *

THE COWBOY'S
SECRET TWINS

Chapter 1

Melissa Monroe couldn't help but wonder if she was making a huge mistake. A fierce case of déjà vu filled her as she drove the Texas road. The lonely highway, the snow coming down from the overcast sky and the Christmas carols playing on the car radio all evoked memories of the last time Melissa had driven on this particular road.

It had been just a little over a year ago, only at that time the snow hadn't been comprised of pretty little flakes lazily drifting down, but rather a blizzard whiteout condition that had eventually forced her to pull over.

A sexy stranger in tight jeans and a cowboy hat had rescued her. He'd told her his name was James and they'd ridden out the storm together in a vacant farmhouse.

It had been a wild and crazy night and she'd acted completely out of character. The consequences of her actions that night were in two car seats in the back.

Joey and James, who were a little over four months old, had been completely unplanned and unexpected, but since the moment she'd realized she was pregnant, they had been desperately wanted and loved.

She glanced back now to check on them and smiled. Snug as bugs they were in their little blue coats and matching hats. They'd been sleeping for the better part of an hour and Melissa hoped to get where she was going before they woke up demanding another meal.

Thirty minutes ago she'd passed the place in the road where she'd had to pull over during the storm a year ago. It was just outside the small town of Rockport, Texas. She was now ten minutes from the Texas town of Dalhart and her final destination.

On that night a year ago she'd been on her way from her home in Amarillo to visit a friend in Oklahoma. Tonight she was on her way to someplace just on the other side of Dalhart.

Tightening her hands on the steering wheel, she hoped she wasn't on some kind of a wild-goose chase. Suddenly all kinds of doubts crashed through her mind. Maybe she was a fool to trust her cyber friend, a woman she'd never met in person but had bonded with over the past year in a chat room for single moms.

MysteryMom had been a source of support, information and friendship over the past year. She'd helped Melissa through the difficult pregnancy. Then once the twins were born she'd been a font of advice on everything from colic to diaper rash.

MysteryMom and Melissa's best friend, Caitlin, were the only two people on earth who knew about the circumstances of the twins' conception.

Melissa suspected that MysteryMom had given her directions to her place, that she was bringing Melissa to her home for a face-to-face meeting and to spend the holidays together.

For the past couple of weeks Melissa had been depressed. Christmas was only four days away—the twins' first Christmas—and she hadn't even had any extra cash to buy a tree or a single present.

She'd always dreamed of giving her children the kind of Christmas she'd never had, with family gathered close and laughter in the air. It wasn't all about a lack of money that had depressed her, but certainly financial worries played a role.

She'd been working at building her own interior design business when she'd found herself pregnant. The pregnancy had been difficult and the business had fallen by the wayside. Since the twins' birth Melissa had been living on her savings, which were dwindling fast.

It had been all she could handle to take care of newborns, but after the first of the year she was determined to somehow provide for them and delve back into her work.

She slowed as she reached the Dalhart city limits. According to the directions MysteryMom had sent her she was to turn off the main highway and onto a country road approximately ten miles from where she was now.

With a new burst of nervous tension kicking up inside her, she pulled into a restaurant parking lot and grabbed her cell phone from her purse and punched in Caitlin's number.

"Are you there yet?" Caitlin asked when she answered.

"According to the map I'm about fifteen minutes from the place," Melissa replied.

"How's the weather? I heard they were calling for snow."

"It's been spitting a bit, but nothing to worry me," Melissa replied.

"I don't know why you just didn't plan on coming to my place for Christmas instead of taking off on this adventure of yours."

Melissa smiled into the phone. "You're going to have so many fancy parties to attend, the last thing you need is me and the boys hanging around." Caitlin was single and gorgeous and working up the corporate ladder at blinding speed. "Besides, look what happened the last time I was on my way to visit you."

"It's not my fault you got stuck in a blizzard and then decided to kick it with some sexy stranger."

"True, it wasn't your fault. I've decided it was all Tom's fault," Melissa replied and tried to ignore the faint pang of her heart at the thought of her ex-boyfriend.

"Ah, don't even mention that snake's name," Caitlin replied. "I thought he was a creep when you first starting dating him and he definitely proved me right."

"Water under the bridge," Melissa replied. "Anyway, I just wanted to check in with you and let you know I'm almost there."

"You'll call me when you arrive? Tell me all about this MysteryMom of yours?"

"Definitely."

"And, Melissa, I hope you have an amazing Christmas. You deserve it."

Melissa put her cell phone back in her purse and pulled her car back on the road. Dusk was falling and she was eager to get to her destination before dark.

As she drove her mind filled with thoughts of Tom Watters. She'd thought they'd marry and build a family together and after two years of dating she'd begun to press him about setting a wedding date. He'd finally told her there wasn't going to be a wedding, that for the past six months he'd been involved with another woman, one who was much sexier, much more a woman than Melissa.

Once again she clenched her hands on the steering wheel as she thought of that moment. She'd immediately made plans to visit Caitlin, needing to get away from her dismal apartment and all reminders of Tom.

Reeling not only with a broken heart, but also

with a damaged ego, she'd been easy pickings for the handsome stranger who had come to her aid.

Her cheeks burned hot as she remembered that night of unexpected passion. James had looked at her with such desire. He'd made her feel so sexy, so wanted. She'd never before experienced that kind of wild abandon and suspected she'd never experience it again.

She cast all these thoughts aside as she drew nearer to the road her directions told her to take. As she left the small town of Dalhart behind, she spied the highway sign where she needed to turn.

In approximately ten miles she should be at the destination that she suspected was MysteryMom's home. Excitement danced in her chest as she thought of finally coming face-to-face with the woman who had been not only a friend, but also a surrogate mom through the trials and tribulations of being a single new mother to twins.

If she didn't like the looks of the place she'd turn around and make the two-and-a-half-hour drive back home. If she got any bad vibes at all, she'd just drive away. There was no way she'd put her babies or herself at risk.

The first surprise was the enormous stone monuments that marked the entry to the address she sought. The second surprise was when she drove down the tree-lined narrow drive and got her first glimpse of the house. No, *house* was too plain a word for the mansion that rose into view.

The two-story home was as big as a hotel, with

several equally impressive outbuildings. Lights spilled with a cheerful welcome from several of the windows as the evening had begun to thicken with night shadows.

"Oh, my goodness," she whispered to herself. The whole place breathed money.

As she drove up the circular driveway she saw that one of the outbuildings was a stable and she was more convinced than ever that this was Mystery-Mom's house. MysteryMom had mentioned that she loved working with horses.

She parked the car and glanced into the backseat where Joey was awake. Of the two boys, Joey was the most laid-back. He rarely fussed and seemed content to take life as it came at him.

On the other hand, James was a handful. Demanding and impatient, he was the first to set up a frustrated cry if he needed a diaper change or a meal or if she took away his beloved rattle. But, he also had begun to belly laugh when happy and the sound of it never failed to delight her.

She looked at Joey, who gazed at her with bright blue eyes. "Are you ready to go meet Mommy's new friend?" she asked. He waved his arms as if to show his excitement.

As she got out of the car she realized it had grown darker, as if night hadn't just stealthily approached but had rather slammed down without warning.

She opened the door to the backseat and first unbuckled Joey and pulled him up on her hip, then went to the other door and did the same with James.

In the past four months she'd become quite adept at not only carrying both boys, but also her purse and a diaper bag all at the same time.

The cold air chased her to the front door, where she managed to use her toe to knock. Her heart hammered with excitement as she waited for MysteryMom to answer. When the door opened her excitement transformed to stunned surprise.

He filled the doorway with his broad shoulders and lean hips, and his blue eyes widened with the same shock that she felt. His gaze swept over the two babies in her arms and his face paled.

James.

For a moment her mind refused to accept what she saw. "Henry? Who's here?" a feminine voice called from somewhere in the house.

Two thoughts flew into Melissa's head. Apparently his name wasn't James and he must be married. Oh, God, this was all a mistake. A terrible mistake.

Before she could take a step backward, before she could even move a muscle, a ping sounded next to her and the wood of the doorjamb splintered apart.

Everything seemed to happen in slow motion. Another ping resounded and James or Henry or whatever his name was leaned forward, grabbed her and pulled her inside the house. He slammed the door behind them.

"Call the sheriff," he yelled. "Somebody is shooting at the house." He opened a drawer in the ornate sideboard in the entry, pulled out a gun then without a backward glance at her, disappeared out the front door.

Melissa stood in the center of the entry, her heart banging frantically. Mistake. This was all some sort of horrible mistake.

What kind of a man was her babies' father that somebody shot at the house the minute he'd opened his door? Was he a drug dealer? A criminal of some kind?

As Joey and James began to cry, Melissa fought back tears of her own.

Henry Randolf clung to the shadows of the house as he tried to discern exactly where the shooter might be. He thought the attack had come from the stand of trees directly in front of the house.

As he moved forward he tried not to think about the woman who had appeared on his doorstep. Melissa, that was her name. She'd crossed his thoughts often over the past year, but he couldn't think about her now or the two babies she held in her arms. He couldn't afford to get distracted while somebody with a gun was on his property.

One problem at a time, he told himself. The shooter first, then he'd have to figure out what to do about his unexpected visitor.

He clenched his gun tightly as he worked his way to the stand of trees, listening for a sound, seeking a shadow that would indicate where the attacker might be. As he thought of how close those bullets had come to Melissa and those babies, a slow seething rage built up inside him.

This wasn't the first time he'd been shot at in the past week. Three days ago he'd been riding his horse across the pasture and somebody had taken a potshot at him. His mount had reared and taken off for the stables as Henry had pulled his gun to defend himself from the unknown.

He was still outside checking the area when the sheriff's car pulled up. Sheriff Jimmy Harrick lumbered out of his patrol car like a sleepy bear exiting a favorite cave. He pulled his collar up against the cold night air as Henry approached him.

"I've checked the area. There's nobody around now. The shots came from that stand of trees over there but it's too dark to see if there's any shell casings or evidence."

He pointed toward the house. "Let's go inside and talk." Henry didn't wait for a reply but headed for the door. He hadn't felt the cold when he'd first burst outside, but now the damp December air seeped into his bones.

"Got company?" Jimmy asked as they passed the older model car in the driveway.

"Yeah, an old friend." Henry's stomach kicked with nerves as he thought of the woman who had stood on his doorstep carrying twins who looked remarkably like he had when he'd been a baby.

Damn, what mess had he gotten himself into? He had a feeling his life was about to get extremely complicated.

As he and the sheriff walked into the living room he saw Melissa seated next to his mother on the sofa, each of them with a baby in their arms.

Melissa's blue eyes were wide with fear. He couldn't blame her. There was nothing like a welcoming committee of bullets to put that expression in a woman's eyes.

Henry tore his gaze from Melissa and focused on the sheriff. "Something's got to be done, Jimmy. This is the second time somebody has taken potshots at me in the past week."

Jimmy shoved his meaty hands in his pockets and rocked back on his heels. "I'm not sure what to do about it, Henry. There's no question that you've made some enemies with your decision to run for mayor."

"And so it's okay for somebody to try to kill me? Because they don't like my politics?" Henry was acutely aware of Melissa listening to every word, watching him with those amazing eyes of hers.

Jimmy pulled his hands out of his pockets. "Now, you know that's not what I'm saying," he protested. "I'm going back out there with my flashlight and I'll take a look around, then I'll head back to town and start asking questions. I'll let you know if I find anything. If I don't then I'll give you a call sometime tomorrow."

"Fine," Henry said curtly. He knew nothing more could be done tonight and in any case he was having a difficult time thinking about anything but the woman who sat next to his mother.

He walked Jimmy to the door, then closed and

locked it and drew a deep breath to steady himself. How had she found him? They'd only exchanged first names on that crazy night they'd shared a little over a year ago and he hadn't even given her his real first name.

And then there were those babies. Henry had decided he was never going to marry and he'd certainly never planned to be a father, but there was little question in his mind about the paternity of those twins. Now he had to figure out what he was going to do about it.

He returned to the living room, where the two women on the sofa didn't appear to have moved, although Melissa and the two little boys no longer wore their coats.

His mother had that look on her face she used to get when he was a kid and had done something he knew he shouldn't do. He definitely had some explaining to do.

She stood and walked over to him and thrust the baby she held into his arms. "I'm retiring to my room. It appears you and Melissa have a lot to talk about."

The little boy smelled of baby powder and gazed up at him with curious blue eyes. As Henry stared down at him the little boy's lips curved up in a sweet smile.

"That's Joey," Melissa said. "And I have James." She said the name with forced emphasis and he remembered that the night they'd been together he'd told her his name was James.

That night he hadn't wanted to be the wealthy Henry James Randolf III. He'd just wanted to be an ordinary cowboy named James. "My name is Henry. Henry James Randolf," he said.

As he looked at her several things struck him. She was still as pretty as he'd remembered her with her long blond hair and those big blue eyes, but she seemed tired and stressed.

Her cheeks grew pink beneath his scrutiny. "I don't quite know what to say. I didn't expect you."

He frowned and tightened his grip on Joey, who wiggled like a little worm. "What do you mean, you didn't expect me? You came here. You knocked on my door. Who else would you be expecting?" He sat in a chair across from the sofa as Joey leaned his head against his chest. To Henry's surprise his heart knocked hard.

"I thought I was coming to spend the holiday with a woman I met last year on the computer." Once again her cheeks warmed with color. "We met in a chat room for single pregnant women and she's been a wonderful source of support through my pregnancy and single parenting. She goes by the name of MysteryMom. She gave me this address, emailed me directions and told me to come here."

He eyed her suspiciously. The story certainly didn't have any ring of truth to it. "And how did she find me?"

Melissa raised a hand that trembled slightly to tuck a strand of shiny hair behind her ear. "I don't know. When we first got close I told her about the blizzard in Rockport and you coming to my rescue. All I knew about you was that your name was James and that you drove a black pickup with a license plate number that started with tin."

TIN-MAN, that's what his plate read. An old girlfriend who had proclaimed that he had no heart had dared him to get the personalized plate, and he never backed down from a dare.

"When I first realized I was pregnant," she continued, "I went back to Rockport and asked around about you, but nobody had any clue who you might be. Somebody tried to kill you."

He blinked at the unexpected change of topic. "I think it was a warning, not a real attempt on my life. Our current mayor was diagnosed with cancer and has decided to resign. The city council has called an emergency election to be held in two months. I decided to run for the position and somebody apparently doesn't like my politics."

James began to fuss, waving his fists in the air and kicking his legs. "They're hungry," Melissa said. "If you could just show me to the kitchen, I'll fix them bottles, then we'll be on our way."

"On your way? You can't leave now," he protested. "It's dark and getting later by the minute and I don't know if the person who fired that gun earlier is really gone from the area." He stood with Joey in his arms. "You'll stay here tonight and we can discuss everything further in the morning."

She stood and gazed at him with somber eyes. "You haven't even questioned if they're yours or not."

For the first time since he'd opened his door to her, he offered her a smile. "They look just like me. They even have my cleft chin. And I know we used no protection that night."

"I'm not here to cause you any trouble," she replied.

Henry nodded, although he wasn't so sure about that. "Let's go into the kitchen and get those bottles ready," he said.

Time would tell if she had really been led to his doorstep by some mystery cyber friend or if she was just another woman who had recognized who he was on the night of the blizzard and had found a way to cash in on the Randolf fortune.

Chapter 2

Melissa snuggled down in the bed in a guest room fit for a princess. The twins were sound asleep in an old playpen that Henry had found in the attic. It had been dusted off and the padding covered with a crisp, clean sheet. The boys were clad in their pajamas and sleeping beneath a cashmere throw that was as soft as a cloud.

She'd called Caitlin just to let her friend know that everything was all right and that it hadn't been MysteryMom's home she'd come to, but rather the man who was the father of her boys. She'd promised to let Caitlin know everything that happened when she returned home in the morning.

She was exhausted now, but sleep refused to come. The night had been filled with far too many surprises. The first had certainly been the sight of Henry as he'd opened the door. The second had been the bullets that had come precariously close to both her and her babies.

Even after the trauma of the shooting had passed she hadn't been able to get a read on Henry. He'd said little as he'd helped her bottle-feed the boys. She knew he had to be as stunned to see her as she'd been to see him.

They hadn't spoken much, just attended to the boys' needs, then he'd shown her to her room for the night with the promise that they'd talk further in the morning.

She didn't know what would happen. She had no idea what to expect from him, if he intended to be part of the boys' lives or not.

She'd resigned herself at the time of their birth to the fact that Joey and James wouldn't know their real father. At least now she wouldn't have to tell them the humiliating story of how she'd gotten pregnant by a stranger in a vacant farmhouse during the middle of a snowstorm.

MysteryMom must have somehow traced him with the partial license plate letters Melissa had mentioned. She obviously had resources Melissa didn't have. If MysteryMom had hoped for some kind of happy ending for Melissa, she was functioning in the world of make-believe.

Despite the intimate night they'd shared, Melissa and Henry didn't know each other at all. He hadn't even given her his real name that night.

Certainly he was in a social position to date all kinds of sophisticated, successful women. And the last thing Melissa was looking for was a man in her life.

Tom's betrayal still burned bright in her heart and if that wasn't enough, she had two little boys to raise. She didn't want a man. She didn't want anything from Henry, except for him to be a father for her boys.

She'd been hoping to spend Christmas someplace where the spirit of the holiday was everywhere. There was no sign of Christmas in the Randolf home and in any case she didn't belong here.

First thing in the morning she'd be on her way back home to her little apartment and maybe on the way home she'd stop at a discount store and buy one of those little metal trees in celebration of the twins' first Christmas.

She finally fell asleep and dreamed of that night with Henry in front of the fire he'd built to warm them through the snowy night. The heat of the flames had been nothing compared to the fire in his kisses, the warmth of his hands on her body.

When she woke up bright sunshine drifted through her bedroom window, not the faint light of dawn she was used to, but full sunlight that let her know it was late.

The boys!

She shot up and looked at the playpen. It was empty. She jumped out of bed and yanked on her robe. Henry had gotten her suitcase from the trunk of her car the night before despite her protests that the gunman might still be out there lying in wait for him. She'd held her breath until he was back in the house safe and sound.

Now her breath caught once again in her throat as she raced out of the bedroom and down the grand staircase to the lower level of the house.

She heard voices coming from the formal dining room and headed there, her heart beating frantically as all kinds of irrational fears whirled through her head. She flew into the room and stopped short.

The boys were in their car seats on the polished mahogany wood of the huge table. Henry's mother, Mary, stood in front of them, shaking a rattle at first one, then at the other as they bubbled with laughter.

"Melissa," Mary said with a smile that faltered as Melissa sagged against the doorjamb. "Oh, dear, we frightened you, didn't we?"

"I woke up and they were gone. I wasn't sure what to think." Melissa's heart slowed its frantic pace.

"It was Henry's idea really," Mary said. "You looked so tired last night and he thought it would be nice if you got to sleep in a bit this morning. So we sneaked into your room around dawn and grabbed these two little bundles of love and brought them down here. We gave them each a bottle and then I gave them a little sponge bath and changed their clothes. I hope you don't mind."

Melissa wanted to be angry that they'd obviously riffled through the diaper bag and taken her boys from their bed. But the look on Mary's face as she gazed at the twins made it impossible for Melissa to maintain anger. Besides, if she were perfectly honest with herself the extra couple of hours of sleep had been glorious.

"You know, I never thought I'd live to see grandbabies. Henry is quite the confirmed bachelor so I'd resigned myself to the fact that there would probably never be grandchildren." She smiled at the twins. "But these two are like gifts from heaven."

Melissa smiled. "You haven't changed one of their messy diapers yet. That might change your mind about gifts from heaven."

Mary laughed. "Oh, good, you have a sense of humor. I'm so glad. And now if you'll get dressed I'll have Etta make you some breakfast. Henry and I have already eaten."

"Oh, that's not necessary," Melissa replied. "I'm not much of a breakfast person and besides, I'd like to get back on the road as soon as possible." She not only wanted to get back to Amarillo, but she was still determined to stop someplace on the way home and pick up a few things to bring Christmas to her tiny apartment.

At that moment Henry appeared in the opposite doorway. He seemed bigger than life, his presence sucking some of the oxygen out of the air.

He looked like the rugged, handsome cowboy she'd met on the road that night. Clad in a pair of fitted jeans and a flannel shirt that emphasized the width of his broad shoulders, he let his gaze sweep the length of her before he smiled and said good morning. Even though he smiled, his eyes remained shuttered, enigmatic.

Melissa was suddenly aware of the fact that her robe was tatty and frayed and her hair was probably sticking out in every direction. She hadn't even washed her face before hurrying down the stairs.

"I'm just going to run upstairs and shower. I'll be right back."

"When you come back down I'd like to have a talk with you," Henry said.

She nodded and backed out of the dining room then escaped back up the stairs. There had been an edge in Henry's tone of voice when he'd said he wanted to talk to her that worried her.

This whole trip had been a nightmare. The unexpected presence of a man she'd never thought she'd see again, bullets splintering a door and now the promise of a conversation she had a feeling she didn't want to have.

He was probably going to tell her to take her babies and leave, that being a dad didn't fit into his lavish single lifestyle. And even though that was fine with her, it made her heart hurt just a little bit for her sons.

She knew what it was like to grow up without a father. She remembered the empty ache his absence had created inside her and she certainly hadn't consciously chosen that for her boys.

Minutes later, as she stood under a hot spray of water she found herself again wondering what MysteryMom had hoped to accomplish by leading her here. Of course, it would be nice for the boys to have a father in their lives. She wanted that for them. But she wasn't in control of Henry's reaction to instant parenthood.

Mary had said he was a confirmed bachelor. It was definitely possible a bachelor wouldn't want to be saddled with two little boys who required a lot of time and attention.

By the time she'd finished her shower and dressed, nervous energy bounced around in her stomach. She certainly didn't know Henry well enough to second-guess what he might want to discuss with her, but it didn't take a rocket scientist to know that it had something to do with Joey and James.

Despite the night of desire they'd shared, since the moment she'd arrived at this mansion Henry frightened her more than a little bit. Oh, she wasn't physically frightened of him. What scared her most was the fear of him rejecting his sons, sons that he'd never wanted and had never asked for.

When she returned downstairs Mary had the boys on their tummies on a blanket in the living room. She smiled at Melissa. "That James, he's a feisty one, isn't he? He reminds me of Henry when he was a baby. Demanding and impatient. There's going to be no holding him back when he starts to walk."

James arched his back, raised himself up and grinned at Melissa, as if relishing the very idea of being independent and mobile. Meanwhile, Joey rolled over onto his back, perfectly content to play with his fingers.

"It must be hard, being a single parent to twins," Mary said.

"I manage okay," Melissa replied with a touch of defensiveness.

"I'm sure you do, dear. Henry is waiting for you in the study," Mary said. "It's down the hall and the first door on your right."

Melissa nodded and with one last look at her contented boys, she went down the hall to the study. The door was closed and she knocked on it with a gentle tap.

She heard him tell her to come in and she opened the door. Henry sat behind a massive mahogany desk and although he smiled at her as she stepped into the room, it did nothing to alleviate her nervousness.

The study was as beautifully appointed as the other rooms in the house. A stone fireplace took up one wall and floor-to-ceiling bookcases filled another. "Melissa, please have a seat." He gestured to the chair in front of the desk. She sank down and tried not to be intimidated by the surroundings, by him.

"Mom said you were eager to get on the road and head home, but I wanted to talk to you about the possibility of you staying through Christmas," he said.

"Oh, I'm not sure…" She paused as he held up a hand to stop whatever she was about to say.

"We're forever linked now by those boys and despite the fact that we had that night together, I don't know anything about you."

Oh, but he did, she thought. He knew she liked

to be kissed just below her ear, that if he stroked her breasts she moaned deep in the back of her throat. A whisper of longing swept through her as she remembered that night and him. She forced herself to focus on what he was saying.

"We stopped having anything to celebrate at Christmastime three years ago when my father unexpectedly died of a heart attack on Christmas Day. Since then Christmas each year has slid by with little celebration in this house. But this year we have something to celebrate. The twins. I'd like to give them a terrific first Christmas, so please tell me you'll stay."

Her first instinct was relief, that he wasn't casting the boys out and that he apparently wanted to get to know them better. Still, there was one thing that made her relief short-lived. "I have to be honest. I haven't forgotten those bullets that flew when I arrived here," she said. "I don't want to put Joey and James in harm's way." She fought against a shiver as she thought of the bullets that had come far too close to them the night before.

"I feel more comfortable with you here rather than going back outside," he replied. "Somebody is being a nuisance, obviously attempting to make me rethink my position in running for mayor, but I won't let any harm come to you or the children."

She considered his words thoughtfully and believed him. There was something solid about him, a strength in his eyes that let her know he wouldn't allow danger to come to her or her babies.

He was their father and all he was asking was for

her to remain a couple more days. Surely there was no harm in that, in giving him and his mother the first Christmas with the boys.

"Okay," she finally replied. "We'll stay through the holiday." She had no idea if it were the right thing to do or if it was possible she was making a terrible mistake.

A wave of satisfaction swept through Henry at her reply. From the moment she'd stepped into the study he'd smelled her, a familiar scent of fresh flowers with a hint of vanilla. It was the same fragrance she'd worn the night they'd been snowbound together and it stirred all kinds of crazy memories inside him.

As she stood and tucked a strand of hair behind her ear he remembered how soft, how silky her hair had been beneath his touch. That wasn't all he remembered. There was the taste of her mouth open to his, the spill of her warm, full breasts into his palms and the moans that had escaped her at his every touch. Desire slammed into his stomach, hot and wild and completely unexpected.

He had no idea if he trusted her, hadn't spent enough time with her to know if he even liked her, but that didn't stop him from wanting a repeat of what they'd shared on that snowy night.

"Good. We'll make it a Christmas to remember," he said and stood.

She backed toward the doorway, as if eager to escape him. "I'm going to take the boys upstairs for their morning naps. I'll see you later."

"Melissa," he said, stopping her before she could disappear from the room. "I don't even know your last name."

She smiled, the first real smile he'd seen from her, and the gesture lit her up from the inside out. "Monroe. Melissa Monroe."

The minute Melissa left the study Henry leaned back in his chair and gazed thoughtfully out the window. From this vantage point he could see the carriage house in the distance. It was a two-bedroom self-contained cottage that was occasionally used as guest quarters.

Henry had been living there before his father's death. His heart constricted as he thought about his dad. Not a day went by that Henry didn't miss him. Big Henry, as he'd been called, had not only been father, but he'd also been friend and mentor to his only son. The two of them had worked side by side running Randolf Enterprises, which was comprised of not only the ranch but also oil wells and enormous financial holdings.

There were people in town who were threatened not only by the financial power Henry possessed, but also by his decision to run for the position of mayor and clean up the corruption he knew ran rife through the city offices of Dalhart.

He had a couple suspicions of who might have taken those shots at him, but suspicions didn't work for an arrest. He also suspected that whoever had shot at him hadn't really tried to kill him but rather was just warning him, hoping he'd decide not to run for mayor.

Those gunshots didn't scare him half as much as the idea that Melissa might not allow him to be as big a part of the boys' lives as he wanted.

"Henry?" His mother entered the study, her features worried. "Is she going to stay?" She sat in front of him in the chair that Melissa had vacated.

"She didn't tell you?"

"I was in the kitchen speaking with Etta about dinner. Melissa took the babies and went upstairs before I got a chance to ask her."

"She's staying until after Christmas." He leaned forward. "I don't quite know what to make of her. The story she told me about some cyber friend giving her directions here sounded more than a little bit shady."

"You think she's after money?"

"It certainly looks like she could use it." He frowned as he thought of the rusted old car out front, the frayed robe that had hugged her curves that morning.

Mary leaned back in her chair and folded her hands in her lap. "You want to tell me how this happened?"

Henry grinned at her. "You need a lesson in biology?"

She scowled at him. "You know what I mean, Henry. I've never heard you mention this woman's name before and yet she shows up here with two babies who are obviously yours."

"Remember the blizzard we had at the beginning of December last year? The night I couldn't get home from Hilary's because of the whiteout conditions?"

"That was the night you broke up with that woman."

Henry nodded. "I was on my way home when the conditions got impossible to drive in. As I pulled over to the side of the road I saw another car there and Melissa was inside. I had no idea how bad the weather was going to get and I'd just passed the old Miller place and knew it was vacant, so I got her out of her car and we holed up there for the night."

Mary raised a hand. "That's all I need to know about the particulars. Is it possible she knew who you were?"

Henry pulled a hand down his lower jaw. "I don't know. I suppose anything is possible. I've always been so careful. I've always recognized how vulnerable I was to gold diggers."

Mary arched an eyebrow upward. "Need we mention Hilary's name?"

Henry smiled as he thought of the woman he'd been dating and had broken up with the afternoon of the blizzard that had brought him and Melissa together.

"Hilary might be a gold digger, but she never kept that fact a secret," he replied. Since the day of their breakup the attractive brunette hadn't stopped waging her battle to become Mrs. Henry Randolf III. She called him or came by at least once a week in an attempt to seduce him back into her arms.

Mary straightened her back and sniffed indignantly. "That woman couldn't wait to marry you and have me shut up in a nursing home someplace. The evil witch."

And that had been the very reason Henry had broken up with Hilary. It was at the moment she mentioned that she thought it would be uncomfortable living with Mary and that Hilary had been searching for a nice nursing home for the older woman when Henry had recognized there would never be a future with her and certainly not a marriage.

"You don't have to worry about that," he said to his mother. Once again he leaned back in his chair and cast his gaze out the window.

"I never really thought about having kids," he said softly. "But now that they exist I want them here with me. I want them to grow up here on the ranch and learn the family business. I want to teach them like Dad taught me."

"Aren't you forgetting one little thing? Melissa might not want to move here. She might have a perfectly fine life, perhaps with a boyfriend or family of her own."

Henry frowned thoughtfully. "I find that hard to believe. I mean, according to her story she took off from her home to meet some cyber friend and spend Christmas with her. If Melissa has family or a boyfriend, why didn't she stay home to spend Christmas with them?"

"I'm sure I don't know. You know her better than I do. But, Henry, you have to remember that just because you want something doesn't mean you can have it. You're talking about a woman here, not a business deal."

Mary stood. "All I know is that I intend to enjoy each and every minute of having those babies in this house. And now I'm going to go make a shopping list. There's only two shopping days left before Christmas and suddenly I'm in the mood to shop."

She practically floated out of the study. Henry hadn't seen his mother this happy since his father had been alive.

Even though he'd had the entire night to process the fact that he was now a father, he still wasn't sure how this was all going to work. The first thing he would have to do was get to know Melissa, find out if she'd come here looking for easy street or if the story she'd told him was true.

But before he could do that he had some phone calls to make. He'd promised Melissa a Christmas to remember and Henry never broke a promise.

His mother was wrong about one thing—this *was* a business deal. Melissa had what Henry wanted and all Henry had to figure out was what price he'd have to pay to get it.

Chapter 3

Melissa stood at the window and watched as a car pulled up out front and Mary got into the car's passenger side. When the vehicle pulled away Melissa wondered if she should be doing the same thing—driving out the main gates and heading for home.

Behind her in the playpen the two boys had just fallen asleep. They usually napped for about an hour in the morning and the same amount of time in the afternoon.

Restless energy coursed through Melissa and she moved to the window on the opposite side of the room to gaze out at the pastures, corrals and outbuildings on the land. In the distance she could see what appeared to be a carriage house.

The dusting of snow that had fallen the evening

before had melted beneath the warmth of the sunshine. It was a beautiful day, cold but clear.

A whisper of noise whirled her around and she saw Henry standing just outside the room in the hallway. He motioned to her and she left the room. "I thought maybe while the boys napped you might want to have a cup of coffee with me. I'd like to get to know you, Melissa."

Once again nervous energy fluttered in her chest. Of course he wanted to know her better. She was the mother of his children. "And I'd like to get to know you better," she agreed. "Coffee sounds wonderful."

She checked on the boys to make sure they were still asleep, then followed him down the staircase to the dining room where Etta, the Randolf cook, carried in a tray laden with two cups of coffee, cream and sugar and two small plates with slices of cinnamon coffee cake.

Henry introduced the older woman to Melissa. "Etta has been keeping the Randolf family well fed for the past twenty years."

"And it's been a pleasure," Etta replied. Then with a friendly smile at Melissa she turned and left the dining room.

Melissa pulled a coffee cup before her and wrapped her fingers around it. As Henry watched her she felt ill at ease and wasn't sure what to say, where to begin.

"This is awkward, isn't it?" he finally said.

She flashed him a grateful smile. At least he felt it, too. "Terribly awkward," she agreed. "I know you have no reason to believe me, but it's important to me that you know that I don't just fall into bed with strangers I meet."

She couldn't hold his gaze and instead looked down at her coffee as she continued. "That morning the man I'd been dating for two years, the man I thought I was going to marry, let me know that he had found a new girlfriend, somebody sexier than me." She felt her cheeks warm with her confession. "That night I just… It all went more than a little crazy."

He laughed, a low chuckle that was both pleasant and surprising. She looked up at him sharply, wondering if he were laughing at her.

"It seems fate had a hand in our meeting that night. I was coming home after ending a relationship with a woman I'd been dating for over a year. Maybe we were both a little reckless that night."

"But that's not who I am," she replied. "I'm usually not reckless."

He took a sip of his coffee, eyeing her over the rim of his cup. "And yet you took off with an address to an unknown place given to you by a woman you've never met before."

"A calculated risk," she replied. "If I didn't like the looks of the place when I arrived, I wasn't going to stop." She tugged on a strand of her hair in frustration. "Okay, it wasn't the brightest thing in the world to do," she conceded.

She wasn't about to tell him that it was an aching loneliness that had driven her to meet MysteryMom.

Although she loved her boys more than anything else on the face of the earth, she'd been hungry for adult conversation. The idea of spending the holiday alone had depressed her.

She reached for one of the plates and a fork. Whenever she was nervous she wanted to eat and it was impossible to ignore the heavenly scent of the cinnamon that wafted from the coffee cake.

"Okay, let's start with the basics," he said. "Henry James Randolf, thirty-five years old, rancher and oil-man. I'm a Taurus. I like my steak rare and sunrise rides on my horse. I've been told that I'm stubborn but I don't necessarily see that as a fault. I'm not a big drinker but I do like a glass of scotch or brandy in the evenings. Now, your turn."

"Melissa Sue Monroe, thirty years old. I'm a Libra and I like my steak well-done. Before I got pregnant I was working to build my own interior design business. I've never been on a horse and my drink of choice is an occasional glass of wine. Oh, and I've been told I have a bit of a stubborn streak, too."

He smiled, although she noticed that the gesture didn't quite warm the blue of his eyes. "What about family?" he asked.

She shook her head and paused to take a bite of the cake. "I don't have any. My father left when I was five, told my mother he wasn't cut out for family life. I never saw him again. My mother passed away two years ago and since then it's just been me…and of course, the boys."

"You have friends who give you emotional support?"

"My best friend lives in Oklahoma, so I don't see her very often. As far as other friends, to be honest the birth of the twins has pretty much put an end to any social life for me."

"How's your interior design business?"

She considered lying. She thought about telling him that she was wildly successful, but he was obviously an intelligent man. He only had to take a glance at her car and note the worn condition of her clothing to know that the money wasn't rolling into her household.

"Nonexistent," she finally said. "The pregnancy was difficult and for the last three months of it, I couldn't work. Since then it's been just as difficult. The boys have required all my time and energy." She raised her chin. "But after the holidays I'm going to try to get back to work."

She took a sip of her coffee and wished he didn't smell exactly like she remembered from that snowy night, a scent of clean male and wintry air and a faint whisper of spicy cologne. It was a fragrance that stirred her with memories of warm hands and hot kisses.

"How have you been supporting yourself?" he asked.

"I had a small inheritance from my mother." She shifted positions beneath the intensity of his stare and took another bite of her coffee cake.

"You have a boyfriend? Somebody significant in your life?"

A small laugh burst from her. "Definitely not. The only males in my life wear diapers and drool."

This time the smile that curved his lips warmed the blue of his eyes. "At least they're cute when they drool." His smile faded. "I'm sorry I wasn't there to help through the pregnancy. I'm sorry you had to go through it all alone and I promise you won't be doing it all alone now."

She wasn't sure why his words, rather than comforting her, filled her with a new burst of apprehension. Maybe if she really knew him, knew what kind of a man he was, she wouldn't feel so worried about what he might have in mind for her and the boys.

"Having grown up without a father figure in my life, I understand how important the role of father is and will be to my boys. I want you to know that I'm open to a discussion about visitation for you," she said.

"There will be time to discuss the particulars of that over the next couple of days," he replied. He took a sip of his coffee and leaned back in his chair. "So, are you originally from Amarillo?"

She nodded. "Born and raised there." This was the kind of talk they might have had if they'd been on a date, the kind they should have had that night instead of falling on each other like two sex-starved teenagers.

"Do you have somebody special in your life? A

woman you're seeing? I don't want my presence here to make any problems for you," she said.

"You don't have to worry. There's nobody special. I don't intend for there ever to be anyone special." There was a firm finality in his voice.

She took another sip of her coffee. God, the man was so good-looking she couldn't imagine the women in the area leaving him alone. "Your mother mentioned that you were a confirmed bachelor."

"I am. The only reason I might have entertained the idea of marriage would have been to have a son to pass the ranch to when I died. You've managed to give me two without the nuisance of a marriage."

Nuisance of marriage? Funny how different they were, Melissa thought. She'd wanted to be married for a very long time, had always thought that by the time she turned thirty she'd be part of a family like she'd never had growing up.

She still hoped for that someday. The only difference her dream had from reality was that in reality her boys would have their real daddy and then maybe eventually they'd have a loving, caring stepfather.

But at the moment, any kind of relationship with a man seemed impossible. She was just too tired to even think about romance. She'd been tired for months, not that she minded. The twins were more than worth any exhaustion they caused.

"You look tired, Melissa," he said as if he'd read her thoughts. "I hope you'll take your time here and allow my mother and me to help so that you can get some extra rest. It can't be easy dealing with twins all by yourself."

"I'm fine," she assured him. "It's gotten easier since they sleep through the night most of the time now."

"Still, I hope you'll let us take some of the burden for the next couple of days."

"They aren't a burden. They're my joy," she exclaimed a bit more vehemently than the situation warranted.

He leaned forward and reached out and brushed the corner of her mouth. "You had a little cinnamon," he said as he pulled his hand back.

She grabbed a napkin and wiped her mouth and tried to ignore the electric jolt his touch had shot through her body. *He just swiped your mouth,* she told herself. A simple, casual touch and yet she felt it from head to toe.

A loud knock sounded on the front door and he pushed back from the table. "You might want to come with me to answer it," he said. "I think it's for you."

"For me? Who would be here for me?" She got up from the table and followed him to the front door.

He looked outside, then smiled and this time his smile warmed her completely. "It's Christmas, Melissa. Christmas has officially arrived at the Randolf house."

Henry opened the door to allow in the four ranch hands who maneuvered a huge evergreen tree through the door. The boughs were tied down and Hank and Tim, the ranch hands bringing up the rear, carried between them a huge pot to stand the tree in.

"It was the biggest one old man Keller had on his lot," Charlie said as they carried the tree into the living room.

"Melissa, can you help me move the coffee table?" Henry asked.

She quickly grabbed one side and he grabbed the other. They moved the table out of the men's way. "Just set it up in the corner," he instructed.

"That's the biggest tree I've ever seen," Melissa said, her eyes round with wonder.

Henry smiled. "I told them to get the biggest one they could find. We'll decorate it this evening after dinner."

"We could string popcorn and cranberries," She flushed and shook her head as if irritated with herself. "That was silly of me. I'm sure you have lovely expensive ornaments."

He could tell she was embarrassed and he found that oddly endearing. "Actually, I've always wanted to do a tree the old-fashioned way. I think it would be fun to string popcorn and cranberries."

The look she gave him was so sweet, so grateful, that he once again felt a stir of desire deep in the pit of his stomach. When he'd brushed the trace of cinnamon from her lip moments earlier, he'd wanted to kiss it off.

He focused on watching his men wrestle the tree into the stand. Something about Melissa touched him, a vulnerability, a wistfulness in her eyes that he hadn't seen in a woman's eyes for a very long time.

He still didn't trust her. The only woman Henry really trusted was his mother, who had no ulterior motive for loving him. Any other woman he'd ever allowed close had ultimately shown herself to be more interested in the Randolf fortune than in whatever Henry could offer her as a man.

He didn't know if perhaps Melissa was just smarter than them all and had managed to trap him like none of the other women had managed to do.

Once the men had the tree up and the ropes off, Henry introduced Melissa to them. "These are some of the best ranch hands in the state of Texas," he said. "That's Hank and Tim, Ben and Mike and Jacob, and that rascal with the black hat is Charlie, my right-hand man."

Melissa's eyes had glazed over and he smiled at her. "Don't worry, there won't be a test later," he said.

She laughed and the sound of her musical laughter shot a rivulet of warmth through him. "Good, because you lost me at Hank." She smiled at all the men. "But it's nice to meet you all."

"I'll be right back," Henry said to her as the men began to head for the front door.

In the entry he touched Charlie's shoulder and motioned for Charlie to stay behind while the rest of them got back to their work.

"You heard about the shots fired last night?" he asked.

Charlie nodded. "Jimmy talked to a couple of us late yesterday evening."

"I want all of you armed while on the property until we know what's going on," Henry said. "And I'd like to work a couple of you in shifts so that somebody is always working the house. Talk to the men and see what kind of schedule you can arrange."

Charlie's eyes narrowed. "You looking for more trouble?"

Henry released a small sigh of frustration. "To be honest, I'm not sure what I'm looking for, but twice now somebody has taken potshots at me and I don't like the idea of anyone on my property attacking me or mine."

"We'll work out a schedule and I'll get it to you this afternoon," Charlie replied.

"Thanks, Charlie. I really appreciate it," Henry replied.

"It's no problem. We can't let the boss get hurt." With these words he stepped out the door.

Henry watched him catch up to the other men. Charlie was a good worker, always pitching in for even the dirtiest jobs. When Henry had broken up with Hilary he'd worried that he was going to lose Charlie. Hilary was Charlie's sister and Henry had feared that Charlie might feel compelled to stop working for him because of sibling loyalty. But Charlie had assured him that he wasn't going anywhere and that he didn't get involved in his sister's affairs.

Henry had gotten the impression that there was no love lost between the two. In any case, he was grateful that he hadn't lost Charlie. Good workers were hard to find.

In fact, he was going to have to let Hank go. He'd noticed the tall, thin man had smelled like a brewery despite the fact it wasn't even lunchtime. Henry had already warned him twice about drinking on the job. There wouldn't be any more warnings.

He closed the front door and returned to the living room to find Melissa gone. She'd apparently gone upstairs to check on the twins. He walked over to the large floor-to-ceiling windows and gazed out to the outbuildings in the distance. The tree was only the first of the deliveries that would take place over the next two days.

The brief conversation he'd had with her over coffee had told him exactly what he needed to know. She had no family and he suspected she had few friends. That would make what he had in mind much easier. All he had to do was convince Melissa that his plan was in the best interest of them all.

He looked up as he heard the sound of her coming down the stairs, a baby on each hip. He hurried to meet her halfway and took one of the boys from her.

As he scooped the little one from her arms he tried not to notice the warmth of her body, that scent of her that half dizzied him with memories.

"Which one do I have?" he asked.

"Joey," she replied.

"How can you tell the difference?" The little boy snuggled against Henry's chest, as if aware that he was held in loving arms. Once again the heart that

Henry didn't know he possessed filled with a strange wonder and a fierce sense of protectiveness.

"Once you get to know them better, it's easy to tell them apart by their personalities," she said as they hit the landing. "But the quickest way is that Joey has a tiny scar in his right eyebrow. He was reluctant to be born and the doctor had to use forceps."

Henry looked at the little boy in his arms and noticed the tiny scar at the corner of his eyebrow. Joey grinned up at him and reached for his nose. Henry laughed as he dodged the little hand.

James kicked his feet and wailed, his face turning red as Melissa wrestled with him. "He's hungry and he has no manners," she said.

"Ah, a boy after my own heart," Henry replied. "Let's go to the kitchen and get them some lunch."

The kitchen was a huge room although Henry and Mary rarely took meals there. This was Etta's space but it was also the easiest place to feed two hungry little boys.

Etta was in the process of preparing lunch, but smiled with welcome as they all entered. Henry got the car seats that were serving as high chairs and placed them in the center of the large oak table. Once the boys were settled he watched Melissa prepare two small bowls of cereal.

As she approached the table he held out his hand for one of the bowls.

"You might want to put on a hazmat suit," she warned as she gave him one of the bowls and a small baby spoon. "They not only like to eat cereal, they also like to blow it and spit it and play in it."

Feeding Joey was a pleasure like Henry had never known before. The kitchen filled with laughter as he and Melissa spooned cereal into their waiting mouths, off the front of their shirts and themselves.

"Well, this sounds like fun," Mary exclaimed as she came into the kitchen.

"Ah, the shopper is home," Henry said as he wiped off Joey's face then handed him his bottle.

"Randy is putting my purchases upstairs in my room." She smiled at Melissa. "It's been far too long since this house had such laughter in it. And the tree, it's going to be just lovely."

"Melissa thought it would be fun to string popcorn and cranberries for the tree," Henry said.

Mary clapped her hands together. "What a lovely idea. We'll have a real old-fashioned tree trimming. I'll make hot cocoa and we'll play Christmas music and have such fun."

Melissa looked from Mary to Henry. "You both are so kind," she said and once again he saw a touch of vulnerability in the depths of her eyes.

"Nonsense, you're family now," Mary replied.

But she wasn't family, Henry thought. She was still a stranger. And she would never really be family, he mentally added. Sure, he had a strong physical attraction to her and she was the mother of his boys, but she would never be anything more than that to him.

His father had spent a lot of years warning Henry

about the women who would want him for his money, women like Hilary who would turn themselves into whatever he wanted or needed to access the kind of lifestyle he could provide for them. As far as his father was concerned, aside from his wife, Mary, women were cunning creatures to avoid except for the occasional physical release, and then only if protection was used.

"I was lucky, boy," his father would often say. "I was poor as a church mouse when I met your mother. I never had to worry about if she loved me for my money or for myself. You won't have that luxury. You'll never really know if a woman loves you or your money."

He knew without a doubt that Melissa hadn't set out to seduce him that night. There was no way she could have orchestrated the blizzard and the two of them being on the road at the same time in the same place.

What he didn't know was that once fate had placed them in that position, had she recognized him and taken a calculated risk of getting pregnant? It had been a mutual seduction that night. She'd been as willing a participant as he had been.

He frowned thoughtfully as he watched her coo and sweet-talk the two little boys. But if that was the case, if she'd recognized him that night before she'd slept with him, why hadn't she contacted him the minute she realized she was pregnant? Maybe she'd been afraid he'd talk her into an abortion.

One thing was clear. Henry wanted his boys living here with him and he would achieve that goal with or without Melissa's help.

Chapter 4

The afternoon seemed to fly by. Melissa was shocked when two baby cribs were delivered and Henry had them set up in the room across from hers. And the beds weren't all. High chairs were also delivered, fancy high chairs that seated infants then changed to accommodate toddlers, along with boxes and packages in all shapes and sizes.

"This isn't necessary," she'd protested. "We're only going to be here a couple of days."

"Then things will be more comfortable for the couple of days that you're here," Henry had replied.

Dinner was a pleasant meal with the boys happily seated in their new high chairs and most of the conversation between Mary and Melissa. Henry had been quiet, watching Melissa with an enigmatic gaze that made her overly self-conscious and more than a little bit nervous.

After dinner they all gathered in the living room for the tree-trimming party. Mary supplied thick thread and needles to string the popcorn and cranberries that Etta provided, and Henry carried the two high chairs into the room and placed the boys in the seats.

"Why don't I put the lights on while you two make the garland?" Henry asked.

Mary smiled at Melissa. "He'd do anything to get out of using a needle and thread."

"Sewing is a woman's work," Henry replied.

"Stubborn and a male chauvinist, what a surprise," Melissa exclaimed.

"I'm not a male chauvinist," he protested. "I just don't like needles."

"Okay, then stubborn and a bit of a wuss," Melissa replied teasingly.

Mary laughed in delight. "Finally, a woman who can put you in your place, Henry."

Henry looked at Melissa and in the depths of his eyes she saw a flicker of heat that stirred something wild and hot inside her.

"Ouch!" she exclaimed as she pricked her finger with the needle. She instantly put her finger in her mouth and Henry's eyes flamed brighter.

"And that's why I don't like needles," he finally said and turned his attention to the string of Christmas lights.

There was definitely something between them,

she thought. Something hot and hungry. She wasn't in love with him, didn't know him well enough to gauge exactly what she thought of him. But there was no denying the strong physical attraction that existed between them.

"I always wanted to do a tree like this," Mary said. "Old-fashioned and simple. Big Henry was into flash and gaudy." A soft smile curved her lips. "That man wouldn't know simple if it tapped him on the head."

"You miss him," Melissa said.

Mary leaned back against the sofa cushion, the smile still lingering on her lips. "He was stubborn as a mule, ridiculously opinionated and could make a saint weep with frustration, but yes, I miss him each and every day." She tapped her heart with a finger. "But he's still with me in here."

That's what Melissa wanted, what Mary and Big Henry had apparently shared, a love that would last through eternity. "I'm so sorry for your loss," she said and covered Mary's hand with hers.

Mary smiled and gave her hand a squeeze and then released it and began to string popcorn once again. "Thank you. I'm just sorry he's not here now to meet his grandsons. He would have been so pleased to know that there will be another generation."

"I'm going into town tomorrow and thought you might like to take the ride with me, Melissa," Henry said. "Mom can babysit the boys for an hour or so."

"I'd be happy to do that," Mary agreed.

"Oh, I don't know," Melissa said hesitantly. She'd never left the boys for a minute since their births.

"I promise I won't beat them or chain them to their beds," Mary said gently.

Melissa laughed. "That never entered my mind." She looked at Henry. "Aren't you afraid to go out? I mean it was just last night that somebody shot at you…at us."

"I won't be a prisoner in my own house," he said with a tone of steel in his voice. "Besides, I've got my men watching the grounds and we'll be safe in town. Nobody would risk trying to hurt me with so many other people around."

Melissa was torn. She was reluctant to leave the boys for any amount of time, yet there was a tiny simmer of excitement as she thought of an hour or two without them. The idea of a trip into town was appealing, but she was surprised by how cavalier he was about somebody trying to hurt him.

"I keep telling you that I don't believe my life is really in danger, that I think somebody is just trying to aggravate me, trying to manipulate me into throwing in the towel on my plans to be mayor," he said.

"Okay, I'll go with you," she finally said, unsure if it was just another reckless decision on her part.

"Good. We'll plan on going after breakfast and we'll be home before lunchtime," he replied.

"It will be fine, dear." Mary reached over and patted Melissa's hand. "I remember the first time I left Henry with somebody. He was just about the twins' age and Big Henry had decided I needed a night out.

I must have called home a dozen times to check on Henry in the two hours we were gone. Big Henry finally decided to bring me home."

Melissa smiled. "They're getting to the age where if you blink you feel like you've missed a first."

"I've already missed too many firsts," Henry said with a touch of vehemence.

He would make a good father, Melissa thought. Whenever he looked at the boys she saw a fierce love shining from his eyes. As crazy as it sounded, there was a tiny part of her that wished that same expression were in his eyes whenever he gazed at her.

She recognized the foolishness of such a wish. He was a confirmed bachelor and in any case he was the kind of man who could choose from a harem of successful, beautiful women if he ever did decide to end his bachelorhood.

She'd be a fool to entertain any kind of happily-ever-after ideas where Henry was concerned. He was right in that they were forever bound because of the boys, but the ties that bound them would be dual parenting and nothing more.

When the phone rang Henry went to answer it, leaving Mary and Melissa alone. Melissa looked at the woman who had been so kind to her.

"I can't imagine what you must think of me," she said.

Mary smiled. "I certainly wouldn't want anyone to look at some of the things I've done in my life and make a judgment. I'm not about to do that to you."

"I appreciate that," Melissa replied gratefully.

As Melissa thought about all the ways coming here could have been so terrible, she was even more grateful to Mary and to Henry for their welcome, for embracing the boys and her into their home.

As Henry came back into the room James exploded in one of his rich belly laughs. Henry froze, the look on his face one of sheer wonder and delight.

"What's so funny, little man?" he asked as he leaned down and picked up the rattle James had dropped. He handed the rattle back to James, and James promptly threw it on the floor once again and looked at Henry and laughed. Henry laughed, as well, and picked up the rattle and once again gave it to James, who tossed it over the edge of the high chair tray yet again.

Melissa laughed. "That's his new game and he'll play as long as you will."

Henry's eyes sparkled with a new warmth she hadn't seen there before. "They're amazing, aren't they? It's obvious already that they're smart."

Melissa smiled. It was fun to see him being a proud daddy, certain that his boys were more intelligent and cuter than any other babies on the face of the earth.

The rest of the evening passed quickly. They drank hot cocoa and strung the popcorn and cranberry garlands on the tree, then added tinsel and ornaments that had been in the Randolf family for years.

Mary knew the history of each and every ornament and Melissa was entranced by the stories she told.

"I picked these up while I was out today," Mary said as she grabbed a box from the bookcase that Melissa hadn't noticed. She took the lid off the box and pulled out two ornaments and handed them to Melissa.

The ornaments were little cowboys and each sported the words *Baby's First Christmas*. For a moment as Melissa gazed at them her heart was too full to attempt speech. "I don't know what to say," she finally managed to sputter. A sudden mist fell in front of her eyes. She quickly blinked them away. "Once again, thank you for your kindness."

"Pick a good spot and hang them on the tree," Mary said. "It's the beginning of a new tradition. There will be an ornament every year for each of the boys to add to the collection. When they leave home and have their own trees, they can take them with them."

Melissa got up from the sofa and approached the tree, vividly aware of Henry's eyes on her. She'd felt him watching her all evening long, an intense, almost predatory gaze that had kept her in a state of anticipation.

It was still there between them, that crazy, wild attraction, that white-hot desire that had exploded out of control on the night of the snowstorm. She saw it in the depths of his eyes, felt the electricity in the air whenever he was near.

She hung the ornaments and then James began to fuss. "It's past their bedtime," she said as she unbuckled James from his high chair and pulled him up into his arms.

"I'll get this one," Henry said and picked up Joey.

"I think I'm going to call it a night, as well," Melissa said to Mary. "Thank you for a wonderful evening and I'll see you in the morning."

Mary kissed each of the boys on their foreheads and smiled at Melissa. "Sleep well, Melissa."

As Melissa went up the stairs she was conscious of Henry just behind her. She could smell the scent of him, felt a stir in the pit of her stomach. It was easier to be around him with Mary in the room. Being alone with him made her think of how his lips had felt on hers, how his eyes had burned electric-blue as he'd taken her that cold, wintry night.

She carried James into the bedroom across from where she'd slept the night before, where the two new cribs awaited. The boys were already dressed in their sleepers, but each needed a diaper change before going to sleep.

"You can just put him in that bed," she said. "And I'll take it from here."

"What else needs to be done?" he asked.

She smiled and unsnapped James's sleeper bottom. "Diaper duty."

"Toss me one of those diapers and I'll take care of Joey," he replied. She looked at him in surprise. "I wrestle cattle. I think I can handle wrestling a diaper on a little bottom," he said with a smile.

Within minutes the boys were changed and half-asleep. Melissa kissed their downy heads then walked to the doorway and turned out the light. A night-light glowed from a socket in the corner as she and Henry stepped back out into the hallway.

"That's it? Now they'll just go to sleep?" Henry asked.

"If we're lucky. If it's a good night," she replied.

"And if it's a bad night?"

He stood so close to her she could feel the heat from his body radiating to her. Memories of the night they'd shared shot through her mind. She remembered the feel of his hand around hers as they'd raced through the blinding snow to the abandoned farmhouse, his gentleness as he'd helped her pull off her wet shoes and socks.

He'd rubbed her feet between his hands, then had gotten a roaring fire started using a stack of wood that had been left by the fireplace.

As crazy as it sounded, that night in the arms of a stranger she'd felt more loved, more cared for, than she'd ever felt in her life. It was a pathetic statement on how lonely her life had been up until now. She suddenly realized that even with Tom she had felt lonely.

She also realized he was looking at her expectantly, that he'd asked her a question she hadn't yet answered.

"If it's a bad night then I usually walk them or rock them until they finally go to sleep," she said. "Hopefully they won't have a bad night while we're here so they won't wake up you or your mother."

"You don't have to worry about them waking up

Mom. Her rooms are on the other side of the house. And I don't mind if they wake me up. I'd be happy to walk or rock a baby back to sleep."

She was quickly developing a crush on her babies' daddy and she found it appalling. "Then I guess I'll just say good-night," she said as she backed away from him.

"Good night, Melissa," he replied then turned his attention back to the bedroom where the boys slept.

It wasn't until Melissa was in her nightgown and had slid beneath the blankets on the bed that the first stir of uneasiness filtered through her.

The new cribs, the high chairs, even the ornaments on the tree suddenly took on an ominous meaning. She'd worried that Henry wouldn't want to be a part of Joey's and James's lives but now her worry was exactly the opposite.

What if those things hadn't been bought to make her visit more pleasant? What if they'd been bought as the beginning to creating a permanent place here for the boys?

Henry certainly had the money and the power to make a play for custody of the boys and Melissa was in no financial position to be able to fight him.

Don't jump to conclusions, she told herself, but she couldn't stop the burning fear that somehow, someway, Henry intended to take her babies away from her.

Chapter 5

"Are we ready to take off?" Henry asked Melissa the next morning when they'd all finished breakfast. She looked so pretty in a bright pink sweater and worn jeans that hugged her hips, but she'd been unusually quiet since she'd gotten up that morning.

She glanced at the boys still seated in their high chairs. "Go on, Melissa. I can take it from here," Mary assured her. "Go enjoy a little shopping or whatever. It's a beautiful day and we won't see many more of them."

"I just need to get my coat," Melissa said.

As she ran up the stairs, Henry walked to the entry hall and retrieved his gun and shoulder holster from the drawer. He quickly put them on and then pulled on his winter coat.

He didn't want the presence of the gun to frighten Melissa, but he also didn't intend to go out the door without it. Although he anticipated no trouble, he intended to be prepared if trouble found him.

As she came back down the stairs he felt a tiny fluttering heat in the pit of his stomach. He was looking forward to spending some time with her, without the boys, without his mother as a buffer between them.

She intrigued him. He couldn't get a handle on her. He didn't know if she was really what she seemed—a nice woman who had acted uncharacteristically the night she'd been with him, a loving mother who had come here to find a friend, or a schemer who was like so many of the other women who had drifted through Henry's life.

"Ready," she said as she reached the landing.

He'd already had Charlie bring his truck to the driveway and as he stepped out the door he was on alert. As Charlie got out of the driver's seat, Henry helped Melissa into the passenger side.

Once she was in he met Charlie at the driver door. "Thanks, Charlie," he said.

"No problem. You watch your back in town."

Henry nodded. "I'm sure we'll be fine. You keep an eye on things here while I'm gone. Oh, and Charlie, tell Hank I'm giving him three weeks' severance pay, but he's fired. I warned him about his drinking, but he didn't take my warning to heart."

Charlie's expression didn't change. "I'll tell him, boss."

Within minutes Henry was in the truck and they were pulling out of the ranch entrance and onto the main highway that led into Dalhart.

He cast her a sideways glance. "You've been rather quiet this morning."

She looked out the side window, making it impossible for him to see her face. "I was up most of the night. The boys were restless and fussy." She paused a moment and then continued. "You know it's not all fun and games, dealing with the boys. You've seen them on their best behavior, but they can be so difficult. They cry and fuss and keep you up all night. They spit out their food and make a big mess."

He frowned, wondering where she was going, what had brought on this little diatribe. "I'm aware that parenting isn't all fun and games," he replied.

She turned to look at him. "How could you possibly be aware of that? You've only been around them for a day and a half." Her eyes were wide and her lower lip trembled slightly.

"Only a fool thinks it's easy to raise kids, and I'm not a fool," he replied.

Once again she cast her gaze out the side window. She appeared at ease, but he could feel the tension wafting from her. Something had put a burr on her butt and he couldn't imagine what had caused it. Maybe she was just one of those moody women who got mad at the world without any provocation. Maybe this was a negative character trait that he would have seen if they'd dated for any length of time.

He figured eventually he'd know what had set her

off. "Are you warm enough?" he asked as he turned the heater fan up a notch.

"I'm fine," she replied. She turned her head and he felt her steady gaze on him.

They rode in silence for only a few moments, then she sighed, an audible release that sounded weary. "You're obviously a man who is accustomed to getting what you want in life."

"I do all right," he replied cautiously. They had entered the town and he pulled into a parking space in front of Nathan's General Store. He unbuckled his seat belt and turned to look at his passenger. "Melissa, something is obviously bothering you. You want to tell me what's going on?"

Her eyes were filled with anxiety as she studied him. She raised a hand that trembled slightly to shove a strand of her long, pale hair behind her ear. "You scare me, Henry. Your power and your money scares me."

He looked at her in surprise. "It's been my experience that most women find my power and my money exciting—even intoxicating."

"Then I'm not most women," she replied. "Maybe those women had nothing to lose, but I do." Her voice thickened. "I need to know if you intend to take the boys away from me."

"What makes you think I'd do that?" he countered.

"Because you can," she replied and her eyes flashed with a touch of anger. "Because it's obvious you've already taken them into your life. You've bought cribs and high chairs and heaven knows what else and don't tell me you bought those things in order to make my visit with you more pleasant."

"I have no intention of taking the boys away from you," he said.

For a long moment their gazes remained locked. He saw the internal battle going on in her eyes, knew she was trying to decide if she could trust him or not.

"Melissa, I'm not going to lie to you. I want those boys living at the ranch. I want them to grow up here. I don't want to just be a weekend dad. I want to teach them to love the land, to be a part of Randolf Enterprises, which will one day be their legacy."

Her eyes narrowed with each of his words and he watched her stiffen in protest. She was a mother bear, sensing danger to her cubs, and he liked that she looked as if she were about to rake his eyes out.

"I have a suggestion so that the boys will remain with you, but I also get what I want," he said.

"And what suggestion is that?" she asked dubiously.

"There's a carriage house behind the main house. It's a two-bedroom fully functional unit. I'd like you to consider moving there with the boys."

"That's a crazy idea," she said immediately. "I have a life in Amarillo."

He raised an eyebrow. "A full life? From what little you've told me, it sounds like a lonely life."

"But it's mine," she replied fervently. "It's my life, not yours."

Henry stifled a sigh of frustration. She'd said she

was stubborn and at the moment that stubbornness lifted her chin and flashed in her eyes. "Look, I'd just like you to consider making the move. It would be great for the boys to have not just me, but my mother in their lives on a full-time basis. Just think about it. That's all I'm asking of you."

Once again those beautiful eyes of hers studied him thoughtfully. "And you promise that you won't try to take the boys from me. You won't use your money to try to get custody of them from me?"

"I promise," he replied.

"How do I know you aren't lying?"

He opened his truck door. "I guess you're just going to have to trust me, just like I'm trusting that the story you told me about some mystery woman bringing you to my house is true. Now, let's do a little shopping and let me show you the charms of Dalhart."

In all honesty, he hadn't really seriously considered going to court to take the boys away from her. They were babies, not some company he could buy or sell.

Besides, he knew how important a mother was to children. He had a wonderful relationship with his own mother and would never deprive his children in that way. He hoped Melissa could put away her fears at least for the duration of their outing and she appeared to as she got out of the truck and offered him a tentative smile.

"I'd like to pick up something for your mother while we're out," she said.

"You don't have to do that," he protested. He knew that money was tight for her.

"It's something I want to do," she replied, her chin once again lifted in that stubborn thrust. "She always smells like roses so I was thinking maybe some rose-scented soap or lotion."

He was surprised both by her observation about his mother and by her thoughtfulness. "Okay, I'm sure we can find something like that in one of the stores. I've got some things to pick up, too."

He gestured her toward the door of the store. Shopping at Nathan's General Store was kind of like delving into a treasure hunt.

The floor-to-ceiling shelves were stuffed full of items with no rhyme or reason for their placement there. Candles sat next to disposable diapers, jars of peanut butter next to boxes of cereal.

"Wow," Melissa exclaimed as they entered the store. "It looks like you could find whatever you need in this one store."

"If you can find what you need," Henry said dryly. "Nathan has an unusual way of arranging things."

"I can see that," she replied. "But that's just going to make this fun." As she drifted toward a shelf, he watched her and wondered what it was that so drew him to her.

Granted, she was pretty, but it wasn't the heart-stopping beauty that could make a man yearn. She was pretty in a girl-next-door kind of way. But she wasn't a girl. She was a woman with lush curves that he remembered intimately. She also had an intriguing aura of a combination of strength and vulnerability. Certainly she had to be strong to take on the job of raising twins alone. But there were times when he saw a wistfulness in her eyes, a yearning for something that he had an idea had nothing to do with his money or his lifestyle.

A blue sweater, he thought suddenly. That's what she needed. A sweater the exact color of her eyes. He'd like to buy her several things, but he wasn't sure if his gifts would please her or make her angry.

He'd like to buy her a new robe to replace the one she'd been wearing yesterday morning. He'd like to buy her a new car to replace the junk on wheels that she'd driven to his house. But besides her strength and stubbornness he sensed more than a little bit of pride.

He liked that about her and yet knew it was that very trait that might make it difficult for him to get what he wanted.

Although he wouldn't mind another night of pleasure with her, he certainly didn't want to marry her. He didn't even want a romantic relationship with her. All he had to figure out was a way to convince her that it was in everyone's best interest for her to move into the carriage house. That's what he wanted more than anything and he would stop at nothing to get what he wanted.

Despite the anxiety that had weighed heavy in Melissa's heart from the moment she'd opened her eyes that morning, she was enjoying the unexpected shopping time with Henry. The talk in the truck had helped ease some of her fear. He'd promised he wouldn't try to take custody of the boys and she only hoped that she could trust that promise. She'd steadfastly refused to think about his offer of the carriage house. She might think about it later, but she didn't want her ambivalence to ruin a perfectly good day out.

They'd wandered in and out of stores and she'd been successful in buying rose-scented lotion and body soap for Mary.

Dalhart was a charming little city that Henry explained got an influx of tourists each summer.

In August there was a three-day celebration that included the largest free barbecue in the United States, a rodeo and three nights of live music and fun.

"See that building over there?" He pointed to a four-story brick structure on the corner. "That's the Randolf Hotel. I bought it six months ago and it is currently undergoing massive renovations. I'm going to need an interior designer when the renovations are done. I'd hire you if you were living here."

"Sounds suspiciously like a bribe," she replied lightly.

He grinned. "Maybe a little one. But I have to hire somebody and it might as well be you."

"You don't even know if I'm good at it," she exclaimed.

"I have a feeling you're good at whatever you put your mind to," he replied.

As they continued to walk the sidewalks Henry

pointed out other places of interest and eventually led her to a café where he insisted they go inside and have a cup of coffee before heading back to the ranch.

She agreed. Although she was eager to get back to the kids, she was also reluctant for this time with Henry to end. He'd been charming, making her laugh with a surprising sense of humor and making her feel as if she were the most important person on the face of the earth.

He'd introduced her to people that greeted them and she'd seen the respect, the genuine admiration Henry's friends and neighbors had for him.

In the café they were led to a table in the back where they sat and ordered coffee. "I thought you said you had things to buy," she said once the waitress had poured their coffee and departed from the table.

"I got them," he replied.

"But you don't have any packages." She reached for the sugar to add to her coffee.

"I always have my purchases delivered to the house."

"I guess that's one of the perks about being you," she said dryly.

He grinned and the charm in that gesture kicked her in the heart. "I'm not going to lie. There are definitely perks to being wealthy. For instance, I never go to bed at night and worry about how I'm going to pay the rent. You'd have that same luxury if you'd move into the carriage house."

"That's not true. I would never expect to live someplace free of charge. I pay my way, Henry." She wrapped her hands around her coffee mug. It was one thing to be independent, but it was another to make the boys suffer from her independence.

"There are two things I'd ask of you," she said after a moment of hesitation.

"What's that?"

She realized this close that his eyes were really more gray than blue. Almost silver, they were the kind of eyes a woman could fall into, eyes a woman could lose herself in.

"I haven't been able to afford to get them health insurance," she said. "Maybe it would be nice if you could put them on your policy."

"Done," he answered without hesitation.

"The other thing is that maybe you could help me with a college fund for them. I didn't have the opportunity to go to college, but I'd like my sons to."

"You didn't have to ask for that. I'd want to make sure they go to college," he replied. "Why didn't you go?"

"There were several reasons. Financially it was impossible, but even with a full scholarship I couldn't have gone." She paused to take a sip of her coffee and then continued. "When I was a junior in high school my mother developed health complications due to diabetes. She lost most of her eyesight and they had to take one of her legs. There was no way I could leave her to go to college. She had nobody but me to take care of her."

"Quite a sacrifice on your part," he observed.

Melissa smiled. "I never considered it a sacrifice. I considered it a privilege to take care of the woman who had always taken care of me."

"One of the reasons I broke up with the woman I'd been dating for a while was because she thought it was time to put my mother into a nursing home."

Melissa looked at him in stunned surprise. "What was she thinking? Your mother certainly doesn't belong in a nursing home."

"My sentiments exactly," he replied. "And you don't even need me to tell you what Mom thought of the idea. Needless to say Mom wasn't upset when I broke it off with Hilary. Now, tell me how you got involved with interior decorating."

As Melissa told him about working in a furniture store and finding her calling in arranging rooms and décor, she once again remembered the thrill of his mouth on hers, the way his arms had felt holding her tight.

"Shouldn't we be getting home?" she asked when she'd finished telling him about her struggling business. "It's been a couple of hours and I don't want to take advantage of your mother."

"We'll head back," he agreed. "But I can promise you my mother wouldn't feel taken advantage of if we were gone all day. She's absolutely crazy over those boys."

Melissa smiled. "I can't tell you how wonderful it is that the boys not only have a father like you, but also a grandmother like Mary. I'm well aware of the fact that James the cowboy could have been a man who wanted nothing to do with them."

He looked at her sheepishly. "I want you to know that night was the first and only time I've lied about my name." He motioned for the waitress to bring their tab. "To be honest, that night I just wanted to be James the cowboy, not Henry Randolf III."

The café had grown busy with the approach of the noon hour and Melissa was aware of several people looking at her with curiosity as she and Henry left their table and headed for the door.

They were just about to reach the door when a tall, willowy brunette walked in. "Henry!" she cried in obvious delight, then her gaze swept to Melissa and her smile faltered slightly.

"Hilary, this is Melissa Monroe, a friend visiting from Amarillo. Melissa, this is Hilary Grant," Henry said.

"Nice to meet you," Hilary said to Melissa, then turned her attention back to Henry. "I was going to stop by your place this evening. I made a batch of that fudge you love and was going to bring it to you."

"That's not necessary," Henry protested.

"Well, of course it isn't necessary, but it's something I want to do. Will you be home this evening?"

"We'll be home, but it's Christmas Eve. It's really not a good time," he replied.

Her lush red lips pursed with a hint of irritation. "Then I'll give the fudge to Charlie to give to you tomorrow," she said. "I made it especially for you, Henry."

He smiled at the beautiful Hilary. "That was very nice, Hilary, and now we'd better get out of here. We're blocking the entrance."

"Nice to meet you, Hilary," Melissa said.

She nodded and returned Melissa's smile but there was nothing warm or inviting in the dark centers of her eyes. She swept past them toward a table where another woman sat as Melissa and Henry stepped out into the cold late morning air.

"Hilary knows Charlie?" Melissa asked.

"They're brother and sister," Henry replied.

She glanced up at him. "That must have been a bit awkward when you broke up with her."

"Actually, it was fine. Charlie doesn't seem to get involved with his sister's life. I get the feeling that they aren't real close."

They had gone only a few steps down the sidewalk when they came face-to-face with a short, squat man. Melissa felt Henry's instant tension. "Tom," he said and gave the man a curt nod.

"Henry. Heard you had some excitement out at your place the other night."

"And you wouldn't know anything about that," Henry replied. His eyes were cool, steely in a way Melissa hadn't seen before.

"Just what I hear through the grapevine. Sounds like there are some folks who aren't too happy about your decision to run for mayor."

"Just a handful, mostly the people who have something to lose if I get into office. You wouldn't be one of those people, would you, Tom?"

"Taking potshots at a man with a rifle isn't my style. You'll see me coming if I come after you." Tom gave Melissa a curt nod, then stepped around them and walked by.

"Who was that?" Melissa asked as they arrived at Henry's truck.

"Tom Burke, city manager and the man who definitely doesn't want me to become mayor." Henry opened her car door and she slid in and watched as he walked around the front of his truck to get into the driver's side.

She could tell he was irritated. A muscle ticked in his strong jaw and his shoulders looked more rigid than usual.

"You don't like Tom Burke?" she asked as he got into the car.

"I think he's a criminal masquerading as an upstanding citizen," Henry replied as he started the truck. "He knows that if I get into office I'm going to do everything in my power to see that he loses his job."

"So, you think he's behind the attacks on you?"

He backed out of the parking space before replying. When he was on the road that led back to the ranch he visibly relaxed. "Yeah, Tom Burke is definitely at the top of my list of suspects. He knows I believe that he's been taking kickbacks from inferior contractors doing work for the city and he knows that if I succeed in being elected, his days are numbered."

"Have you told the sheriff this?"

He nodded, his dark hair gleaming in the sunshine

that danced into the truck window. "Jimmy knows. Unfortunately Tom isn't the only councilman who I think is on the take. The corruption in this town runs deep and I'm determined to do some housecleaning."

"And what do the townspeople think?"

"I think they're behind me, but nobody has been brave enough to speak up. I'm hoping they'll speak by voting for me."

Melissa admired what he wanted to do. Like an old Wild West hero he was riding into town filled with outlaws with the intention of cleaning it up.

"She's very beautiful," she said.

He didn't pretend not to know who she was talking about. "She's okay."

She'd been more than okay, Melissa thought. Hilary Grant was stunning. Tall and slender, with lush long dark hair and exotic olive eyes, she'd looked like a model in her long, fashionable coat and boots.

"What does she do?" she asked curiously.

"She's a beautician and she does some local modeling gigs. She and Charlie had a pretty rough life and mostly Hilary is looking for somebody to change all that rather than figuring out how she can change it herself."

"She's in love with you, you know," she said.

"She was never in love with me," he scoffed. "She was always in love with my money."

"Were you in love with her?" Melissa was surprised to realize that his answer mattered. It mattered much more than it should to her.

"No, but there was a weak moment when I considered marrying her."

"You'd marry somebody you weren't in love with?" Melissa asked with surprise.

"I considered it a business deal," he replied with an easiness that astounded her. "Hilary would have made a good wife when it came to giving parties and acting as hostess for social affairs. In return she would have been able to live the lifestyle she desperately wants."

"And you'd do that? You'd marry as a business arrangement instead of for love?" Melissa asked.

"As far as I'm concerned love is overrated." He cast her a wry look. "I suppose you're one of those hopeless romantics?"

"Absolutely," she exclaimed. "I'll only marry for love. I want to marry somebody who loves me mindlessly, desperately, and I want to love him the same way. I want somebody to laugh with, to love, somebody to grow old with and love through eternity. And I won't settle for less."

As if to punctuate her sentence there was a loud pop. The truck careened wildly to the right side of the highway as Henry muttered a curse.

Melissa saw the deep ditch in front of them and knew they were going to hit it—hard. She squeezed her eyes closed and screamed as she felt the truck go airborne.

Chapter 6

Henry fought the steering wheel hard, trying to keep the truck on the road, but he lost the battle as the vehicle flew far right, hit the lip of the ditch and flew with all four tires off the ground. It came down with a crunch and a hiss, jarring the teeth in his head as it finally came to rest.

His heart raced and he quickly looked at Melissa. "Are you all right?"

She opened her eyes and gave a slow nod, but her face was chalky pale. "I'm okay." She drew in a deep breath and her hand shook as she shoved her hair away from her face. "I hope you have a spare," she said.

He pulled his gun from his holster with one hand and reached for his cell phone with the other. Melissa's eyes widened at the sight of his weapon. But he didn't have time to deal with her fear.

He handed her the cell phone. "Call Jimmy." He rattled off Jimmy's cell phone number. "Tell him we're three miles from my place on the highway and somebody just shot out my tire."

As she made the phone call, Henry kept his gaze on the wooded area on the right side of the highway. He was ninety-nine percent certain that a mere second before the tire had blown he'd heard the unmistakable faint crack of a rifle.

"Jimmy said he's on his way," she said, her voice higher than normal in tone.

He felt her fear radiating across the seat, but he didn't look at her. Instead he kept focused on the area where he thought danger might come. He didn't know now if the attack was over or if the blown tire was just the beginning. Was somebody approaching the truck now, knowing it was disabled and that he and Melissa were sitting ducks?

Minutes ticked by—tense minutes of silence. He was grateful that Melissa understood his need for focus, for complete concentration, and didn't attempt to engage him in any way.

His heart continued to bang unusually fast, but as the fear began to recede, anger took its place. Who was behind these attacks? Dammit, there had to be something he and Jimmy could do to figure out who was responsible and get them behind bars.

Henry didn't relax until he saw Jimmy's patrol car pull up on the side of the road. Henry lowered his gun and opened his window as Jimmy got out of his car, gun drawn, and headed across the ditch toward them.

"You're becoming a full-time job, Henry," Jimmy said as he reached the driver side of the truck. "You both okay?" He bent down to look at Melissa. "Ma'am?"

"I'm fine," she replied, her voice a little stronger than it had been moments before.

"You sure the tire was shot out?"

"I heard a crack right before the tire blew. I think it was a rifle shot."

Jimmy scanned the area. "You have any idea where the shot came from?"

"Somewhere in those trees, about a quarter of a mile back," Henry replied. "I'm sure whoever it was is gone now. If the intention was to do more harm, then he would have come after us while we were sitting here waiting for you."

"Any ideas on who might have taken the shot?" Jimmy asked.

"The usual suspects," Henry replied dryly. "Oh, and I have a new one to add. I fired Hank Carroll this morning before we left for town. You might want to check him out. Can you get somebody out here to take us home?"

Jimmy nodded. "I'll radio for Gordon to come out and give you a ride. Meanwhile I'll check out the woods and see if I find anything. You armed?"

Henry showed his gun. "Nobody is going to sneak

up on us. You see what you can find and we'll wait here for Gordon."

Jimmy nodded, hitched up his pants then turned to walk back to his patrol car.

Henry shot Melissa a quick glance, pleased to see some of the color had returned to her cheeks. "I don't think we're in any danger," he said softly. "And I appreciate the fact that you haven't fallen into hysterics."

She offered him a faint smile, although her lips trembled slightly. "I'm really not the hysterical kind of woman. You fired Hank?"

He nodded and returned his gaze to the outside. "I'd warned him twice about drinking on the job, but he was half-lit when he carried in the tree yesterday."

"I noticed," she replied. "Would he do something like this?"

Henry frowned thoughtfully. "To tell the truth, I don't know. He hasn't been working for me very long. I hope this doesn't change your mind about living in the carriage house."

"I haven't made up my mind about living in the carriage house," she replied. "And I'd say now is definitely not a good time to ask me how I feel about living here."

At that moment a deputy car pulled up and Gordon Hunter got out. Jimmy returned as Henry and Melissa were getting into the backseat of Gordon's car.

"I couldn't find anything. I don't suppose you'd do me a favor and stay inside that secure castle of yours until I can figure out who's after you? I mean, tomorrow is Christmas, surely you don't have to be out anywhere."

"I won't be out and about for the next couple of days, but, Jimmy, I'm not going to become a prisoner in my own home," Henry replied.

Jimmy frowned. "I know, Henry. I'm doing the best I can but these drive-by shootings, so to speak, aren't giving me much to work with."

Henry clapped his hand on Jimmy's shoulder. He knew Jimmy was as frustrated as he was by these sneak attacks. He also knew Jimmy was a good man who took his job seriously.

"I'll arrange for Willie at the garage to pick up your car," Jimmy said. "And I'll be in touch in the next day or two. In the meantime, try to have a merry Christmas."

Henry nodded and got into the back of Gordon's car next to Melissa. "Okay?" he asked her.

"Never a dull moment with you, is there?" she said.

There was still a tiny flicker of fear still in the depths of her eyes and he reached over and took one of her hands in his. She immediately curled her cold fingers with his as if she'd desperately needed the contact with him.

He was surprised by the sudden surge of protectiveness that filled him holding her small, slender hand in his. He wanted to keep her from harm. Surely it was only because she was the mother of his children and nothing more.

Still, he was equally surprised to realize that he had no desire to release her hand until Gordon deposited them at the front door of his house.

Melissa grabbed her shopping bags and Henry ushered her into the house, where Mary met them at the door. "What happened?" she asked, worry thick in her voice.

"Nothing serious, just a blowout," Henry said quickly before Melissa could reply. "The spare was flat and Gordon just happened to be driving by so we hitched a ride home with him."

The last thing he wanted to do was worry his mother, but he wasn't sure if Melissa would play along with his story.

She did, not countering his story to his mother. "How were the boys?" Melissa asked. "Did they behave for you?"

Mary's face lit up. "They were absolute angels," Mary said as Henry flashed Melissa a grateful smile.

As Melissa and his mother disappeared into the house Henry headed for his office. He needed to call the garage about his truck and he needed to talk to Charlie to see how things had gone with Hank.

The main thing he needed was some distance from Melissa. Even with the concern that somebody had shot out his tire, he couldn't stop thinking about how nice her hand had felt in his, how the scent of her had dizzied his senses all morning long.

He wanted her. He wanted her naked in his arms, gasping beneath him as she'd been on the night they'd shared. But she'd made it clear what she was looking for—that happily-ever-after and love forev-ermore nonsense. That definitely wasn't what he'd be offering to her.

Would she be interested in a night of passion with him with no strings attached, no promise of love or commitment? It was possible.

He knew she wasn't immune to the sparks that snapped in the air between them. He'd seen an awareness in her eyes when he got too close to her, noticed the way her gaze lingered on him when she thought he wasn't looking.

He sank down at his desk and realized it was much easier to speculate on how to get Melissa into bed than trying to figure out who in the hell was trying to kill him.

"You're perfectly safe here," Henry said later that evening to Melissa. "The house has a state-of-the-art security system. Nobody can get in here without me knowing about it."

Melissa nodded and took a sip of her wine. Mary had just gone to bed, the boys were also down for the night, and Henry and Melissa were sitting in the living room with the glow of the Christmas tree lights the only illumination in the room.

There was no question that the safety of her sons had been on her mind all afternoon and evening. How could she even consider moving here knowing that somebody wanted to do harm to Henry? Know-ing that it was possible she or her boys could be ca-sualties in whatever war was being waged?

"I can't seriously consider moving here until the issue is resolved, not that I'm seriously considering it anyway," she said, giving voice to her thoughts.

"But I want you to consider it seriously," Henry said. He paused to take a sip of his scotch. "The special election is in February. Certainly by then I'm confident that Jimmy will be able to figure out who is hassling me. It would probably take you that long to make the move anyway."

"Hassling you?" She raised one of her eyebrows at him. "Honestly, that's a pretty weak description for what's happened just since I've been here. That tire blowout could have killed us both. The truck could have rolled and we wouldn't be sitting here right now."

"I swear I won't do anything to put you or the boys in danger," he replied.

She shrugged. "It doesn't matter now. I plan on going home tomorrow afternoon."

"But it will be Christmas Day," he protested. "You can't leave tomorrow. You'll break Mom's heart."

She smiled at him. "Ah, first you try to bribe me with a job offer and now you're using your mother to manipulate me. You should be ashamed of yourself."

He laughed and that familiar warmth shot through her at the pleasant sound. "I refuse to feel guilty if it forces you to stay a little longer. Besides, Etta will be making a traditional Christmas feast for lunch tomorrow and what difference does another day or two make?"

"You just want more time to try to talk me into moving here," she said.

He nodded, his eyes teasing her. "There is that," he agreed.

"Okay, I won't leave tomorrow. But the next morning we've got to get back home."

He finished his scotch and set the glass down on the coffee table. "And what then?" The teasing light in his eyes vanished. "When will I see the boys again?"

Melissa realized that her life was about to get more complicated. She'd been thrilled that Henry wanted to be a part of the boys' lives, but now she was faced with the logistics of how they would make it all work.

"I guess I can commit to twice a month driving here for a weekend visit," she said. "I know it isn't ideal, that you'd like to see the twins every day," she added as she saw the dismay on his face. "But, Henry, you have to work with me here."

"I know." He leaned back against the sofa and frowned thoughtfully. "I never knew how kids would make me feel, how much they'd make me want to be there for them, to protect them and teach them. I never dreamed that thoughts of them would be so all-consuming."

She smiled, finding him even more attractive than ever with love for his children—for her children—shining from his eyes. "Welcome to parenthood."

He shook his head and smiled. "I never knew it would be like this." His features were soft in the glow from the Christmas lights and Melissa found herself wishing for things that could never be.

She wished she and Henry were married and tonight after checking on their children they'd get into bed together and make love all night long. She wished they'd share breakfast the next morning and talk about their shared dreams, laugh over secret jokes and know that they would face each other over their first cup of coffee every morning for the rest of their lives.

Foolish wishes, she knew. Wishes brought on by the glow of the Christmas tree and the warmth of family that permeated this house. She was slowly being seduced by Henry and his mother and she knew she'd be a fool to hope for anything except weekend visits for the boys and nothing more.

Still, she'd allowed him to talk her into staying another day because she'd been reluctant to leave this house of warmth, reluctant to leave him.

"Are there twins in your family?" he asked, pulling her from her wayward thoughts.

"Not that I know of. What about yours?"

"I think there were twins on my father's side of the family," he replied.

The doorbell rang and Henry checked his watch with a frown. "Who could that be?" Melissa watched as he rose from the sofa with a masculine grace.

When he disappeared from her sight, she leaned back in her chair and released a sigh. She'd enjoyed the day with him far too much.

His ideas about marriage had shocked her. Was he

so afraid a woman would take his money? Did he not believe that he was worth anything simply as a man? What good was it to have money if all it made you do was worry about who might take it away from you?

She wondered what had made Henry so cynical about love. Had some woman hurt him in the past? Certainly Tom had hurt her, but even the pain of his rejection hadn't made her belief in true love waver.

When he returned he carried his car keys with him. "That was Willie from the garage. He delivered my truck." He pocketed the keys and sat back down on the sofa.

"Henry, do you have a computer?" she asked. She knew he had never really embraced her story about MysteryMom and more than anything she wanted him to believe that she had no interest in any of his money for herself.

"Sure, in my study. Why?"

"I was wondering if maybe you could let me use it to see if I can connect with MysteryMom. This is the time of the evening when I normally could find her in the chat room. It's important to me that you believe what it was that brought me here to you."

"You haven't given me a reason not to believe you."

She heard the faint edge of doubt in his voice and the *yet* that had remained unspoken. What he meant was that she hadn't given him a reason not to believe her *yet*.

"Maybe not, but for my own peace of mind I'd like to show you."

Once again he got up from the sofa. She finished her wine and then followed him down the hallway to the study. The room had seemed enormous the first time she'd been in here, but as he gestured her into the chair behind the desk and he stood immediately behind her, the room seemed to shrink.

They waited for the computer to boot up, and she was intensely aware of his scent, that provocative scent of clean male and spicy cologne. She could feel his warm breath on the nape of her neck and she fought a shiver of pleasure and hoped he didn't notice that she was suddenly breathless.

"There you go," he said. "You're internet connected and can go wherever you want to go."

She placed her hand on the mouse and began to maneuver her way to the chat room where night after night for months she had talked to MysteryMom and other single mothers and mothers-to-be. But when she tried to find the room where she had spent so much of her time, bared so much of her soul, it was gone.

"I don't understand," she muttered softly as she clicked and whirled the mouse in an effort to locate the chat room. "It's not here." She felt a sick frustration welling up inside her.

"Melissa, it's Christmas Eve, that's probably why nobody is there." He placed his hand on her shoulder.

"No, you don't understand. The room always had a virtual sign welcoming single mothers and it's gone. The room itself isn't there anymore."

She looked up at him, surprised to feel thick emotion rising up inside her. She'd wanted to prove to him that it had been MysteryMom who had brought her here and not his money or the lure of a life on easy street.

"Do you have an email address for this Mystery-Mom?"

She shook her head negatively. "We always just talked in the room. If we wanted to talk privately we instant messaged each other. I only got one email from her and that was the directions here, but when I tried to answer her back my reply bounced back to me." She covered his hand with one of hers. "You have to believe me, Henry. It's so important to me."

He gazed at her for a long moment. It was a piercing gaze, as if he were looking into her very soul. "I believe you, Melissa. You don't have to prove anything to me."

He pulled his hand from her shoulder and turned off the computer. "Come on, it's getting late and Santa will come early in the morning."

She was ready to get out of the study, ready to get away from him. His scent, the gentle touch of his hand and the way he'd gazed at her had all combined to make her feel more than a little weak in the knees.

They left the study and as they walked back through the living room Henry turned out the Christmas tree lights, then turned on a switch that illuminated the stairs. They climbed up the stairs side by side and again Melissa was struck with a wistfulness that things were different between her and Henry. Everything would have been much less complicated if they'd dated for a long time, fallen in love and then she'd gotten pregnant.

And if wishes were horses, I'd have a whole herd, she thought. When they reached the top of the stairs she went into the boys' room and Henry followed right behind her.

She went to Joey's crib first and her heart expanded in her chest as she saw him sleeping peacefully. He had a little smile on his lips, as if his dreams were happy.

She then checked on James, unsurprised to see that he'd managed to wiggle himself sideways in the crib and had worked the blanket off him. She didn't attempt to move him from his position, but covered him again with the blanket, then backed away from the crib and into the hallway.

"James is a restless sleeper. He's more easily awakened than Joey and never keeps his blankets on," she said softly as she moved across the hall to her bedroom doorway. "I guess then I'll just say good-night."

"Melissa, I enjoyed spending the morning with you." He took a step toward her and stood so close she could feel the radiating warmth of his body.

"I had a nice time with you, too," she replied as her heart drummed a little faster.

There was a heat in his eyes that excited her and when he reached up to smooth a strand of her hair back from her face his simple touch electrified her.

"I thought about you often after that night," he said, his voice a husky whisper that stirred a simmering fire inside her. "I wondered if you'd gotten where you were going okay, if somehow, someway, our paths would ever cross again. I can't believe how little we shared and yet how much we shared."

"It was a crazy night," she replied half-breathlessly.

"I'm feeling a little crazy right now." He didn't give her time to think, time to process what he'd just said. He pulled her into his arms and his lips claimed hers.

It never occurred to her to step back from him, to deny him and herself the pleasure of kissing him. Just as she remembered, his lips were a combination of tenderness and command, of controlled hunger.

She opened her mouth to allow him to deepen the kiss. His body was rock-hard against hers as his hands slid down her back and pulled her closer to him.

Their tongues swirled and danced and Melissa felt herself falling into a sensual haze of instant desire. No man had ever been able to stir her like Henry. No man had ever made her feel as alive as she felt in his arms, with his mouth on hers.

He released her suddenly and stepped back, his eyes hooded and dark. Melissa fought for composure when all she really wanted was to grab him by the arm and pull him into the bedroom with her. Then she was struck by a thought that dashed all desire away.

"You've tried bribery and manipulation to get me

to agree to move here. Is seduction your next weapon to use?" she asked.

A slow grin curved the edges of his mouth upward. "I promise you I will never seduce you in order to get you to move into the carriage house. The only reason I would seduce you is strictly for my own personal pleasure and nothing more."

He reached out and touched her lower lip with his index finger. "And I do intend to seduce you, Melissa. But, for tonight, sleep well and I'll see you in the morning."

Chapter 7

Henry awakened the next morning with a sense of excitement he hadn't felt since he'd been a very young boy. The air smelled of Christmas, of baking cinnamon rolls and fresh evergreen boughs and the cranberry-scented candles his mother loved to burn.

For a moment he remained in bed, thinking about the day ahead and the night before. Kissing Melissa had been an early Christmas present to himself. He'd wanted to kiss her all day.

As he'd watched her wander through the stores, her lips pursed thoughtfully as she considered her purchases, all he'd thought about was capturing that lush mouth with his own. Even in those moments immediately after the blowout he'd wanted to cover her trembling mouth with his and kiss her until the fear in her eyes transformed to something else.

Kissing her had been just like he remembered. Her lips had been soft and hot and welcoming and he hadn't wanted to stop. He'd wanted to take her by the hand and lead her to his bed.

Afterward he'd told her good-night and he'd gone back downstairs and spent the next several hours wrapping presents and placing everything he'd bought and the items that had been delivered over the past twenty-four hours under the tree.

By the time he'd finished it looked like toy land had come to the Randolf home. As pleased as he was about what he'd bought the twins, he couldn't wait for Melissa to open her presents from him.

It had been a long time since Henry had been excited about giving to somebody else. Sure, he was a generous contributor to a variety of charities, but buying for Melissa had given him a special kind of pleasure.

He pulled himself from bed and after a shower left the master suite. It was just after six when he passed Melissa's door and glanced inside to see her still in bed.

She was nothing more than a short, lean lump beneath the blankets, her hair the only thing visible. He wanted to crawl beneath the blankets with her, pull her into his arms and make love to her as the sun crested the horizon. That would definitely make it a Christmas to remember.

Instead he backed away from the doorway and

checked on the boys, who were still sleeping soundly. He drew in a deep breath of their baby scent and felt a piercing ache at the thought of having to tell them goodbye even for a brief time.

He continued down the stairs. The tree was lit up, candles burned on the mantel and two stockings were hung, each with one of the boy's names in big glittery letters. His mother had been busy already.

He found her in the dining room, sipping a cup of coffee. She stood as he entered and gave him a kiss on the cheek. "Merry Christmas, Henry," she said, her eyes twinkling as brightly as the lights on the tree.

He hugged her and returned the greeting. "You're up early," he said as he poured himself a cup of coffee from the silver coffeepot in the center of the table.

"I couldn't stay in bed another minute. I can't wait for Melissa to see everything we've bought for the boys. I can't wait to see them in the little outfits I bought for them." She smiled and shook her head. "Christmases are going to be wonderful from now on."

"When Melissa and I sit down to discuss the visitation, I'll insist that the twins are here at Christmastime," he replied, although the words certainly brought him no comfort.

He wanted the boys here all the time. He wanted to see their first steps, he wanted to hear the first time they said da-da. He didn't want to wait days or weeks at a time between visits.

"You haven't managed to talk her into moving here? Staying in the carriage house?" Mary asked.

"Not yet. But I still have until tomorrow to make my case," he replied.

"She's leaving tomorrow?" Mary's dismay showed on her features.

"That's what she says."

"It would be nice if we could talk her into staying until after New Year's Eve."

Henry grinned knowingly at his mother. "Then we could try to convince her to stay until after Valentine's Day, or maybe Easter."

Mary laughed and nodded. "I don't have a problem with that." Her smile grew thoughtful. "It's not just the boys. I like Melissa. She's the kind of girl I once dreamed that you'd marry and build a family with."

Henry scowled. "You know that's not happening so don't even start." Most of the time Mary seemed to respect his decision to remain single, but occasionally she launched a sneak attack in an attempt to get him to change his mind.

"If not Melissa, then surely you can find some nice woman to fall in love with," she continued as if he hadn't spoken. "I hate the idea of you growing old alone. I want you to have what your father and I shared."

He paused to take a sip of his coffee. "I have sons who will keep me company as I grow old and that's all I need."

"I'm just saying it would be nice if they all could be here full-time."

Henry leaned back in his chair. "I have a feeling she isn't going to make a decision about moving here until I can assure her that it's safe. The greeting committee of bullets flying has to play a role in her not even considering it right now."

"Jimmy still doesn't have any idea who is responsible?" she asked with concern.

Henry shook his head. "He's coming over tomorrow and we're going to sit down and discuss the whole thing."

At that moment Melissa appeared in the doorway, a twin on each hip. Both Mary and Henry jumped up to take the boys from her.

"Merry Christmas," she said, her eyes sparkling brightly. She looked beautiful in a cheerful red sweater and jeans. Her cheeks were flushed with color and her hair was shiny and smooth to her shoulders.

"And the same to you," Mary said as she took Joey from Melissa's arm.

Henry took James, who offered him a half-cranky smile, then fussed and kicked his feet. "They're hungry," Melissa said. "I'll just go make them some cereal and I'll be right back."

Henry watched her disappear while he put James into his high chair. The fussing stopped, as if James knew he was about to get what he wanted. Within seconds Mary had both boys giggling as she made funny faces and silly noises. The sound of their laughter welled up inside Henry, filling him with such love it brought unexpected tears to his eyes.

Sons.

His sons.

He still couldn't quite wrap his mind around it and he was thankful for the blizzard that had brought him and Melissa together for that single night that had resulted in Joey and James.

There was no way he wanted a long-distance relationship with them. What if Melissa tired of the drive back and forth from Amarillo to here? What if eventually she fell in love and married a man who resented sharing the boys?

Fear clutched his heart at the very thought. He had to convince Melissa to move into the carriage house. It was the only way Henry could get what he wanted—a full-time position in his sons' lives.

He smiled as she came back into the room carrying two cereal bowls. "You sit back and enjoy your coffee. Mom and I will do the honors," he said as he took the bowls from her. "Did you sleep well?"

"Like a log," she replied. She poured herself a cup of coffee and sat in the chair next to Henry. Instantly he could smell the scent of her, clean and floral and intoxicating.

"Etta should have breakfast ready in about fifteen minutes," Mary said as she spooned cereal into Joey's mouth. "And after that we'll go in and see what Santa left for us."

"Santa has already given me more than enough," Melissa said. Her eyes were filled with warmth as she looked first at Mary, then at him. "The welcome you've both given me is more than I ever expected to find this Christmas."

"Maybe later today you would let Henry show you the carriage house," Mary said, surprising Henry with her forwardness. "Just have a peek at it before you definitely make up your mind one way or the other."

"I guess I could do that," Melissa agreed slowly, but she lifted her chin in the gesture Henry had come to know as stubborn pride.

At that moment Etta entered the dining room carrying a tray of fist-size biscuits, a bowl of gravy and a platter of scrambled eggs.

Breakfast was pleasant with he and his mother telling tales of Christmases past and Melissa sharing some of her fond childhood memories of the holiday when her mother had been alive. Henry found his gaze drawn to her again and again. She looked so soft, so inviting, and it was more than memories of the sex they'd shared that attracted him to her.

He loved the sound of her laughter. He liked the habit she had of shifting that shiny strand of hair behind her ears when she was thinking or when she was nervous.

He felt a little like he had in seventh grade when he'd had a crush on a girl named Angela. She'd been blond-haired and blue-eyed like Melissa and it had taken him months to work up his nerve to ask her to a school dance. The experience had been his first taste of how materialistic women, even very young women, could be.

He shoved the ancient painful memory away as he focused on the conversation and the musical ring of Melissa's laughter.

When they were all finished eating they adjourned into the living room, where the first thing his mother insisted they do was dress the boys in the little Santa suits she'd bought for them.

As the women dressed the little ones, Henry moved the high chairs into the room, as excited as a kid to distribute the presents to everyone. When the boys were in their little Santa suits, Mary took dozens of pictures and Henry knew she'd be sporting those photos all around town, bragging about her grandbabies.

Henry donned a Santa hat that James found incredibly funny. As the little boy laughed that rich burst of joy, Henry knew this was definitely going to be a Christmas to remember.

Melissa sat on the sofa next to Mary as Henry began to unveil the bigger presents hidden under sheets. Rocking horses and walkers and stuffed animals as big as Henry himself were just the beginning. There were boxes of clothes and diapers and educational toys. Of course, the boys liked the shiny wrapping paper best of all.

Mary opened her gift of the lotion and soap from Melissa and exclaimed that it was the brand and scent that she loved.

Melissa was already feeling overwhelmed when Henry gave her a present. "You shouldn't have," she said to him.

He smiled. "Open it, Melissa. I picked it out just for you. It's the exact color of your eyes."

Melissa couldn't help the way her heart fluttered at his words. She carefully removed the wrapping paper and opened the box to display the most beautiful blue sweater she'd ever seen in her life. It was soft as a whisper and she was touched by his thoughtfulness.

"Oh, Henry. It's beautiful." She felt the ridiculous burn of tears at her eyes.

"That's not all." He handed her a larger package. "I hope you won't be offended by the more personal nature of this gift, but I couldn't resist it."

She frowned at him, wondering just how personal the gift might be, aware that his mother was seated right next to her. It was a robe, a beautiful long burgundy robe with a satin collar and belt. He must have noticed the worn condition of her robe.

One of the things she was grateful for was that although he had been extravagant with the things he'd bought for the boys, the things he'd bought for her had been ordinary presents, as if he'd known she'd be displeased if he went overboard for her.

"I have something for you, Henry." Melissa got up from the sofa and grabbed the small present she'd slipped under the tree when she'd come downstairs that morning. He looked at her in surprise, took the gift and sat in one of the chairs to open it.

"There's not much I can buy for a man who appears to have everything," Melissa said. "But I know it's something you don't have, something I think you'll want to have."

He looked at her curiously, then ripped the paper off to expose two small frames. Inside the frames were the newborn pictures of the boys and two cigars with bands that exclaimed, "It's a Boy."

His eyes filled with emotion as he gazed at the gifts, then back at her. "It's the most perfect present you could have given me." He stood and kissed her on the cheek. "Thank you."

Her skin burned with the press of his lips and once again she felt overwhelmed by the warmth, by the feel of family and by the gifts he and Mary had bought for her sons.

By ten o'clock most of the mess from the morning had been cleaned up and the doorbell rang to announce a guest. Henry went to answer as Melissa finished placing the last of the wrapping paper into a large garbage bag.

She tensed as she heard the familiar female voice. Hilary. The sharp pang of jealousy that roared through Melissa stunned her. She shouldn't feel jealous of any woman Henry might have in his life. She had no right to feel that kind of emotion.

As Hilary walked into the living room she stopped short at the sight of the twins in their chairs. She looked at the boys, then at Henry, and her pretty features tightened with stunned surprise.

"Hello, Hilary," Melissa said. The woman was

exceptionally beautiful and sophisticated in a gold sweater and tight black slacks. Her dark hair was pulled up and gold earrings danced at her dainty ears. She carried in her hands a platter that Melissa assumed was the famous fudge she'd promised Henry the day before.

"Merry Christmas, Mary and Melinda," Hilary replied.

"Melissa. My name is Melissa."

"Of course," Hilary said, then turned her attention to Henry. "Could I speak to you privately for a moment?"

"Okay. Let's go into my study." Henry gestured her down the hallway.

"I can't imagine what he ever saw in that woman," Mary said the minute they had disappeared.

"She's very beautiful," Melissa said as she put the last of the wrapping paper into the trash.

"Maybe on the outside, but it's inner beauty that really matters. Now, if you'll excuse me, I'm going to go help Etta with the lunch preparations."

"And I'm going to put the boys down for their nap," Melissa replied.

Minutes later Melissa stood in the doorway of the room she now thought of as the nursery. Joey had fallen asleep almost immediately and James was almost there, fussing a bit as he fought sleep.

As he finally gave up the battle, Melissa turned from the door and gasped in surprise at the sight of Hilary in front of her.

"He won't marry you, you know," she said softly.

"I don't expect him to marry me," Melissa replied.

Hilary smiled. "He's not going to marry me, either. I'd hoped that eventually I could wear him down, but Henry has no interest in being married. You seem like a nice woman and it would be a shame for you to get hurt."

"I appreciate your concern, but trust me, Henry has made it clear to me a hundred different ways that he's not the marrying kind. Besides, what makes you think I would want to marry him?"

Hilary looked at her and released a dry laugh. "You're kidding, right? I mean, he's good-looking and nice and wealthy. Why wouldn't you want to marry him?"

Melissa couldn't believe she was having this conversation with a woman who had been Henry's lover. "My life is in Amarillo. I'll be going home tomorrow to my life."

"Well, in any case, I just came up here to tell you that it was nice to meet you and I hope you have a safe trip home." With a curt nod, Hilary turned around and walked down the stairs.

Melissa drew a deep breath and went into her bedroom. While the morning had been one of the happiest she could ever remember, she felt a sudden burn of tears in her eyes.

There was no way she'd ever to be able to provide for the twins like Henry could. Would she be denying her sons by choosing not to move here? She didn't want to do the wrong thing, but she didn't know what was the right thing. Maybe she should just take a look at the carriage house and keep an open mind.

Still, she couldn't ignore the fact that somebody was trying to hurt Henry and it was possible she and the boys might become accidental victims.

"Melissa?"

She whirled around to see Henry standing in the doorway. "Everything all right?" he asked.

"Everything is fine," she replied.

"I know Hilary came up here. She didn't say anything to upset you, did she?" He gazed at her worriedly.

Melissa smiled. "Not at all. She simply told me that it was nice to meet me and she hoped I had a safe trip home."

He seemed relieved. "Hilary tends to have a bit of a sharp tongue."

"Don't worry, Henry. I'm a big girl and I can take care of myself."

He nodded. "I was wondering if while the twins are napping now would be a good time to take you to see the carriage house." He smiled, that slow sexy grin that heated every ounce of blood in her body. "I was also wondering when I was going to get to see that blue sweater on you."

"Why don't you give me five minutes and I'll meet you downstairs and we can take a look."

"Great. I'll meet you downstairs."

The minute he left the room she closed the door and pulled the sweater out of the box. It fit perfectly and was exactly the color of her eyes. The fact that he'd even thought about her eyes made her heart flutter just a little bit.

It was only as she was walking down the stairs that she realized the terrible truth—she was more than a little bit in love with Henry Randolf III.

Chapter 8

The morning had gone far better than Henry had hoped. The living room had been filled with laughter, warmth and a feeling of family that had been missing from the house since his father's death.

Melissa had teased him as if they'd known each other forever, and in many ways that's the way he was beginning to feel about her. She was comfortable, and yet made him simmer with expectancy. He couldn't remember a woman who had done both for him.

He pulled on his holster and his gun and then covered it with his winter coat. Despite the fact that it was a holiday and the season of peace and joy, Henry couldn't let down his guard. He was eager to have a sit-down meeting with Jimmy the next day to see if the lawman had come up with any evidence as to who might be after him. They needed to come up with a plan to force the person out into the open.

He turned as Melissa came down the stairs, clad in the blue sweater and the jeans that did amazing things for her legs and curvy butt. Something about her stole his breath away.

Lust, he told himself. That was it. Lust and nothing more. If he slept with her again he was certain these crazy feelings would go away.

Her plans were to leave in the morning and short of locking her up in a tower, there was no way he could stop her. He pulled her coat from the closet and held it out to her. "Ready?"

She nodded. "Ready."

"I've got to say, you look sexy as hell in that sweater."

"I'll bet you say that to all the girls," she replied lightly, but her cheeks flushed as she pulled on her coat.

They stepped out the door, and Henry threw an arm around her shoulder. He told himself it was because he wanted to protect her if somebody came at them, but the truth was he'd been dying to touch her all day.

She didn't pull away but instead snuggled into him as the cold wind whipped her hair against his face. They walked briskly, not speaking. Henry kept his gaze bouncing left and right, relaxing as he saw Charlie and several of his men in the distance.

When they reached the carriage house he unlocked the door and ushered her into the foyer. "You might want to keep your coat on. We just have the minimal heat running in here right now."

She nodded, stepped into the living room and caught her breath. "Oh, my gosh. This is four times the size of my apartment."

It was an open floor plan, the living room flowing into the kitchen. The living-room flooring was a soft beige carpeting and the kitchen had an attractive tile in Southwest colors. The furnishings were simple but tasteful and the kitchen was fully equipped with every pot and pan that a chef might need.

"If you wanted to bring in your own furniture we could store all of this," he said, unable to read the expression on her face. "Let me show you the bedrooms." He led her down a short hallway to the first bedroom. It was definitely large enough to accommodate two cribs and later two twin beds for the boys. From the window the stables and corral were in view, perfect for two little cowboys.

From there he led her into the master bedroom, which was huge, with an adjoining bathroom complete with a Jacuzzi tub. For a moment his head filled with a vision of how she'd look in that tub with her shiny hair piled up on her head and her body surrounded by scented bubbles. He tried desperately to shove the provocative vision out of his mind.

She wandered around the room and when she finally turned to look at him, tears glimmered in her eyes. Instead of looking pleased, she looked achingly miserable.

"What's wrong?" he asked.

The tears spilled from her eyes onto her cheeks. "I don't know what to do. I'm so confused. I'm so overwhelmed by everything."

Henry realized at that moment he didn't like to see her cry. He walked over to her and captured her pretty face between his palms. The look in her eyes was slightly wild, as if she wanted to escape him and the entire situation.

"Melissa, don't cry," he said gently. "Tell me what's wrong."

She jerked away from him and took several steps backward. "You don't understand. This place is so wonderful and all the things you bought for the boys were unbelievable. I know they could have a wonderful life here, but they could have a wonderful life with me in Amarillo, too."

She raised her chin and swiped angrily at her tears. "Lots of children just see their father on the weekends and they survive just fine. People get divorced or never marry and visitation is worked out okay."

He stared at her for a long moment. "But that's not what I want," he said. He shoved his hands into his coat pockets and leaned against the wall. "I don't want to be a weekend dad. What can I do to make this work for you? Of course, I'd take care of all your moving expenses and if you have a lease that needs to be broken, I'll take care of that, too. If you're worried about work, I'm sure I can find you some clients for your interior decorating and there's always the hotel that you could be contracted to do. I can take care of all your needs, Melissa. We can make this work."

As he'd spoken, her tears had dried and she gazed at him with an inscrutable expression. When he finished she shook her head and offered him a small, somehow sad smile.

"Henry, there are some things your money just can't buy. You can't buy me. I don't care about money or things. My mother and I didn't have money, but we were happy." She paused and frowned.

"So, this is a no?" he asked flatly.

"It's an I don't know," she replied with obvious frustration. "I've known you and your mother for a couple of days. I refuse to make a life-altering decision that quickly. What I suggest is that I go home tomorrow and think things through without your influence. I want to do what's best for everybody, Henry, and that includes what's best for me."

Although he was disappointed with her decision, he couldn't help but admire her strength in not succumbing to an easier life than the one he thought she was currently living.

"You know I won't stop trying to change your mind," he said lightly, hoping to dispel some of the tension that sparked in the air between them.

She offered him a smile. "Why am I not surprised by that?" She walked out of the bedroom and he followed just behind her.

"I told you I was stubborn," he said.

"Just be aware that you might have met your match," she replied.

As they stepped out of the carriage house he noticed that the sun had disappeared beneath a thick layer of clouds and the air felt colder than it had before.

What he needed was a good old-fashioned blizzard that would make Melissa stay long enough for him to get her to agree what he wanted.

But Henry knew there were two things he couldn't control. The weather was the first and apparently Melissa was the second.

It began to snow at nine o'clock that evening. Melissa stood at her bedroom window and stared out in dismay. If this kept up there was no way she could leave after breakfast in the morning like she'd planned.

She checked on the boys, who were sleeping soundly, then went back down the stairs where she knew Henry was probably having a glass of scotch. Funny, after such a brief time she'd begun to know his habits. He usually sat in the living room to unwind after his mother excused herself for bed.

Sure enough, he was seated in his chair, a glass of scotch at his side as he stared at the lights still twinkling on the Christmas tree. He smiled when she appeared in the doorway. "How about a glass of wine?"

"That sounds nice," she agreed and sat on the sofa while he went to the bar and poured her drink.

It was odd, anytime she was near him a sizzle of

anticipation raced through her and yet she was also comfortable with him. He was an easy man to be around, easy to talk to and share things with.

As he handed her the glass of wine, she again wondered if somehow somebody had hurt him in the past. Had somebody made him believe that he had nothing to offer a woman except for his bank account and a lavish lifestyle? His money seemed to be the only bargaining chip he knew how to use to get the things he wanted in life.

"Looks like your plans to take off tomorrow morning might have to be postponed," he said as he returned to his chair.

"Don't look so smug about it," she replied teasingly. "Actually, I'm hoping it stops soon and the roads will be all right for travel by morning."

"And I'm hoping it snows until March and you're forced to stay here and I'll have all that time to convince you to move into the carriage house."

She laughed. "You're positively relentless." She took a sip of her wine and eyed him curiously. "Tell me why you're such a cynic when it comes to love. Haven't you ever been in love before?"

"The last time I was in love I was in seventh grade. Her name was Angela and I was absolutely crazy about her." He took a drink of his scotch and then continued. "It took me months to get up the nerve to ask her to a school dance that was coming up."

Melissa sensed a sad tale ahead and there was

nothing worse than young love scorned. "Did she go to the dance with you?"

He smiled, and she saw a hint of sadness, a whisper of loneliness in the depths of his eyes. "She did. She told me she knew I was rich and if I'd buy her a gold bracelet she'd go with me."

"So you bought her the bracelet?" A tiny pang pieced Melissa's heart, a pain for the boy he'd been who had learned early that his worth was in his wallet.

He nodded. "Bought her the bracelet, took her to the dance and thought it was the beginning of a wonderful love match. Then when I took her home that night she told me that she'd only gone out with me for the bracelet and that I shouldn't bother her anymore." He smiled again and this time it was the smile of the cynic he'd become. "That was my first and only experience with love."

"That's horrible," she exclaimed.

He shrugged. "It was a long time ago. Tell me about the man you were dating before we met that night. Were you in love with him?"

"I believed I was at the time." She thought of Tom, who she'd once thought she would marry. There had been a time when any thought of him brought pain, but all she felt now was relief that she hadn't married a man who had cheated on her, a man who hadn't valued her.

"I loved what I thought we had. I loved the idea of getting married and building a family. I loved the idea of waking up with the same man I went to bed with day after day, year after year. We'd dated for over two years and it had become comfortable. I just assumed we'd take the next step and get married but now I'm glad we didn't. He didn't love me the way I wanted to be loved."

"Mindlessly, desperately," Henry said.

"Exactly," she replied, surprised that he'd remembered she'd said that before.

They fell silent, but it was a comfortable quiet. Melissa sipped her wine and found her gaze going again and again to him.

He was such an attractive man with sharp, bold features and that sexy cleft in his chin. But it wasn't his physical qualities that drew her. She loved the teasing light that so often lit his eyes. She loved the respect and caring he showed to his mother. He was a good man and he would make a wonderful role model for her children.

"I think I'll call it a night," she finally said. "I'm still hoping to be able to get home in the morning." She stood and finished the last of her wine, then headed for the kitchen to place her glass in the sink.

"I think I'll call it a night, too," he said and followed behind her into the kitchen. "Jimmy is coming over tomorrow and we're going to sit down and discuss what's been going on and what we're going to do about it." He placed his glass in the sink next to hers.

"What can you do about it? You don't know who is after you." She looked at him worriedly. "Even if the person is just trying to scare you, there's nothing that says he won't make a mistake and actually manage to shoot you." She was shocked by the fear that rocketed through her, fear for him.

"Yeah, that thought has entered my mind, too," he said dryly. "I'm sure Jimmy and I can put our heads together and come up with a plan to figure out who is responsible and get them behind bars. Don't you worry about it. I'll get it all taken care of."

"I can't help but worry about it," she replied. "You're now a part of my life." Emotion began to well up inside her. "I mean, I don't want my boys to grow up without their father," she said hurriedly.

As they left the kitchen and headed for the stairs, Melissa tried to get her emotions under control. It was true, she didn't want anything to happen to him for the twins' sake. But it was also true that as a woman she'd be devastated if anything happened to him.

He turned off the Christmas tree lights then together they climbed the stairs. As always, the first thing Melissa did when she reached the top of the stairs was go into the boys' bedroom to make sure they were still peacefully sleeping.

Henry followed her in and a soft smile played on his face as he looked first at Joey and then at James. That smile, filled with such love, with such tenderness, created a warmth inside her.

She would never have to worry about her sons being loved. If anything ever happened to her, Henry would make sure they not only had what they needed to survive, but he'd make sure their world had the love he refused to believe in for himself.

"Melissa." He grabbed her hand as they left the room.

She knew immediately what he wanted, what she wanted from him. For months after that night of the blizzard she'd thought about the pleasure she'd found in his arms.

She wanted it again. She wanted him again and she could tell by the heat in his eyes that he wanted the same.

She stepped closer to him and raised her face to him and he took the unspoken invitation by crashing his mouth down on hers.

His mouth was hot hunger against hers and she felt as if she'd been waiting for this since the moment he'd first opened the door to her.

Allowing him to deepen the kiss, she leaned into him, wanting him to have no question in his mind that she wanted him.

His tongue danced with hers as his hands slid down her back and pulled her hips into his. His arousal was evident and fed the flames of desire inside her.

The kiss seemed to last forever before he finally dropped his hands from around her and stepped back. "You look beautiful in that blue sweater, but I remember how beautiful you looked naked. I want you, Melissa. This has nothing to do with anything but you and me."

"I want you, too," she said, her voice a husky whisper.

"You know I'm not making any promises. I need you to understand that there's no future with me. I'm not the man to give you your happily ever after."

"As far as I'm concerned, tonight you're a handsome cowboy keeping me warm on a wintery night and nothing more," she replied. His eyes flamed as he pulled her into the bedroom and back into his arms.

Chapter 9

This time his kiss left her breathless and aching. When he pulled her sweater over her head she was more than ready for him. There was no embarrassment as she stood before him in her wispy bra. The light from her bathroom spilled into the bedroom and she could see the flames that lit his eyes while he gazed at her.

Every bone in her body weakened and she reached out to unfasten the buttons on his shirt. The heat from his body radiated to her, urging her to unbutton his shirt and sweep it off his broad shoulders.

He was beautiful, with his chiseled chest and flat abdomen. He pulled her back into his arms and as he kissed her he reached around her to unfasten her bra. He tugged the straps off her shoulders and when it fell away he embraced her again and she delighted in the feel of his bare skin against hers.

"I've wanted this since the moment you arrived," he said, his breath hot against her throat.

"I've wanted it, too," she confessed.

Within minutes they were both naked and beneath the blankets in bed. Even though she'd only made love with him once, his skin felt just the way she remembered, warm and firm as he pulled her against him. The familiar scent of him filled her head and she knew any other man who ever wore that particular brand of cologne would always evoke memories of Henry.

As his kisses made her mindless, his hands cupped her breasts and a low moan escaped her lips. He pulled his mouth from hers and looked down at her. "You are so beautiful," he whispered.

She felt beautiful beneath his gaze. That was part of Henry's gift. He'd made her feel beautiful and desirous that night of the blizzard, and he made her feel that way now.

He lowered his mouth to capture the erect tip of one of her breasts and she tangled her fingers in his rich, dark hair. Sweet sensations sizzled through her.

He teased her nipple, swirling his tongue and using his teeth to lightly nip. Melissa closed her eyes as all concerns about the future melted away beneath the heat of his caresses. She couldn't think about anything but him and the magic of his touch.

She ran her hands down the length of his broad back, loving the play of muscle beneath her fingertips. She felt safe with him, not just physically protected, but emotionally, as well. She felt as if she could say anything to him, tell him her deepest, darkest secrets and he'd keep those secrets safe.

The love she'd tried not to feel for him welled up inside her, a love she knew would never be reciprocated. But at the moment that didn't matter. She had this night with him and she knew it had to be enough for her. She wouldn't allow this to happen again but she intended to enjoy every moment of it.

"This is much nicer than a hardwood floor beneath the scratchy blanket from my truck," he said, his voice thick with desire.

"I have very fond memories of that scratchy blanket and the hardwood floor." She could speak no more as his mouth once again claimed hers.

Every inch of her skin was electrified, for each and every place he touched, he kissed, sizzled in response.

His heartbeat was strong and quick against hers, the heart that didn't believe in love, the one that refused to believe that anyone could love him for himself.

She slid her lips down his neck, wanting him to feel loved, to feel as desired as he made her feel. Her mouth moved down his chest and she licked first one of his nipples, then the other.

He gasped, a quick intake of breath that made her even bolder. He rolled over on his back as she moved down the length of his body, kissing and nipping and teasing his fevered skin with her lips.

Tangling his hands in her hair, his entire body tensed as she kissed his inner thigh. He was fully erect and although this was something she'd rarely done for Tom, she wanted the utter intimacy with Henry.

As she took him into her mouth she let out a low groan and every muscle in his body tensed. "Melissa," he moaned as his hands tightened in her hair.

She loved the strained sound of her name on his lips, loved the pleasure she knew she was giving to him. But it didn't take long for him to push her away and roll to his side.

"Now, it's my turn," he said, his eyes gleaming with promise. He ran his hand down her body and rubbed against her. "I want you gasping for air and crying out my name."

As he moved his fingers against the very center of her, a rising tide of pleasure began to build inside her. She arched her hips up to meet his touch, needing release, wanting the wave to consume her.

And then it did, crashing through her as she cried his name over and over again. She shuddered with the force of it and tears filled her eyes. But he wasn't finished yet. He rolled over and grabbed a condom from the nightstand and while she was still weak and gasping, he moved between her legs and entered her.

For a moment neither of them moved. The pleasure of him filling her up was so intense she feared if she moved she'd lose it again.

He froze, his arms holding him up from her chest. From the light shining in from her bathroom she could see his features. His eyes were closed, his neck muscles corded as if he were under enormous strain.

He opened his eyes and looked down at her, then slowly slid his hips back and thrust forward. That single slow movement broke everything loose between them.

Fast and furious, he stroked into her and she encouraged him by clutching his buttocks and pulling him into her.

Lost. She was lost in him and once again she felt the wild tide rushing in. As it washed over her she felt him tense and moan against her, knowing it had claimed him, too.

He collapsed on her and she wrapped her arms around his back, wishing she could hold him there forever. But all too quickly he got up and padded into the adjoining bathroom.

Melissa turned her head to one side and fought a sudden rush of tears. Of all the foolish, reckless things she'd ever done in her life, this was probably the worst. She'd chosen to make love to a man who apparently wasn't capable of loving her back.

MysteryMom couldn't have known that she was sending Melissa into a new heartbreak. The woman had probably simply wanted to unite a man with his sons, ease the burden of single parenting for Melissa. She'd accomplished that. Melissa would no longer be alone in the task of raising her sons. She knew in her heart, in her soul, that Henry would always be a support and help in the parenting process.

But MysteryMom couldn't have known that

Melissa would fall mindlessly, desperately in love with Henry. She couldn't have known that Melissa would repeat the same mistake that she'd made on that snowy night over a year ago. At least he'd used a condom and there wouldn't be another accidental pregnancy.

As he came out of the bathroom she assumed he'd leave to go to his bedroom, but instead he surprised her by sliding back beneath the sheets and taking her in his arms. He kissed her on the temple, a sweet, soft kiss that touched her more than anything that had occurred between them.

"Definitely better in a bed," he said. He lay on his back and pulled her into his side. His hand stroked her hair as she placed her head on his chest. "I really hate to see you take off tomorrow."

"It's time, Henry. It's been a wonderful holiday but now it's over and I have to get back to my real life." It was more important than ever that she leave here as soon as possible. Her heart had gotten involved in a way that already would ache when she left. More time here would only make the ache sharper when she did go home.

She raised her head to look at him. "You know I'll do whatever I can to make it easy on you to see the boys."

"I know that." He raised his hand and trailed a finger down the side of her cheek, across her lower lip. "I can't think of a better woman to be the mother of my boys."

The tears that had hovered just under the surface

sprang to her eyes at his words. "You're just saying that now because you have me naked in bed with you," she replied with a choked little laugh.

"You know that's not true," he chided. "You have the values I want the boys to have. I know you'll teach them to have integrity, to have strong but gentle hearts."

She ran her hand across his chest and placed it on his heart. Her last thought before she fell asleep was that the one thing she would teach her boys was to believe in the power and wonder of love, something apparently nobody had ever taught Henry.

Henry stood at the window in his study and watched the snow swirling in the air. It had snowed about two inches overnight, effectively postponing Melissa's plans to leave first thing that morning.

He was now waiting for Jimmy to arrive. Jimmy had called earlier to tell Henry that the snow wouldn't keep him from his appointment.

Staring at the carriage house in the distance, Henry thought of the night before. Making love to Melissa had been amazing and he'd been in no hurry to leave her bed.

Henry couldn't remember the last time he'd slept with a woman in his arms. He'd never stayed the night with Hilary, had always preferred the comfort of being alone in his own bed. But sleeping with Melissa had been not just comfortable, but comforting in a way he'd never imagined. It had been nice to feel the warmth of her next to him as he'd drifted off to sleep. And it had been equally as nice to wake up with her curled in his arms.

Surely these crazy feelings he was developing for her were nothing more than gratitude. After all, she'd given him the greatest gift a man could get—children.

He wasn't going to mention the carriage house solution to her again. He recognized that over the past two days he'd become a bore and bordered on becoming a bully in trying to get her to do what he wanted.

Whatever she decided, they'd make it work because it had to work. Even though they weren't married, he knew they'd do whatever was in the best interest of the twins.

At the moment Melissa and his mother and the twins were all in the kitchen. It was Etta's day off and they were in the process of making dinner.

As he'd walked to his study he'd heard the sound of laughter and merriment coming from the kitchen. The house would feel empty once Melissa and the boys were gone.

Actually, the house had felt empty for a long time. And if he thought about it long enough he'd admit that his life had been fairly empty for a very long time. He frowned, irritated with the direction his thoughts were taking. Maybe it was a good thing Melissa was leaving soon. She was messing with his mind in a way that was distinctly uncomfortable.

He turned away from the window as a knock fell

on his door. The door opened and Jimmy poked his head in. "Your mom told me to come on in," he said.

Henry motioned him inside. "How are the roads?" he asked as he gestured his friend into the chair in front of the desk.

"A little nasty but not too bad. The road crews are out working so if we don't get any more accumulation we should have everything under control." He eased into the chair. "You got any of that good scotch hidden away in here?"

Henry walked to the minibar in the corner and poured himself and Jimmy a drink, then handed Jimmy his and sat at the desk with his own.

Jimmy took a deep swallow and sighed. "I don't know if Willie told you or not, but he found the bullet that shot out your tire still in the rubber that was left on the truck. It was a .22 caliber. I know it wasn't Hank. At the time your truck was fired on, Hank was down at Lazy Ed's, completely sauced."

Lazy Ed's was a popular tavern for the ranch hands in the area. "I'm not surprised. His drinking is what caused him to get fired in the first place," Henry said.

"Before we get into all this, I want to know about those twin boys that your mother introduced me to in the kitchen. They sure do have the Randolf chin. You been holding out on me about your love life?"

Henry smiled and knew in an instant he wasn't about to tell Jimmy the truth about how the twins were conceived. Although Henry certainly wasn't a prude, he didn't want to give anyone in town a reason to think less of Melissa.

"Melissa is a friend from Amarillo. She's a terrific woman and we've been close for some time. When she got pregnant we agreed that we'd share the parenting of the boys and remain friends."

"I never even knew you wanted kids," Jimmy said.

Henry smiled. "I didn't know I wanted them until they were here. I got to tell you, Jimmy. They change your life. They make you want to be a better man. That's why it's so important we get this mess cleaned up, these attacks that are happening on me. I can't have them around if it's not safe."

Henry leaned back in his chair. "You know who is at the top of my suspect list."

Jimmy nodded. "Tom Burke. You scare him, Henry."

"He should be scared," Henry said with a scowl. "You and I both know he's a criminal."

Jimmy nodded. "I've been in contact with the FBI and I'm hoping they're going to look into his actions as city manager. The problem is we both know he's a likely suspect. What we don't have is any proof."

"Did you question him about his whereabouts at the time my tire was shot out?"

Jimmy nodded. "According to his wife, he was at home with her."

Once again Henry frowned. "You know damn good and well she'd lie for him."

Jimmy nodded. "I've put a couple of my men on Tom. Full-time surveillance as long as I have the manpower. If he tries anything we'll be on top of him. It's the best I can do, Henry."

Henry nodded. He knew Jimmy was as frustrated as he was by what had been happening. He took a drink of his scotch.

"If this had all started the night that Melissa showed up here with those babies, I would ask you if you thought Hilary might be playing a woman scorned," Jimmy said.

Henry laughed at the very idea of Hilary hiding out in the woods with a gun. "No way. I'll grant you she wasn't too happy to discover I had two babies, but Hilary knew the score where I was concerned. Besides, she'd never risk breaking a nail to do anything like this."

"And the first attack happened to you before Melissa arrived on the scene," Jimmy said.

Henry nodded. "I'm telling you it's Tom Burke or it's somebody he's hired. He's the only person who has a hell of a lot to lose if I become mayor."

Jimmy tilted his glass up for another drink of the scotch. "I just wanted to come out here and tell you that I'm doing the best I can."

"What about a ballistics test on the bullet Willie dug out of my tire?" Henry asked.

"Unfortunately the bullet hit your rim and was pretty mangled. Besides, in order to do a ballistics test you have to have a weapon to compare it to and Tom Burke insists he doesn't have a rifle."

Henry snorted in disbelief. "I don't know a man

in this entire county who doesn't own a rifle. This is Texas, for God's sake."

"You're preaching to the choir, Henry."

For the next thirty minutes the men spoke about other potential suspects. There were only two that Henry could think of, both council members and friends of Tom Burke.

"You definitely have the support of the people," Jimmy said. "People like you, they admire your integrity and they trust you. If you can stay alive until February there is no doubt in my mind that you'll be voted in as mayor."

"That's nice to hear," Henry replied.

Jimmy glanced toward the window. "I've got to head back into town." He stood.

"I appreciate you coming out on such a crummy day." Henry stood, as well.

"I swear I'm going to get to the bottom of this, Henry," Jimmy said as they left the study.

"I just hope you do before this mysterious shooter gets lucky," Henry said dryly.

The two men walked to the front door, where they said their goodbyes. The snow had begun to fall again and as Henry closed the door he realized that he was more worried now about whoever was trying to hurt him than he'd been before Melissa had arrived at the house.

Before, he'd just been irritated by the whole thing. But now all he could think about was if anything happened to him the boys wouldn't have their father. He had every reason in the world to want to stay alive…for them and for Melissa.

The laughter coming from the kitchen pulled him away from the front door and to the source of the sound. Once there he found his mother and Melissa finishing up dinner preparations.

As he walked into the room, the twins flashed him smiles that as always filled him with warmth. "Something smells wonderful," he said.

"Melissa can cook," Mary exclaimed.

"It's just spaghetti with meat sauce," Melissa replied as she took a pot of boiling pasta off the stove top.

Henry took a seat at the table and watched as she dumped the spaghetti noodles into an awaiting colander. "You don't understand. Mom would think you were amazing if you could just boil an egg. She's the worst cook in the entire state of Texas."

Melissa shot a quick glance to Mary. "Don't worry," Mary said with a laugh. "He's quite right. It's one of the reasons Big Henry hired Etta. He knew if we tried to live on my cooking we'd all starve. Henry, why don't you set the table and I'll get the salad."

As always, dinner was a pleasant time. They chatted about favorite foods and Mary regaled Melissa with some of her war stories at the stove. The boys kept up their end of the conversation by babbling and cooing.

At one point James blew a raspberry. He looked startled and as they all laughed, he grinned and blew another one.

Henry smiled at Melissa. "You might have gotten his very first smile, but at least I didn't miss out on his very first raspberry."

After they'd finished eating Mary took the boys into the living room while Henry and Melissa cleaned up. "Dinner was terrific," he said as he stacked the dishes she'd rinsed into the dishwasher. "Do you like to cook?"

She nodded. "I do, but most of the time it seems like a lot of trouble to cook for one. When my mother was alive I did a lot of cooking, but not so much since she passed."

"You miss her."

She smiled with a touch of sadness. "Every day. Unfortunately diabetes is a ruthless disease and I think she was tired of fighting. It's some comfort to know she's not in pain anymore."

"I miss my father, too. He and I weren't just father and son, we were friends." Henry smiled at thoughts of his dad. "He was bigger than life, one of those colorful characters that people didn't forget after meeting him."

Melissa handed him the last plate. "And he taught you everything you need to know about being a wonderful father."

Henry smiled. "Yeah, I hadn't thought about it before, but he was a wonderful role model." He took the towel she offered him and dried his hands.

"It worried me that I was all alone," she said, her expression somber. "I worried about what would happen to the boys if I got hit by a car or had a sudden heart attack. Now I don't have to worry anymore. I know if anything happens to me you'll love them and take care of them."

"Nothing is going to happen to you," he assured her. "You and I are going to parent those boys until they're hulking adults and we're old and gray."

She smiled. "I like that plan, and speaking of the boys, I think it's probably time for a diaper change."

The rest of the evening passed and by nine o'clock it was time to put the boys down for the night. Mary said her good-night and retired to her wing of the house while Melissa carried Joey and Henry carried James up the stairs to their room.

Once the boys were settled into their beds, Melissa motioned Henry into her room. "Do you think I'm going to be able to head home tomorrow?" she asked.

Henry walked over to her window and peered outside. A light snow was still falling. He turned to look at her. "Why don't you make a decision in the morning? It's snowing now but maybe it will stop before too long. I can call Jimmy in the morning and ask him about the condition of the roads."

What he really wanted to do was have a repeat of the night before. But something in the way she stood with her arms crossed in front of her chest made him think she wouldn't be open to the idea.

"You want to go back down and have a glass of wine or something?" he asked.

She shook her head. "No, I think I'll just call it a night now. I really am hoping that we'll be able to travel in the morning. Besides, it's been a long day and I'm exhausted."

He realized she was already distancing herself, preparing for the goodbye. He was surprised at the edge of sadness that took hold of him. It wasn't like it was going to be goodbye forever, he told himself. Most likely one way or another he'd be seeing her every weekend. If she didn't want to drive here, then he'd drive to Amarillo. But somehow he knew that once she left here things would never be the same between them again.

"Then I guess I'll just say good-night," he said. He couldn't help himself. He stepped closer to her with the intention to deliver a kiss to her forehead, but instead found his mouth claiming hers.

The minute their lips connected the window where Henry had stood moments before shattered. As Henry saw the device that lay on the floor in the bedroom fear screamed inside him.

He shoved Melissa toward the door and they fell into the hallway as the bomb went off.

Chapter 10

One moment Henry had been kissing her and the next Melissa found herself on the hallway floor with Henry on top of her. The back of her head had connected hard with the floor in the fall and she was dazed and confused.

The loud explosion still rang in Melissa's ears, making her momentarily deaf. As Henry got off her, her hearing began to return. Above the din of the house alarm ringing she could hear the cries of her babies and her heart slammed into her chest with enough force to steal what little breath she had left.

"Check on the boys," Henry yelled as he pulled her up off the floor. He raced back into the bedroom and tore down the curtains that had caught on fire. As he stamped out the flames, she ran across the hall to the boys' room. They were safe, but scared by the noise.

She took them into her arms, and her heart beat so fast it felt as if it were trying to burst out of her chest. She stood in the center of the room, afraid to move, unsure what might happen next. She tried to calm the boys but with the alarm ringing discordantly it was impossible. Tears raced down Melissa's cheeks as she tried to still her own fear.

Somebody had thrown a bomb of some kind into the window of the bedroom where she'd slept, at the window where Henry had been standing only moments earlier. Her head couldn't wrap around it.

The blast could have killed him. It could have killed her. Had Henry not reacted as quickly as he had, they both could have been seriously hurt or worse.

She hugged the boys even closer to her chest and breathed a sigh of relief as the alarm suddenly stopped ringing. Now what? Had the danger passed? Was there more to come? Too afraid to move, she remained in the center of the room.

A moment later both Henry and Mary rushed into the room.

"You okay?" Henry asked her, his features taut with tension.

"We're fine," she said and felt a new press of tears as Mary put an arm around her shoulder.

"Jimmy is on his way," Henry said as he took Joey from her arms. "Let's go downstairs to wait for him."

By the time they got down the stairs several of

Henry's ranch hands were at the front door. Henry opened the door to allow them inside and they all gathered in the living room.

"We heard the explosion," Charlie said, his features grim. "Then we saw the fire at the window. I'm just glad to see you're all okay."

"You didn't see anyone?" Henry asked as he shifted Joey from one arm to the other.

Both Charlie and Randy shook their heads. "Didn't hear a car, didn't see a soul," Charlie said. "Dammit, it's like it's a phantom."

"It wasn't a phantom that threw a bomb through the window," Henry said, his anger rife in his voice. He handed Joey to his mother. "I want to go out and take a look around. With the snow there should be some footprints that can be tracked."

Charlie frowned. "Unfortunately, Randy and I might have messed up any prints," he admitted. "When we heard the blast we both ran to that side of the house. I didn't even think about footprints."

"There still might be some prints that don't belong to the two of you," Henry said.

"Please, Henry, wait for Jimmy before you go out," Melissa said. She had no idea what other danger might await him if he ventured outside and she couldn't stand the thought of anything happening to him.

"Yes, Henry," Mary spoke up, her voice filled with a mother's worry. "Please wait for Jimmy. I don't want you out there."

Melissa could tell by Henry's expression that he

was chomping at the bit, needing to do something, anything that might find the guilty party.

"If you want, Randy and I can go back out and take another look around," Charlie offered.

"Trust me, if there's anyone around I'd be happy to tie him up and beat his ass until Jimmy shows up," Randy exclaimed.

Henry clapped him on the back. "I appreciate the sentiment, Randy, but the last thing I want is for anyone to get hurt. Why don't we all sit tight until Jimmy gets here?"

Charlie and Randy sat on the two chairs while Melissa and Mary sat on the sofa with the twins. Henry paced the room, looking like he wanted nothing more than to punch something or someone.

There was no question that somehow, someway, Melissa had to leave here as soon as possible. She couldn't place her children at risk. The idea that the pipe bomb could have easily been thrown through the window of the bedroom where the twins slept filled her with a kind of terror she'd never felt before.

"Randy, what I'd like you to do is see if you can find a piece of plywood in the shed to put over the broken window after Jimmy takes a look around." Henry turned to look at Melissa and his eyes were dark as midnight. "Melissa, I want you to pack a bag for you and the boys."

She looked at him in surprise. "But where are we going?" She knew the roads were snow-packed and her tires weren't in the best shape. There was no way she'd take off at this time of night for home.

"I'm going to have Charlie check you into a motel until the roads are safe enough for you to travel home." Henry looked at his mother. "You might want to pack a bag, too."

"Nonsense," Mary scoffed. "I agree with you that Melissa should take the twins and go but nobody is chasing me out of my home."

Henry nodded, as if unsurprised by his mother's decision to stay put. He returned his attention to Melissa. "The latest weather report I heard said that the snow is going to stick around for at least another twenty-four to forty-eight hours, so pack enough things to last you and the boys for a couple of days."

"But what about you?" Melissa asked. She wanted him to come with them, to leave this place of danger and hide out with her someplace where she knew he'd be safe.

"I'll be fine as long as I know you and the twins are safe." He took James from her arms. "Come on, I'll go up and help you get your things together."

"I'm going to head out to the shed," Randy said. "It's been long enough now I imagine whoever threw that bomb is long gone."

"And I'll wait here with Mrs. Randolf," Charlie added.

Henry said nothing as they climbed the stairs back to the room where the blast had occurred. The scent of smoke and gasoline lingered in the air.

"It must have been loaded with fuel," he said as he surveyed the damage. "At least it wasn't filled with any kind of shrapnel."

Melissa shuddered at the thought. She pulled her suitcase from the closet and quickly packed what little she'd brought with her. They then moved into the boys' room, where she packed their clothes and diapers.

"I'll have Charlie get you settled in at one of the motels and I'll call you first thing in the morning," he said. She turned to face him and saw the worry in his eyes, a worry coupled with rage.

He stepped up to her and placed his palm against her cheek. She turned her face into the warmth of his hand. "He could have hurt you tonight. He could have hurt you and the boys."

"But that didn't happen," she said softly.

"Not this time, but I can't take another chance. I thought you were safe here, but I now realize I can't guarantee your safety. You'll be safe in a motel until the roads are clean enough for you to go home."

"Henry?" Jimmy's voice drifted up the stairs.

Henry dropped his hand from her face and stepped back from her. "Come on up, Jimmy."

Melissa and Henry met the lawman in the hallway. "You can have a look around. I'm sending Melissa with Charlie to a motel for the rest of the night. I'll be back up here as soon as I get those arrangements made."

Henry didn't say a word as they went back downstairs. Once there, as Melissa and Mary began to put the coats on the boys, he disappeared into his study.

Minutes later he came out. "I've got you set up in a room at Ed's Motel. It's clean and comfortable and the owner is a friend of mine. The room is registered in the name of Hank James. Nobody will know you're there and the key will be waiting for you in the office."

A muscle knotted in his jaw. "Charlie will get you there safe and sound and I'll call you in the morning." He shoved a wad of cash into her hand. "There's a diner right next door to the motel. They'll deliver whatever you need to your motel-room door."

It was crazy, but as Melissa pulled on her coat and Charlie grabbed her bags, she had a sudden terrible fear for Henry.

"Please, stay safe," she said as she held the twins in her arms.

He kissed Joey and James on the forehead and then gently shoved a strand of her hair behind her ear. "Get out of here and let me do what I need to do."

It took only minutes for her and the boys to be loaded into Charlie's four-wheel-drive vehicle. While they pulled away from the house Melissa looked back to see Henry silhouetted in the front door.

Once again she was struck with the strong, inexplicable fear—the fear that she was never going to see him again.

"Henry, where are you going?" Jimmy asked as Henry pulled on his winter coat. They had just spent the last hour picking through the rubble in the bedroom.

Jimmy had collected the pieces of the device to

use as evidence and now Randy was hanging the plywood over the broken window.

Charlie had returned to the ranch after dropping Melissa and the children at Ed's Motel. At least Henry had the comfort of knowing she and the babies would be safe there until she could leave town.

With each moment that had ticked by a rage had grown in Henry, a seething sick rage that begged to be released. And he knew exactly where to vent it.

"I'm going to Burke's house." Henry buttoned his coat but didn't reach for his gun in the drawer. He knew if he had it on him he might use it and as much as he wanted to hurt the man he believed was responsible for the pipe bomb, he didn't want to kill him. He was a father now, a man who had too much too lose by letting his rage get the best of him.

"Dammit, Henry, you can't go off half-cocked," Jimmy exclaimed in frustration.

"Trust me, I'm not half-cocked, I'm fully loaded," Henry replied dryly.

"Just stay put," Jimmy said. "I'll go talk to Burke."

"Then I'm coming with you." Henry didn't give Jimmy another opportunity to talk him out of it, but instead slammed out the door and walked into the snowy night.

Minutes later he and Jimmy were in Jimmy's patrol car navigating the slick roads as they headed into town. All Henry could think about was how devastating the results might have been had that bomb been thrown into the boys' room. The thought of such a tragedy stoked the flames of his rage even hotter.

"He could have killed my kids, Jimmy. He could have killed Melissa," Henry said, breaking the silence in the car.

"I know," Jimmy said. He grunted as the back of the car threatened to fishtail out. He steered into the slide and straightened the car. "We'll check out Tom's alibi for the time that the bomb was thrown through the window."

"It's possible he didn't personally throw it, but instead hired somebody." Henry frowned. "I've got to put an end to this." He stared out into the dark night. "Maybe I should withdraw from the election."

Jimmy shot him a stunned look. "You'd do that?"

"If I just had myself to worry about then I'd never quit. But it's not just me anymore, Jimmy. I've got kids and Melissa and they are going to need me."

"So they win and the corruption in Dalhart continues." Jimmy released an audible sigh. "Just give me a few more days before you make a decision. You're running on pure emotion right now. Give yourself time to calm down and let me sort this out."

Henry didn't reply. He knew Jimmy was right. He was definitely running on emotion, but as he thought of Melissa and Joey and James, he couldn't help but be filled with emotion.

He'd wanted to be a hero to the town, to clean up the mess that had been allowed to go on for far too long. But he now wondered if the stakes were too high. He'd rather be a father than a hero.

He sat up straighter in the seat as they approached town. The only other vehicles they'd passed were snow trucks laying down salt and pushing snow.

Tom Burke lived well above his means and salary in a five-bedroom luxury home on a three-acre lot. The first thing Henry noticed was that Tom's car was parked in the driveway. Not only was the car relatively clean of snow, but tire tracks showed that it had recently been driven.

The rage that had slowly begun to wane during the drive now roared back to life inside Henry. He was out of the car before it had come to a complete halt.

"Henry, dammit, wait for me," Jimmy cried as he parked the car and got out.

Henry didn't wait. He headed for the front door with a single-mindedness and once he got there he banged on the door with his fist.

By the time the door was opened by Tom, Jimmy had reached the porch. Henry didn't say a word, but rather grabbed the short man by the front of his pristine white shirt and dragged him out the door.

"Hey, get your hands off me," Tom yelled and jerked out of Henry's grasp. "What the hell is wrong with you, man?"

"Have you been out to my place tonight, Tom? I see your car has been driven. Did you come to pay me a little visit?" Henry glared at him and became aware of Deputy Gordon Hunter joining them on the porch.

"I don't know what you're talking about," Tom

exclaimed, his beefy face red. "I haven't been any-where near your place tonight."

"Then you hired somebody to throw that pipe bomb through my window." Henry took a menacing step toward him. "I had babies in the house, you bastard."

Tom looked from Henry to Jimmy. "A pipe bomb? I don't know a damn thing about a pipe bomb."

"Then where did you go tonight?" Henry demanded. "Your car has been driven recently. Where did you go?"

"To the damned grocery store," Tom exclaimed in frustration. "We're supposed to get more snow. I needed to get a gallon of milk. Is that a crime now?"

"It's true," Gordon said. "I've been watching him, tailing him all evening. The only place he went is to the grocery store."

Henry stared at Gordon, then back at Tom. "I'm warning you right now, Tom. If anything happens to anyone I care about, I'll be back here to see you and I'll beat your ass to a pulp."

Tom looked at Jimmy in outrage. "Did you hear that? He threatened me with bodily harm."

Jimmy shook his head. "Nah, he didn't threaten you. He promised you." Jimmy clapped his hand on Henry's back. "Come on, Henry, nothing more can be done here for now."

Henry shot Tom another killer glare, then stalked back to Jimmy's car and got into the passenger's seat. As Jimmy and Gordon spoke to Tom for another few minutes, Henry steamed.

How were they ever going to get to the bottom of this? Whoever was responsible was smart enough to leave no clues behind, to do the kind of sneak attacks that made it impossible to investigate.

One thing was clear. He couldn't allow Melissa and the boys back into his home until the situation was resolved, and that angered him more than anything.

It was a tension-filled ride back home. Jimmy talked the whole way, detailing his plan to investigate what had happened.

"We might be able to find fingerprints on the pieces of the bomb that survived the blast. There might be specific traceable material that was used. Don't you worry, Henry. I'm going to get to the bottom of this."

As he babbled on, Henry stared out the window, his mind drifting to Melissa and the boys. What were they doing at this moment? He glanced at his watch and realized his sons would be sound asleep and tonight he wouldn't be able to stand in the doorway and smell their scent, watch their little faces as they dreamed. Tonight he and Melissa wouldn't be able to sit together in the living room, enjoying quiet conversation after his mother had gone to bed.

The fact that some nut had taken these particular pleasures away from him reignited the fire of his anger. But by the time they finally reached the house the anger had burned itself out and he was simply exhausted.

Randy and Charlie sat with his mother in the living room and he quickly told them what had happened with Tom, then Charlie and Randy left.

"Are you all right?" his mother asked as he walked to the bar and poured himself a healthy dose of scotch.

"No. I'm angry and frustrated and I'm wondering if I shouldn't just pull out of the election." He sat on the sofa next to her.

"Is that what you want to do?"

"I don't want anything to happen to Melissa and the boys."

Mary smiled at him. "That didn't answer my question. Besides, as soon as the roads clear Melissa and the boys will return to Amarillo. You still have to live here with any decision you make."

Henry released a sigh and dropped his head back against the cushion. "I've never really been scared in my life, but the thought of how close danger came to Melissa and the boys put a fear in my heart I never want to feel again."

"Parenthood brings with it a multitude of fears." Mary patted his hand. "The first time those boys get on a bicycle your heart is going to race with fear. The day you put them on a bus to go to school you're going to be filled with a terror as you think of all the things that can go wrong. But you'll also know a joy greater than anything you've ever experienced with them."

Henry nodded.

"And then there's Melissa," Mary said softly. "You light up in her presence, Henry."

"She's the mother of my children," he replied.

"I think she could be more than that to you if you'd just open up that heart of yours," Mary said.

"I don't want her to be any more than that," he replied with forced lightness.

Mary sighed. "Your father was a wonderful man, Henry, but he was obsessed about some woman stealing your money. I worry that instead of making you careful, which was his intention, he made you incapable of allowing anyone close to you."

He was in no mood for one of his mother's attempts to get him to change his mind about love and marriage. He tipped his glass up and drained his drink, welcoming the hot burn down his throat. "Mom, it's been a long day and I'm exhausted. I have a lot of things to think about and I don't want to have a conversation about my decision to stay single."

"You're right. I'm sorry." She got up from the sofa. "I'm going to bed. I'll see you in the morning and hopefully by then Jimmy will have this all figured out and we can get back to a normal life."

"Good night, Mom." He watched her disappear up the stairs, then once again leaned his head back and released a long sigh.

He hoped Jimmy had some answers in the morning, but he didn't expect him to have any. He looked over at the phone. What he'd like to do is call Melissa, just hear her voice before he called it a night. But it was late and he didn't want to wake the boys. Besides, he'd told her he'd call her first thing in the morning.

He got up from the sofa and walked to the window. It was snowing again. Yesterday he'd hoped for snow so that he could keep Melissa and the boys here longer. Now he prayed for it to end so she could take the boys back to Amarillo where they would be safe from the madness that had become his life.

Chapter 11

It was the longest night of Melissa's life. The motel room was typical of motel rooms all around the country, equipped with a king-size bed, a television in a cabinet and a desk. It was spotlessly clean and once she'd placed the desk chair and a barricade of pillows along one side of the bed, the boys fell asleep almost immediately.

Unfortunately sleep remained elusive for her. She took a fast shower and changed into her nightgown, then got into bed and tried not to relive the events of the night.

What was happening at the house? Were Henry and Mary all right? If anything happened who would come to tell Melissa that something had gone wrong? Surely somebody would keep her informed.

She tossed and turned with worry and fear and it was during those long hours of sleeplessness that she realized the depth of her love for Henry James Randolf III. And in that realization she knew she would never be able to give him what he wanted.

The idea of making her home in the carriage house, so close, yet not a part of his life, was physically painful to consider. She could easily imagine the kind of routine they'd fall into over time.

The twins would spend a lot of their time in the big house with Henry and Mary and occasionally the desire Henry and Melissa felt for each other would rear up and explode and they'd make love. There would be no commitment, no love, just an arrangement. She couldn't do it. She couldn't sacrifice her own dreams of a marriage and love forever just so that Henry could get what he wanted—full-time access to the boys and an occasional release of sexual tension with her.

As soon as possible she was heading home and she and Henry would work out a viable visitation plan, one that didn't involve her living in his backyard.

She finally fell asleep around dawn and awakened around eight with a sliver of sunshine drifting in around the edges of the curtains. The boys were still asleep. The disruption from the night before had apparently exhausted them.

She got out of bed and pulled on the luxurious burgundy robe Henry had bought her and moved to the window to peer outside. Although it had snowed another inch or so overnight, the sun was a welcome sight. Surely by late evening or first thing in the morning the roads would be cleared enough that she and the babies could go home.

She needed the reality of her little apartment, away from Henry, where she could think clearly. Being with Henry definitely muddied her mind.

The ring of the telephone on the desk pulled her from the window. She grabbed up the receiver and said a soft hello.

"You okay?" Henry's deep voice filled her ear.

"I am now that I know you're okay," she replied. "I couldn't sleep last night. I've been worried about you."

"I almost called you last night to tell you that everything was fine, but I was afraid I'd wake the boys. I've got a glass company coming out first thing this morning to replace the broken window in the bedroom. Jimmy and his men went over it with a fine-tooth comb looking for anything that might be evidentiary. How are the boys?"

She glanced over to the bed. "Still sleeping. What happened after I left last night?" She listened as he told her about going to Tom Burke's home and confronting the man he thought responsible.

"You didn't really expect him to confess, did you?" she asked when he was finished.

"No, but it would have been nice if we could have settled all this last night. I'm hoping Jimmy will be able to get something from the pieces of the device he collected last night, something that will be enough evidence for an arrest."

"You know I can't come back to the house," she said, her heart heavy as the words left her mouth.

"I don't want you and the boys back here," he replied. "Not until this is all resolved. Last night was too close for comfort and I'd never forgive myself if anything happened to you or Joey or James."

Melissa squeezed the receiver closer to her ear as she heard the passion in his voice. He cared about her. She knew he did, but it wasn't enough for him to invite her fully into his life.

"You have everything you need there? The roads are still pretty bad but you should be able to get home sometime tomorrow."

"That's what I thought when I looked outside the window a minute ago, and yes, I have everything I need—we need."

"I'll have Charlie or one of the other men deliver your car later today or first thing in the morning. I don't want to be seen there with you." He paused a moment. "So I won't be able to tell you or the boys a personal goodbye."

She could hear the regret, a true longing in his voice, but she was almost glad that there wouldn't be a personal goodbye. There were going to be enough goodbyes in their future and she had a feeling she'd find each and every one of them difficult. "You'll let me know if anything changes?"

"Of course," he replied. "I'll call you later this evening in any case. And, Melissa, I'm so sorry about all this."

"You don't have to apologize. Just take care of yourself, Henry. My boys need their daddy."

"And I need them," he replied softly, then with a murmured goodbye he hung up. By that time the boys were awakening and she changed diapers and fixed them each a bottle of formula.

While they ate their breakfast she made a pot of coffee in the coffeemaker provided, then studied the menu she found on the desk from the diner next door.

She was starving and she knew part of it was probably stress-related. She picked up the phone and called in an order for an omelet and toast. While she waited for the food to be delivered she got dressed for the day.

The boys had just finished their bottles when her food was delivered. She sat at the desk to eat and kept one eye on the twins, who entertained themselves by playing with their fingers and toes and gurgling to each other as if sharing a secret language.

The omelet was excellent and after she'd cleaned up the mess she stretched out on the bed and played with her sons.

Maybe it had just been the spirit of Christmas that had her feeling so strongly about Henry. The days she had spent in his home had been like a fantasy of everything she'd ever wanted in her life. She didn't care about the lavish gifts or the fancy mansion; she didn't care about personal cooks and sterling silverware. She didn't need any of that.

It had been the warmth of family that had seduced her, the caring both Mary and Henry had offered to her and her children. It had been the shared laughter and the comfortable small talk.

Henry was going to make a tremendous father, but he'd warned her all along that he wasn't interested in becoming a husband. Still, somehow he'd made her want to be his wife.

Instead of thinking of what would never be, she tried to focus on what she intended to do when she got home. She was more determined than ever to jump back into her decorating business. She'd contact old clients, solicit for new ones and hopefully the business would grow.

Somehow she and Henry would work out a solution to the visitation issue, one that would allow each of them the independence to continue their own lives. Eventually perhaps she would find a man who would love her like she wanted to be loved, a man who would bind his life with hers. Although at the moment the idea of any man other than Henry filled her with repugnance.

What she'd once felt for Tom was a pale imitation of her feelings for Henry. She realized now that she hadn't loved Tom. She'd never loved like she loved Henry.

The day passed achingly slow. When the boys fell asleep for their naps, she turned on the television and watched two soap operas that she'd never seen before.

Around four o'clock she placed another order at the diner, deciding that an early meal and early bedtime would be the best thing.

The sun had continued to shine throughout the day and she'd heard the rumble of street plows working, letting her know that she should be able to leave first thing in the morning.

By five-thirty she'd eaten her dinner, fed the boys and the sun had gone down. She was considering changing back into her nightgown when a knock fell on her door.

With the chain on the door she cracked it open a mere inch to see who was on the other side. "Charlie," she said and quickly unfastened the chain to open the door. "Henry said you might come by to bring my car."

"Actually, Henry sent me here to take you and the boys back to the house," Charlie replied as he stepped inside the room.

"What?" She looked at him in surprise. "Has something happened?"

Charlie nodded. "Tom Burke has been arrested and the danger is over. Henry wants you all back at the ranch."

"When did all this happen?" she asked, a wave of happiness sweeping through her.

"Just a little while ago. I don't have any real details. Henry just told me to come here and collect you and the boys and bring you home."

Melissa looked around the room. "It's going to take a few minutes for me to pack everything up again."

Charlie smiled. "Take your time. I just know Henry

doesn't want you here another night since it's safe now for you to be back at the house."

Melissa was thrilled by the news that Tom had been arrested and Henry was no longer in danger. Charlie entertained the twins with silly faces while Melissa scurried around and quickly packed her things.

She was going to have to say goodbye in person. The thought broke her heart just a little bit. It would have been easier to take off in the morning without any long goodbyes to Henry. But she knew Henry probably wanted to spend time with the twins one last time before she left for home the next day.

Tonight she would have to tell him about her decision not to move into the carriage house. It would be difficult but she was firm in her decision and he was just going to have to accept it.

Finally she had her things ready to go. While Charlie carried her suitcase back to his SUV, she got the boys into their coats. "You're going to see Daddy again," she said, buttoning Joey's coat.

"I'll carry this little guy," Charlie said as he came back into the room and picked up James. "I've still got the car seats so everyone will ride safely."

Within minutes they were all packed in the car and Charlie started the engine. "Do I need to check out or anything?" she asked.

"Nah, Henry will take care of it." He put the vehicle in Reverse and backed out of the parking space.

"So you don't know what kind of charges have been pressed again Tom?" she asked.

"No, but I'm assuming it's attempted murder or something serious like that," Charlie replied.

"I'm so happy that it's finally been resolved, that Henry is safe and can get on with his life." She stared out the window and frowned. "Shouldn't we be going the opposite direction?"

"No, I'm going exactly where I need to go." Charlie turned and smiled at her, but in the depths of his eyes she saw something cold, something calculating and the first whisper of fear edged through her.

Her throat went dry. "Do you have an errand to run before you take us home?"

"Yeah, an errand that's going to change my life." He reached into his coat pocket and pulled out a gun. "And I suggest you sit back and enjoy the ride."

Melissa stared at him with a rising sense of horror. Charlie? Why was Charlie holding a gun on her and where was he taking her?

Fear screamed inside her head, a fear for herself, but more important, a fear for the two babies who were in the backseat.

It had been a busy day but no matter what Henry did his thoughts were on Melissa and the boys. It ached in him that he wouldn't be able to give the boys a final kiss on their sweet cheeks before sending them back home, that he wouldn't be able to fill his lungs with the sweet baby scent of them.

He would have liked the opportunity to tell Melissa goodbye in person, too. One last look at that shine in her eyes, one more of her lovely smiles to end the holidays would have been nice.

But he reminded himself that this wasn't a permanent goodbye. Whether they liked it or not they were in each other's lives for at least the next eighteen years.

Etta hadn't made it in because of the snow so at dinnertime he and his mother had a quiet meal of ham and cheese sandwiches. In fact, throughout the day the house had been far too quiet.

He hadn't realized how much Melissa and the boys had filled it up and brightened every dark corner. He told himself this was just temporary, that eventually they'd be back and the house would come alive once again.

It was almost six o'clock when he sat down in his study and picked up the phone to call her. The phone rang at the motel room once…twice…three times. Henry frowned as it rang a fourth and fifth time.

He finally hung up but stared at the phone with confusion. Surely she wouldn't have taken the boys out anywhere. She didn't have a car and it was frigid outside. *Maybe she's in the shower,* he thought.

Picking up a pen, he tapped the end of it on his desk as a vision of Melissa in the shower filled his head. He could easily imagine her slender body beneath a steaming spray of water, visualize the slide of the soap across her full breasts.

He threw the pen down, irritated with these kinds of thoughts. He'd believed that if he made love to her one more time she'd be out of his system. He thought that the crazy physical attraction he felt for her would wane, but instead of diminishing, it seemed to have grown stronger.

He picked up the phone and tried her number again. It rang and rang and still there was no answer. How long did a woman spend in the shower?

He got up from the desk and paced the room, a thrum of anxiety inside his chest. Moving to the window, he stared out in the direction of the carriage house. He still hoped to talk her into moving in there. It would make everything so much less complicated.

They were going to work well together as a team in raising the boys. He was incredibly lucky that a woman like Melissa was the mother of his children.

He returned to the desk and tried to call her once again. When there was still no answer, the anxiety that had whispered through him screamed with alarm. Racing out of the study, he headed for the coat closet in the foyer and yanked out his coat. He grabbed his gun from the drawer and stuck it in his pocket.

"Henry? Where are you going?" Mary appeared in the foyer.

"I can't get hold of Melissa on the phone. Nobody answers and I've got a bad feeling."

Mary's hand flew up to her heart. "Maybe she was in the bathroom, or stepped outside for a moment. Maybe she went to the office for something?"

"Maybe," he replied grimly. "But I won't be satisfied until I go there and check it out."

"Should I call Jimmy?" she asked worriedly.

"No, I'll call him if I need him. It's possible there's a perfectly logical explanation for her not answering the phone." He leaned over and kissed his mother on the cheek. "Don't worry."

"You'll call me?"

"The minute I get there and know that everything is all right." He didn't wait for her reply, but instead braced himself and hurried out into the cold evening air.

Minutes later as he pointed his truck toward town, he thought of all the logical explanations for the unanswered calls. Maybe she'd gone to get ice. Maybe one of the boys had been crying and she hadn't heard the ring of the phone.

There could be a dozen innocent reasons, but the possibility of those wasn't what made his heart bang in his chest. And his heart was banging fast and furious. He felt as if a wild beast had been let loose in his chest.

Fear. Rich and raw, it clawed at his guts, made him sick with worry. He'd never felt like this before. He'd never known this kind of fear.

The going was slow as the roads were slick and nasty. His hands clenched the steering wheel tightly as he prayed that nothing was wrong, that nothing bad had happened.

A lump lodged in the back of his throat. Had one of the boys gotten ill and Melissa had somehow taken them to a doctor? Surely if that had happened, she would have called him.

By the time he reached the city limits he was almost nauseous with worry. Ed's Motel was on the south side of town along the main highway. It was a typical one-story building with connecting rooms that faced the parking lot. The office was in the center, but Henry went past it. He knew Melissa was in Room 112 and it was in front of that unit that he pulled up and parked.

He cut the engine and jumped out, his heart banging faster than he could ever remember it beating before. "Melissa?" He banged on the door. "Melissa, it's Henry. Open the door."

Nothing. No answer, no door opening. Absolutely nothing. He hammered on the door with his fist, then tried the door. It opened into a dark room.

He flipped on the light. The bedspread was wrinkled with pillows lined up against one side, but there was no suitcase, no babies and no Melissa anywhere in the room.

Maybe he got the room number wrong, he thought, but even as he grabbed onto that idea, he smelled the faint familiar scent of Melissa lingering in the air. She'd been here. Oh, God, so, where was she now?

He wouldn't have thought his heart could beat any faster, but it did, thundering in his chest with painful intensity.

He left the room and ran across the parking lot to the diner. Maybe she'd decided to take the boys there for dinner. Although he couldn't imagine her packing them up and carrying them across the way when the diner would deliver whatever she needed, he clung to the hope that this was the explanation for her absence.

Although on a normal evening at this time the diner would be packed, the weather conditions had the place nearly deserted. Henry took two steps inside the door and instantly knew she wasn't there.

His heart crashed to the floor. He stepped back outside and pulled his cell phone from his pocket. His fingers trembled as he punched in Jimmy's phone number.

"Jimmy, it's me," he said when the sheriff answered. "I need you to meet me at Ed's Motel. Something has happened to Melissa and the boys."

With Jimmy's assurance that he'd be right over, Henry walked back to the motel and into the office. Maybe he'd gotten the room number wrong. Maybe he'd only imagined the scent of Melissa in the room.

The owner, Ed Warren, was at the front desk and greeted Henry with a friendly smile.

"Henry, didn't expect to see you tonight," he said.

"Ed, that room I rented from you by phone. What room number was it?"

"112," Ed replied without hesitation. "I know because it's the only room I've rented in the past couple of days. This damned weather has practically closed me down. Why? Is there a problem?"

"Have you noticed anybody around the room? Have you seen a car or anything parked in front of it?"

"No, to be honest I haven't moved from behind

this desk all day. I know a pretty lady came in for the key last night and that's all."

"The pretty lady isn't there now and she had a couple of babies with her. You haven't seen them this evening?"

Ed shook his head. "Sorry, Henry. I can't help you."

Henry reeled back out the door, almost blinded by the sickness that welled up inside him. Where were his babies? And where was Melissa?

Chapter 12

Melissa had never known such terror. There was no escape. She couldn't open the car door and jump out, not leaving Joey and James still in the car with Charlie. She was trapped and she had no idea why this was happening, what Charlie had planned for them.

As they left the city limits and began to travel on dark, lonely country roads, the terror clawed up the back of her throat and twisted her insides.

Joey and James had fallen asleep, unaware of the drama taking place. "Where are you taking us?" she finally asked, her voice reed thin.

"Don't you worry about it," Charlie replied. "If you do what I tell you to do then there's no reason anybody has to get hurt and you and your kids will be fine."

"What do you want, Charlie? Why are you doing this?" She needed to make sense of it. "Is this because of your sister? Because Henry didn't want to marry her?"

Charlie laughed, the sound not pleasant. "I don't give a damn about Hilary. That stupid bitch dated Henry for over a year and couldn't close the deal. If she'd gotten Henry to marry her then I would have been on easy street. As Henry's brother-in-law I wouldn't have been shoveling horse crap anymore. I could have worked a respectable job with all the perks. Now I have to take matters into my own hands."

Henry had believed that somebody on the town council was responsible for the attacks on him. But he'd been wrong. "You were trying to kill Henry?" she asked.

Charlie glanced at her and laughed once again. "Trust me, if I'd wanted Henry dead, he'd be dead. I just wanted to disrupt his perfect little life, make him go to bed at night a little nervous."

"But why? What's he ever done to you?"

"I hate him!" Charlie exclaimed with vehemence. "I should be living his life. I should have his money. All he did to earn it was be born. I've been working my ass off for all my life. I came from nothing, but those babies in the backseat are my ticket to something."

It all crystallized in Melissa's mind. Kidnapped. Charlie was kidnapping her and the boys and was going to demand a ransom.

Henry had spent his entire life worrying that some woman might try to take his money from him and now because of her and the boys his fear was coming true, except it wasn't a woman about to take him, but a madman.

What if he didn't pay? Even as the possibility entered her mind she dismissed it. She'd only spent a couple of days with Henry, but she knew the man he was, she knew what was in his heart. He'd turn his bank account inside out to assure the safety of his children.

But what if something went terribly wrong? What if Charlie snapped or things didn't go as he planned? There was no question that to Charlie she and the boys were expendable. Nobody knew where they were, nobody would suspect Charlie of wanting to hurt Henry or having anything to do with her disappearance.

They were in mortal danger and at the moment she saw no way out of it. Maybe when they arrived to wherever he was taking them she'd be able to do something—anything—to get away. She grabbed on to that hope, that somehow, someway, she'd be able to figure out a plan.

She glanced at her wristwatch. It was just after six. Henry had said he'd call her sometime this evening. Had he tried to call? Did he even know they were missing yet?

It seemed like they drove forever before Charlie finally pulled to a stop. In the glare of the headlights stood a small shanty. It was dark and isolated, surrounded by trees laden with snow. There wasn't a light from a neighbor or a sign of civilization anywhere.

A shudder worked through Melissa, a shiver that had nothing to do with the cold as Charlie opened his car door. "Get the kids and don't try anything stupid. You're worth nothing to him or to me and I won't hesitate to kill you if you give me any trouble."

She believed him. The coldness in his eyes, the hardness in his voice let her know he meant what he said. Charlie knew Henry would pay whatever the demand to get his children back, but she was definitely expendable. Henry didn't love her.

She was grateful that the boys didn't awaken as she unfastened them and pulled them from the car seats. She held them tight as Charlie motioned her into the shanty with the barrel of his gun. Once inside he turned on a light that illuminated the dismal interior.

There was a sink, a small refrigerator, a two-burner hot plate, a microwave and a small table along one wall. On the other side of the small room was a single-size cot and a door she assumed led to a bathroom. A small electric heater blew warm air, but not enough to heat the entire room.

"Put the kids on the bed," he commanded.

On trembling legs she moved to the cot and gently placed the sleeping twins in the center of the small area. Tears blurred her vision as she straightened up and turned to face her captor.

"Unfortunately this is going to be your home away

from home for the next day or two," he said. "Sit down." He pointed to one of the chairs at the table.

With one backward glance at the sleeping twins Melissa did as he asked. "You threw that bomb through the window, didn't you?" she asked and was appalled by the quiver in her voice.

Charlie opened the cabinet beneath the sink and pulled out a heavy chain. The sight of it shot a new wave of fear through her. "Yeah, it's amazing how easy it is to build a little pipe bomb. I shot out the tire on Henry's car, too. My original plan was to waylay you as you left town, but Henry's decision to move you into the motel made it all so easy."

He straightened and locked one end of the chain on a metal hook that had been driven into the wall and then approached her with the other end.

"Please, you don't have to do this," she said, the tears not only blurring her vision but running hot down her cheeks. "I can talk to Henry. I'm sure he'll give you whatever you want. Just please, let me and my babies go."

"Shut up," he said. He bent down and grabbed her ankle. She instinctively kicked at him, the survival instinct roaring to life.

He stepped back from her, the gun pointed at her head. "Don't make this difficult. I told you that if you cooperate, you won't get hurt. But I won't hesitate to put a bullet through your head if you give me any trouble. You understand?"

She drew a deep breath, gulped back a sob and nodded. She didn't want to give him a reason to kill her. She had to stay alive. She had to figure out a way out of this and save her boys.

"Now, I'm going to put this chain on your ankle. There's enough length for you to move around the room, take care of the kids and use the bathroom. There's some grub in the refrigerator and you should be fine until I get back here."

He fastened the chain around her ankle and she shuddered at the cold bite of steel against her skin. "I'll bring in your things so you should have everything you need."

With that he disappeared out the door. Instantly Melissa grabbed the chain in her hands and began to attempt to pull it out of the wall. She yanked and pulled, but there was no give at all.

She quickly dropped the chain as Charlie came back in carrying her suitcase and the diaper bag. The one thing he didn't have was her purse with her cell phone inside.

"Don't look so worried. You should only be here a couple of days, however long it takes him to get the cash for me. I'm not even going to make a ransom demand until tomorrow. I'll give him a night to worry. It will put him in a better mood to deal with me and my demands."

"Please, Charlie," she said one last time. "If you let us go now I won't tell anyone what you did."

"If and when you get a chance to tell anyone I'll be long gone. I'll be a rich man on some tropical beach living under a new name."

"Henry will never stop looking for you," she insisted. "He'll hunt you down wherever you go. You'll live your life looking over your shoulder."

He smiled, obviously not concerned by her words. "But what a great life it's going to be. I'll be back later." He dropped the suitcase and diaper bag to the floor, then left the shanty. She heard him lock the door from the outside and then she was alone with just her sleeping babies to keep her company.

"Henry, there's no sign of a struggle or forced entry," Jimmy said. He'd arrived at the motel room with two of his deputies. "There's nothing to indicate that anything bad happened her. Maybe she just went home."

"Without her car?" The urgent burn in Henry's gut had only intensified over the past half an hour.

"Maybe she had somebody pick her up," Ben Whitfield, one of the deputies, said.

Henry shook his head. "She wouldn't have done that. She wouldn't have left without telling me goodbye."

"Maybe the scene at your house last night scared her more than she let on. Maybe she was afraid to tell you she was going home because she was afraid you'd try to change her mind," Jimmy said.

A new sick feeling swept through Henry. Had he been pushing her so hard the past couple of days that she might have taken off without telling him? Afraid that he'd push her to do something she didn't want to do? Even though their time together had been relatively brief, he believed he knew the kind of woman Melissa was and he was convinced that wasn't the case.

"I'm telling you, Jimmy, something's happened. We've got to find her." He looked at the sheriff. "She's in trouble. I know it. I feel it."

"Ben, you and Jake hit the streets, see if you can find anyone who might have seen something," Jimmy said.

"What about Tom Burke?" Henry asked.

"I already checked with Gordon. Tom is home with his family and can't have had anything to do with Melissa or your boys."

Henry grabbed Jimmy by the shoulder. "We have to do something, man. We have to find them." The emotions that filled Henry left him weak, a combination of the worst fear he'd ever known in his life.

"We'll find them, Henry. Why don't you go home and wait. Maybe she'll call."

"I can't go home. I need to do something," he said in frustration.

"Henry, take a deep breath. We don't even know that something bad has happened," Jimmy repeated.

But Henry knew. He felt it in his gut. There was no way that Melissa would have left town without speaking to him, no way she would have left her car at his house and taken off with somebody.

Something was wrong.

Something was horribly wrong.

"I'm going to drive around and see if anyone has seen her," Henry said. He couldn't go home and tell his mother that Melissa and the boys were missing.

Telling Jimmy he'd be in touch, Henry got into his truck and started to drive down the street, looking for anyone who might have seen Melissa and the boys. For the next hour he stopped at each and every business that was open and questioned anyone he found in the place.

Where could they be? What had happened in that motel room? Jimmy was right, there had been no sign of a struggle. Whoever she left with, she'd apparently gone willingly.

Surely if she'd planned on having somebody pick her up and take her back to Amarillo she would have said something to him when they'd spoken earlier on the phone. She would have made arrangements to get her car.

It was almost nine when he finally headed back to the ranch. He didn't know what else to do, where else to look. He only knew the terror that filled his heart.

The drive back to his place was the longest he'd ever made. Tears burned behind his eyes but he refused to let them fall. Tears implied sadness, grief and he absolutely refused to grieve for Melissa and the boys. He needed to stay strong.

His mother met him at the door. "What's going on?"

"They're gone." The words fell from his lips and suddenly the tears that he'd fought so hard to control spilled from him.

"Melissa and the boys aren't at the motel. We can't find them, Mom. We don't know where they are."

Mary reached for him and wrapped her arms

around him, attempting to comfort him like she had when he'd been a little boy and had skinned his knee. But he wasn't a little boy and this was far worse than a bruised knee.

He stuffed back his tears and straightened. "I don't know what to do. I don't know what's happened. I've never felt so helpless in my life."

He allowed his mother to lead him into the living room, where they both sagged down to the sofa. "Jimmy and a couple of his men are out looking. I drove up and down the streets and asked everyone I saw, but nobody had seen them."

"Maybe she called a friend," Mary said, but Henry could tell by her tone that she didn't believe her own words.

"You and I both know she wouldn't have left town without telling us goodbye. That's not who Melissa is." He leaned his head back and closed his eyes and prayed that somehow this nightmare would end.

Both he and Mary jumped as the doorbell rang. Henry shot up off the sofa and raced to the door. He opened it to see Charlie.

"I just heard," Charlie said. "Is there anything I can do to help?"

Henry motioned him inside the foyer. "Last night when you dropped Melissa off at the motel did you see anybody around?"

Charlie frowned. "Not that I noticed. I made sure we weren't followed when we left here. I can't be a hundred percent certain that nobody saw her when I let her and the boys out of the car. God, man. What can I do?"

Henry raked a hand through his hair. "I don't think there's anything anyone can do at the moment. Jimmy and his men are out searching in town and I don't know what else to do."

"I'm heading home. You'll call me if I can do anything?"

"Thanks, Charlie. I will." Henry watched as the man left the house and walked to his vehicle in the driveway.

The night was dark and cold and Melissa was out there with his babies. "Maybe we scared her away," his mother spoke from behind him.

He turned to look at her.

"Maybe we came on too strong. We bought so many things, made it look as if we were making a home here for the twins." Mary wrung her hands together. "Maybe she's afraid you'll take those babies from her and so she ran away."

"No, she wouldn't do that." He knew in his heart, in the depths of his very soul, that she wouldn't just disappear. He turned back to the door and stared outside. "I think somebody has them. I think somebody took them from the motel room."

"But why?" Mary cried.

Once again he turned to face her. "Maybe as a final attempt to make me pull out of the election. I don't know. We won't know for sure until whoever has them contacts us."

"Surely whoever has them wouldn't hurt them." Mary's voice trembled with her fear.

He didn't attempt to give her false pacification. "I don't know, Mom."

"So, what do we do now?" she asked.

Henry's stomach clenched. "We wait."

Melissa wasted no time the minute Charlie left the shanty. First she worked to try to get the chain off her ankle. He'd secured it with a padlock and she was hoping maybe she could use something to pick it open. But a search of the two drawers in the kitchen area yielded nothing more than two spoons. Even the handle of the spoon was no good in trying to pick the lock.

The boys remained sleeping soundly. She was grateful for their silence. She needed to think. Even if she did manage to get herself free from the chain, then what? She had no idea where they were, no idea how far she'd have to walk with the twins in her arms to get help.

But she figured her odds were better braving the elements than staying here until Charlie returned. Henry had said that his breakup with Hilary hadn't seemed to matter to Charlie. Apparently, it had.

Charlie had seen Hilary and Henry's marriage as a ticket for him off the ranch. When that had fallen apart, she'd made the mistake of coming here and giving Charlie a new bargaining chip. She glanced at the twins. No, two bargaining chips, she thought.

What scared her more than anything was that

she didn't think Charlie intended to let her live. The twins couldn't identify their kidnappers, but she could. If she died then Charlie would be safe. He'd never have to look over his shoulder to see if somebody was after him.

For the next hour she pulled on the place where the chain was connected to the wall, hoping to break it loose. She finally sat on the floor, exhausted by her efforts and overwhelmed with defeat.

Silently she began to weep. She would never see her babies grow up. She'd never see their first step or hear them say mommy. She wouldn't be there to put them on the bus for their first day of school, to straighten a tie when they went to their first school dance.

Pain flooded her as she stuffed a hand against her mouth to keep the sobs from ripping out of her. She wept until there were no more tears to weep and then she prayed. She prayed that no matter what happened to her, the boys would be safe. She prayed that they would live a long and happy life with Henry and Mary.

Thoughts of Henry brought more tears. She'd never see him again. She'd never see that slow slide of a sexy grin across his lips, the simmering sparkle of pleasure in his eyes.

Surely by now he knew they were missing. She looked at her watch. Almost ten. He would have called the room and gotten worried when she hadn't answered. He was probably looking for her now. Unfortunately there was no way he'd ever suspect his right-hand man on the ranch, the worker he depended on. The last person he'd suspect would be Charlie.

She pulled herself up and looked in the cabinets, seeking something that could be used as a weapon. He might intend to kill her, but she'd like to be able to hurt him before he did. She'd like to be able to mark him in a way that might bring up some questions.

Her fingernails were kept too short to do damage to his face. But surely she could use something in the cabinets.

She searched every nook and cranny on the room and found nothing. The cabinets held only a handful of canned goods, some soup and pork and beans and corn. The refrigerator had a gallon of milk, a loaf of bread, a package of bologna and a small jar of mayo. The freezer contained five frozen dinners.

She had a feeling the food had been brought in specifically for her and there was just enough for a couple of days. This hadn't been a spur-of-the-moment decision on Charlie's part. He'd planned this and that depressed her even more.

Finally, she sat next to the bed where the twins slept and laid her head back. She could smell her babies, the sweet scent of innocence and love.

She closed her eyes with the weary knowledge that at least she knew they'd be loved by Henry for the rest of their lives, even if she wasn't around to share it.

Chapter 13

"Henry, Hilary is on the phone," Mary said.

Henry frowned. "I don't have time to talk to her now. Tell her I'll call her back later." He returned his attention to Jimmy, who sat on the chair opposite the sofa where Henry was seated.

"We're treating the motel room as a crime scene," Jimmy said. "Even though we don't know if a crime has occurred. I've got a couple of my boys lifting prints to see what we find."

"It's a motel room. You're probably going to find the prints of people who stayed there ten years ago," Henry said with a weary sigh.

"Ed's place is pretty clean. It's possible we'll lift fresh prints."

"And then what? Unless you have a matching set on file the prints won't tell us anything."

"Henry, we're doing the best we can," Jimmy replied patiently.

"I know, I know. You tell Tom Burke that if he had anything to do with this, then he wins. If he'll let them go unharmed, I'll leave him alone. I'll pull out of the race for mayor and he can continue his business practices as he sees fit."

"Henry, I don't think it's Tom," Jimmy said. "Or anyone he's hired. I've known Tom for most of my life. Sure, he's a scoundrel, he's a white-color criminal but this isn't something he's capable of."

"Would you stake Melissa's life on that? Stake the lives of my boys on it?" Henry replied.

"Of course not. I'm just telling you what my gut is telling me and that's that Tom isn't responsible."

"Then who is?" Henry asked as a hollowness threatened to swallow him whole. "Jesus, Jimmy, who is responsible? Who could hate me this much?"

Jimmy swiped his broad hand down the length of his face. "I don't know. It might not be about hate. It might be about greed. If this is some kind of kidnapping then I'm guessing that you'll hear from the kidnapper."

Henry looked at his watch. It was after ten. "We don't even know how long they've been missing. I spoke to her this morning but didn't speak to her after that."

"I checked with the diner. Dinner was delivered to

the room at around four-thirty so we know she and the boys were there then," Jimmy said.

"I've made coffee," Mary said as she stepped into the living room.

Jimmy stood. "Come on, Henry, let's go have some coffee. It looks like it's going to be a long night."

The last thing Henry wanted was to sit around and drink coffee while Melissa and his boys were out there somewhere. He wanted to beat on every door in the town of Dalhart until he found the place where Melissa and the twins were being held.

But he followed Jimmy into the kitchen, where the two men sat at the table while his mother poured them each a cup of the fresh brew.

"Shouldn't we call the FBI or something?" Mary asked. She looked as if she'd aged ten years in the past couple of hours.

Jimmy shook his head. "They won't be interested until I have evidence that a crime has occurred. She's only been missing for five or six hours and we don't know if she made the decision to go missing of her own free will."

Henry frowned and wrapped his hands around his coffee cup, seeking the warmth to banish the icy chill that had taken possession of his body the moment he'd entered the empty motel room.

"If this is a kidnapping for ransom I wish to hell somebody would call me," Henry said.

They all froze as Jimmy's cell phone rang. Henry's stomach clenched as Jimmy answered. He listened for a moment. "Just keep me posted," he finally said then hung up. "That was Jake. He and Ben have questioned everyone in the block surrounding the motel and nobody has seen Melissa."

"Why doesn't he call?" Henry cried. "If somebody has them why in the hell haven't they called to tell me what he wants?"

The frustration, the fear and the rage that had been building throughout the night exploded and Henry slammed his hands down on the table. "If anybody hurts them I'll kill them. I swear, Jimmy. I'll kill the bastard responsible for this."

At that moment the doorbell rang. Henry leaped up from the table and hurried to the door, his heart thundering in the hope that it would be Melissa.

It wasn't. It was Hilary.

"Henry, I heard about Melissa and the babies missing. I need to talk to you." There was a trembling urgency in her voice.

"Hilary, this really isn't a good time," he said, unable to stop the crashing waves of pain that coursed through him.

She reached out and placed her hand on his shoulder. "Please, Henry, I think maybe I know who is responsible."

He stared at her, wondering if this was some crazy ploy to get close to him. "What are you talking about?"

He was aware of Jimmy and his mother stepping into the foyer.

"Charlie was real upset when we broke up. He

thought if you and I got married then you'd get him a job that paid well, a job in a fancy office somewhere. A couple of days ago he told me he had plans to get enough money to blow this town and live the easy life. When I pressed him for details he refused to say anything more."

The words exploded out of her in a rush, along with a torrent of tears. "I might be a lot of things, Henry, but I saw the way you looked at Melissa, I saw the look in your eyes when you saw those babies and I can't condone this. I think Charlie has done something terrible and I just had to tell you."

Henry stared at her in confusion. Charlie? Henry's mind buzzed. Charlie knew where she was staying. Melissa would have trusted Charlie. She would have gone with him without questions. Still, he was reluctant to believe it. "But he was here just a little while ago. He offered his help."

"I'm just telling you what I think, Henry, and I think he has Melissa and the boys," Hilary said.

Henry pulled his cell phone from his pocket and punched in Charlie's phone number. His heart crawled into his throat as he heard it ring and ring. "There's no answer," he said as he clicked off.

"I know where Charlie lives," Jimmy said with a frown. "There's no way he could have Melissa and the twins stashed in that tiny little apartment of his. Somebody would hear the boys crying or would have seen him bring them all inside."

Henry was processing everything in the span of seconds. Charlie could have easily taken the shot at him when he'd been out riding in the pasture. Charlie would have known that Henry and Melissa had gone to town and would have known about when they would be returning home. Charlie, who then tramped through the snow to obscure his own footprints, could have easily tossed the pipe bomb through the window.

Charlie. He still had trouble wrapping his mind around it. Charlie had been his right-hand man, his go-to guy for everything around the ranch.

"Charlie has a little shack, a place he goes hunting. Maybe he has them there," Hilary said.

"Why? I trusted him. I've always treated him fairly," Henry said.

"I think he hates you, Henry. He envies your money, your life and I think he knew how much you cared about Melissa and the boys, cared enough to pay whatever ransom he might come up with."

The slow simmering rage that had been building in Henry throughout the night once again rose to the surface. "Where's the shack?" he asked.

Hilary wiped her tears with the back of her hand. "I hope I'm not sending you on a wild-goose chase. I don't want anything to happen to Melissa or those precious babies."

"Where's the shack, Hilary?" he demanded. He suddenly felt like too much time had been wasted.

As Hilary gave them directions to the shack, Henry was already pulling on his coat. He grabbed his gun and looked at Jimmy expectantly.

"Let's go," Jimmy said with a nod. He looked at

Hilary. "If Charlie contacts you, don't tell him you spoke to us. Don't say anything to warn him or I'll see you behind bars for obstruction of justice."

"Please be careful. I honestly don't know what he's capable of," she said.

As Henry stepped out into the cold dark night he had a last glance of Hilary reaching for his mother's hand. He hoped to hell she was telling the truth and he prayed that they wouldn't be too late.

Melissa was cold. She didn't know if it was because the little heater simply couldn't warm the interior of the cabin or if it was fear that had her freezing.

Waiting. Wondering what happened next, that was what had her blood icy in her veins.

She certainly couldn't sleep, although she was grateful that the boys slumbered soundly. Seeking internal warmth, she finally opened a can of tomato soup and emptied it into a pan, then set it on the hot plate to warm.

As she waited for it to heat she wondered if Charlie had contacted Henry, if he'd already demanded a king's ransom for the return of the boys. He'd said he'd wait until morning, but maybe he'd gotten impatient. She just wanted this over.

She winced as she stood to stir the soup. She'd worked so long at trying to get the chain off her ankle she'd made it bleed.

Maybe she should be sleeping. Maybe Charlie didn't intend to return tonight and she should be getting what little rest she could. But even as she thought that, she knew there was no way she could sleep. She wanted to hold her boys. She wanted to squeeze them to her heart. She wanted to hear James's belly laugh one last time, see Joey's sweet smile. She stirred the soup as tears began to course down her cheeks once again.

Henry, her heart cried. She would never see him again. The only thing she could hope was that he would tell the boys about her, about how much she'd loved them, about what a good mom she'd wanted to be.

She froze as she heard the sound of a vehicle approach. Headlight beams flashed into the window. Sheer terror leaped into her throat. Had the deal gone down? Had Charlie come back to kill her?

The footsteps on the porch sounded loud, like gunshots, and when the door opened Charlie came inside. "Hi, honey, I'm home." He snickered, as if finding the joke amusing.

Melissa turned away from the hot plate. "Have you contacted Henry?"

"Not yet. I told you I was going to give him a little time to worry. I just figured I needed to stop back here and check on my investment." He leaned against the door and looked down at her ankle. "Looks like you worked hard to get out of that. Short of chewing off your foot, you aren't going anywhere."

Melissa had never hated anyone as much as she hated him. She'd never believed herself capable of killing anyone, but she'd kill for her children and if she got the chance, she'd kill Charlie without a blink of her eyes.

He kicked out a chair and sat at the small table and she backed up against the cabinet. "You're going to kill me, aren't you?" She didn't wait for him to answer. "I won't tell that it was you. I'll say that I don't know who took us, that he wore a mask and I didn't recognize him."

She hated that she was begging for her life, but she wanted to live. She had all the reasons in the world to want to stay alive.

"Lady, I wouldn't trust you as far as I could throw you," he replied.

With those words Melissa knew that he had no intention of letting her live and a new wave of grief crashed through her.

She turned back to the soup at the same time the front door crashed in. She whirled back around and everything seemed to go in slow motion.

Henry stood at the door, bigger than life, his eyes wild and dangerous. At the same time Charlie jumped up and drew his gun and lifted it to point at him.

In an instant Melissa knew Henry was about to die. Without thinking, she picked up the pan of hot soup and threw it at Charlie. As it splashed across the back of his head, he yelled and his gun dropped to the floor. The twins began to cry as Henry let loose a thunderous roar and tackled Charlie to the floor.

Melissa kicked Charlie's gun under the bed, then ran to the twins as Henry and Charlie wrestled with each other. Her heart pounded as she pulled the screaming boys into her arms and watched the life-and-death battle between the man she loved and the man who would kill her.

A sob escaped her when Henry pressed his gun barrel into Charlie's temple, halting the fight. At that moment Jimmy burst into the room.

"I got it, Henry. Drop your gun," he said.

Henry didn't move. His handsome features were twisted into a mask of rage. His entire body trembled and it was obvious how badly he wanted to put a bullet through Charlie's head.

"Henry, don't do it," Jimmy said and touched Henry's shoulder. "Come on, man. Let him go, I'll take it from here."

Henry squeezed his eyes closed, the internal battle he was waging bringing a new fear to Melissa. She knew if he shot Charlie his life would never be the same. It might feel good at the moment but eventually it would destroy him.

"Henry." She spoke his name softly. He opened his eyes and met her gaze. In the depths of his eyes she saw the torture he'd suffered over the past couple of hours. "Let Jimmy take him away. Please, I need your help with the boys."

With a strangled sob, he lowered his gun and rolled off Charlie. Jimmy immediately handcuffed Charlie and hauled him to his feet.

Henry rushed over to her and knelt in front of her. He cupped her face between his palms, his gaze intense. "Did he hurt you? Oh, God, did he hurt you or the boys?"

"No, I'm okay. We're all okay." The boys had begun to calm.

He glanced down at the chain around her ankle and as he tensed as if to spring up again, she grabbed his arm. "It's okay."

Henry turned to look at Charlie and Jimmy. "Search him, Jimmy. I need a key to get this chain off her."

A moment later he unlocked the chain and removed it from her ankle. As he gently rubbed her skin, she remembered how he'd rubbed her cold feet on the night that they had been snowbound together.

Then she was in his arms, weeping in the aftermath, and he held her tight, as if afraid to ever let her go again. Eventually he did let her go. Gordon arrived along with several other deputies who would process what was now part of a crime scene.

Jimmy left to take Charlie to jail and Melissa and Henry and the boys got into Gordon's patrol car so he could take them home.

The car seats were shifted from Charlie's vehicle to the back of Gordon's car and once the boys were settled in they immediately fell back asleep. Melissa sat between them, happy yet exhausted by the turmoil and the lateness of the hour.

As they drove home Henry told Melissa about Hilary telling them that she thought Charlie might be involved. When they got back to the house Mary and Hilary stepped out on the porch to greet them.

Henry carried the twins and when Melissa reached the porch Mary pulled her into a bone-crunching hug. "Thank God," she said. "Thank God you're all okay."

As Mary released her, Melissa grabbed Hilary's hands. "Thank you," she said to the beautiful woman. "You saved my life."

Tears shone in Hilary's eyes. "I'm so sorry. I can't believe he did this. I always knew Charlie had a mean streak, but I never knew he was capable of something like this." She pulled her hands from Melissa's. "I'm going home now. I'm sure you all need some time alone."

An hour later the twins were asleep in their beds upstairs and Jimmy arrived to take a statement from Melissa.

It was near dawn when Jimmy left and Mary led Melissa to one of the spare bedrooms. As they passed the boys' room she saw Henry sitting in a chair just inside the door, as if guarding the king's treasure. Daddy on duty, she thought, and knew he'd probably be in that chair until dawn.

Minutes later as she lay in bed, even though she was exhausted she couldn't shut off her mind. Not only did her brain whirl with all the events and emotions of the night, but thoughts of Henry also filled her head and her heart.

She needed to get home. She couldn't stay here any longer. She'd allowed him into her heart in a way no other man had ever been. Each and every moment she spent with him only deepened her love for him.

It was time to go.

Chapter 14

Henry felt sick.

She was leaving. They were leaving. Even though he'd known this time would come, he wasn't ready to tell them goodbye, even if it was just a temporary goodbye.

It was midafternoon and the sun shone through the window as she finished the last of her packing. "I hate to see you go," he said.

"I know, but it's not like this is a final goodbye." She shut her suitcase and smiled at him, but her smile looked forced. The sunshine found her hair and sparkled in it and a press of emotion rose up in Henry's chest. He swallowed against it, unsure why this was so difficult.

She pulled her suitcase off the bed and set it on

the floor. "I need some time at home, Henry." Her eyes weren't as bright as they usually were. "I need some time to process everything that's happened."

He nodded. "I know. At least we know now that there's no more danger here. The next time you come back things will be completely different. You'll have no reason to be afraid."

She gazed at him with an enigmatic expression on her face. "I'm just glad it's all over for you…for us."

"I'm sorry, Melissa. I'm so sorry that you and the boys were put in any danger."

She held up a hand to stop him. "Don't apologize. It wasn't your fault. You couldn't have known about Charlie. You have nothing to be sorry for." She glanced at her watch. "And now, I really need to get on the road."

He nodded and reluctantly picked up her suitcase. Together they went down the stairs, where Mary and the twins were in the living room.

"You'll come back, won't you?" Mary asked worriedly.

"Of course," Melissa replied. "And anytime you want you're welcome to come to Amarillo for a visit."

Mary smiled. "I might just surprise you."

"I'd love a visit from you," Melissa replied. She leaned down and picked up James from the blanket on the floor where they had been lying.

"I'll get Joey," Mary said. As she picked up the smiling little boy tears filled her eyes. She looked at Melissa and gave her a teary smile. "I don't know what's worse, saying goodbye to these precious boys or saying goodbye to you."

"I packed up some of the Christmas presents in the trunk," Henry said as they all left the house and walked to Melissa's car, and Mary put Joey in his car seat. "If you need or want anything else, just give me a call."

"We'll be fine," Melissa said, then leaned into the backseat to buckle James into his seat. When she straightened, her gaze held Henry's for a long moment.

In the blue depths of her eyes Henry saw words unspoken and a shine of emotion that momentarily stole his breath away. It was there only a moment, then gone.

"Thank you. Thank you both for your generosity," she said. Once again her gaze met Henry's and he thought she was going to say something more, but instead she slid into the driver's seat and waved goodbye.

As he watched her car disappear down the driveway, he was struck with the fiercest wave of loneliness he'd ever felt.

"You're a fool, Henry James Randolf," his mother exclaimed and started back into the house.

"What are you talking about? I didn't do anything," he said.

"That's right. And that's why you're a fool." She went into the front door and slammed it behind her.

Henry swiped a hand through his hair and sighed. Women. He'd never understand them. His mother was probably upset with him because he hadn't managed to talk Melissa into moving into the carriage house. But after the trauma she'd suffered the night before, he hadn't wanted to pressure her any more about it.

There might be a time in the future to bring up the subject again. In the meantime he had some things to take care of that would hopefully take his mind off the empty ache inside his chest.

For the next three days Henry stayed as busy as he could. Everyone in town was stunned to hear what Charlie had done and Henry was shocked and warmed by the amount of support he received from friends and neighbors.

He also made a difficult apology to Tom Burke, who surprised him by saying he was resigning his position as city manager and he and his wife were moving to Florida.

It was each evening after his mother had gone to bed and he sat in his chair with a glass of scotch when thoughts of Melissa and the boys filled his head.

It was amazing how much they had imbued the house with warmth, with joy. He missed seeing her smile and hearing that musical laugh of hers as she teased him. He missed talking to her, just sharing moments of time that could never be recaptured again.

She was a wonderful woman and someday she'd make some man a wonderful wife. He couldn't help it that he wasn't the man to fill that role in her life.

He would be the best father that he could be, but that's all he had to offer her. He hadn't pretended to be anything else but what he was —a confirmed bachelor.

The time with Henry at his house had taken on the quality of a wonderful dream as Melissa threw herself back into her real life. The boys settled back into their normal routine as if they'd never been away from home and Melissa tried to do the same.

It was Thursday morning when she sat at her computer in her living room working to build a brand-new slick webpage to advertise her business.

The twins were on the living-room floor, babbling happily to her and to each other. At least they didn't appear any worse for the drama that had taken place in that little shanty. Even Melissa was surprised by how easily she'd managed to put it all behind her. She had a life to build and couldn't dwell on that night with Charlie and how close she'd come to losing everything.

She tried not to think too much about Henry. She was in his life by accident and she couldn't forget that. It hurt to think of him, to love him and know that she would always be the mother of his children but never the woman of his heart.

For the past four nights she'd spent hours on the internet trying to reconnect with MysteryMom but she hadn't been able to find the woman in any of the chat rooms she'd visited or anywhere else. It was as if she'd been a figment of Melissa's imagination.

Melissa would have liked to tell her that she'd successfully united Joey and James with their daddy and in that respect the story had a happy ending.

And someday maybe Melissa would find her happy ending with a man who would love her, a man who wouldn't be able to wait to marry her. At the moment the idea of romance with anyone left a bad taste in her mouth. It would take her a while to heal, to get over the heartbreak of loving Henry.

At least he hadn't spoken again about her moving into the carriage house. If he brought it up again she was afraid she would confess that the reason she didn't want to live there was because she was in love with him. She didn't want to burden him with her love. The last thing she wanted to do was complicate their relationship.

It was important for the boys' sake that Henry and Melissa's relationship remain calm and pleasant, not filled with stress or tension.

She stopped working on the webpage at six and fed the boys a bottle, then snuggled with them on the sofa. This was the time of the evening when loneliness struck her the hardest.

As the twins got sleepy and fell silent, the quiet of the apartment pressed in on her. She couldn't help but remember those nights with Henry when they'd sat and talked and just shared little pieces of each other.

She had to make sure in the future she maintained an emotional distance from him. She was going to have to see him on a regular basis but somehow, someway, she had to uninvolve her heart where he was concerned.

When the boys had fallen asleep she carried them one at a time to the cribs in their small bedroom then returned to the living room. She sat back down at the computer, but her thoughts were still consumed by Henry. He'd called every day since she'd been home, short chats about the twins that had only made it more difficult for her to gain the emotional distance she needed from him.

He'd wanted her to drive back to Dalhart this weekend, but she'd told him that she wasn't ready to make the drive again. He'd been disappointed but seemed to understand and they'd made plans for him to come to her apartment the following weekend.

There was a motel nearby and he could stay there and when she went back to Dalhart she would stay at a motel and he could visit the twins there. It was important that she set boundaries when it came to the visitation. He was her weakness and it would be far too easy for her to fall into his bed if he wanted her every time they were together for visitation.

Even now as she thought about being with him, kissing him and making love with him, she was filled with a longing that knew no bounds.

She was just about to stop working on the webpage and turn on the television when a knock fell on her door. She opened the door and her breath caught in her throat.

Henry. He stood before her as if conjured up by her thought, by her deep longing for him. "Surprise," he said with a smile that looked distinctly uncomfortable.

"Henry... What are you doing here?" She opened the door to allow him inside and as he swept by her she caught the sweet familiar scent that belonged to him alone. She closed the door and turned to face him.

He looked wonderful in a pair of worn jeans and a flannel plaid shirt and his winter coat. He looked just like the sexy, handsome cowboy who had rescued her on that snowy night over a year ago.

"I couldn't wait until next weekend or the weekend after that," he said.

She frowned. "But you've come so late. The boys are already asleep for the night. You should have called and let me know you were coming."

He shrugged out of his coat and laid it across the back of the sofa. "I would have called, but I didn't know I was coming until I was in the car and on my way." He stared at her for a long moment, his gaze inscrutable. "We need to talk."

He seemed nervous and ill at ease and suddenly she was afraid. Had he come to tell her that he'd changed his mind, that he'd decided he was going to fight her for custody of the twins? Had being away from them made him decide he'd do anything to keep them with him?

"Talk about what?" She sank down on the sofa, afraid that her trembling legs wouldn't hold her up any longer. She motioned him into the chair opposite the sofa but he remained standing with his back against the door, as if he might escape at any moment.

"I want to talk to you about the carriage house," he said.

"Henry, I..."

He held up a hand to stop her from saying anything more. "Please, just listen to me for a minute. I've never offered something to somebody and then taken it back, but that's what I'm doing now. I don't want you to live in the carriage house."

Even though she hadn't intended to move in there, his words shot a sliver of pain through her. He didn't want her there. He didn't want her that close to him.

She nodded and told herself it was for the best. It hadn't been something she wanted to do anyway. "Okay," she replied.

"No, it's not okay. Nothing has been okay since you and the boys left." He shoved off from the door and walked the width of the room to stand in front of her. He stared at her, his expression impossible to read.

He finally drew a deep breath. "I thought I had my life all figured out, then you arrived with the boys and everything got all screwed up."

"I'm sorry. It was never my intention to mess up your life," she replied. Could this get more horrible? She fought back the sting of tears, refusing to allow him to see the depth of emotion inside her where he was concerned.

With one smooth movement he sat next to her. "My mother told me that my father might have done me a disservice in pounding into my head that all any woman would ever want from me was my money. Certainly my relationship with Hilary proved him right."

"But he was wrong, Henry," Melissa exclaimed fervently. "You're a wonderful man and you'd be a wonderful man with or without your money."

He smiled then, that slow sexy grin that would always have the capacity to warm her. "Last night I was sitting in the living room alone and thinking about the boys and what the future might hold. When I thought about them mounting a horse for the very first time, you were there in my vision. When I visualized putting them on the bus for their first day of school, in my vision you were standing beside me and holding my hand. Each and every fantasy of the future I imagined had you in it."

He frowned and his gaze never left hers. "And it wasn't just the boys' future that I fantasized about. I thought about your laughter and the way your eyes light up when you're happy. I thought about sleeping next to you, making love to you and I realized there was no way I wanted you living a separate life in the carriage house. I don't want you dating. I don't want you to be alone."

She didn't say a word. She was afraid she was misinterpreting what he was telling her. She remained frozen, her gaze locked with his.

"I realize now why it's been so easy for me to

be a confirmed bachelor," he continued. "It's because I'd never met a woman I wanted to share my life with, a woman I loved mindlessly, desperately, until I met you."

Melissa's heart soared. "I wasn't going to move into the carriage house because I'm in love with you and I couldn't live there and see you every day and not be a real part of your life."

Her words seemed to break something loose in Henry. His eyes flared bright and he reached out and placed his palm against her cheek. "God, I was hoping you'd say something like that."

"I love you, Henry, but are you sure your feelings for me aren't because of the boys?"

"Melissa, I love you as the mother of my children, but my love doesn't begin and end there. I love you because you're strong and beautiful. I love you because you make me feel like I've never felt before in my life. I want to spend my life with you. Marry me, Melissa. Marry me and move into my house. Let us be a real family together."

His mouth took hers in a kiss that tasted of desire, but more it tasted of the future, of promises made and kept and the family she'd always wanted.

"You haven't answered me," he said when he finally pulled his mouth from hers. "Will you marry me? Will you share the rest of your life with me?"

"Yes," she replied breathlessly. "Yes! Yes!"

He pulled her into his arms and she leaned her head against his chest, listening to the strong beat of his heart.

"I wonder if MysteryMom has any idea what she's managed to accomplish?" she said.

"I have a feeling she knows," he replied. "I'll give you the world, Melissa. Whatever you want, whatever you need to be happy."

"I don't need or want anything but you and the boys," she replied.

"There is one thing you can eventually give me, if you're willing."

She rose up and looked at him. "What on earth could I possibly give you that you don't already have?"

He smiled, his eyes lit with love. "Twin daughters."

Melissa's heart swelled inside her. She was filled with such love, such joy, that she couldn't find her voice. She could only nod as he once again claimed her mouth with his.

She would forever be grateful for the blizzard that had brought them together on that night so long ago and to a woman named MysteryMom who had led her to happiness that she knew was going to last a lifetime.

Epilogue

She sat in front of her computer and stared at the email she'd just written, but hesitated in hitting the button that would send the message on its way.

MysteryMom picked up the cup of coffee sitting next to her at the desk and took a sip, her mind whirling with the words she'd just typed.

It was amazing what kind of information could be gained when money was no object and you had contacts everywhere in the world. For the past year she'd used those contacts and her money for a mission— the mission of uniting people for the sake of their children.

It had begun when she'd started dropping in on various chat rooms and began to hear stories about women who didn't know where the father of their children were or how to get in touch with them to let them know they were fathers.

The stories had torn at her heart until finally she'd decided to try to do something—use her resources to bring some sort of reunion to the men and women who had parented children.

So far she'd been successful with several couples, but this one worried her. She reread the email she'd composed and thought of the man and woman involved.

A terrible fate had pulled Emily Grainger and Jagger Holtz apart after a single night together. The result of that night had been a daughter named Michelle.

MysteryMom now had the pieces of the puzzle that could potentially bring together Emily and Jagger. She knew the information contained in the email could save a man's life, but might also bring extreme danger to both him and Emily.

He's already in danger, she thought to herself. And if the email wasn't sent then in all probability he would die.

She owed it to Jagger Holtz to send the email and she prayed that when she did Emily Grainer would survive whatever consequences might come.

Drawing in a deep breath, the woman who called herself MysteryMom hit the send button.

* * * * *

Read on for a sneak peak of
THE COLTON BRIDE by Carla Cassidy,
available October 2013
from Harlequin Romantic Suspense

Chapter 1

The three Colton sisters sat in the parlor area of Catherine's bedroom suite, each of them pretending to carry on a casual conversation and ignore the reason they were gathered together.

The pregnancy test Catherine had just taken was in the adjoining bathroom and none of them had looked at it yet to see the results.

The suite was three rooms—the sitting area, the bedroom and the bath—and all were decorated in a splendor of pinks and black with silver accessories. This was Catherine's haven, the place she felt most safe and secure, but at the moment her nerves screamed inside her.

"Jim Radar's bull got himself all tangled up in a mess of barbed wire this morning. It took me hours to get him unwound and cleaned up," Amanda said. At twenty-eight, Amanda had a successful large-animal veterinarian practice and a six-month-old daughter, Cheyenne, who was the love of her life. "I gave Jim a lecture about the dangers of barbed wire, but I think it went in one ear and out the other."

"How's the barn project coming along?" Catherine asked her younger sister, Gabriella. Gabby had a dream of turning an old red barn on the property into a center for troubled teens. She was not only devoted to her project, but also planning a Christmas wedding with Trevor Garth, head of security here at the Dead River Ranch.

"Slowly," Gabby admitted, her green eyes sparkling with happiness. "I keep getting distracted by wedding plans. It's already October and that doesn't give me much time to have a perfect wedding by December."

"It's going to be a beautiful wedding and hopefully it will bring some joy into this place," Catherine replied.

Amanda sighed with a touch of impatience. "We've only got an hour before dinnertime. Shouldn't somebody go in there and check and find out if the answer is yes or no?"

Once again Catherine's nerves jumped erratically inside her veins, as if attempting to make a hasty escape. How had she gotten herself into the situation where she'd even have to take a pregnancy test? Before the question fully formed in her head, she knew the answer…she'd been such a fool. They'd always been so careful, always had what she assumed was safe sex, but apparently it was possible that at some point a condom hadn't done its job.

She stood from the dainty pink-and-white chair where she'd been seated, an anxious dread attempting to weigh her back down. "I guess I'll go find out."

Gabby jumped up off the chaise where she and Amanda had been seated. She grabbed hold of Catherine's cold hand. "I'll go with you, Cath."

The whole thing felt surreal. When Catherine had missed her first period she'd chalked it up to all the stress and madness that had been taking place over the past couple of months at the ranch. When she'd missed her second period, she'd finally decided it was time to take the test. And now, it was the moment of truth.

She squeezed Gabby's hand tightly as they entered the large, plush bathroom. The plastic test container was on the back of the stool and within five steps of it she could see the result. The positive sign glared up at her.

She was vaguely aware of Gabby's small gasp, but a curious numbness swept over Catherine. Pregnant. She was pregnant. The words went around and around in her head, but she couldn't grasp the concept.

She picked up the test and threw it into the small trash can next to the commode and then she and Gabby returned to the sitting room. Gabby gave a nod to Amanda as Catherine sank back down on her chair.

"So, what are you going to do, Cath?" Amanda asked.

"I don't know. I'm not sure. I need some time to think," Catherine replied. "Neither of you can tell anyone about this. It has to be our secret until I figure things out."

Amanda nodded solemnly. "My lips are sealed."

"Pinky swear," Gabby said. "You know your secret is safe with us."

Catherine did know. She and her sisters had always been a team, confiding in each other, trusting each other, especially lately when there was such tension, such a sense of uncertainty and a faint simmer of danger in the house.

"I need to go check on Cheyenne," Amanda said as she stood.

"And I've got some things to get to before dinner." Gabby gazed at Catherine in concern. "Are you going to be all right?"

"Of course." Catherine forced a smile to her lips.

"Do you need to talk or something?"

Catherine shook her head. "I just need some time to process everything. I think I'll head out to the petting barn for a little while before it's time to eat."

She'd be able to think more clearly among the little creatures that depended on her for their care. She'd always found peace in the petting barn and she definitely needed some peace at the moment.

Thankfully, as she made her way downstairs and

to one of the back doors, she encountered nobody. She didn't want to see anyone right now, didn't want to have to indulge in idle chitchat. She needed to embrace the fact that she was pregnant by a man she'd thought she might be in love with, a man she now abhorred.

The Dead River Ranch was one of the most prosperous spreads in Wyoming. The two-thousand-acre ranch was located in the Laramie Mountains, forty miles from Cheyenne.

The enormous mansion housed not only the three sisters, but also their sickly father, other relatives and staff and ranch hands. It was an entire community unto itself, and for the past three months the community had been folding in on itself, but she couldn't think about all that right now.

Not only was the house huge, but there were also outbuildings everywhere and the remains of several that had burned in a horrible fire that had occurred two months before.

Old barns competed with new ones, stables and sheds dotted the landscape against a backdrop of blue, endless skies and thick woods of a variety of trees.

As she stepped outside, she drew in a deep breath of the fresh, slightly bracing October air. It smelled of evergreen-tinged wind from the mountains and of pastures browning with the cooler air. Cattle were visible in the distance, enjoying the late-afternoon sunshine while they grazed.

She headed toward the miniature barn, where

the petting area was located next to the huge stables building. The petting barn had been built two
years ago when Catherine had found herself the unexpected owner of two friendly ferrets.

The owner of the ferrets, a friend of Catherine's,
was getting married and moving and she didn't want
to take her little babies to the local animal pound.
Catherine had taken them and then had talked her
father into building the petting barn.

She'd known her father, Jethro, would like the
idea of a place where school and scout groups could
come. He loved the idea of anyone visiting the ranch
and admiring all that he'd built.

The minute she opened the waist-high white gate
that surrounded a small outdoor arena, Inky and
Dinky, the two miniature donkeys, brayed a greeting and competed with two sheep, three pygmy goats
and a potbellied pig to get her attention.

She laughed as she was nudged and head-butted
by the variety of animals all vying for an ear scratch,
a belly rub or the nuggets of grains she often carried
with her before coming into the enclosure. "Sorry,
kids, nothing for you this afternoon," she said. Her
words didn't lessen the enthusiasm of the furry,
fluffy creatures who loved her with or without treats.

It took several minutes for her to make sure that
each and every one of them got a little special time
and then she headed inside the miniature barn that
housed the smaller animals. Rabbits ran in a fenced
area and ducks quacked their happiness as they swam
in a small pool that was continuously fed fresh water.

A large cage held Frick and Frack, the two ferrets who were favorites among the school and scout troops that came to visit the hands-on animal barn.

During those visits, Catherine acted as spokeswoman, educating the kids on each type of animal and their natural habitats and origins. It was something she loved to do when she got the opportunity.

There were stalls to house the outdoor animals during the harsh, cold winters and the entire barn was heated to keep everyone toasty while the snow flew outside and the temperatures dropped to subzero numbers.

Today as she checked food and water containers, petted and stroked each and every animal, her mind was a million miles away.

Pregnant.

She was pregnant.

Catherine admired Amanda for her veterinarian business, and Gabby for her commitment to troubled teens. At twenty-six years old Catherine hadn't yet figured out what she wanted to do with the rest of her life.

All she'd ever really dreamed of was being a wife and a mother. She'd once believed that would happen with Gray Stark, one of the ranch hands whom she'd loved with every fiber of her being when she'd been a teenager. Then one day she'd awakened to discover that he'd left Dead River Ranch and her behind without a word of explanation.

It had taken her a long time to realize he wasn't

coming back, that whatever they'd shared was over, and eventually she got on with her life.

She lowered her hand to stroke a small circle across her still-flat lower stomach. Pregnant. Be careful what you wish for, she thought ruefully as she headed back toward the gate. She'd gotten half her wish, but the timing couldn't be worse.

She and the father of the baby had broken up two months ago and nothing and nobody would fix that particular relationship. She didn't want it fixed under any circumstances.

An attempted kidnapping, a couple of murders and a dozen other crimes had created a houseful of distrust and wariness. Her father was on his death-bed and she and her sisters had been working hard in an attempt to locate their half brother, Cole, who had been kidnapped over thirty years ago.

Now wasn't the time for her to be an unwed mother, and yet that's exactly what she intended to be. The minute she had seen the positive sign on the test she'd known she was going to have this baby.

She paused at the gate, nervously twirling a strand of her hair with one hand while the other moved to her stomach once again.

Despite the fact that she'd grown to hate the man she'd been dating, the man who had fathered the baby, she already loved the life growing inside her. This was her baby and there was no way she'd let the scoundrel father, Dirk Sinclair, know anything about it. He'd shown his true colors and she didn't want him anywhere around her or her baby.

A wave of light-headedness swept over her as she stepped out of the gate. She clung to the fence, waiting for the feeling to pass, but it seemed to get worse.

Stress.

It was all too much.

Her head spun with memories of the night somebody had attempted to kidnap her little niece Cheyenne and the unsolved murder of the governess, Faye Frick, who had tried to intervene. The poor cook's assistant, Jenny Burke, had been murdered in the ranch kitchen pantry and her killer had not yet been found.

Flashes fired off in her brain of her father in his bed, looking like death as he drifted in and out of comas because of the cancer that ate at him. So much, there was suddenly too much spinning around in her head.

And now in all the chaos and uncertainty she was pregnant. Everything whirled faster and faster in her mind and then light-headedness overwhelmed her. She slumped to the ground with her back against the fence. She just needed a minute to rest. She'd be fine if she could just rest a bit, she thought as darkness claimed her.

He smelled her long before he saw her. Ranch foreman Gray Stark had a history with that distinctive fragrance of exotic spices and mysterious flowers. Catherine Colton had worn it for the year and a half he'd loved her, for the five years that he'd hated her and now for the past four years of his cold indifference toward her.

He only had to take a couple of steps out of the stable and he knew she was someplace nearby. The scent eddied in the air, rising above the smell of animals and hay and oiled leather.

She was probably at the petting barn. He glanced at his watch and noted that it was nearing dinnertime. He wondered if she knew how late it was getting.

Although his usual pattern was to avoid being anyplace where he thought she might be, he decided to walk over to the small barn and let her know that it was almost time to eat.

He knew she often lost track of time when she was with the little animals in her care. She'd always loved the creatures of the earth and was a natural at nurturing all the ones in her care.

As he ambled toward the small barnlike structure, he steeled himself to see her. He'd believed he'd cast her out of his head, out of his heart, in the five years that he'd been away from Dead River Ranch and working on a ranch in Montana.

Four years ago when his father, the former ranch foreman, had become ill, Gray had come back to Dead River Ranch, and when his father had passed, Gray had become the new foreman.

In all that time there were moments he almost forgot that he'd once loved Catherine Colton, there were increments of time that he almost forgot the depth of her betrayal. But, seeing her always wrought myriad emotions in him, emotions that he consciously schooled to indifference.

She had no place in his life and he had none in hers. He'd learned that lesson when he'd been eighteen years old, a hard lesson that he was likely never to forget.

Any indifference he might have felt for her fled as he rounded the corner to the petting barn and saw her slumped on the ground against the fence.

Adrenaline roared through him as he raced to her side, his gun pulled and at the ready. Had she been attacked? He hadn't been that far away in the stables and he hadn't heard her cry out, hadn't heard anything that would warrant action or warn of any danger.

It took only a quick assessment to assure him that she didn't appear to have any wounds anywhere. He tucked his gun back into the holster, sat next to her on the ground and pulled her into his arms.

"Catherine?" Everyone around the ranch called her Cath, but when Gray had returned to Dead River Ranch, he'd decided he'd never call her by that affectionate nickname again. He also refused to call her Miss Catherine as all the other staff did. Cath had been a woman he loved. Catherine was just one of his bosses.

He felt the side of her neck, where her pulse was steady and strong. "Catherine," he said louder, as if by the sheer strength of the command in his deep voice alone he could bring her around.

It worked. She drew a deep breath and slowly

opened her eyes. For just a moment he was eighteen years old again and she was seventeen. Her indigo-blue eyes held sweet softness and her long blond hair spilled over his arm like a sheet of honey-colored silk. As if in a trance, her lush lips turned up in a smile of such pleasure that he felt an ache deep inside him.

Like a time warp, it was as if they were both momentarily trapped in the past, in a time when they'd loved one another more than anyone else in the world, in a time when he'd been foolish enough to believe that a wealthy Colton might really choose a future with a dirt-poor ranch hand.

The moment snapped and she bolted upright at the same time he released her. He quickly rose to his feet. "What happened?" he asked. Reluctantly he held out his hand to help her up, unsure if she'd accept his aid or not. They hadn't exactly been on friendly terms for the past few years.

She slipped her small hand into his and he pulled her up, both of them breaking the physical contact instantly once she was on her feet.

She looked around, as if momentarily confused. "I don't know. I guess I fainted." She frowned and her hand went to her stomach. "I got really light-headed and sat down and that's the last thing I remember."

"Why would you faint? You've never been the fainting type before." He looked at her in disbelief.

A new, tiny frown danced in the center of her forehead. "I...uh...didn't sleep well last night and I missed lunch."

His disbelief deepened. A night of little sleep and a missed meal wouldn't make somebody as healthy and strong as Catherine faint. There had to be something else going on with her.

"I'm pregnant." The words blurted from her lips. Her eyes widened as she slapped a hand over her mouth. She slowly raised her hand to her hair and twirled a strand of it, a remembered indication to him that she was upset. "I took a test just a little while ago and it was positive. I'm going to have a baby."

A whole new set of emotions flew through Gray. "I'm sure Dirk must be very happy. Is there a wedding planned for the near future?" He knew she'd been seeing the society playboy Dirk Sinclair for the past six months or so. Their pictures had graced the society pages more than once in recent months.

"There won't be a wedding," Catherine said as she started walking toward the house. "Dirk and I broke up two months ago when he discovered I wouldn't get my inheritance until I turned thirty."

Gray fell into step beside her. Everyone who lived and worked at the ranch knew that Catherine's father, Jethro, had stipulated that all heirs had to live at the ranch until they turned thirty years old and only then would they receive their inheritance, a substantial amount of money.

"Only my sisters know about the baby and I've sworn them all to absolute secrecy. Dirk will never know. He made it obvious to me that he was courting my money, not me, and I don't want him in my life for any reason."

"I'm sorry about you and Dirk," Gray said, only because it was expected of him.

"I'm not." She raised her chin. "I'm just grateful he showed his true colors before I accepted his stupid proposal." Her hand slid down her light blue sweat-shirt and lingered on her stomach, her eyes darken-ing. "This is my baby and nobody else's."

Gray's stomach clenched with an unexpected tightness. He was surprised to discover that it both-ered him more than a little bit that she carried an-other man's baby. It was a stupid reaction that he refused to give weight. He was never meant to be the father of her children. Far better men than him were destined for that particular role in her life.

What her information did do was make him rec-ognize that this would make her a particularly de-sirable victim to any kidnapper with a brain—two Colton heirs for the price of one.

"If you're smart you'll keep this a secret for as long as you possibly can. It puts a huge target on your back," he said and then hurriedly added, "Not that it's any of my business."

He thought she saw a faint flinch jump across her pretty features. "You're right, it isn't any of your business," she replied coolly, making him wonder if he'd seen the flinch or just imagined it. He couldn't imagine that there was anything he could say to her that would actually hurt her.

Whatever he'd thought they had together years ago had been nothing but an illusion, and in the four years that he'd been back at the ranch she'd dated a variety of men befitting a Colton, confirming to him that she'd never really cared about him anyway.

Still, when they reached the back door, where she would enter and he would continue on around the mansion to the entryway for staff, he took her by the arm.

He wanted to ask her what in hell was she thinking? There was danger all around them. This was the worst time to let people know a new Colton heir was on the way. It had only been three months since somebody had tried to kidnap the youngest Colton heir, Cheyenne, the first time. A second attempt had been made less than a month after—thankfully both had been unsuccessful—but the first attempt had left his best friend's mother dead.

At the moment Catherine and the baby she carried lived in a crazy world, in a house that suddenly felt mad with a simmering, sick energy.

"I'm serious, Catherine. You need to be careful and you should keep your pregnancy a secret."

She pulled her arm from his grasp, as if unable to abide his touch. "I've been taking care of myself for years. I'm sure I can take care of myself now." She didn't wait for a response, but turned on her heels and went inside the house, leaving him only the whisper of her perfume lingering in the air.

He muttered a curse and headed for the employee door. He'd have just enough time to head up to his Spartan room in the male staff housing area, take a quick shower and then get down to the employee dining room for dinner.

Minutes later, he stood beneath a spray of hot water and tried to keep his thoughts away from Catherine, but it was next to impossible.

Holding her in his arms for those brief moments had picked the scabs off scars he'd thought long healed. In the five years that he had been away from Dead River Ranch, he'd occasionally dated other women. But none of them had managed to evoke in him the depth of tenderness, the wealth of desire, the overwhelming rush of love that Cath had so many years ago.

Cath. She'd always been his Cath but since his return to the ranch she was Catherine in his heart and mind, the distinction necessary for him to forget what had been, what he knew would never be.

In the four years since he'd been back at the ranch, as if by mutual agreement she and he had steered clear of each other, rarely speaking to one another unless it was absolutely necessary.

She'd stopped being his problem almost nine years ago and there was no reason for anything to change now. Still, he couldn't help the simmering anxiety that tightened in his chest as he thought of what a perfect target she would make for a kidnapping and ransom scheme.

The crime had been attempted before with the result being the wrong child kidnapped and a beloved governess dead, and the second attempt had only intensified the feeling in the house that both crimes were probably inside jobs.

The family was a convoluted mess, with an ex-wife, illegitimate children and sundry other relatives living in the mansion while the patriarch, Jethro, battled leukemia and drifted in and out of consciousness depending on the day. His illegitimate son, Dr. Levi Colton, had come to do what he could for the man who was his father.

He'd not only brought a bag of medical tricks with him, but also the baggage of a child who had never been acknowledged. At least in the past month Levi had found some peace and had fallen in love with pastry chef Katie McCord.

Gray had no idea how well the staff had been vetted. Mathilda Perkins, the head housekeeper, was in charge of the hiring and firing of employees. He'd never had any reason to doubt that Mathilda did adequate background checks on the people she hired and that she had the best interests of the family at heart at all times. She'd been a devoted employee for many years.

As he pulled on a pair of clean jeans and a denim shirt, he reminded himself that Catherine and her situation wasn't his problem. All he had to worry about was ordering supplies, overseeing the other ranch hands and keeping the horses and cattle healthy and happy.

Catherine Colton wasn't part of his job, nor was she a part of his life, and he definitely intended to keep it that way.

Don't miss
THE COLTON BRIDE
by Carla Cassidy
Available October 2013
from Harlequin Romantic Suspense

WIN *Vegas*

A **TRIP** TO

& **TICKETS**
TO CHAMPIONSHIP
RODEO EVENTS!

Who can resist a cowboy? We sure can't!

You and a friend can win a 3-night,
4-day trip to Vegas to see some real
cowboys in action.

Visit
www.Harlequin.com/VegasSweepstakes
to enter!

See reverse for details.

Sweepstakes closes October 18, 2013.

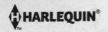

ROMANTIC suspense

LAST CHANCE REUNION
by Linda Conrad

Twice the romance and suspense!

Two stories of Chance County, Texas, have the
Chance siblings fighting for justice and finding
second chances at love.

Look for Linda Conrad's 2-in-1 novel
next month from
Harlequin® Romantic Suspense!

Available wherever books and ebooks are sold.

Heart-racing romance, high-stakes suspense!

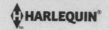

ROMANTIC suspense

COLTON BY BLOOD
The Coltons of Wyoming
Melissa Cutler

Embracing a future with the sweet, sexy pastry chef who's captured his heart means Dr. Levi Colton must settle the score with his past, including the secrets that bind him to Dead River Ranch. Standing in his way is a faceless enemy who will stop at nothing to keep the secrets of the ranch buried...no matter what the cost.

Look for *COLTON BY BLOOD*
by Melissa Cutler, the next title in
The Coltons of Wyoming miniseries,
coming next month from
Harlequin® Romantic Suspense!

Available wherever books and ebooks are sold.

Heart-racing romance, high-stakes suspense!

www.Harlequin.com

HARLEQUIN®

ROMANTIC suspense

He'd never intended to see her again....

To protect her, he broke her heart,
but when Nathan intercepts a kill order for his
former flame, he'll do anything to save her—even
if she hates him.

Look for Kimberly Van Meter's exciting new book
THE SNIPER next month from
Harlequin® Romantic Suspense!

Available wherever books and ebooks are sold.

Heart-racing romance, high-stakes suspense!

HRS27839